Dedications

To:

All the TRUE'S and REAL CREW of *Time Will Reveal's Crew Nation,*
Author Black Coffee
&
True's Relate Publishing supporters page,
The Organization group-
[All on Facebook]
Plus
Twitter, Instagram, Tumblr, Flickr, UniteBlue, LinkedIn, MySpace, all social net followers and digital readers too.
But to> *#Crew4Life*,
this series is *always* for you. *In a minute!*
Enjoy!

I0658553

III

TIME TO SHOW-RELOADED-Time Will Reveal 6

TABLE OF CONTENTS

Chapter 61 The One Son Rules……………………..5

Chapter 62 Not Gone Be Able To Do It…………………26

Chapter 63 Angel Returns [Like A Bad Rash]…………50

Chapter 64 What's Going On?………………………......79

Chapter 65 Those Who Survive…..…………………104

Chapter 66 The New World Order……………………..132

Chapter 67 Giving Unto Your Young…………………165

Chapter 68 The Past Revisited…………………………192

Chapter 69 Family First……………………………..…223

Chapter 70 The Legacy Lives On………………………247

Chapter 71 No More Exile……………………………..269

Chapter 72 Breaking The Cycle…………………………290

Chapter 73 Jerica's Crew…………………………………312

Chapter 74 The Revelation…………………………..327

"We will give unto our young, the knowledge needed. Not only to persevere but to lead and continue with forward change. While reaching another and teaching another."
#CREW4LIFE

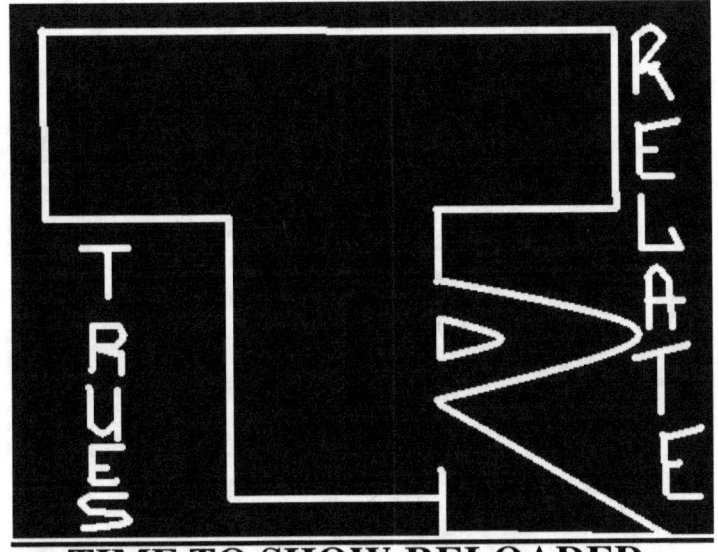

TIME TO SHOW-RELOADED-
Time Will Reveal part 6
By
Author Black Coffee #ABC

TIME TO SHOW-RELOADED-Time Will Reveal 6

Published by True's Relate Publishing
Time to Show-RELOADED-Time will reveal: Part 6
Library of Congress Control Number: 1-2374534651

REGISTERED TRADEMARK-MARCA REGISTRADA
ISBN: 978-0-9844701-9-8
Printed in the United States of America
Set by: True's Relate publishing
Cover design: Gregory Spencer of Misvision Graphics info@misvisiongraphics.com
Logo design by: JayRocOne [@ age 9
Requests for information on ordering, scheduling the author for signings and
appearances should be addressed to:
Black Coffee's websites:
www.truesrelatepublishing.com
www.blackdollone.com
Twitter.com/AuthorBlkCoffee
http://www.linkedin.com/in/lovelybrown
www.facebook.com/TheTimeWillRevealRELOADEDCrewNation#Crew4Life

Manuscript Preparation: Black Coffee
True's Relate publishing company
P.O. Box 2911
Gulfport, Ms. 39505
Email: blackdollone@att.net

PUBLISHER'S NOTES

II

TIME TO SHOW-RELOADED-TIME WILL REVEAL 6   Black Coffee

CHAPTER 61

THE *ONE* SON *RULES*

Its before day on Christmas morning, 2005. Ajay gets Ebony, Lil Ajay, Lannie, Aaliyah and their baby girl triplets; Ariel, Arianne and April, home from the hospital. He gets Lil Ajay, Lannie and Aaliyah into their beds safely by 3am. Dr Susan Mahoney came home with them to monitor the triplets and Ebony too. It doesn't take any effort from Ajay to get their oldest children to go right to sleep either. It's been a long Christmas Eve at the hospital. They were more than ready to lay down. After Ajay gets lil Ajay, Lannie and *Lea* resting comfortably. He heads back down to the master suite to check on Ebony and their less than a day old triplets.

He enters the master bedroom with a big smile on his face. After all, it's been quite a busy week. He and his Cavaliers team had traveled to Chicago and beat the Bulls, 3 nights ago. They returned to Cleveland and triumphed over the Indiana Pacers, 2 nights ago. After that win, Ajay set his mind on his 5 member family, his home and the more than $50,000 Christmas he has packed away in their 6-car garage. But since that Indiana win, his family increased in numbers by 3. And in just 2 days, Ajay is reeling with the pride and the joy of being a new father, once again. He'd purchased a 2006 Cadillac Escalade for Ebony, his wife and most prized possession. He had his father big Al to store it in their garage, out in Shaker Heights.

But at this 3am hour, all Ajay has on his mind is making sure Ebony is comfortable. She'd done a most *professional* job in labor and delivery, last night and into the morning. Their triplets: Ariel, Arianne and April are at home now. Safe and secure. They've been accompanied home by their on-call pediatrician, Dr Susan Mahoney. She has come to their estate to insure Ajay *and* Ebony that their new baby's are healthy and ready to spend their 1st Christmas in the world, with their entire crew family.

Ajay walks over to his large California King-sized bed. He's still smiling. Ebony is looking into his eyes. She's all smiles too.
Ajay is chuckling now as he says, "I got the oldest Jackson *Tre,* sleeping comfortably. They went right out too. It didn't take *any* effort."

"They probably feel like they've already *had* Christmas," Ebony

says with a giggle. "After watching their three little sisters being born."

"Don't be fooled, baby," Ajay says while still chuckling. "They know it's Christmas. Ant and *Lannie* do and I'll bet you they've already made sure Lea knows to expect *big* things too. I'll let big mama and doctor Sue help you and the triplets get settled. I'm heading to the garage aka the North Pole and put that fortress of goodies together. I wanna get it all set up and around the tree before they get up again. Are you good?"

"I'm fine, baby," Ebony says, "Thank you for bringing me home for Christmas. I have to admit. You *are* the man."

She smiles at him and he blushes. Then he says, "I've been *trying* to tell you. I'm gonna wish you a happy birthday, right now. But you know I've got something planned for later. Even though I know I can't get *all* the way in. I'll make sure you enjoy your day."

"*All* the way in?" big mama asks with a chuckle. "You two didn't wait six weeks after the other kids were born. How long will you take off *this* time around?"

"Six weeks," Ebony says quickly and laughs.

"Until her body starts calling me," Ajay says to big mama. "I just obey her body when it talks to me, big mama. She knows I'm not taking it. That body has had control over my mind for thirty years."

They all laugh including Dr. Mahoney. She's use to *this* couple by now.

"No he's not taking it, big mama and doctor Sue," Ebony admits, "My body can't do without him. Not for *too* long."

Ajay sticks his chest out and smiles even bigger. He likes that comment. He knows their triplets won't be a month old before he feels the inside of his wife again. Ajay, Ebony, Dr. Mahoney and big mama laugh hard before Ajay heads out to the garage apartment to take on yet another large job for his wife and his children.

Ajay and Ebony's apartment, above their 6-car garage

When Ajay arrives at the garage apartment, he's still all smiles. He greets papa and poppa, who are already putting together the bikes, doll houses and a lot more while they wait for Ajay to join them. They'd already planned to help him with the Christmas toys and gift setup before Ebony went into labor, last night. But they can't just let Ajay walk in and get started. Not without a jab or two.

"When did Santa Claus start wearing a smile *before* his work is even started?" poppa asks Ajay as he chuckles loud.

Then poppa adds, "You're looking like you just had some *dessert*."

"And we *both* know he didn't," papa says with more laughter. "Because just over 2 hours ago, they brought *three more* baby girls into this world. Dessert is off the menu for *awhile* for you, Ajay."

They laugh more as poppa says, "*Please*, Jackson. Now tell me *when* did this man and Ebony *ever* wait like a normal couples does, after a new baby comes? Just name *one* time when *these* jack rabbits *ever* went the entire six weeks. *When?*"

"Hold on," Ajay asks with a guilty smile. "Does everybody know about me and my wife's sex addiction?"

"Hell *yea*," papa answers and laughs loud too. He adds, "Even your kids know it by now. And that's most likely the reason why you don't have much trouble getting them to go to bed. They don't want the kind of punishment they would get from you and Ebony, if they cock block y'all. They know their parents want their private time."

"I know *Lil Ajay* knows it," poppa says, "Because he wasn't the baby for *five* minutes."

They howl with laughter as they get back to putting the toys together. They have a lot of toys to assemble. They manage to get them all done in under 3 hours.

Ajay, papa and poppa transfer all the Christmas assemblies into the house. They set everything up around the very large Christmas tree, in the 1st floor of the family room. When they're done with the setup, they head back to the garage apartment for more male bonding time.

Poppa and papa continue to tease Ajay about his *very* obvious sex life. But it isn't long before Lil Ajay's name comes up again. They've seen a lot of growth and maturity in him. Same as they did with Ajay when he was 6 years old, which is Lil Ajay's age now. They want to get an update on what Ajay is feeling about his namesake.

"Ajay I have to admit," papa says, "Lil Ajay is *straight* from Al Jackson senior and Allen Saul's mold."

"Oh yes indeed," poppa agrees, "That young man is *already* as stern as a Jackson man and as *dedicated* to respectful treatment as a Williams man. I've seen it in him since he was old enough to make eye contact."

"And he won't waste time getting that Johnson beef bullshit out the way either," papa says, "Amongst other things."

"That's for damn *sure*," Poppa agrees, "That asshole's beef won't survive another generation of *this* crew. *Hell*. It was hard enough keeping

7

Chill's crew stationary so we could wait for Jake's dumb ass to pull something. Since the early eighties, y'all have wanted to go look for him and his *half ass negroes*."

"I can assure the both of you, old man Jake won't die of old age," Ajay says with a serious face. "My crew, me *and* my son have already declared that."

"Lil Ajay plans to look for 'em, Ajay," papa says, "Here's what he said to me, Percy, Al and John at the fourth of July celebration, *this* year. He's gonna arrange for the killing of the people who hurt his parents and his *whole* crew. And he's gonna kill the girl that killed his big sister. He said he's going to do it *himself*. Now *this* was three weeks before he turned six years old. Do you *hear* me?"

"And he didn't even bat an eye," poppa adds and chuckles.

"I already know he wants to put together a plan to kill old man Jake's clique," Ajay says, "He wants to kill Tim too. Because my fight with him, got me shot. And he *definitely* wants to be the one who kills that bitch, Angelise *not* a damn Angel, Taylor." Ajay sighs and adds more.
"And even though pop keeps telling me, he has my impatience. I keep telling pop that my son's mood is *more* intense. He's like a thirty year old in a six year old body."

"Ajay *you* was the same way," papa adds.

"Yea. He was," poppa agrees, "You have always been *way* more mature than your years."

"When he use to take piano lessons with me," papa says, "He would say shit that simply amazed me. I never worried about you doing something good or bad. *Without* thinking it through first, that is."

"Unless love came into play," poppa adds and chuckles.

"Oh yea," papa agrees and chuckles too. He adds, "Once he laid eyes on our granddaughter. He developed a presidential type of attitude. *Shit*. He didn't even want John to whoop Ebony if she did something wrong. So then, he got close with John. Just to see if he could help solve it before Ebony had to be punished."
Ajay laughs hard. Then he says, "I always felt like I had to protect my baby. It was in her eyes and she still looks at me the *same* way, today."

"Yea but it's about sex now," poppa says and they laugh.

"I knew she was gonna fall in love with Ajay," papa says, "*Hell*. We was ready to guide her to you, if she wouldn't have gone on her own."

"Our wives was all for it too," poppa says.

"Pearline sure was," papa says, "She use to pull John's ear about

it, all the time. Until him and Al finally admitted they was working on it too."

"Then me and Eloise had to get with y'all, John and Al, so we could get Pearl and Joanna on board," poppa says and they all laugh again.

Papa says, "It came together *well*, I must admit. You and Ebony went through some things in y'all young lives. But it was never any doubt in my mind that y'all would be *right* where y'all are today."

"Mine either," poppa says, "Eloise and Pearline knew it before any of us did. They use to say y'all would be successful in y'all finances. And that y'all would get married and have a big family. The biggest family of y'all generation. I couldn't wait to see y'all first born son come into this world because I knew he would be a soldier. By his *birthright*."

"He's got all of y'all blood in him," Ajay says, "And then some. But I have to admit something too. I've learned what fear is for the first time in my life. Because I'm scared to death of losing my son. Don't get me wrong. I worry about my girls too. But I know they aren't gonna be out there like Ant will. Well, Lea might be. She's a strong willed female. Like her auntie Lynn. I might have to tell her about the Johnson beef when I tell Ebony. I'm sure y'all already know me and Ant talk about the beef and everything else."

They all laugh as Ajay continues, "But Ant is gonna be a beast. For the first time in my life, I *know* the fear my pops had. But at the same time, I know I'm gonna keep the communication open between me and my junior. Because he loves his mother, just like I love mine. But *his* is just a bit more intense. My son idolizes his mother, just like I idolize mine."

"That's because he looks up to you, Ajay," papa adds, "And he sees how you treat Ebony. He knows you don't bullshit and he knows she has to be the woman *above* women, for you to love her the way that you do. So he's gonna be what he needs to be, to his mother. So he can keep you calm. That's the same way you was and still is, with Al. Jo had the same kind of fool bothering her, back in the day. Jake Johnson's son. Only your father got rid of that asshole who was threatening and bothering Jo, before you got wind of it."

"And knowing you like I do, Ajay," poppa adds, "You will always honor that respect that Lil Ajay has for you. And you'll continue to treat his mother like the queen that she is. Because you don't ever wanna lose his respect. You know what that respect stems from, already. It comes from you."

"You're right. I don't wanna lose it and I won't lose it," Ajay says,

9

"Ant is *very* angry that he don't have an older sister like both me and my pops do. He blames that on the bitch that it's suppose to be blamed on too. It's not a week that goes by that he don't ask me have I heard anything more about a release date for Angel Taylor. And why don't we go on and put a plan together to take her off the map. I told him we'll do that plan after this NBA season is over. So we'll be ready to do her in before the release date is *even* announced."

"She's being moved from upstate and back here to the county, next month," papa says.

Poppa says, "That damn girl is a lot safer *in prison* than she'll ever be, *outside* of it. We *still* have a lot of crew who are *still* doing time since the civil rights movement. They're thoroughbreds in the system. They'd get it done if we just give them the word."

"She'll die before she has a year of freedom," Ajay says sternly. "I'm with my son on that one. That's his birth right. And I'm gonna make *damn* sure I give him the chance to honor it. Do y'all know that bitch is still writing letters to me? She sends them to my Rec center. She use to send them to the spot. Any *damn address* she has that she know is crew property. She'll send letters. All of them shits get returned too. But that *still* hasn't stopped her. That's what keeps my blood *boiling*."

"She's obsessed with you, son," poppa says, "And any other time I'd say just keep telling her, she doesn't have a chance. But not with her. I'm with you, *one hundred percent*. She needs to die."

"That's the only way she'll go away and *stay* gone," papa adds, "We've got folks in leadership status, these days. And they're documenting her too."

"Absolutely," poppa says, "And just know this. We could've been had her whacked. Like I said earlier. If we wanted it done, that way. But the matrons knew that this was one that you *wanted* to be involved in. Just like that Raymond White so called *sweet Ray*, situation. We know it's the same deal and we respect that. And at the same time, we can relate to those feelings. So we won't deprive you and Lil Ajay of that addiction. Not at all." They all laugh. Then Ajay says, "Thanks so much. Because Ant's got photo's of that bitch. They already out at the chamber. He's damn near at marksman status too."

"I heard he's a damn good shot, *already*," papa says.

"He *is*," Ajay says, "And he's got his *own* pistol. *This* Christmas. I didn't put it under the tree though."

They laugh hard as papa says, "No! You don't wanna put a gun for your

son, *under* the Christmas tree. Because Ebony would know about it, right off hand. She'd stall on that dessert for the whole six weeks, if she saw that."

"For sure," poppa agrees and chuckles.

"I know that's right," Ajay says, "I'm keeping it out here. I'll give it to him on our next trip to the chamber. It's a nine millimeter. Y'all know my weapon was a forty five. Right?"

"Or whatever you got your damn hands on, when you needed one," poppa says and laughs.

"Shit yea," papa agrees, "A bow and arrow if he was desperate." They laugh hard as they head back toward the house.

Ajay and Ebony's Mansion, Christmas morning

It's 7am, Christmas morning. On their way back toward the mansion, papa, poppa and Ajay know Lil Ajay, Lannie and Lea will be up very soon to see what else Santa Claus brought for them. They started off this day with 3 new little sisters. On the way home from the hospital, Lil Ajay told Lannie and Lea that whatever they get from Santa can only be extra. Because they got 3 little sisters that all 3 of them have to take care of and watch out for. And he told them that's the best present he could asked for. More sisters to look out for. He also said he was more than ready to do so.

As soon as Ajay, papa and poppa make it into the family room, Lea comes down the huge set of stairs and into the family room. She's wide awake.

"*Chria Muss*!!" 2 ½ year old Aaliyah yells with *very* bright eyes.
Ajay and Ebony have laid it out very nice for their kids. Every popular toy on the market. Every popular dress item and shoe is boxed and wrapped. There are many boxes of jewels which are either setup around their large Christmas tree. Or it's in 1 of over 400 nicely wrapped presents which Ebony had been setting up since they decorated the tree, 3 weeks ago.

"Yes. It's Christmas day, daddy's girl!" Ajay shouts, "Come give daddy a big kiss!"
Lea does so with lots of giggling. She looks around for her big sister and brother but they haven't come downstairs yet.

"I wan Lannie and Ajay, daddy," she says in an impatient voice.

"She speaks *so* well and she's only twenty months old," poppa says.

"She's getting it on out the way," papa says, "The three new

triplets from last night may not even be the babies in this spot, for long."

"My wife said we can't stop until we break that *one son's rule*," Ajay says with laughter. He says, "I tried to tell her that I meant it like, *One son rules the world*. She said it sounds like I'm trying to say, having one son rules the way it suppose to be."

"Oh God," papa says, "You'd better add some more rooms, then. That's baby girl, right there. She has never given up on a dream. Not in her whole lifetime. *Shit*. She made you stay straight, didn't she? Progress!"

"Amen, papa Brown," Ajay says.

They laugh loud as Lil Ajay and Lannie make their way down the stairs and into the family room. Within minutes, they're tearing into the presents with their names on them. It isn't long before Ajay's cell phone rings.

"Goodness," papa says, "Baby girl won't even let him have a day off? She's calling him back into the bedroom, already."

"And I'll come a running too," Ajay adds.

He's laughing hard when he answers his phone. He knows it's Jacobson.

"Hello Jacobson," Ajay answers, "Merry Christmas."

"Same to you, Ajay," Jacobson says, "And congratulations on the triplets, man. That's just awesome."

"Thanks, man," Ajay says.

"I just wanted to let you know," Jacobson says, "I got Ebony's brand new two thousand six Escalade, from your father's garage. I'm at the front gate with it now. Is the coast clear?"

"I haven't gotten her out of bed yet," Ajay says, "So you can bring it on around. We'll park it in the stall where the two thousand four usually sits. She doesn't even know it's not in there."

"I'm on my way," Jacobson says and they hang up.

Ajay goes into the master bedroom again. This time he's going to get Ebony up and moving around, for her 30th birthday. She's just finished breastfeeding the triplets. All 3 of them did well. Mahoney assures Ajay and Ebony, she won't even have to monitor them longer than today.

"They're thriving," Dr. Mahoney says, "It must be the mansion flavor and the fact that they already have a huge nursery upstairs waiting on them."

"That's all good, doc," Ajay says, "I really appreciate you coming home with us. Here's your bonus."

He hands Dr. Mahoney a cashiers check in the amount of $7000.

Her eyes are dancing as she says, "The fee was fifteen hundred *each*!"

"Well the extra twenty five hundred is your Christmas present from the Jacksons," Ajay says and smiles. "After all. It *is* Christmas day."

"Yes and you have some gifts under the tree too," Ebony adds, "I had the mothers to put you and your baby some under there. After doctor Weston told us, you would be coming with us, of course. It's Christmas, doctor Mahoney. We had to show you how much we appreciate you doing this for us."

"Well *thank* you!" Mahoney yells, "I'll baby-sit too. If you'd like?" They laugh as big mama joins them. She's come in to help them bring the triplets into the family room to join the rest, who are already having a wonderful time with a room full of *everything,* for Christmas.

Suddenly the door bell rings. Ajay knows it's Jacobson but he plays it off like he's surprised by it. He turns to Ebony.

He says, "Baby? Who in the *world* is visiting us on Christmas day and your birthday? Our new Tre ain't even a whole day old yet."

"It's no telling, daddy," Ebony says and smiles. "You know their grandmothers said they'd be here with the sunlight."

"Well I'm gonna need you to accompany me to the door," Ajay says and smiles, "So I want hurt our mothers."

"What are you up too?" Ebony asks as she giggles.

"Just come on, woman," he says, "Without the quiz."

He helps her to her feet. They walk to the door together, leaving big mama and Dr. Mahoney to bring the triplets into their family room.

Before Ajay gets their front door open completely, Ebony squeals with excitement. She can see her brand new 2006 Escalade through the glass trim on each side of their double doors. Jacobson has brought the SUV out and parked it in front of the main doors.

It's all white. Just like the other 2 that Ajay had gotten for her. But this 1 is trimmed in platinum.

"It's so shiny, baby!!" Ebony screams.

Ajay has already grabbed 1 of Ebony's coats out of the foyer closet.

"Let's go check it out," he says slyly.

Jacobson hands Ebony the keys as he retreats inside their home to escape the frigid Cleveland weather. Ajay picks Ebony up and carries her to the her new SUV. He's already started it up *remotely*. He presses another button and the driver's door opens. Ebony squeals again.

"There's a button on here for all the doors, baby," he says, "So you can have the door open before you even come outside with our kids. You've got a button to start it. A button to regulate the temperature and all of that.

Hell. There might be a chauffer up in that fancy ass truck too. It *can* be."
They both laugh as he seats her in the drivers seat. He hurries around and jumps into the passenger seat. Ebony looks toward the back and smiles.
As Ajay jumps in, she says, "You already got 4 car seats and a booster seat, in here."

"Yes indeed," Ajay says still smiling because he knows what's going to come next.
She says, "Let me guess. There's no a seat in here for Ant. Right?"
"No ma'am," Ajay says, "He'll be riding with his pops and learning how to drive. Because he can see over the steering wheel, baby."

"He really *is* going to be you," she says and giggles.

"Tried and true," Ajay says proudly. "*Now.* You got this Queen branded automobile running and warmed up. See how it rides for you. That way, if I need to change anything. I can have it done before we hit that long road trip, in a little over three weeks."

"Okay," she says, "And we've got the Bulls tomorrow. I want you to get some rest, baby. You've got a game plan meeting tonight. I want you to get your rest so you'll be ready to run on them again."

"I'll be rested," he says, "My triplets aren't even a day old. So I know there's *no* chance I'll be getting some of my pussy tonight. *Right*?"
He smiles.

"Not tonight, daddy," she says and blushes.

"You know that's my game enhancer, baby," Ajay tries, "I'm gonna lose my spin if we don't get back to fucking, as soon as possible."
She cracks up laughing and says, "Oh. No *pressure.*"

"None at all," he adds as he laughs with her. Then he says, "This Escalade is big enough to fuck in though."

"Oh my God," she says and she laughs.
"Let me see what this *new* baby can do."
They laugh as she puts it in gear and heads down their long driveway.

Pittsburgh, Pa. Christmas day 2005

Farah, Alana and Darlene get together while they're in Pittsburgh visiting their families. Alana has to be back in Cleveland tonight to dance at *The Juice Bar.* Their plan is to be back in Cleveland by late afternoon. But Alana has some news she wants to share with Farah and Darlene.

"I'm taking Libby back to Cleveland with me," she says and smiles. Then she adds, "It's about time. She wants to go and I want her to go too."

"Really?" Darlene asks and her expression is one of both shock and surprise.

She adds, "Did grandma say it was okay for you to takeover as her mama?"

"Yes, auntie," Alana says, "She's helping me get my custody of Olivia back and she said since I've been sending her money to support Libby. She thinks I'm ready to be a mother, *fulltime*."

Farah says, "Well she knows we'll be there to help you out. *Right*?"

"Yes. She knows we all live together," Alana says, "And auntie Darlene, she was gonna talk to you anyway, about being a guide for me. And since Jamal is doing so well with his two kids. She said I should be able to raise my daughter too."

"It's not like she's a baby anymore," Darlene says, "She's fifteen years old now, Alana. And she's about to have a birthday."

"She'll be *sweet* sixteen on February twelfth," Alana says and smiles. "I'm gonna ask my bosses if I can have her a sweet sixteen party at the spot two."

"Best way to get her, *in the know*," Farah says, "And she might get her one of those crew boys. That would be the best way to come into Cleveland. With a crew male as a boyfriend."

They laugh loudly. They all *really* like *that* idea which Farah had just mentioned. Then Darlene tries to think of which young boy in the crew, is Olivia's age.

"She's already older than *all* of the kids from those in Chill and Renee's crew," Darlene says, "Except their son, Kenny. But he's twenty two already and getting married on *Valentines day*."

"Big June's brother Brandon," Alana says, "He just turned nineteen, last month and he's attending college in Natty. The *crew's* college."

"But Brandon dates Stoney's youngest sister, Charlotte," Darlene says, "And the rest of the crew guys are younger than Libby. The next crew guy in *that* line is Junior and Tonya's oldest son. They call him, Lil Brad."

"Hmmm," Farah says, "He just made fourteen and his daddy is really high up the chain of rank, in the crew."

"We'll have to see what's up," Alana says, "But now that I have my *own* car. I'm putting Libby in the same school as the crew. She's going to *MLK*. And I'm hoping she can ride to school with her aunt *Farah*? Hint. Hint."

Alana laughs as Farah says, "Of *course* she can. She'll be great company for me, on that ride into school too. I use to talk to Matt on my way to work.

15

I really miss him. I've gotta find me some more dick in Cleveland. *Damn*. I hope Chill and Renee are having a rough Christmas. Maybe he'll set it out for me again."

"I'll bet you'd better not fuck Ajay," Darlene says, "That's all I gotta say about that."

"And you'd best not fuck *my man* Jeremy no more either, *Farah*," Alana says, "Or we're gonna have a *serious* problem. Girlfriend, that shit pissed me off *royally*."

"I didn't know I was gonna fuck him *that* night," Farah says, "I wanted to fuck Chill. And I *still* wanna fuck Chill."

"And you wanted to fuck Ajay too," Darlene says, "But he didn't wanna fuck you. He's real stingy with that good ass dick of his. It's been a damn decade and half, since I had some of that fourteen inch dick. And I swear. I *still* think about it."

"*Damn!!*" Farah screams. She adds, "Since nineteen ninety?!!"

"Yep," Darlene says sadly, "Ebony was living in Houston, *that* summer. Him and his mother had an argument about something and he left *their* block to come live with me. But as soon as Ebony's ass came back to visit for Christmas, that year. He went right back to Shaker Heights and he never moved back with me. He stayed with Chill and Renee until he got his own apartment."

"And them crew girls jumped on us at the crew party, that night that you went to ask him why he moved, auntie," Alana says.

"That wasn't the first fight during the Christmas break either. Was it, Alana?" Darlene asks as they reminisce.

Alana smiles and answers with, "Nope. I got into it with the crew girls a few times during that Christmas break. When Anita's hoe ass was still around."

"For sho," Darlene says, "But on that last night when six of us went. I just wanted to try to get Ajay to move back in with me. That shit ended in a mêlée. Ebony was fighting me. She had help though. But she *can* fight. I give her that. And I don't blame her because she had just found out who I was. She knew Ajay had been living with me. That night pretty much ended my hopes of getting with him again too."

Alana says, "For real. Because even when she went back to Houston. Ajay didn't wanna give you none of his time."

Darlene adds, "He messed with that bitch Angel, after that. And the world knows how that shit went down. Ajay was dedicated to Ebony. *Period*"

"She went back to Houston, for a minute," Alana says, "It wasn't long afterwards, when Ajay got his own place. When Ebony came back to

16

Cleveland, for good. That apartment was his and hers."

"So he always did move shit for Ebony, ha?" Farah asks.

"I guess you can say that," Darlene says, "I have a better chance of getting some of Ajay, then Angel ever will. Like I told y'all the other day. When Angel's ass gets out and starts stalking him again. I'm gonna offer my services to him. I'm gonna tell him I'll whoop that bitches ass, *for* him. If he'll just let me taste his chocolate ass dick again."

They howl with laughter. But Darlene is *quite* serious. She's willing to do anything for some of Ajay's time and attention.

"You need to let him know that and see what he says, Dee," Farah tries. "I mean, *who knows*? He might take you up on that offer."

"Shit," Alana says while giggling. She adds, "I think Ajay would kill Angel in a heartbeat, if she came near him or *his*. And I know for sure that she is *definitely* planning to hunt him down until she gets a chance to talk to him."

"Fatal attraction ass, *bitch*," Darlene says in disgust.

"You should be more forward, Dee," Farah suggests. "I'm not saying, be stalker like. Like Angel has and will be. But let him know you're still interested in him. Hey. You never know. It could lead to something worthwhile."

"Like the dick *you* can't seem to get over," Alana adds.

"And I'll never get over it," Darlene says, "I guess because I've been knowing him since the early eighties."

"Yep," Alana adds, "She was twenty one and fucking an eleven year old with thirteen inches of dick. That has *got* to mean something!"

"Correction," Darlene says, "It was thirteen and a half inches."

They laugh and continue to talk about the men and boys of the crew.

Jackson Heights, on Wilson's Way-December 25, 2005

The deceased Matt Johnson and his daughter Kelly have been dead for nearly 6 months. Genia Johnson has tried to move on without them but her life has been *very* hard. She hangs around CrewLand mall a lot since their deaths. Her relationship with Renee and Tonya has grown much closer since May, as well. Genia spends this Christmas day with the crew. Greg Jr and the Lions beat the New Orleans Saints, the day before. After the win, he flew straight home. He wanted to be in Cleveland for Christmas. His home in Jackson Heights was completed months ago. He had invited

17

Genia to visit him for Christmas and she accepted. Genia knows Kelly loved Greg Jr and he loved her back. She's here today for her deceased daughter.

Greg Jr and Genia spend Christmas day at Jr and Tonya's house. It was on *this* day that Jr has a long talk with Genia. He wants to know if she knew Matt was related to the same family of Johnson's that the crew has had beef with for decades.

"I don't even know his relatives that live here," Genia says, "Matt never even mixed with them. He grew up in the south and they never got along, once we moved here. They wanted him to be dumb to certain things but he wasn't willing to be. For that reason, they disowned him. He always said that worked just *fine* for him."

"I know he didn't have any connections with them," Jr says, "Because we keep up with their movements. Or lack there of. We keep them *well* monitored. Just to make sure they're not close to *us*."

"They had no dealings with each other," Genia says, "But since Matt and Kelly was killed. Even shortly before that, actually. When Matt was kidnapped and it made the news. That's when they started trying to get in touch with him. Still, he never responded to them. He said they were always gonna be seen as *fake as hell* to him. He just figured they was probably trying to gain some fame and didn't give a damn that someone was trying to take his life."

"No Genia," Tonya says, "They were trying to get a link to *our* family, on the low. What they were trying to do was use Matt and Kelly as a way into our business. As a way to get close to *our crew*. They've always wanted to kill members of our crew and family. Since way back before any of us was even born."

"For *real*?!!" Genia shouts.

"That's real, mom-in-law," Greg Jr adds, "I use to talk to Kelly about it. She knew about it. Pops Matt put her up on the *whole* thing because Chill and Junior made sure he was clean before Tonya could hire him to work in her shop. Or be near Ebony, for her wedding. He was totally down with our crew. That's why he was okay with Kelly dating me. He knew it showed the Johnson's that he wasn't with them, in *anyway*. When he met Tonya at CSU, they brought all of that out, *then*."

"Well I definitely need to let y'all know something because this fakeness has really been on my mind," Genia says, "They have *really* been contacting me since Matt and Kelly was killed. They said they wanna be my family. So I won't be alone."

"Oh *really*," Jr says.

"That's not what it's about, Genia," Tonya says, "They're trying to use you to get close to us."

"Oh hell no," Genia says, "Y'all are family to *me* and all the family my husband and my daughter had."

"I feel you," Jr says, "But we can use them trying to get to you, to our advancement. That is, if you're down wit it."

"Advancement?" Genia asks, "In what way?"

"We'll get together on it, a bit more. Later on," Jr says to her. "But rest assured. Kelly was making sure we knew how they was trying to move toward her. And we've got a score to settle."

"And we're gonna get it settled too. Very soon," Greg Jr adds.

"You're down with us and I know that," Tonya says.

"No shit," Genia says, "Let me know what I can do. Because y'all showed me nothing but loyalty. To my child and my husband too. When y'all attorney refused to represent the bitch that murdered them."

"We'll get with Chill and Renee on it," Jr says, "But I just wanna make sure *you* know. We won't be leaving not *one* of them around who's not cool with our crew. We won't leave any of them with a life to live."

"Just know that I *am* crew for life," Genia says, "I was looking forward to knowing this family, back when Matt first got connected with y'all. But with him trying to run his playboy lifestyle. He never brought me around because he was trying to hide *that part* from me. And that's what took his life too. We split up twenty one years ago, this past October. We remained friends because of Kelly and our love for her. But we wasn't sexual *at all*. As I said before. He grew up in the south. North Carolina. Just like I did. We got together in ninth grade. It was hard for me to date others, after we separated. Because he always blocked me. But that didn't stop him from fucking whomever he wanted too. Kelly was the mediator. *All* the time. But she didn't want me back with him either. Because of his ways when it came to women. My loyalty is definitely with the only family I have. And that is *this* crew. Crew only!"

"She is, Brad," Tonya says, "She's been in our lives since the day she found out about Kelly dating Greg junior. Matt just wasn't pushing for her to be around us or him bringing her around. Only because he wanted to keep *his* affairs a secret. They were still *legally* married. You know."

"Yea I knew that," Jr says, "That's not how crew do *marriage*. But he was valuable to my wife as far as the business side went. We didn't have no beef with Matt. He just brought a lot of drama to our places of business. Through his ho's."

"There are two Johnson's who *are* crew, though. Crew for life," Tonya tells Genia.

"Don't they live overseas?" Genia asks.

"Yes. They live in Europe," Tonya says.

"They are on Rebbie's *maternal* side," Jr says, "Mama Rena's mother is big Jake's sister. Her name is Jessie Mae. Big Jake's oldest grandson is crew also. His name is Albert Johnson. He moved to England to get away from his father and grandfather and this whole beef with our crew."

"Those are the very ones who Matt always said, the ones here in Cleveland would tell him, *not* to mix with," Genia tells them, "And Matt always kept in touch with them. He didn't take Old Jake's advice. *Ever*."

"We know he stayed in touch with our Europe crew," Jr says.

"Just let me know what y'all need me to do," Genia says, "Talk me through it. I'll do *whatever* I need to do to make things smooth for this crew family. Y'all have been the strength for me."

"We'll get to it," Jr says, "Just keep that link open with them."

"And we'll coach you through it," Greg Jr adds.

Jackson Heights: Ajay and Ebony's

Ajay and Ebony have arrived back at their estate, after a great ride in her 2006 Escalade. They're heading back inside to open gifts with their kids, Mahoney and the grandparents too. Erica has arrived with Kimmie, Leilenne and Alan Anthony. The hardest job poppa, papa and big mama had was keeping all the kids from tearing open *all* of their gifts before Ajay and Ebony returned. Now that they're back, the *total* unwrapping can proceed.

"Is it finally time for us to open *all* the big stuff?" Lil Ajay asks impatiently.

"Son, you had all this stuff that was sitting out already," Ebony says and smiles. "Are you telling me that with all of these gifts you have visible. It wasn't enough to keep you busy for fifteen minutes?"

"Yes ma'am. It was," Lil Ajay says, "But I wanna give out the gifts I bought too. While everybody is here and waiting for their stuff from me." Ajay chuckles as he leans over and whispers in Ebony's ear.

He says, "Ant's got a lot of gifts for Kimmie."

"Uh huh. I know," Ebony says, "I helped him pick them out."

"I did too," Ajay says and laughs hard.

"Oh wow," Ebony says, "Let's get to it then. But first. Doctor Susan is still here. She's going to monitor the triplets while we open gifts. That's why you see all of the monitoring equipment has been moved in there. Her and our papa's set it up, over on that side."

"Doctor Susan," Ajay says, "Will your daughter be mad at us for having you here working, on Christmas day?"

"My daughter is at Nina's house with Jerica," Dr. Mahoney answers as she giggles. She adds, "She went home with them from the hospital. And your family moved all of her gifts while you all were being released to come home. We've got some gifts under this tree too. I've already been made aware."

"You do," big mama says, "We've got everybody covered."
They all laugh as they begin to tear open the hundreds of gifts. Dr Mahoney has the triplets hooked up to their monitors, in no time. She joins the gift giving and they have a wonderful morning.

Ajay keeps a watchful eye on his son and Alan Anthony as well. The 2 of them are huddled together. They have all of their boy toys, all around them. But they aren't really playing with them. What they're doing is watching Kimmie and Lannie. They want to see what kind of reaction the 2 girls will have to the gifts they're giving to them. At that moment, Ajay decides to join Lil Ajay and Alan Anthony's huddle. He wants to have a *guy* talk with them, on this special day.

"What's up, fellows?" Ajay asks.

"Merry Christmas, pops," Lil Ajay says.

"Merry Christmas, big Ajay," Alan Anthony says.

"Merry Christmas to you too, Ant and to you, Alan Ant," Ajay says, "Are you two young men okay?"

"I'll know in a minute, pops," Lil Ajay says.
He's very focused on how Kimmie's face lights up when she opens gift after gift, from him and his family. He's watching Lannie too. He's interested in how she reacts to gifts from Alan Anthony and his family.

"Alan," Ajay says, "You really laid it out for Lannie. Didn't you?"

"Yes sir," Alan Anthony says, "I just wanna see her smiling and happy when she opens the stuff I bought. My sister found out what she wanted from me. And I asked Lil Ajay too. I had my big brother Eric, set it out for her."

"Just stay in line though," Lil Ajay steps in and says. He adds, "I'm watching *everything*. Just know that."
Ajay smiles and just listens.

21

"I *want* you to watch it, bro," Alan Anthony says, "That's why I was emailing you *back*. So you would know what I was trying to get for her too. Not just to answer your questions about what Kimmie wanted."

Ajay laughs. Lil Ajay has to smile too. He knows Alan Anthony likes his twin sister. He's just trying to find a way to be okay with it. Because he likes Alan Anthony's little sister and Alan Anthony doesn't have a problem with that part. Ajay can't help but reminisce on his days as a young boy. When he went through these *same* emotions with Jb and Tank. He has to make a comment.

He says, "The two of you remind me, of me and big Tank when we was y'all age. *Man*. This is what it must've looked like to my pops and big John, back then."

"We do?" Alan Anthony asks.

"Yes indeed," Ajay says, "I just wanna know. What are y'all plans for tonight?"

"We're going to the spot two," Lil Ajay answers, "Lil Jb is here and so is lil Rob. They're gonna go. Rich-the-third is going too. You know it's a lot of girls that be up in there, pops."

"The crew girls who are thirteen or older, can go too," Ajay says, "But the ones who are y'all ages, can't go. Girls in this family don't go to crew parties. Not until they turn thirteen. Unless they have a clique and someone in that clique is thirteen already."

"Like Destiny, Jada and Jerica," Lil Ajay says, "They can go because CJ is already thirteen. Right, pops?"

"That's exactly right," Ajay says.

"I'm glad it's like that in our crew," Lil Ajay says, "That way, Alan knows Lannie won't be going to nothing that we go too."

Ajay and Alan Anthony laugh. Alan says, "I'm cool with that."

"See my pops already know about the goods I've been telling you about, Alan," Lil Ajay says.

"You do, big Ajay?" Alan asks.

"For sure," Ajay says, "My son is always gonna tell me about his actions. I told his papa Al about my actions and he advised me, all the way. At that age, that's the *only* way you'll know how to move correctly."

"Yes sir, pops," Lil Ajay says, "And I already told you about *my* action. And they're all *older* than me. Just like it was for you. But that don't matter to them. For me, they're still not ready though, pops. Not for the *real* thang, they're not. I want a girl who's already been doing it. So she don't try to fall in love with me, just cause she let me hit it. You know I'm

22

the little you, pops. I told you about the oral part. I like it too. But that's getting *old*. I wanna get to the real thing but I don't want no girl thinking I'm gonna be with her or be kissing on her. There won't be *none* of that. I already see the girl I wanna kiss, whenever she's ready for that move. I told you about that. Right, pops?"

"Yea you did and I know about the head too, son," Ajay says and laughs. He adds, "And you *definitely* should only kiss the girl you plan to have and hold onto for life. But there's one thing I wanna make sure you understand. Just remember this. You don't wanna have this conversation with your mama. She's always gonna see you as her *young* son. She's not gonna be okay with all the girls that's *serving* you. Or the ones in line to serve you, either."

"I know and I won't tell her about that," Lil Ajay says and smiles. Ajay makes his voice very low as he says, "Especially about the sex part. You can always come to me about that side of things. Especially with you being six years old, son. You *are* the little me. So you're wise beyond your years. That's how the men in this crew are raised and all the crew men know the moves of the other men. The women know too. Once they're married and have a son. But your mother, even though she knows what you come from. She's never gonna be okay with any girls touching you in that way. Not until *she* feels you're old enough. So play the role as she wants you to, in her eyes. We'll always talk about whatever you and me *need* to talk about. *Cool*?"

"Cool," Lil Ajay says as he gives his father some dap.

"This crew thing will go on *forever*," Ajay says, "As long as us men remember. Always keep our women in mind when we're moving outside of their presence. And if you love your woman, like I love mine. You'll handle yourself *correctly* when you're in those streets."

He laughs. Lil Ajay and Alan Anthony laugh too. They get it and Ajay can tell, they get it. They also realize where Ajay is going with that comment. They have to carry on as young boys around the females in their family. And also make sure the females see them as respectable.

They decide to play with their Playstations and leave the girls to enjoy their dolls, tea sets and jewelry.

"Let's go up to my room, Alan," Lil Ajay says, "We need to talk anyway. We need to hit up lil Jb, Rich-the-third and lil Rob on their cell phones. So we can get up on what the plan is for CrewLand. Let's hit it."

"Cool," Alan Anthony says.

They grab their Playstations, along with a couple of the new games and

23

head up the stairs. Ajay gives each of them some dap and smile as they head off.

As the boys are heading upstairs, Ajay glances over at Lannie and Kimmie. They're sitting together watching as Lil Ajay and Alan Anthony make their way up the stairs. Ajay shakes his head and smiles.

"Parenthood is *no* joke," he says to himself as he heads back to Ebony's side.

He's still smiling when he takes his seat next to Ebony and gives her a kiss. He says, "Happy Birthday. Again. And Merry Christmas. Again."

She smiles and says, "Thank you, baby. Are you gonna open your gifts?"

While still smiling, he says, "I'm about too, right now. But I have to tell you something."

What is it, daddy?" Ebony asks as she continues to smile.

Ajay says, " I now realize why my pops was the last one to open his gifts on Christmas day, when y'all was at our house. Or we was at y'all house."

"Why," Ebony asks, still smiling.

"Because he was watching how we all reacted to the gifts from each other," Ajay says and laughs.

"He knew what was going on way back then. Ha?" Ebony guesses.

"He sure did," Ajay says and chuckles as he grabs his first gift and starts to tear it open. He says, "We'll talk about it tonight."

"Okay baby," she says with a giggle, "I know that's going to be a *revealing* conversation."

"It's time to *show*, baby," Ajay says and laughs. "It's been revealed for years."

They laugh harder as her and Ajay finishes opening up all of their gifts and the gifts for their new triplets too.

The crew ladies arrive by 11:00am and proceed with the cooking. They have everything prepped from yesterday. With the multiple ovens at Ajay and Ebony's estate, it won't take them long to finish.

By 4pm, they have everything done and ready to set the tables. The crew men and offspring have arrived. Jarvis Rhodes Sr is here too. Him and Ajay have a game shoot around, for later tonight. They'll have to be at *Quicken Loans arena* by 8pm to go over tomorrow's game plan for the *Chicago Bulls*.

"Can you behave yourself during dinner, Lil bro," Ajay asks Jarvis with a slight smile. "I just need to know *that* much. That's all I'm gonna bring up at *this* time."

"I will, big bro," Jarvis Sr says, "I give you my word. I won't get out of line at all. Unless she wants me too."

"Y'all asses are gonna behave at my house," Ajays says as he smiles. "You got me? It is the *entire* crew that will be here today. You wanna make it into the crew. *Correct*?"

"Absolutely, man," Jarvis says.

"Then be on your pee's and cue's," Ajay advises him. "No matter how tempting Ree Ree is to you. You gotta hold it together. For crew sake. If she *really* wants to have a future with you and not June. Then she's gonna be on her best behavior too. But if anybody is going to show a fucked up side. Let it be her, not you. You got me?"

"I got ya, bro," Jarvis says, "You got my word on it. I will hold it together. I promise."

"Cool," Ajay says, "Let's eat."

CHAPTER 62

NOT GONE BE ABLE TO DO IT!

Parma Heights

Farah, Darlene and Alana have made it back to Cleveland. Alana's daughter Olivia returned with them. They're all going to call her *Libby,* for her nickname. Olivia is already raring to get out and see what the city of Cleveland has to offer her.

"I'm finally back in the city I was born in," Olivia says, "And I wanna go to that underage club out there by where you work at, mom."

"The spot two?" Alana asks, "You're ready for it too, ha?"

"Yes I am. I've heard so much about it from Jamal and Holly," she says. "So I *can* go. Can't I?"

"Yes you can," Alana says, "We'll all be out there at the spot. So that's the best plan. I just didn't want you to go by yourself."

"I'll meet some people while I'm there," Olivia says, "I hope the basketball and football players from this Cleveland Crew, be up in there."
Alana, Farah and Darlene look at each other and smile. They already see where this is headed and they don't have a problem with it.

"Be sure and let everybody know that you'll be enrolled at MLK for the spring semester," Darlene says.

"Oh I will," Olivia says, "I *definitely* will. I'm gonna make me some new friends while I'm up in there. That way I'll know somebody when I start school in January. Somebody besides, a *teacher.*"
She laughs and so do the ladies, at Olivia's comment to Farah. They're all laying out there gear for their Christmas night at CrewLand. They're getting prepared for a club night while having some of their *usual* conversation.

"I know a girl who's your age," Alana says, "And she already goes to the spot two. She's Angel's stepsister, *actually*. But she's fifteen too."

"Can you call her for me?" Olivia asks, "I wanna know what she's wearing. Like, how do they dress for *this* club? Dressy or sporty?"

"I know Alana's got a good phone number for some of Angel's people," Darlene says with a annoying look on her face. She asks, "Don't you, Alana?"

"Yes I do," Alana says and laughs, "I'm dialing it, right now."
She continues to laugh while Darlene smirks at her and Farah stays out of that part of the conversation.

Alana is calling Angel mother's cell phone. Angel's mother's name is Angela Graham, who answers on the 3rd ring.

"Hey Alana," she says, recognizing Alana's number on her caller ID. Mrs. Graham says, "Merry Christmas. I talked to your buddy today."

"I figured she would've called me, by now," Alana says.

They're speaking of Angel.

Alana adds, "I know she'll call me before Christmas is over. Or first thing in the morning, so I can bring her up on all of the happenings at CrewLand tonight. I know she's gonna want and *need* her fix."

Alana laughs and so does Mrs. Graham.

Then Mrs. Graham says, "Angel is being moved to Cleveland, some time in the next 3 months."

"She told me that," Alana says, "But she didn't know exactly when. Do you know what day it will be yet?"

"Nope," Mrs. Angela Graham says, "I still don't know that part and I won't know it until the day of. Or maybe, the day before."

"I've gotta let her know my daughter is living with me now," Alana says, "My grandmother is helping me to get custody back."

"Oh that's awesome," Mrs. Graham says, "How old is she now?"

"She'll be sixteen in February," Alana says, "February twelfth."

"Okay," Mrs. Angela Graham says, "So she's gonna go to school, *here* in Cleveland?"

"Yes. At MLK," Alana says and giggles, "Just like me and Angel did. The only thing is. She don't know anybody her age here. I was trying to see if your old man's daughter was still around. Ain't she the same age as my Libby?"

"Jaylisa," Angela says, "Jaylisa Mangrove is her name. And yes, she's fifteen. She's here now. Me and Tony are still together too."

"That's what's up," Alana says, "Do you know if she's going out tonight?"

"I know she is, honey child," Angela says, "She never misses a chance to go to the kids club, over by the U....."

"The spot two," Alana finishes her thought and says, "Ask her if she wants to ride with us. We'll come by and pick her up, if she wants us too. That way, Libby will have someone her age to go in with."

"Okay. Hang on," Mrs. Graham says.

She relays the information to Jaylisa and Jaylisa takes the phone, so she can say hi to Alana. Then she asks her to put Olivia on the phone. Alana does.

From there, Jaylisa and Olivia make their plans for the night. It's

all set. Olivia and Jaylisa trade cell phone numbers before they hang up. Then Olivia turns her attention back to the Alana, Darlene and Farah.

"It's all set," Olivia says after hanging up with Jaylisa. "She's getting a ride over here, so she can ride out there with us."

"Well alright then," Farah says, "You see what your mom did? She got you a partner to kick it with, on your *first* day home."

"I'm so ready to see what my birth city has to offer," Olivia says as she smiles seductively.

Darlene knows that look. She'd worn it many times. So have Alana and Farah. Darlene know there's going to be some run-ins with the crew's next generation of females too. The same type of run-ins which her and Olivia's mother had and still have, with the females of their era.

"Here we go again," Darlene says as she gives Alana a warning look and smile.

"Who knows, auntie?" Alana asks, "Libby might open a bigger door for us. She might have the juice to get all of us in good with the crew. Let's see how it goes."

"Yes, Dee," Farah agrees, "Libby might have a easier time than we all have. And maybe, *lesser* time to getting in as well."

"Whatever," Darlene says, "I'll just remind y'all. We are going to be bringing a connection to Angel around the next generation of Ajay's crew. How the fuck is *that* gonna open a bigger door? Unless somebody's shoving all of our asses through it?"

Darlene laughs. But they all know she's quite serious. They hurry and get dressed for their Christmas night out.

CrewLand, The Spot II

Lil Ajay and Alan Anthony arrive at the spot II with Rich III, Lil John and Rob Jr. Rich III is 10 years old now. The other 3 haven't made it to double digit ages yet. Other than Alan Anthony, the other 4 are crew by birth. And each 1 of them have big shoes to fill.

At 6 years old, Lil Ajay is the tallest of all 5 of these boys. Just like his father Ajay, he stands at nearly 5 feet tall at age 6. With his *wise beyond his years* legacy in tact, he appears to be older than the others as well.

Lil Ajay gets attention from the girls from the time he enters the spot II. Mainly because he's not trying to make eye contact with any of them. That seems to make the girls want his attention, even more. He can tell they think he's older than what he is. He's okay with that part too. The

girls can think that he's older. Whatever it takes to keep their questions at a minimum.

He gets Olivia's attention as soon as he walks past the concession stand, where her and Jaylisa are standing.

"Who is *that*?" Olivia asks Jaylisa.

"He's crew," she says, "His daddy plays for the Cav's too. Ajay Jackson is his daddy."

"He is *fine*," Olivia says, "Is his girl in here?"

"I don't know about that part," Jaylisa says, "I know Brandon and Bradley, though. He's standing with them. I already had some of Bradley. He's related to him. I know that much too. Let's go over there and see what's up with them."

"Word," Olivia says.

Her and Jaylisa walk over to where Lil Ajay is standing with Alan Anthony, Rich III, Rob Jr, Jb III, Brad III and Brandon James. Of course, their *of same age* crew girls are very near them as well. CJ, Destiny, Jada and Jerica give Olivia and Jaylisa a very unpleasant look. They don't say anything. Not just yet. They're watching these 2 girls, cautiously though. At the same time, they're keeping their eyes on Brandon and Bradley. Bradley turned 14, this year. Destiny will turn 13, July of next year. Her and Bradley have already been selected to be a couple.

Bradley's parents are Jr and Tonya. Destiny's parents are Chill and Renee. The most senior couples in the 3rd generation of the crew and lifelong best friends. Thus Bradley and Destiny are connected from the mold which the ideal crew couples are made from. Same as Ajay and Ebony. So of course, CJ and the girls are going to check Bradley, if he tries to have a warm conversation with any other girl right in front of Destiny. Charlotte is upstairs working the VIP section of *The Spot II*. Brandon James, big June's younger brother is her man. The crew girls will inform Charlotte if anything happens out of the ordinary with Brandon as well.

Jaylisa and Olivia make their way over to where Bradley and Lil Ajay are standing.

"Hey Brad," Jaylisa says, "What they hitting foe?"

"Jay, I know you wanna be seen as cool, right?" Bradley asks.

"For sho," Jaylisa answers.

"Then don't approach me talking like you're a dude," he says and laughs. He adds, "That shit is unattractive as *hell*."

"Okay," Jaylisa says, "My bad. I just wanted to know what you got up for tonight."

"I don't know yet," Bradley says.

"Well my girl wanted to meet your boy, here-"

"My name's Ajay," Lil Ajay checks her immediately, "My name is not boy. If you wanted to know it. All you had to do was ask me. Okay? I have a name."

"Oh okay," Jaylisa says, impressed by Lil Ajay's sternness. Quickly she adds, "Ajay, I'm sorry. There was no disrespect intended. I wanted to introduce you to-"

"Hi. I'm Olivia Casey," Olivia cuts in and introduces herself. After all, Jaylisa was batting zero with *both* guys. Ajay looks her over as she smiles with her hand extended. He shakes her hand.

"What's good, Olivia?" he asks.

"*I am.*"

"Is that right?" Lil Ajay asks, "How would I know?"

"I can definitely show you," Olivia says boldly.

"Cool," Lil Ajay says, "But tone it down."

"Okay," she says, "I would love it if we could find somewhere to talk. In *private.*"

"We can do that," he says, "But it depends on what you wanna talk about."

"Me and you," she says.

"What about me and you?" Lil Ajay asks.

"Like, us going somewhere where it's not *so* many people around," Olivia says, "I'd like to get to know *more* about you."

"What do you wanna know?"

"Do you have a girlfriend?" she asks, "I love tall guys. You're over five feet tall. Do you play basketball?"

"I shoot. Yea. I'm a good shot," Lil Ajay says and smiles slightly. He's referencing to basketball and the chamber. Whether he has a girl or not, isn't her business. But Olivia wouldn't know any of that, just yet. She's just trying to keep this conversation going with him, as long as she can.

"You must be single," she says, "Cause if you was my man. I'd be standing right here with you."

"Are you single?" Lil Ajay asks her.

"Yes. I am now," she says, "I just moved to Cleveland today. I was born here though. But I grew up in Pittsburgh."

"You look like you grew up too," Lil Ajay says, running his game.

"So you think I'm fly?" she asks as she giggles.

"You look like you're working with something," Lil Ajay says as he

cuts to the chase. He adds, "What do you do with all that work?"

"I can work it," she says and grins. "That's for *damn* sho."

"Is that right?"

"That's right," she says, "I haven't had a complaint yet."

"So you're fuckin?" he asks bluntly, "Cause I'm not about to fuck with no virgin."

That's his *only* interest in a girl with this type of forward conversation. If she wants to serve him. They can get to it. But if she's looking for a guy who wants to be her boyfriend. She'll have to keep looking.

"Oh I'm not a virgin," she says, "*Trust.*"

"So how long are you out tonight?" Lil Ajay asks, cutting to the chase, even more.

"Until the club closes," she answers him, "My ride is grown folks. They're at the adult club. So when this one closes, me and Jay are gonna hang out at the bar and grill until they get ready to leave. Unless we can get into something else."

Lil Ajay is thinking about exploring the real sex side of things, *this* Christmas night. And if he can get in touch with Kilo or Arthur. It's going to happen *tonight*. He knows Greg Jr would let him use his condo too. All he needs is a ride.

Meanwhile, Jaylisa is barely getting any conversation out of Bradley. He's on guard because he knows Jerica and his 1st cousin CJ are going to get things riled up with Destiny. He doesn't even want to go there. His mother *and his* father would get in his shit, if he did that.

"So can we hook something up tonight?" Jaylisa asks.

"I'm out with my crew brothers," Brad says, "Wherever I go. They go. Is your girl wit that?"

"She is," Jaylisa answers, "She's into your crew brother, *already*. That's how it looks from here. She's been talking to him the whole time."

"My crew brother Brandon is our wheels tonight," Brad says, "I'll see what he's got up. His schedule is crazy. He's gotta head back to Natty, this week. Are you bringing your girl? Because y'all gonna have to take care of Ajay. I know he's got an appetite and very little patience for bullshit. Same as me."

"I'm not gonna fuck over your time," she says, "I can promise you that much."

"Alright, look here," he says, "Why don't y'all kick back for awhile. Go grab a couple more of your girls too. Just let us see what big Tank needs for us to do, around the spot. After that, we'll get back with

y'all when we can. Just kick it around the club and have a good time."

"Okay," she says and smiles, "I'll get Olivia and we're gonna hit the dance floor."

"Cool," Bradley says.

He steps back and waits for Lil Ajay to shed Olivia. Then they get with the rest of their crew brothers and head upstairs to Tank's office, so they can see what duties he has for them to handle tonight.

Ajay and Ebony's Estate, Jackson Heights

Ajay and Jarvis has returned from Quicken Loans arena. Of course, Ebony is home with her and Ajay's, 5 girls. Most of the mother's are still here too. The fathers are helping run the 2 clubs and Stoney's Bar N Grill. Nina is here with Lil Tank. T-baby is here. She's pregnant and didn't want to club it tonight. Rebbie's here with Orian and her twin sons. The rest of the crew ladies who don't have small kids, are out at the clubs. Ajay isn't going out tonight. Him and Jarvis have a home game tomorrow. They're saving their energy.

Jarvis is happy to see Rebbie is still here. More importantly, he's glad June isn't here. Ajay walks over to Ebony and gives her a huge hug and kiss.

"The oldest two triplets are almost a day old," he says with a smile.

"Yes they are, baby," Ebony says, "And they're *really* good babies, Anthony. They have all eaten, at least four times each today."

"*Hell.* I wouldn't turn down Henny and Penny *either*," Ajay says and smiles.

Ebony giggles and says, "They didn't. All three of them ate their share and they have been calm, all day."

"I think they like company," he says and they both laugh.

"Well the house has been full, all day," Ebony says, "They should feel like they're in heaven."

"It'll be wrapping it up shortly though," Ajay says, "I need some time with my wife and my girls."

"Okay baby," Ebony says, "It *has* been a long couple of days."

"You were amazing, baby girl," he says, "I'm so proud of you."

He gives her a sweet kiss. Then he says, "It's time to clear out the house."

"That's the second time you've said that," she says and smiles.

"I wanna have some private time with my wife. I told you."

"You know we're not able to..," she starts but he finishes her

sentence, ".. I know we can't fuck tonight. You'll need a couple more days." They both crack up laughing and he adds, "Nah really. Mom is gonna get all this company cleared outta here. And you and me are gonna rest our bodies and talk."

"I'm all yours, baby," she says, "And the girls too. Since Ant is at the kids club."

"Let him make it, baby," he says, "He *is* the little me."

"He's six, Anthony."

"Six in Ajay years. Is sixteen for other guys. He's all good."

By this time, mama Jo comes over to them. She lets them know that she's about to shut down the Christmas day celebration at their home and get all of the guest on their way.

"Is that okay with y'all?" mama Jo asks.

"Have at it, mama," Ajay says with a big smile.

"Anything for my *only* son," mama Jo says.

Jo giggles as she heads over to the front of the family room and grabs the microphone.

She gets everybody's attention. Then she makes the announcement.

"It's time to depart, so Ebony and the triplet's can get some rest, crew!!" Mama Jo says into the microphone.

Everybody starts to wind down and pack up their kids and gifts. They're all heading for the door. It's at this time, when Ajay recognizes that Jarvis and Rebbie *aren't* in the room. Ajay looks at Ebony. She doesn't seem to notice it, right away. He has to bring it to her attention.

"Did you notice that *one* of your foursome sisters is missing?"

Ebony spots Nina and T-baby but not Rebbie. That's when she notices that Jarvis is missing too.

"Oh no," she whispers to Ajay. "Where are they?"

"I'm about to find out," Ajay says as he grabs his cell phone and dials Jarvis' phone.

It takes more than 5 rings but Jarvis finally answers.

"Hello," Jarvis says, sounding as if he knows he's about to be taken to task.

Impatiently Ajay says, "I know you are not on *my* property misbehaving. Right?"

"No big bro," Jarvis answers, "I'm not on your property. I told you I wouldn't do that."

"Where are you? And I know Rebbie's with you. Correct?"

"I'm at Greg Jr's house," he says, "No one saw me come here."

"How did you get in, Jarvis? Don't play with me. I know Rebbie has a key to that house. All the *wives* have keys to all of the homes out here. Are you there with Rebbie?"

"Yes bro."

"I'm gonna hang up this phone and clear out my home," Ajay says, "I hate to say this. But y'all have to stay there until all of these people leave my house or y'all will be busted. You feel me?"

"Yes."

"I'll call you back as soon as everybody is out of the gates," Ajay says, "Don't go too far, Jarvis. Trust me. That's not the way to do this. And I don't even wanna talk to Rebbie, right now. Y'all are on my last nerve. Later."

He hangs up and helps his mother get all the guest packed into their cars, so they can all head home. While Ebony relaxes and takes care of their girls.

As soon as their house is cleared, Ajay puts Lannie and Lea to bed. Then he helps Ebony move the triplets bassinets into their master bedroom. Big mama is still here. She's still staying in their guest house, along with poppa and papa. Poppa and papa are at Stoney's Bar-N-Grill with Al and John.

Ajay assist big mama in getting her stuff to the guest house and getting comfortable.

"It's been a long day, big mama," Ajay says.

"It's not over with yet," big mama says, "I want you to be sure and let Rebbie and Jarvis know that it's time for them to get to *their* homes. The homes they share with their spouses. Can you handle that part for me?"

Ajay doesn't even look shocked. He's not surprised that big mama Eloise knows about the rendezvous. Not at all. Big mama always knows what's going on. She always has. Ajay just simply hugs her.

Then he says, "Big mama, I'm about to call him now and tell him to clear out of there. I don't even wanna be around when that comes out."

"Rebbie wants it, Ajay," big mama says, "It's something about it that feels right to her. All I'll say is this. June was never forgiven by her. When he broke her heart. He broke *his* relationship. He never learned from it. You go on and call him. Then you get some rest. You're handling yours, Ajay. I'm so proud of you. And Lil Ajay is following in your footsteps. He's going to be a lady killer in his young life too. Just like you were. But he'll grow out of it. Just like you did and all of his male role models too. You're doing your job. Don't you dare stress out over somebody else's mishaps. Do you hear me?"

"Yes ma'am."

"Go on and get some rest," big mama says, "And then score forty points tomorrow. Goodnight, son."

He hugs her again and bends down so she can give him a kiss on the forehead.

"Goodnight, big mama," he says, "I love you."

"I love you too," she says, "Goodnight and kiss all of them babies goodnight for me again. That includes Ebony."

"I sure will," he says, "And I'll try not to get turned on."

She laughs hard before saying, "Ajay, I already know that won't work for either of you. But y'all are just gonna have to bid your time. Goodnight, son."

"Goodnight, big mama."

Ajay heads back toward his main house. He reaches the patio and walks on through the patio doors and inside of his estate. He's all smiles as he calls Jarvis' cell phone back. Jarvis answers on the 3rd ring, this time.

"We're heading out, right now," Jarvis says.

"Uh huh," Ajay says, "And you'd better show up in the game tomorrow, bro. That's all I'm gonna say to you about this, for tonight. Goodnight and tell Rebbie I said goodnight too."

"Okay. Goodnight, big bro."

Ajay hangs up and heads to his bedroom. All he wants to do is take a shower with his wife and get comfortable. After they shower, they're going to lay down, cuddle and talk about all of the events of today. He's going to find away to let Ebony know that their son isn't *such* a little boy anymore.

Greg Jr's duck off, CrewLand Condominiums

Brandon hooks up with Bradley, Alan Anthony, Lil Ajay, Rich III plus Lil Jb. They all leave *The Spot II* headed to Greg Jr's condo. Greg Jr's condo is *this* generations hook up spot. Similar to how Chill and Stoney's houses was, for Chill's crew. And how Ajay's apartment at the U was the hook up spot for Bruce and Greg Jr's crew. Rob Jr is with them. Two of Ron and Carolyn Banks sons, Ron Jr and Jonathan are in Cleveland for the Christmas holidays. They make this *crew thangs* trip with their Cleveland crew brothers as well.

Ron Jr is 17 years old. He'll turn 18 on the 13th of next month and he'll graduate high school in May 2006, down in Houston. He likes Valene Hamilton. She was a flower girl in Lynn, Jan and Bre's wedding, back in

1995. She has a younger sister named Aaliyah who turned 12 in August. Valene and Aaliyah's parents were killed in Twin Tower 1 of The World Trade Center on September 11, 2001. Valene and Ron Jr met through her uncle Ced, who's married to Bre, Bradley's aunt. Ron Sr and Carolyn work out of Atlanta, a lot. That's how their oldest son met and came to like Valene. Her and Aaliyah live in Atlanta with their uncle Ced and aunt Bre, during the school year. They use to spend their summers in New York with their grandparents. Only that changed in the last 2 years. Valene wants to stay in Atlanta, year round. Because she knows Ron Jr is going to be coming to visit her. It's worked out well so far. Valene will turn 16, very soon. Aaliyah and Lil Jb are already liking each other too. Even though she's older than Lil Jb by 3½ years.

Ron Jr has a younger brother named Jonathan. They call him Jon, for short. He turned 12 in September. Jon likes to visit Atlanta too. But he loves to visit Cleveland, more than Atlanta. Nina and Tank's daughter Jerica is the reason why. Jon and Jerica met 3 years ago while they were both visiting in Atlanta. It was during the summer of 2002, right after Jerica's baby brother Jeremy Jr was born. Jerica went to visit her aunt Lynn and uncle Jb for the summer. While Nina and Tank recuperated from the delivery of Lil Tank. And while they got The Spot II renovated to the upscale class teen club, it is today. Jon likes Jerica and she likes him too. Both of their parents are already aware of their fondness for each other. For now, they're keeping a close eye on them. This way they can bring them into a relationship, along the crew legacy lines. Ron and Tank are thrilled that their children like each other. They both see it as a way to bring the Cleveland and Houston crews together by bloodline, in the future. Neither Valene, Aaliyah nor Jerica are here at Greg Jr's condo. Because tonight isn't about expanding *crew relationships*. Tonight is all about *crew thangs*.

The 9 guys who are here tonight: Brandon, Ron Jr, Bradley, Jon, Rich III, Lil Jb, Alan Anthony, Lil Ajay and Rob Jr. These 9 young crew men are on 1 of many, of their *crew thang* missions. They do them just like their fathers had done. Before they settled down to be husbands. After knowing it was going to be 9 guys going to Greg Jr's condo. Lil Ajay suggested to Bradley that he tell Jaylisa to bring a couple more girls with her. She most definitely did. It's about to get *very* revealing up in Greg Jr's condo, this late Christmas night.

Jaylisa and Olivia are here with the 9 crew brothers. This is *exactly* where they wanted to be. Even before they'd ever made it *to* the club. At Bradley's request, Jaylisa brought along 2 more of her girl friends who

were also at The Spot II. The other 2 girls names: Shalom Wittman and Rioshauna Fields. Both of these girls are from families who have, not so pleasant history with the extended Cleveland crew. Just as Olivia's mother and her aunt Darlene does. And just as Jaylisa's stepsister Angel does.

Shalom Wittman is the daughter of Miss Wittman. Debra Wittman, the ex-school teacher. Debra has history with Chill, Stoney, Jr, Rob, Jb and Ajay. But she was actually caught spending time with Ajay. She was caught by Ebony, Nina, T-baby and Rebbie. Debra Wittman also suffered an ass whooping or 2, at the hands of Ajay's female crew. That will most likely be an experience Debra Wittman and her daughter Shalom will connect on, in the very near future.

Rioshauna Fields' history is a little bit different but negative nonetheless. *Deadly,* as a matter of fact. Rioshauna's mother's name is Mallory Fields. Her father's name is Draper Watts. Neither of her parents have history with the crew. Or none that stands out, at this time. But Mallory's older sister and 2 of Draper's older brothers, who are all deceased now, had negative history with the crew. The 3 deceased went by the names: Malaysia Fields, Carlos Watts and Mike Watts. Their history was with the male crew, by way of Ajay. Ajay fought with Carlos Watts during his 4th grade school year at Abe Lincoln middle school. That school fight extended into the summer of that same year. Ajay and his crew brothers were at the gym playing pick up basketball games. Carlos Watts had shown up with his brother Mike and their gang. Their intent was to beat up Ajay. But Ajay wasn't alone. He had his crew with him and he wanted the mass fight to happen. It didn't happen though. That only made Ajay more angry. He knew why Carlos had started the fight with him at school, as soon as he'd seen his brother Mike at the gym that day. It was for 2 reasons.

1) Carlos was friends with Jacob aka Lil Jake, Old Jake Johnson's grandson. And 2) Because Ajay was fucking Mike's girlfriend. That girlfriend's name was Malaysia Fields. Once Malaysia found out there was beef between Mike, the boy she called her boyfriend. And Ajay, the boy she *wanted* for her boyfriend. She set the wheels in motion to make sure they fought over her. That fight over Malaysia never happened either. What the crew did do, was set her up. Ajay did have sex with her, one last time. It was at the chamber aka *The crew's killing floor.* Ajay had sex with Malaysia while both Mike and Carlos had to watch from a chained up position. Which they were in, at the same time. None of the 3 survived that evening. Malaysia had her last sexual encounter with Ajay. A boy who would never

TIME TO SHOW-RELOADED-Time Will Reveal 6

Ebony and Ajay's Estate, Jackson Heights

Ajay and Ebony have had their shower. She has breastfed Ariel, Arianne and April and the triplets are sleeping soundly in their bassinets, next to their parents bed. Ajay and Ebony are in bed now, laying in each others arms. They would both like to ravish each other. But it's *much* too soon for sex. Even for them. Ajay knows he has to talk to Ebony about their only son and the advancements he's already experiencing. He also knows Lil Ajay could be going even further before he returns home. But Ajay has to find a way to ease into that conversation with Ebony. He figures out an opening to get the conversation going and goes for broke.

"Mmmm," he says, "This is the life, baby girl. This is the way I've always wanted to start and end *each* day of my life. Since the day I first set eyes on you."

"I'm glad you pursued me and had eyes for me too," Ebony says, "You led me *all* the way, Anthony. And then, at the same time. You let me move at my own pace. You were always *such* a pro."

"I was raised to know that it had to be all about what you wanted to do," he says, "My pops was a master when it came to teaching me how to take my time and just follow my heart. Big John was too. Chill and Stoney added their levels as well. But big mama was the factor. She knew I'd seen who I wanted. The girl who gave *nobody* special attention. Except her parents and grandparents. I had to get your *special* attention."
He kisses her and smiles. She smiles and blushes. She likes where this conversation is going right now.
Ajay continues. "Ebony, I knew if I was able to have you. I would get to everything else I *needed* and wanted in my life. But I knew I had to come correct though. Because you was big John's daughter. He treated you like a princess. I *knew* I had to treat you like one too. I always looked up to my pops and he was always best friends with yours. That was an added plus for me and pressure too. Because I *knew* your pops could kill a man with his *bare* hands. I've never wanted to disappoint big John or make him mad."
They both laugh as Ajay's text alert goes off. It's a text from Lil Ajay. He's making his father aware of 2 things:
1. *"There's 4 girls here at Gee Jr's spot who wanna have REAL sex with me. U know I'm Da man's son, right? ;)"*
2. *"And all 4 ho'z got crew history & all 4 will be apart of MY past, very soon. \o^o/ haha"*
Ajay chuckles which makes Ebony curious.

She says, "That's Ant, isn't it?"

"Who *else*?" Ajay answers and smiles. He adds, "It's one in the morning, baby. Only a person who's in my life *and* yours is gonna be contacting me at *this hour*."

"Is he okay?" she asks.

"Yes he is," Ajay says, "He's the *little* me."

"Is Ant sexually active, Anthony?" she asks suddenly, "Is he?"

"Is he sexually active?" he repeats. Then he says, "He's active, Ebony. But he hasn't penetrated nothing. *Yet*."

He chuckles before she all but yells, "He's getting *oral* sex?!!"

"Ssshhh," Ajay says with a smile, "You don't wanna wake up *Tre'*, do you?"

"I wanna know where my son is and who's touching on him."

"What makes you think somebody's touching on him?" he asks.

"Because he's the *little* you," she says.

"Then you know he's straight. *Right*?" Ajay ask as he looks into her eyes, while brushing her hair back from her face with his hand.

"I pray to God he is," she says, "How old are these girls?"

"Older than him," he answers.

"How much older?" Ebony persists.

"They're not grown, baby," Ajay says, "I'd never be okay with that. Not when he's less than double digits in age, that is. Now when he breaks ten. Who knows?"

He chuckles again, trying to keep his wife from stressing too much.

"How much older are these girls?" she presses.

"Five to ten years."

"*What*?!!" she yells again.

"Calm down, baby. That's my *only* son and my *first* born," Ajay says, "Do you think I'd allow any harm to come to him?"

"Is he alone with them?"

"No way," Ajay says.

"Who's with him, Anthony?"

"*Crew*."

"Like whom?" she asks.

"His crew, baby," Ajay says.

He's trying to give her solid answers without giving up too much of Lil Ajay's privacy.

"How many crew?" she asks.

"Eight plus him. Nine."

"How many old *behind* girls?" she asks.

"Four."

"Let me guess," she says, "Our *six* year old son is already participating in *crew thangs*?"

"Yes. Hell it wouldn't even be a thang, if he wasn't there," Ajay says and chuckles.

"Let me read the text," she asks.

"You know I can't do that," he says, "You do know that. *Right,* Ebony?"

"I do but I don't have to like it," she says.

"No you don't," Ajay says, "But our son has to know he can trust me. The last thing he wants to do is break his mother's heart or disappoint you. So I have to make sure he can trust me with his private actions. Because that's the only way he'll come to me with *everything*. Which is the only way I can make sure he follows the right guidelines. *My* guidelines. What's more important to you? Running his life? Or knowing that he's making sure *I* know every move he makes?"

"Both," she says with a smile.

"Both is impossible."

"It's one *ay em* and our six year old son is at an orgy," she says, shaking her head. "How is *that* safe?"

"Because he's a Jackson man and he's with his crew," he answers.

"Did mama Jo know about you, when you was out there at a young age too, Anthony?"

"Not as fast as you know about our son *now*," he says and laughs. "Because cell phones wasn't available for the average income people, back then. But my pops knew and Chill knew. Chill would make sure Renee told mama Brenda and mama Rena. They would tell aunt Deb and she made sure my mama knew. Other than what my pops would tell her."

He's chuckling now. Ebony smiles at him but he can see it in her face. He can tell she's still very worried about their young son.

She asks, "How is he gonna get home?"

"Brandon is driving him home," he says, "And you know he can drive and we can trust him driving. Because I let him drive my Benz the night of Erica's bridal shower. He did damn good. He's good, baby."

"So this is how it's gonna be, on the *mother's* side of a Jackson male?" she asks.

"A Jackson *man*," he says with emphasis, "And yes. I suppose so."

"I see why mama Jo was so glad when she could except us being a

couple," she says, "She was just glad to see you settle down in your *mid teens.*"

"I know she was happy I liked you," he says, "She knew you was the best for me and she also knew you was the only person who could get me to calm down or open up too. Remember when my papa Al died? Who did her *and* Chill bring to the house to get me to come outta my room?"

"Me," she says and smiles.

"Jackson men are very fixed and focused, when we get our minds made up," he says, "And determined too."

"I'm gonna loose my mind before Ant turns thirteen," she says, "Does big Al know about all of this too?"

"Of course," Ajay says, "He knew it and expected it. This is how it is in a Jackson man's life."

"Ant isn't a man, baby," she tries.

"He's more of a man than any guy who's the same age of the girls that's coming at him," Ajay says sternly. "He's very mature, baby. And you *know* he is. You've said it *yourself*. For him, same as it was for me. It's just something about getting that curiosity about sex out of the way, at a very young age. And not just sex either. But sexual curiosity comes early for us Jackson men. It's just how our minds work. We see shit *long* before it actually happens and we have to get it out of the way, as soon as possible. So we can focus on the next lesson. Trust me, baby. Ant and I have been talking about this, for three years. And he brought it up *first*. His mind and body is *way* more advanced than mine was at age six. Ebony, trust me when I say this. Ant knows how to handle himself. The talks I have with him. They blow *my* mind," he chuckles and continues. He asks, "Do you wanna know how our first real conversation about growing up, started off?"

"How?"

"He ask me what did I have to do to get a woman like you."
She smiles as her eyes well up with tears.
Ajay figures this is the best time to crack a joke. Just to keep her calm.
He tries, "Ah baby. Don't start crying because you're gonna make me cry too. I can't let my triplets see me crying before they even turn a week old. They're gonna think their daddy is an ole softy."
Ebony laughs while her tears are still shedding. She reminds him,
"Baby, you cried when they was born."

"I know," he says, "And that's natural. But I can't do it no more. Not until somebody pisses me off for messing with them the wrong way."
Ebony cracks up laughing while he continues to wipe her tears dry.

He asks, "Are you gonna be okay, hearing this?"

"Yes baby," she says, "And I like that he asked you that. That touches my soul. My son sees me as the ideal woman."

"Hell *yea*, he does," Ajay says, "Which means I can't fuck up at all. Or he'll be pulling a me, *on me*."

She laughs more. She likes that, a lot. She asks, "Did you tell him?"

"For sure I did," he answers.

"Everything?" she asks, looking shy all of sudden.

"I didn't sugarcoat any of it, baby," he says, "I told him about my life. How I grew up and that I knew I wanted you to be my girl. Before I was even in school. Ant started talking to me in detail, when he was barely three years old. By the summer of 2003, when Eric started bringing his family around a lot more. That's when he started talking to me everyday. Even if he had to call me on the phone. He talked to me. Or he called pops or big John and they called me, for him. Ebony it wasn't long after that. He told me that he sees Kimmie in the same way I describe, how I felt when I first saw you. He said that to me. We was riding in my car, heading to our Rec center. He blew my mind. Because before he said it. My biggest worry was how was I gonna get him to understand that there could only be one special girl in his life."

"That's really amazing," she says, "He is *so* much like you, baby."

"Yes he is," Ajay says, "But even more intense. I have to keep him feeling comfortable about telling me what's on his mind. I will not fuck that up. Not for anything or anybody. You know what I mean, right?"

"Yes I do," she says, "I understand it, Anthony. Now that you've broken it down, like this. I understand it. This is all about his safety and him staying safe. Isn't it?"

"And out living me," he says, "*Exactly*. His conversation is on a man's level and he knows Kimmie isn't near bout there. Just like I knew that about you. Ant knows he has conversation that she's not ready for yet. And he don't even want her to be ready for it, right now. He just wants her to be a little girl, as long as she can. With trust in him until she's ready to grow up. And he wants her to grow into loving him."

"Really?" she asks in astonishment.

"Pretty much. Yea," he says.

"But if he likes her," she says, "Why is he out with other girls, right now?"

Ajay tries to explain a Jackson man's logic and way of thinking.

He says, "Because she's not ready for what he's ready for, right now.

He wants her to fall in love with him. But he's not looking to fall in love. Not right now. Because he hasn't even experienced the things he'd have to know, in order to make her love him. But when he's ready to love. He's going to show that to Kimmie and Kimmie only. Everybody around him will know he cares for her. Even before she does. Because just like I did. He's gonna make sure that anyone who comes in contact with her. Knows that he has picked her. So don't fuck with her. And baby, he's gonna be best friends with Alan. I see that already. The way they are, right now. Is exactly how me and Tank was."

Ebony laughs as she remembers those days with Ajay. And how Tank was okay with her talking to Ajay. So was Jb and Chill was too.

"Big Chill use to tell me about you," she says, "Tank and Jb did too."

"Because they knew I didn't give a fuck about a whole lot of people. And *no* girls, at all. Not in *that* way," he says, "Baby, Ant is the same way. Only ten times stronger. With these other girls, he's not looking to fall in love. He's only getting past that *experience* factor and he's gonna make sure they know that, from jump. He's not a liar. Just like I didn't lie to none of them either. If they ever get to fuck with him. It's gonna be on *his* terms. He's in a battle with his *own* mind, right now. That's *it*. He's ready to get to the man phase. Because his body is already there. In his mind, he's already a man. That's how we are, baby. That may be why God only puts one Jackson male in a family, at a time. I don't know. But I was the same way. So was my pops and both of my grandfathers. It's in his blood."

"So this is a normal thing from a Jackson man? Before he's of age?" she asks, "Passed down for generations?"

"Yes," Ajay says, "It's apart of the *one* son rule, I guess. And our son *is* an only son. He's just doing what comes natural to him and it feels natural too. Without it. He's gonna lose patience and fuck some shit up."

"Wow," she says, "Maybe I'd better stop at one son, then."

She looks at Ajay and giggles. He laughs too. Then he leans in and gives her a kiss.

He says, "I hope you don't. But for me. I started getting head when I was going on seven. He got his first head, over a year ago. He had been five for less than 2 months. It was in September, two thousand four. The girl was eleven. Do you remember in two thousand three, when Lannie was telling you about Ant's girl named Jamela?"

"Yes," she says, "But she was also talking about a boy named Reginald too."

"Yea," he says quickly, not wanting to talk on a boy subject. Not with his daughters name in the conversation.

He says, "That boy was going to Granny's House daycare, with Ant and Lannie. Back when Lannie was talking about them. But Jamela was his older sister. She use to pick him up from daycare, to catch the city bus, after she got out of school. That's when she first saw Ant."

"I'll kick her ass, if I ever find out where she is," Ebony says.

"You won't," he says, "She's history. She started looking at him in a serious way, by that next summer and he ended it. But before that. She was going to the sixth grade. Ant was gonna be starting Kindergarten. Mrs. Gates class. They started school after labor day. Jamela saw him at school when she dropped her little brother at his classroom. She wanted to do Ant. September, Oh four. She came to my Rec center to make it happen too."

"What?"

"*And* baby," he says, "He told me about it *before* it happened. That's the conversation he was having with me, pops and big John. When Lannie was upstairs with you and mama Pearl, snitching on him."

He laughs and so does Ebony.

He continues, "She did him, about once a week. I was just glad I got that option to come and play in Cleveland. Because I knew his keenness for sex was only gonna grow."

"So he was telling you, in two thousand three. About an eleven year old girl who was liking him and he wasn't even four yet?"

"Yes," he continues, "The moving toward him, happened shortly after that. But baby it was because of his conversation. Not hers. You have to understand how he's talking to girls that he don't wanna do nothing with but sexual things. That's the part you aren't familiar with. And you never will be. Because you have always been wanted by me. I had to find away to make sure *you* wanted me. Ant talked upon that head. Not the other way around. Understand that. But I made sure he knew to strap up, long before he got to that point. He won't be nothing like that with Kimmie. He could care less about Jamela or any of the girls that's at their hook up spot, right now. The girl he wants to have feelings for. Is the girl he's gonna kiss on the mouth. And he's only gonna kiss, *one* girl in his life. I have a feeling *that* girl is Kimora aka Kimmie. He sees Kimmie as a reflection of you. So he's not gonna try anything with her. He just wants to make sure she knows she's *his*. That's it."

"Then he should be saving himself for Kimmie," she says, "Why can't he just save himself for her?"

"Because he doesn't want her to fuck, right now," he says and smiles. "And right now. He *wants* to fuck. He wants to learn what females like and don't like, in every area. That way, when it's time for him to actually *date* Kimmie. He'll know what he needs to do to please her. He wants to honor her and make her smile. He wants to protect her virtue, Ebony. The same way *he knows* his father did and *still* do with his mama. That's what this is about. Learning life. Finding his manhood. These are his growing years. For a Jackson man, that comes *very* early. And you need to know that now. Especially since you're gonna have me another son."
He smiles.

She smiles and says, "As hard as it is to be okay with this. I *do* get it, baby. I really do. I remember how mature you *always* were. So were you learning how to know *just* how to please me, like you have done from day one?"

"Exactly."

"Wow," she says.

"I've never wanted to make any mistakes when it came to pleasing you. I learned that from my pops. And now, Ant is learning that from me."

"So, if he *does* have sex tonight," she says, "Is he gonna tell you?"

"He sure will," he says.

"And are you gonna tell me?" she asks.

"Do you want me too?"

"Yes I do," she says.

"Then of course I will," he says, "As soon as he tells me. I'll make sure you know. But promise me you're not gonna bring this up to him."

"Well-"

"Promise me," he says sternly, "Because if he loses trust in me. He'll stop talking to me. Do you understand?"

"I do understand," she says, "And I'll try not to bring it up-"

"Don't bring it up, Ebony," he says, "It could cause a gap in me and Ant's relationship. That would break my heart and his too."

"Okay," she says, "I would never wanna do that. Just please. Keep me aware. That's all I ask. And make sure he's protecting himself. *Always.*"

"Done," he says, "Now. There *is* something else I have to tell you and it's been going on for longer than either one of us have been alive."

"What is it?" she asks.

"It goes back to both of my grandfathers, on both sides. Allen Saul and Allen Devante senior. Also Chill's grandfather, Paul Payne senior."

"What is it, baby?" she asks as she sits up, still facing him. She says, "Please tell me. What is it that's lasted as long as our crew has?"

"The Johnson beef."

Greg Jr's duck off, CrewLand Condominiums; 2am

Lil Ajay is in the main bedroom of Greg Jr's Condo. He has Rioshauna and Shalom in there, with him. Olivia had to settle for the other 8 guys and she wasn't happy about that at all. Lil Ajay wasn't interested in her, once they got to the condo. Because she was *too* clingy. Besides, he's smart enough to know Olivia isn't going to be hard to bring in. Because her mother works for him and his crew. He brought Rioshauna and Shalom into the room with him. That was 10 minutes ago. *Now!* Their both giving him head. Getting head isn't new. But 2 girls at the same time, is very new to him. He's enjoying this feeling, *big time*. He's wearing a Trojan condom. *Size?* Large. He calls his dick, his *Jackson*. Not Johnson. And his Jackson is 7 inches long and as hard as a rock, right now.

He's definitely considering using it, in both of these pussies who are sharing this king sized bed with him. They're all over his balls and his dick too. Like they're starved for the taste of it. He likes the rush. But in his mind, he feels he needs to know more about them before he gives either of them the pleasure of being his 1st and 2nd pieces of pussy. He picks up his cell phone off the nightstand. He looks at the 2 girls while they're parlaying on his south end. He has to keep them focused on his dick, so they won't be distracted by him typing on his phone.

"I'm bout to text another mouth," he says, "I can't tell if y'all really want me. Or if y'all just wanted to beat out the other two ho's, out there. Show me what y'all working with. Or do y'all wanna switch. I want a nut. Is y'all wit that? Let me *know*."

"Yesss, Ajay," they squeal together.

"Then show me that. *Shit*," he grunts, "I'm bout to see if them other two ho's want more than y'all do. I want some pussy tonight."

He starts to text his dad, right in the middle of getting head. He wants to know what, if anything, his father knows about these 2 girls ages 12 and 14, who are sucking him off, very nicely.

His first text.

"Pops. I know you knew some ho's with the last names Wittman and Casey. How bout Fields and Mangrove? Same Fam? Hit me back. ASAP!"

Ajay text back.

"Debra Wittman> Ex-teacher/ho. Alana Casey> Ex-ho>Uncle Tank. Malaysia Fields>YoungHo/1ˢᵗdrop>Watts/Jake=Beef>connect.

47

& A+ *"Tony Mangrove." Prison bitch/ho> step dad. Holla back."*
Lil Ajay text.
"If I wanna push to empty my clip status. Get Fields N Mangrove chasing. Bet?"
Ajay text him back.
"Status. Sooner than later. Game plan type action."
Lil Ajay text.
"Bait n switch. On deck. Out. #Crew4Life"
Ajay text him back.
"They know Da man is in that bitch. #Crew4Life"
They're done with the texting. Lil Ajay has all he needs to know to move forward. He reaches down to Shalom and stops her from tasting him. He tells her to leave but she doesn't want too. He has Rioshauna to pause long enough for him to get up, wrap a towel around him and guide Shalom out of the room. Then he finds Jaylisa who's being had by Bradley and Ron Jr, this round. Lil Ajay leaves Shalom in the living room with them and brings Jaylisa with him. They head back into the room. He has an instant request.

"I wanna fuck," he says, "I'm tired of head, for tonight. Let's get to the real shit, if you're wit it. Or I'm bout to get up outta here."
With that said, Jaylisa moves up close to him. She's interested. She's *Very* interested.
She says, "I wanna fuck you, Ajay."
"Lay on the bed," he says and she does.
He straps on a new Trojan and looks at Rioshauna.
"Lay down next to her," he says and she does.
He mounts Jaylisa first. It doesn't take him long to find the inside of her pussy. The feeling takes him, instantly. He knows this is an action he's going to love and participate in, a lot. He fucks Jaylisa for a few minutes. Then switches to Rioshauna. She tries to kiss him but he refuses. He tells Jaylisa to kiss Rioshauna while he fucks her. She does. This action really gets him aroused.
"Kiss her like you would kiss me," he says, "I wanna know what it would look like."
"Mmmm," Rioshauna moans.
Lil Ajay is fucking her, very well. She's enjoying him. Jaylisa loves his aggressiveness. He switches pussy again and the girls continue to kiss each other while he takes care of their southern ends. Lil Ajay isn't going to be leaving the G Jr spot. Not for, *at least* another hour. He has it in his mind now. This is a crew plan that he was born to see through. His plans are to

smoke out old man Jake Johnson, for sure. And at the same time. He's setting the wheels in motion to make murderer Angel Taylor, think she has an in, through her stepsister. That is. Until the opportunity comes for him to make Angel Taylor feel as though she can trust him as a friend. For tonight, Lil Ajay is going to enjoy this feeling of fucking. Because it feels awesome. He's got 2 pussies at his disposal. He's been uptight for over a year. And now, he knows why. His body needed to get to a *released* state. He feels good. His body is tensing up but only in the best way. He likes this feeling. This is the good part. The best part is still, yet to come. But he can feel that it's going to come, sooner than later. Because it has already started. Right here and right now.

CHAPTER 63

ANGEL RETURNS [Like a bad rash]

Ajay and Ebony's Estate, Jackson Heights, 3am

Ajay and Ebony are still awake. The triplets will be ready to eat again, in another hour or so. Ajay has filled her in on the *complete* history of the crew's *Johnson beef*. After hearing the *whole* history, Ebony is astonished, annoyed and flat out angry. Not to mention, very emotional.

"They killed Chill's mom *and* dad," she says as she sniffles from the cry which started shortly after she learned that there are people in this world who's lives are all about taking theirs.

Ajay says, "Yes. On the night they killed mama Willa. They thought big Paul was in the car. Mama Willa was on her way home from work. Her and mama Pearl rode together every night, when they was scheduled together. On that night, mama Pearl had to work a double shift. Mama Willa would've stayed too. But she had other business to handle for big Paul. She took care of the business and was headed to Shaker Heights. They ran her off the road. It was the same cliff Angel ran you off of. Mama Willa didn't make it. Now can you understand how scared I was when Chill told me what cliff your car went off of? From jump, all the men thought it was Old Jake Johnson who did it. That was until Michelle made Alana and Darlene come to the hospital and tell the crew what they knew. You was in recovery when they came. I was back there with you, when they came. Still thinking this crew beef almost took my heart. I knew Lil Jake and his boys were dead already. I was trying to figure out who Old Jake had sent after you."

"And Angel isn't apart of this beef?" she asks.

"Hell no. That bitch was after *my* beef," he says.

Ebony can't help but giggle. Because she knows her husband isn't lying about why Angel tried to take her life. But Ajay isn't laughing at all. He's in the zone while having this Johnson beef conversation.

He continues, "We did look at that angle. But I already knew she wasn't. The Johnson's angle was always about looking for a come up, through the crew. And that shit has *not* changed, to this very day."

"This is *insane*," she says, "So Lil Jake was his grandson?"

"Yes," he says, "He was one of the three who killed Stoney."

"Because he lived away from us and they couldn't get to Chill or you, right?"

He says, "That's the part I told you, when we first started this crew talk.

And yes, that's right. We never wanted Stoney to stay on Union alone. Chill and Renee tried to get him to come home with them. Chill's vibe was on. But that night, Stoney wasn't having it. That night, in particular. He didn't wanna come to Shaker Heights and he didn't want nobody to stay with him. He was feeling down because it was the holidays and mama Jackie didn't come up to visit and she hadn't really called him to say she was coming up. Only Chaundra and Charlotte called. But they always called him."

"Is this beef the reason you killed that dude named Eddie?"

"Yes," he says, "He was sent by Old Jake to infiltrate us. He was acting like he wanted to sell weed for Chill. But he was suppose to gain our trust and then get me off to myself. So those same guys who eventually killed Stoney, could kill me."

"But you got him first," she says, "And when I came home to visit for Christmas, that year. That's when y'all went to the U and killed them?"

"We got the two that was still walking. Yes," he says, "Stoney had shot one of the three, while they was in his house. Before they shot him. The dude he shot, name was Danny Washington. He went to intensive care with brain damage. But when he came home, that spring. We got him too."

"And you said Bre shot him?" she asks.

"Yes she did," he says, "She was pregnant with CJ when she did him in. She told us she felt like Stoney had helped her pull the trigger. And we added some new members to the murderers side of the crew. Because of that Danny Washington hit."

"Who is it?"

"Well you know we already knew Joe and Dre," he says, "Then Woody is a boy who use to live in the point with his grandma. Before they turned it into a retirement age neighborhood. But you know Pac Man. Well, his mom use to fuck with Danny Washington. Danny abused her and eventually killed her. He said he would kill Pac Man if he ever snitched on him. From there. Pac Man grew into a killer. He trained for it. See, after his mama was killed. He had no other family. He went to foster care and got abused, *real* bad. And from there. He only wanted to be able to protect himself with his bare hands. So he learned the art and he's *vicious* too."

"Has he done any work with the crew?"

"Marvin," he said.

"Marvin Huntley?" she says in a whisper, "Farah's ex?"

"Yes," he says, "Baby, that's what that whole crew thang night was all about, with Farah. It was never done just to fuck Farah. Marvin had been stalking her and we knew it. We knew we could get *him*, if we involved

51

Farah. That's *all* it was. Marvin had tried to buy a contract hit to have Matt and Chill killed. Just because Farah was fucking Matt and she wanted to fuck Chill."

"And I got mad at you. Because I thought y'all was just doing *popular* male stuff," she says, "But it really *was* about a mission, ha?"

"It always has been, for me," he says, "I've never went to a crew thang, just to fuck no ho."

He laughs. She has to laugh too.

Then she adds, "I believe that. It's never been hard for you to get *any* girl you wanted."

"Oh it was *hard* work to get the girl, *I* wanted," he says and chuckles. He adds, "You're the only girl I've ever *wanted*. Real talk. The rest of them was just filling in the gaps until I could get to you."

"My life with you has always been such a thrill," she says, "And I didn't even know about this part, that you just finished telling me. This is wild, baby. It's like a movie. But you know. When I heard about Marvin's death on the news. I had a feeling the two things went together. But I had no way to link them. And Matt's kidnapping..-"

"....Was a crew rig," he says, "The guy Marvin went to, to buy the contract, was Joe. You know how far back we go."

"Yes. They was around long before the Houston hood rats saga," she says.

"Hell yea," he says, "They're apart of *Chill's* generation of our crew connection to west Cleveland. They keep us updated on whatever they hear from Old Jake and his posse. Or anybody else. Like Marvin. I'm gonna bring you up on a lot of things, that you will see *more* clearly, after this talk. We have a six year old son. It's time for me to make sure *you* know how he is to move. Okay?"

"Okay," she says, "I'm just wondering why me and my girls didn't know about *any* of this?" she ask as she looks into his eyes.

"This is a crew *male* thing. *Only*," he tells her. He says, "It's not until the females become mother's of sons. That we're allowed to tell y'all. And only after the sons are moving around, outside of their home, on their own. That's when we have to tell our wives. So y'all will understand just how deep it goes. Now *you* know the history and we are *very* deep. Because Old Jake's main anger was toward my papa Alan Saul, papa Allen Jackson senior and Chill's grandpa, Paul Payne senior. So he always wanted to get to me and Chill or our loves. Our girls. You know? When it comes to protecting the crew families. Us males, we must always move together."

"I've always wanted to ask you something about an incident that happened," she says, "This is from, way back. But I felt like it was something dangerous going on. Because that was the only time my daddy told me I couldn't go with him. I remember when me and you first started being *good* friends. We was suppose to shoot basketball, one day. My daddy was home, that week. Him, your daddy and your uncle Rich got beat up that night before. On the next day. Most of the males left together. I wanted to go, *so bad*. But my daddy told me it was just for my big brothers and girls couldn't go. I cried when y'all left."

"You was standing in y'all side door. Looking at me when I came out of our house to leave with them," he says and gives her a kiss.

"I remember," she says, "You had something under your shirt. It was pocking out too."

"That was the gun my papa Al gave me," he says, "I know you saw it. I was planning to tell you about it, later. But the grown men told me I couldn't tell you. Not until you was my wife and we had a son."

"Where did y'all go?" she asks.

"Down by *The Landmark*," he says, "Mid-city. We got Old Jake's son, Jake junior, on *that* day. He was Lil Jake's daddy. My pops and your daddy, they beat him *senseless*. But big John took him all the way out. That was the day I saw him kill that dude with his bare hands. He snapped his neck. I can still see the vision of it now. We killed more than ten of Old Jake's posse, that day."

"Oh my God," she says.

"Big John and my pops knew Old Jake had plans of coming after you, to get to me," he says, "Because all the crew men knew, I wanted you as my girl. Way back then. That's why, when you went over that cliff. The men all thought it was Old Jake, who set it up."

"But we know now that it was Angel aka the demon devil," she says and rolls her eyes. Then she asks, "So has he ever come after me? Do you know if he has?"

He says, "Oh yes. He has, baby. We was in high school, when he went for broke."

"In what way?" she asks.

"Carl. Craig, Justin. Tim," he says, *"More than four admirers."*

"What?!!" she screams, "They were apart of this *beef*?"

"Carl and Craig was related to Old Jake," he says, "That's why I was so scared for you. Because I couldn't tell you what it was about. I just had to get you to understand that no matter what. You and your girls

couldn't be going off with nobody. Boys or girls. Crew don't do that, baby. For *no* reason. Not unless it's approved by the elders and watched by the crew."

"So the older ladies know about all of this?" she asks.

"Oh yea," he says, "All the mothers and grandmothers know. Renee has known for almost two decades. Tonya knows. Bre found out after Stoney was killed. Because she was carrying his unborn. Plus she wasn't gonna rest until we told her why someone would go after Stoney and what it was about. So we brought her into our meeting," he says and pauses. Then reminding her, he says, "Do you remember when we was at Chill's house, after Stoney was killed? And we sent all the females to mama Deb's house with Bre?"

"I remember," she says, "Because I didn't wanna leave your side. But you made me go. You was so tensed that day. Your eyes were *very* distant."

"My mind was in kill mode," he says, "We knew who did it and why. We was already mad because earlier, on that same day. I did Eddie in. Lil Jake and his boys was suppose to meet me and Eddie in mid-city. If he could've got me into that trap. But we knew they plan. Still we was mad that they bitch asses didn't come back. Cause we was gonna do them too. If we'd gotten them that day. They wouldn't have been alive to take Stoney."

"I never knew *any* of this," she says, "Thinking back on that whole Tim and his boys thing. I was in danger of being killed and didn't have a clue. I just know I didn't wanna be there. Even before y'all came to the mall. But T-baby was so determined to make Rich feel pain. And Nina wanted to get back at Tank too. Me and Rebbie didn't want them in our booth. Then when they came up with the movie thing. We tried to talk Nina and T-baby out of going. But they was determined to go. No matter what. The only reason I went, was because I had a car and could drive me and my girls. I didn't want them riding with boys, they had just met. But they was so determined to get back at Rich and Tank. That they would've had them to come pick them up."

"There is no way they would've came to our block," Ajay says, "They would've gotten them to meet them somewhere. And picked them up from there."

"They knew y'all knew who sent them?" Ebony asks.

"Carl and Craig knew," he says, "But they know our formula. They know we don't involve our ladies until a son is born and involved. Or daughters, who roll deep."

"I never liked Tim," she says, "I need to make sure you know that. Even back then. Did you know that?"

He clears her question up, by saying, "Baby I knew you was never gonna mess wit Tim and I knew you didn't like him, in *any* way. You thought that was the reason I was acting upset that night, when we was at the apartment. But it wasn't even about that. It was about what their whole plan was. He was planning to do to you, what Raymond tried to do."

"Oh no," she says and her tears come back. She adds, "I was so naïve. I hate that part about my life. Always going against my first mind. Or giving folks the benefit of the doubt. I had to learn that *all* people don't have common decency. Becoming a mother has made me not give so much credit to people, I don't know. Big mama said that's my mother's gene. She said that gene can see things vividly. And when you have kids. You're less likely to trust other folks around them. Not if you don't have a lot of history with them. And now I know. She knew about this beef too."

"Big mama knows everything," he says, "She knew it because it started when they were the active crew. It was building during their prime years. During their generation. With all the other shit going on with civil rights and all of that bigotry shit. Still, black folks had to worry about their own race, *then* too. Because some black folks was playing that nigger role and owning it, way back then."

"I'm *so* sorry I went near Tim," she says as she still cries.

He wipes her tears and says, "We watched y'all, the whole time. We had folks in the theatre with y'all and in *Pizza hut* too. While we waited outside. We have people, baby. We always have. On the streets and in prisons too. So I need you to really understand this. Angel will be killed when she gets out. She could be dead already. But I want to watch that bitch's eyes roll back. She took a part of me. It's *my* call as to how she leaves this earth."

"I don't have a problem with that," she says as she looks into his eyes. She says, "I know she's not rehabilitated. She won't give up on her mission to be in your life. I *want* her gone. I can't even lie."

"She'll definitely see the chamber," he says, "If I can hold out that long."

"The Chamber," she says, "I've had my time there. But I had no idea that it's been there, for this long and for this reason."

"Oh yes," he says, "And baby. Ant has been there."

"I'm not surprised," she says, "*Afraid*. But not surprised."

"He's already planning to take Angel out," he says, "I need you to know, expect and accept that, Ebony. Because as he says it. She denied him

55

of his legacy. His birthright. He would've had an older sister. Just like me and pops and papa Allen too."

"What does he do at the Chamber?"

"Shoot," he says and smiles. "He's a great shot too. And Ebony. One of his gifts was his own pistol."

"Anthony," she says.

"Ebony, it's how it's done," he says, "Pops and big John helped me to pick it out."

"I'm just so afraid," she says.

"He's not," he says, "Neither am I. He has to be ready to protect himself. He's a Jackson. He's gonna help me to protect you and all five of his sisters too. And baby, he's *so* ready."

"Anthony, Old Jake started this, more than a half century old beef. Because our families wouldn't pay his bills?"

"Exactly," he says, "Like I said earlier. He made damn good money. Just like my papa and every other man. But he didn't manage his money correctly. The way I was told. He was always having parties. Buying women. Getting used by women who wanted to get his money. Just that kind of craziness. And he hated that Jeb Baker was close to our crew. Even though, there was nothing bigoted about mister Jeb Baker. Old Jake just couldn't give him the benefit of the doubt. And when his son, Jeb junior met and fell in love with Old Jake's sister. That sealed it for him. He was trying to convince our crew heads that Jeb Baker was bad. Just because he was white. Yet, there were white folks threatening him when they found out that Jeb junior and his sister was together. And he would do whatever they told him to do. They was trying to get him to mess up the businesses our crew had going. Our crew wasn't willing to be bullied. Not at all. Mister Baker fixed the books, so it would look like he owned it. Then he just cashed the checks and gave the cash to my papa Al. So he could pay everybody their cut."

"And Old Jake tried to talk to mama Jo's, mama," she says, "Before it even got to all of the business stuff, right?"

"Yep," he says, "My grandpa Alan Saul told my papa Al senior, not to trust him and only give him a starter share in the business. Still it was more than enough to take care of what he had and save some too. But he was the type that tried to lay out money. He had a bunch of *good time* friends. They used him. Then left him hanging when he went dry."

"And you said he convinced the ones who were as dumb as him. That it was our crew's fault that his money went dry, ha?"

"Yes he did," Ajay says and chuckles, "He made sure they knew our money was good. And they needed to do whatever they could, to take our money and take us down too."

"I'm so glad you told me all of this, baby," she says, "I've smiled, laughed and cried. But now that I know all about it. So many more things make sense to me. I get it now. But I have one more question."

"What's that?" he asks.

"Do I get to talk about this with my girls," she asks, "So I can be sure they know what to look for?"

"Your girls had girls, first. Except for T-baby," he says, "But Richie Rich was so fucked up, that he never even brought her up on this. So his son would be protected. Wes is handling it, these days. But you can't tell them. Not first, you can't. It's a husbands job to make his wife aware. You see T-baby haven't told you, right?"

"No she hasn't," she says, "Secrets. I can't believe I don't get it, still. How come I just can't accept the fact that my girls have kept some secrets from me. The only secrets I have from them. Is my personal business with you."

"And that letter Richie Rich left with Keno," he reminds her.

"Oh yea," she says, "I'm just trying to figure out how to tell T-baby about it."

"That her first love wanted *my* girl," he says, "And never had a chance in hell of getting you."

"That's the truth," Ebony says, "I'll figure out a way to tell her. But I want you to be there too."

"Bet," he says.

Suddenly they hear the kitchen door chime. It's Lil Ajay coming in from his 1st night of real sex, at Greg Jr's condo. Ajay knows his son will want him to meet in the upstairs library. Before Ajay can even hint about it. Ebony suggests that he go check on their son to make sure he's okay.

She says, "I want you to go check on Ant. I wanna make sure he's okay and not stressing over *anything*. Then you need to come to bed and get rested up for your game, later tonight. You fly to Newark after the game. We'll continue our talk after you return from your Nets game. That way, you can get to sleep before sunlight," she says and laughs.

Then she adds, "Because it's four in the morning already. So don't be too long. Okay?"

"Okay baby," he says.

He gives her a kiss and heads to the back staircase, which leads to the 2nd floor and on to their children's upstairs library. That's where Lil Ajay is already waiting.

Stoney's Bar N Grill, CrewLand Mall

Olivia, Jaylisa, Rioshauna and Shalom had been dropped off by Brandon, Ron Jr and Jon, on the 1st trip from Greg Jr's condo. The guys had gone back to the condo to get their other 6 crew brothers and take them home. Then they head back out to *Stoney's* in Brandon's *Excursion*, to grab a bite to eat and go over the pointers of the night.

When they arrive back at Stoney's Bar n Grill, they can see that Olivia is still thoroughly pissed off with all 3 of her party girls. She's heated with Jaylisa, Shalom and Rioshauna. *Why?*

Because all 3 of them had some of the other 8 guys and they had some of Lil Ajay too. Olivia had the other 8 guys and that was it. She didn't get any of Lil Ajay nor his time, after they had arrived at the rendezvous spot. She's wondering why he didn't give her any of his private time. And why he kept Rioshauna in their with him, until he was done fucking. *Period.* Shalom got to suck his dick earlier. Before he switched her out for Jaylisa. But he never requested Olivia. Nor did he join in on any of the fuck sessions that Olivia was apart of. She's very angry that she didn't get to fuck him. She feels *she's* the reason he had wanted to hook up with them, in the first place.

"I'm the one who got him to come," Olivia says, "I talked to him at the club, the whole time. So I know he was interested in getting with me. But y'all bitches must've did something behind my back."

"No we didn't, Libby," Rioshauna says, "He did the choosing. He kept me in there and sent Shalom out. That's when he asked for Jaylisa to come in. After that, we fucked all *kinda* ways. Then when he was done with us. He didn't even participate in the group stuff, in the rest of the condo."

"Not unless he was rubbing my tits while his boys was fucking me," Shalom says and laughs.

"He saw me fucking Brandon and Ron," Olivia says, "But he didn't come over by us. He barely looked over there. That's because y'all said something to him while y'all was in that room."

"No we didn't, Libby," Jaylisa says, "I *swear*. There was no talking going on. He had us doing him and each other. He wouldn't even let us talk to him. Unless we was telling him how good that dick felt."

She bursts out laughing.

"Y'all bitches are *dead* wrong!" Olivia says loudly.

Big Al reminds her to hold her voice down.

He says, "This is a place of business, young lady. Respect all of our customers and keep the bad language to a low. Or not at all. *Understand*?"

Olivia says, "I understand. But I just got some dirty friends, on my first day back in Cleveland. I didn't mean to get too loud."

Al motions to her that all is well, as he goes on with his duties. Big John, Dre and Woody just laugh. The look on Brandon and Ron Jr's faces, tell them everything they need to know. Another generation of crew thangs had gone down tonight. And there is yet another set of side pieces, left to argue over the ruins. Olivia continues to make her case, in a less loud voice.

"I know he told one of y'all to switch and come get me," she says to Jaylisa and Rioshauna. "And Rioshauna, how did *you* get to take part in all of the fuckin that Ajay did, *all* night?"

"I don't know," she answers, "But I'm not complaining. His boy told me that Ajay wanted me to come with y'all."

"Me too," Shalom says, "I got a chance to give him some head. Then he took me to the door and called Jaylisa. And once he came out, while we was doing the other guys, he kept coming to my group and playing with my breast."

"Cause you've got some big ass titties," Jaylisa says and bursts out laughing.

Shalom laughs and says, "I know I do. I get em from my mama. Wittman tits are naturally big."

They all laugh. All except Olivia. She's convinced that they'd stabbed her in the back when it came down to time with Lil Ajay.

"It don't make sense how we got along while we was next door," Olivia says, "But then when we get to the fuck spot. He acted like I wasn't even there."

Ron Jr decides to get in on their conversation. He brings Jonathan and Brandon along with him.

"What y'all chickens over here cackling about?" Ron Jr asks, "Wit all of the dick y'all chickens done had tonight. Y'all should be too tired to speak. Let alone, argue."

The boys laugh, as do the girls. All except Olivia again. She has a question for the 3 guys.

"How come I didn't get none of Ajay?" she asks.

"How you gonna asked us about Lil Ajay's personals?" Brandon asks her.

"He speaks for himself. You heard me? He did what he wanted to do."

"He had two, all night," Ron Jr adds, "Dude might've been tired, after that."

The guys howl with laughter. The other 3 girls have to laugh too. But Olivia doesn't find it funny.

She asks, "Did one of my *so called* friend girls tell him something negative about me or something? Because he was feeling me when we was at the teen club. Then we get out to the condo and he didn't say *one* word to me. It just don't match up."

"Lil Ajay do what he wants," Jon adds, "I don't know why you thinking somebody else made up his mind. You definitely don't know my crew brother. *Trust*. He did what and who, he wanted to do."

The crew guys know exactly why Lil Ajay chose the 2 girls, he'd chosen. They also know neither girl knows why he chose the way that he did. It's only a matter of time before all 4 of these girls will be out of the picture with Lil Ajay, totally. But for now. Lil Ajay needs them as a part of his ultimate plan. So he's going to keep them handy. Olivia will not be one of his handy though. But that won't stop her from going after him, each and every time she sees him. After all, she's got her mother's blood and her lack of common sense too.

Olivia sends a text to her mother's phone. She's ready to leave. She's only waiting for her mother, Farah and Darlene to come out of the adult spot and get her away from these 3 girls. Until she can come up with a game plan of her own. She's going to tell her mother, aunt Darlene and Farah about this back stabbing by the other 3 girls. At least, that's how her mind wants to see it. Then she'll seek the adult ladies assistance in helping her get another chance to talk to Lil Ajay. That's only going to open up a bigger can of foul worms. Nevertheless, she's going to do what she feels she needs to do to get to the son of a professional NBA player.

Nina and Tank's home, December 26, 2005

Erica is on the phone with Nina. She has to make her aware of the new face which was around CrewLand, last evening.

"What's up, Lil sis?" Nina asks, "You partied out last night?"

"Yes indeed," she says, "Me and Eric had a ball in the Chill Spot with the crew. You know how we do it. But I tired out, so easy."

"I know you'd better get a pregnancy test today," Nina says and laughs. "Who is the new face you sent me the text about?"

Erica says, "I am going to get a PT test today. And the new face? Alana's daughter is back in Cleveland."

"Oh *really*," Nina says, "I had a feeling that's who Kim was talking about. She called me. Her and Ashanti. They said she left with the younger guys in the crew."

"Heading to Gregory's condo," Erica says, "The new fuck pad."

"They just doing what all the males before them did," Nina says, "I know my Lil Jeremy is gonna be doing the same. No sooner than he turns five years old. Jeremy already threatening to take him to the teen club and he probably has already."

They crack up laughing before Erica adds, "Lil Tank got two more years and he'll be running with Lil Ajay and the rest of their pack. But I wanted to tell you that Alana's daughter was all up in Lil Ajay's face, while they was at the spot two. I'm talking about, like she *owned* him. While he was playing it just like his daddy would do it."

"Ashanti told me that Charlotte said, 'nine of them went to the condo," Nina says, "And took four girls."

"Yep," Erica says, "Olivia was one of the four. But when me and Eric went in *Stoney's*, before we came home. She was mad as hell. Why do you think that was?"

Nina cracks up laughing and says, "Maybe because she didn't get none of whoever she wanted. Most likely, Lil Ajay. Our nephew is Ajay *warmed* over, Erica. He don't get it."

"He's harder than Ajay, Nina," she says, "He don't compromise at all. If he don't want it. He's not gonna have it."

"And he won't give you a reason *why* he ain't having it either," Nina says and laughs.

"I'm gonna see what all I can find out before my doctors appointment," Erica says, "I'll see you at the game tonight."

"Cool, sis. And let me know the results," Nina says, "In a minute."

"Will do," Erica says, "See ya."

Parma Heights

Olivia wakes up with the same anger she'd gone to bed with. It's now, late afternoon of the day following Christmas. 12/26/05. Alana, Farah and Darlene had given her their word on the way home from CrewLand. They'll do whatever they can to help her work out a way to see Lil Ajay. They're all up by 2pm. Planning another night at the clubs. Darlene likes

that her grand niece likes Ajay's son. She's full of giggles over this knowledge. She has to make a comment.

"I see you got my blood *and* my ways," Darlene says and while still giggling, she adds, "Do you know how old he is?"

"I heard he wasn't seven yet," Olivia says, "Which means I should be able to run that. *Shoot.* But he's taller than I am. He has a young face. But his body is already a teenager and his conversation is on point too."

Farah jumps in and adds, "Your aunt Darlene use to fuck his daddy. She's ten years older than him. And he still got her ass spellbound, to this day."

They all laugh before Darlene says, "If he's anything like his daddy. Then he's probably packing dick already. Let me just tell you that, right now. Ajay had a twelve inch dick when he was twelve. It's fourteen inches now. Or at least, that's the size it was, the last time I got some of it."

"You're thirty eight now. Right, auntie?" Olivia asks.

"Yes. Thirty eight years young," Darlene says, "And still got it."

"I'll be sixteen in February," Olivia says, "When is his birthday?"

"July," Alana tells her daughter. "He has a twin sister. They was born on the twenty fifth of July. He'll be seven in seven months."

"And going on seventeen," Farah says and laughs. "It sounds like maturity runs in his blood. So Olivia you just might have a damn good chance to get some of that. If he's like his father. He'll like older women."

"Ajay's wife is younger than him, though," Alana says.

"And that bitch Angel was too," Darlene says as she cuts her eyes at Alana.

"He fucked Angel?" Olivia asks, "Jaylisa's stepsister?"

"Hell yes and she fucked herself up for life, with him too," Darlene says, "She's in prison right now. Because she ran his *then* girlfriend, now wife Ebony, off a damn cliff and killed the baby she was carrying."

"For *real*?!" Olivia asks in astonishment.

"Hell yea," Darlene says, "And knowing Ajay, like I do. There's no love there. *Period.*"

"And he wouldn't want his son fucking her relatives either. Would he?" Olivia asks.

"I would think not," Darlene says.

"Well Jaylisa fucked him last night," Olivia says.

"Lil Ajay probably don't even know they're related," Alana offers.

"*Well*, he will now," Olivia says, "I'm getting her ass right on up out of the picture."

"*Excuse* me?" Alana asks, of the curse word her daughter just used

in front of her. "I do have to *act* like I'm your mother, Libby."

"Okay. Sorry mom," she says and smiles.

Then they all bursts out laughing. Just then, the house phone rings.

Farah looks at the caller ID and says, "Speak of the fuckin devil. And you ain't my mama, Alana. So I can curse."

They laugh again as Alana picks up the cordless phone. It's Angel, on a call from prison.

"Hello," Alana says. Then she waits for the pre-talk before Angel is connected.

"What's up, Ay?" Angel says, "Merry day after Christmas."

"Same to you, Angel," Alana says, "I heard you're getting ready to be moved. Do you know when yet?"

"I still don't know," she says, "But I know it's sooner than later."

"That's what's up," Alana says, "How are you? I know you got some good news."

"I heard about my stepsister going out with your daughter, last night," Angel says, "And she already told me she done fucked my stepson." Angel cracks up laughing. Obviously she likes that part.

"Libby wanted some though," Alana says, "And she said she had Lil Ajay's attention the whole time. But Jaylisa backstabbed her when they got to the fuckin condo. I think that's low down."

"Jaylisa told me Lil Ajay *wanted* to fuck her," Angel says, "Well anyway. I'll get her straight for you. Tell Libby I said so. Cause I can't have them on bad terms. They gotta be buds. Because we are."

Alana doesn't answer because she knows Angel is up to something. And it's going to be something she's going to want her to do.

Alana finally says, "Angel, what are you pushing up on? Go head. Tell me."

"I told you I got the new number for the club," she says, "And you know I need you and Farah to hook me up. But I wanna do it when Ajay is in town. They play Chicago today. Then they fly out tonight, going to New Jersey."

"*Damn* girl," Alana says and laughs. "You know more about the Cav's than I do. And I'm right *here*. But I know why you keep up."

"Hell yea," Angel says, "That sweet dick stays on my mind. I have to keep up with his ass. Him and that bitch done had triplets. She needs to stop trying to have all them damn kids, so she can hold onto him. I know that's all she's about."

"Well she's got six for him now," Alana says, "One boy and five damn girls. And his son is already fuckin!"

They both laugh hard, before Angel says, "And if he's anything like his daddy. Then he's gonna have the girls going crazy."

"My baby already is, Angel," Alana says, "And she haven't even had none of him yet. But we're gonna work that shit out. He ain't had the best. Until he's had some Casey. Just know that."

"Have you talked to your man again?" Angel asks, "And you know who I'm talking about."

"What do you think?" Alana asks, trying to lead Angel into believing she's talk with Tank.

"I know you have," Angel says, "Keep the communication open for your girl too. I'm gonna make up for what I did to him. I've gotta make him understand that I never wanted to hurt him. Not at all."

"I'll keep the lines open," Alana continues the lie. "So what's been on your mind lately. Other than thinking about that fourteen?"

Alana cuts her eyes at Darlene and motions with her hands, like she's just trying to keep up the idle chatter. Darlene rolls her eyes in anger.

Angel answers, saying, "Nothing else but that fourteen. *Shit.* I'm just ready to get out of here. And I am damn sho ready to get on with moving to that Cleveland jail. Hopefully by New Year's. You *know*? I'll be rehabilitated a lot faster, if I can be closer to my man."

She laughs hard and Alana laughs too. Darlene walks over closer to Alana. She leans the receiver outward so she can hear. She wants to hear what Angel is saying about Ajay. Alana tries to keep the subject on Angel's move to avoid getting busted in her, *both* sides of their game stance.

"Well I hear ya, girl" Alana yells, "I wish you knew when you was moving."

"I told you. They don't tell us *that* part," Angel says, "I just hope you'll come visit me and bring Olivia and Farah too. But leave your old ass auntie at home. I'm not even trying to see her *yamp* ass."

"*And I'm not trying to see yours either*," Darlene yells toward the phone. Interrupting as Alana still holds the receiver to her own ear. "*You through anyway, when it comes to Ajay. So give it up.*"

"Your ass is the one that's through," Angel says, "Crusty bitch!"

"Hey Angel," Alana says as she moves away from Darlene and prevents her from hearing Angels end of the conversation.

Then she says, "Just talk to me, Ay. Before your fifteen minutes is up. I don't want y'all arguing over him. Not with me in the middle."

She tries to keep her name out of it. As if she hadn't already told Angel she'd hook her up. But she's got to keep it a secret from Darlene.

"I'm gonna call you back when I get another call," Angel says, "I wanna know when you can hook me up. You know? As I said. I got the new number for the club and I hope you and Farah will hook me up. Before the holidays are over. Cause they go on a long road trip, January twelfth through the twenty first. They'll be on the road a lot in January. I'll be in C-town by then too. So I know I'll be itching to hear his voice, even more then. Than I do now."

Alana tells her, "I told you before, what my plans are on that, Ay. But you've gotta be cool on all of that phone arguing. Because we all pay this phone bill. Okay? And if you don't keep cool. My auntie might make it where you can't even call me. That would be fucked up. Wouldn't it?"

"Hell yea," Angels says, "And knowing her. She would do just that."

Then she prepares to end her call. She says, "It's about two minutes left, so I'm gonna go on and bell. But I'm gonna work something out with Jaylisa, so I can make sure her and Libby stays cool. Okay?"

"Tell her *my* Libby wants some of that Lil Ajay rod," Alana says and cracks up laughing.

"Bet," Angel says, "I got you. Just make sure you got me. Okay?"

"Bet," Alana says, then the calls ends.

Alana hangs up her end and tries not to make eye contact with Darlene, at all. She already knows there's going to be tension between her and Darlene behind that *Angel* call. She tries to smooth it out instantly.

Alana says, "Auntie just humor her, if you can. Think about it. What chance does she *really* have at hooking up with Ajay? After what she did, which is the reason she's in prison. I believe Ajay would definitely fuck with you. Before he would fuck her. That's the way I see it."

"And I'm gonna make sure Lil Ajay knows about that Angel heifer," Olivia says, "Then he can push Jaylisa on to the other side and let me in."

"Or over a damn cliff," Darlene adds, "Along with her murderess stepsister, Devil!! That bitch ain't no Angel."

"Come on y'all," Farah says, "Let's get ready for the game. Don't let that phone call ruin our plans for tonight."

"For real," Alana adds, "I'm trying to get my baby girl in with Lil Ajay. No way I'd be trying to push for Angel. Not knowing that the whole crew hates her, by now."

She turns to Darlene and says, "Auntie. You've gotta give me a little bit of credit here. Okay?"

She laughs and Darlene laughs with her. Within a few minutes, all 4 of them are cracking up as they start to get ready for the Cavaliers game against the Bulls.

December 28, 2005, John Hopkins Airport, Cleveland

Chill rides with security to pick up Ajay from the airport. The Cavaliers had won their home game against Chicago, the day after Christmas. Today, they return from a losing night in New Jersey against the Nets.

"What's up, bro?" Ajay asks as he and Chill hug each other.
Security grabs Ajay's bags and they head for the vehicles, through the private hall.

"That was a close one, last night, Ajay," Chill says, "But y'all are gonna make that up against the Pistons, on New Years Eve."

"And my eighth Anniversary," Ajay says, "I wish I could fuck my wife." They both laugh. Then Ajay adds, "That would regulate my game, like a muafucka."

"I hear ya," Chill says and laughs. "You only got a few more weeks to go, bro."

"I don't know if I can make it, man," Ajay says, "I *needs* my fix."
They laugh again as they hop into the security SUV and head to Jackson Heights.
Ajay says, "I told Ant, we're gonna talk about *my* life some more today. He's been opening up, real good and he's already hitting splits."

"I knew Lil Ajay was gonna beat your damn record, when it came to the age he started fuckin, bro," Chill says and laughs. He adds, "I knew if *anybody in this world* could beat it. It would be him. Hell, he'll be six feet in another year."

"He's already hooping *real* nice too," Ajay says.

"He'll be in them State polls, in no time," Security Joiner adds.

"Just like his daddy did it," McDaniel adds.

"I can retire then," Ajay says and laughs.

"Without a ring?" Chill asks.

"A ring is my goal," Ajay says, "But I wanna get it in Cleveland."

"And you can," Joiner offers, "This is the best team I've known us to have. We can get it."

"Just play your best," Chill says, "You and Lebron can get us there."

"My *fix*, me and Bron," Ajay says and they all laugh again.

Chill has news on Angel and he wants to share it with Ajay immediately.

He says, "You know when I meet you at the airport. It's because it's some shit that can't wait until we bump into each other at CrewLand. Right?"

"Let me hear it, Chill," Ajay says with eagerness and impatience.

"I got a lick from our Department of Corrections hook up," Chill says, "Angel is being transferred to the Parma Detention Center, one week from today. Wednesday. January fourth. She'll be right out there in her girl *Alana's* district. And you already know, Farah is the one who's been keeping her lawyer paid."

"Just let me know when she walks," Ajay says, "You know I don't plan on being harassed."

"I'd say we open it up for her to harass you by phone," Joiner says. "It'll strengthen your case."

"He's right," McDaniel says.

Even the crew security know about the crew missions now. And they are going to make sure that whatever the crew feel they have to do. They're protected, all the way.

"They're right, Ajay," Chill says, "When you do interviews. Add in when you're hanging out at our club. She'll call, for sure. She's already got the new number. I know that because I sent it through our corrections hook up."

"I just wanna know when I can watch her eyes roll back in her fuckin head," Ajay says, "Set it however it needs to be, to give me that. That is Ant's birthright. I told y'all. That's how he sees it. And his pops is gonna bring it right to his damn feet."

"I'm on it," Chill says, "A chamber date will be scheduled before she walks outta that prison gate. Just know that."

They ride the rest of the way to Jackson Heights with regular conversation. It's clear. On the day that Angelise Taylor gets released. Her life clock will start ticking down.

Ajay arrives home. Him and Lil Ajay have their talk, first thing. Then they join Ebony and the girls for lunch.

Ebony lets them know, she has some new info to share with them. They're going to have a huge family event and 5 additions to a home in Jackson Heights. When Ebony shares the first bit of new information, Ajay pretends to be angry. He isn't angry though. He's just trying to make their kids laugh.

"Erica had a pregnancy test, yesterday," Ebony says, "And she's

going to be a mommy. So far, that's three crew babies coming next year."
Ajay says, "Okay. It's Arthur and Michelle. T-baby and Wes. And now, Erica and Eric. *Ugh*. Eric asked me if he could marry my little sister. But he didn't asked my permission to knock her up. He's crew to the heart though. So we'll let him make it, son."
Lil Ajay laughs. He likes when his daddy makes jokes. So does Lannie and Lea. They're all laughing. Then Ebony reminds them of the new crew wedding bells which will be coming soon.

"We've got a quadruple wedding in February," she says, "Crew Gear is almost done with most of the cuts. It's gonna be massive."

"Who all's getting married, mommy," Lannie asks.

"Lil Kenny and Chaundra. Uncle Jesse and Roo. Sam junior and aunt Pam. Plus Reaper and Brit decided to get married too," Ebony says, "Four brides and four grooms."

"This will be the biggest crew wedding *ever*," Ajay says, "Reverend Tucker's gonna forget who's marrying *who*."
They all laugh again. Ebony has saved the best news for last.

"And lastly, there's going to be some new students, who'll be going to school with Ant and Lannie," she starts out and smiles. She adds, "And those new students are going to be living with Eric and Erica."
Today, Lil Ajay finds out Kimmie and Alan will be making Cleveland their home. He likes this a lot. They'll start school with him and Lannie at Beachwood Elementary. This brings a huge smile to Lil Ajay's face. He's looking forward to going back to school already. Ajay acts surprised, initially. But he actually played a huge part in making this happen. He wants his son to grow up with the girl he plans to have as his own. He knows Alan Anthony likes Lannie. So he figures he may as well be here too. That way, him and Lil Ajay can keep eyes on him and make sure he's molded correctly. Ajay knows Alan Anthony is planning on Lannie being his girl, in the future. But he still has to make a joke, before it's done.

"I'm glad Kimmie will be in C-Town," he says, "Now my son can keep his nerves calm and focus on getting his school education. But son, when it comes to Alan. We can go on ahead and do him in. He can be target practice. Just in case we decide to go on and do Eric in, anyway."
They all crack up laughing. Ajay is on a humor roll today. He's always in his best mood when he's in his home and around his wife and kids. They're all looking forward to the New Year.

Ajay and Ebony will celebrate 8 years of marriage on New Year's eve 2005. With the 6 kids they've added during those 8 years.

Right now is when Ajay decides, their anniversary is when he'll tell Ebony about their son's newest sexual experiences. And also, his new links to their chamber game plan. And that Lil Ajay is no longer a virgin to pussy.

The Chill Spot, December 30, 2005

Jr, Chill, Tonya and Renee meet up at The Chill spot to go over the year end books. But that's not their *only* reason for meeting up. They get the sheets done early. Because they have a more pressing issue to attend too.

They have invited Genia Johnson to come by CrewLand today. Pac Man, Woody, Joe and Dre are apart of today's meeting as well.

When the 5 of them arrive, Kilo and Arthur are with them and so is Greg Jr. He has a home game in Detroit, on Sunday. *New Years day*. He'll be flying out, late tonight. Chill gets everyone seated for this 12 member panel and they get down to business. The crew *history* behind their businesses.

"Junior put me up on the newest lead with you, Genia," Chill says, "I already know who's been contacting you and most likely, what their real reasons are for doing so. We've come up with a plan to do *two* things. Those two things are, getting rid of unneeded and/or unwanted individuals in *all* of our lives. You will be a huge part of this venture and the crew will guide you, every step of the way. Genia, we won't allow you to be in harms way. Nor will we let you take *any* chances. Okay? We will have people near you. So you'll be safe, the whole way."

"Okay," Genia says, "I just need to know what to do. Step by step. Because this is very new for me."

Jr starts by saying, "Here is the first part of this plan. We're gonna stage a public argument. It'll happen at the salon. It will start inside and spill out onto the breezeway and into parking lot."

"An argument?" Genia asks, "With whom?"

Jr says, "It will be between you, Renee and Tonya. I know all three of y'all know how to bring the drama. Let's see if y'all can do it together."

"No way!!" Genia says, "I have *nothing* to argue with them about."

"Oh we know," Chill says, "We've made up a whole plot for the three of y'all to act out."

"And we'll make sure it's hot enough that it makes the news too," Tonya says and she laughs.

"We've got the scene *already* planned out," Renee says, "When the guys are ready to go. We have to be ready. So in the next few days. Me, you

69

and Tonya will go over our parts to make sure we got them down pact. Okay?"

"Okay," Genia says as she giggles, "This sounds like a movie."

"Movie of the week," Greg Jr adds and laughs.

"These guys are going to be your voice and your link to us, during this *whole* plot," Chill says as he points to Pac Man, Woody, Joe and Dre. He introduces them all by name. They shake Genia's hand and lets her know, they're ready for whatever.

"And we don't play to lose," Dre says, "*Ever.*"

"You know they work for big John's trucking company now, right?" Greg Jr asks Genia.

"Yes. Well I've seen them here, around CrewLand," Genia says.

"Well, we're gonna keep you connected through them," Chill says, "After you, Renee and Tonya have the blown out argument, that is."

"It *will* be public," Jr says, "The argument is going to be, *you* blaming the crew for the loss of Matt and Kelly."

"And these guys are gonna have to respond to the media," Greg Jr says, "Because we're public figures now. It'll be a *big* deal. The media will wanna know what our response is to women in our family misbehaving in public."

"And we'll tell the news, we're going to offer you a peace offering," Chill says, "That's where these guys will come in."

"We'll be coming by your home," Pac Man says, "A least three days out of the week. Me, Joe and Dre grew up on the west side of Cleveland. Woody grew up in *The Point*. But we all know the Johnson's and those who run with them. We know they watch your house already."

"*What*?" Genia asks with fear in her voice. She had no idea she was being watched by the Johnson family.

"Yea they do," Dre says, "We want them to see us too. So we'll be coming by your house and bringing things with us, to redecorate your whole home."

"One room at a time," Woody adds, "So that it takes awhile."

"You'll get a house full of new furniture outta the deal," Renee says and smiles, "Floor to ceiling."

Genia smiles too, before asking, "But can I keep it? Because I sure do need some."

They all laugh before Tonya tells her, "You can keep it. Of *course*."

Then Chill speaks again.

He says, "Once they see anybody come near you, who they know can get to

us. They'll reach out to you and try to get through to us, through you. By using you to see what they can learn about our movements. Through these guys. And these guys are gonna play the role."

"Hell yea, we are," Joe says, "I love when we get a crew caper. It's very rewarding."

They all laugh. Then Chill says, "When they come to you to find out why is someone who works for the crew. Coming to your house, so much. This is what you will tell them."

Kilo says, "You'll say. They offered to buy me. Because its their fault that my husband and my daughter got kidnapped and killed."

"That *is* what their asses said already," Genia says, "*Every* time they contacted me, afterwards. Plus when this makes news. They'll wanna get some popularity out of it. So I know they're gonna reach out to me again. That's exactly what they did, after Matt and Kelly's deaths. Well actually. As I told Renee and Tonya already. They reached out to me when Matt's kidnapping made the news. I wasn't having it, then. Because as you all know. Matt didn't fool with them and they wasn't in our lives at all. Not in the eighteen years that we've lived here."

"Well we *are* responsible for Matt's kidnapping, actually," Jr says and smiles.

"We are," Greg Jr adds, "We did it to save his life. He knew about it, once he got to the warehouse though."

"We're the guys who picked him up and took him to the warehouse," Woody says.

"Yep. I heard you screaming when we pulled off too," Joe says, "But it was all about the plan we had to make work, to save his life."

"The boyfriend of Farah was a rich kid," Dre explains. "He knew she was fucking Matt. He put a contract out on Matt."

"He put one on my husband too," Renee says, "Because she wanted to fuck him. That never happened but she *did* screw my son."

"Wow," is all Genia can say.

"So we grabbed Matt to make sure Marvin thought his contract was on," Pac Man says, "But that's when Chill and Lil Kenny went to Farah's house. So we could get the boyfriend *Marvin*, who wanted *our* crew leader killed. He would spy on Farah's house, *every* damn night. He spied on CrewLand too. But he had to do it from a distance. Because he was banned and he knew CrewLand has awesome camera protection."

"He bought all of his spy ware from my store," Arthur tells Genia. "It's right down the sidewalk. He didn't know how tight we roll."

"But we want you to know that we are tight," Chill says, "We're going to be your family, now that Matt and Kelly are gone. So just know this. Any contact you have with us. Will be done through these guys. And they will do the renovating of your house too."

"Renee and Tonya will be calling you through our phones," Joe says, "And things like that."

"And don't worry," Renee says, "You won't miss any of our events. We'll get you here."

"This sounds so organized," Genia says, "Matt always said y'all was so well put together and his relatives was fucked up. He knew that was why they didn't like y'all. But Renee. I have one question before we go any further with discussing *this* plan."

"What is it, Genia?" Renee asks.

Genia says, "Farah did fuck my husband and she was trying to fuck yours. I'm hoping there's going to be a plan to whoop her whore ass, soon."

Tonya cuts in and says, "Genia, you can count on it. Crew females know how to bid our time. Just long enough for these whores to fall in our laps."

"Yes indeed," Renee adds, "And we push their asses to the ground and get to stomping the dog shit out of em too. That will happen. *Trust*!"

"Okay and I wanna be in on *that* plan, for sure," Genia says.

Renee and Tonya assure her that she will be. Genia is happy to know she'll get some reciprocation for the whore who fucked her husband to death. *Literally*. Because he died on her front porch.

She says, "Matt was right about one thing. This crew is *very* well put together. This is how black families survived, back when I was a little girl. I want this so much. And I'm so proud to be down with y'all."

"That's how we were raised," Jr says, "Like the old school."

"The things that got our ancestors to freedom and the right to vote," Tonya says, "Was diehard loyalty and sincere dedication to each other. And that's how we give back to those who paid those dues, for us to have our freedoms. We stick by each other. No matter what."

"We're just carrying it on," Chill says, "And our kids have to do the same. I don't give a fuck what's trending or what is the popular way their generations are acting. Ours are crew. And they will represent with crew style."

"I love this, so much," Genia says, "Renee and Tonya have been my rock since losing my child. This crew didn't tell Matt to fuck that white woman. His *dick* did. Just like it told him to fuck the woman that shot my child and him. Kelly was trying to take up for her daddy and lost her life.

So the Johnson's can say whatever bullshit they want. But I know why my family is gone. It was because of Matt. *Their* relative. He's the reason I lost my only child. So there's no way I want *any* of them in my life. Matt didn't fool with them and he and I were legally separated, before we ever moved here. The house was owned by Matt's great-great grandfather. It was left to him. He wanted to move here to get away from his dirty laundry, down in Carolina. Now that's the truth of the whole matter."

"We're gonna get you some separation from that blood, Genia," Renee says, "We've got the formula and we're gonna move forward. Are you ready?"

"I'm ready to be rid of them," Genia says, "But I have to pretend to be angry with my *rocks*? That's gonna be the hard part."
She laughs and they all laugh with her.
Then Chill says, "I think a newly renovated home is an incentive. *Right*?"

"I'll put my *all* into it," Genia says and they all laugh again.
The meeting is adjourned and they all start to file out. Greg Jr and Kilo meet Genia at the door, just before they step out into the hallway.
Greg Jr grabs her elbow and asks, "Mom-in-law. Can I speak to you about something else?"

"Sure," Genia says, "What is it?"
"This is KeJuan. We call him, Kilo," Greg Jr says.
"How are you?" Kilo asks Genia.
"I'm great," she says, "After this meeting. I'm in the best family I could be in, here in Cleveland. I'm so happy that Matt met Tonya at CSU. Because now I have family here. Renee and Tonya are like the little sisters I've never had. But always wanted. What else do y'all have for me to do?"

"I've been alone since Kelly's life was taken," Greg Jr starts. "How would you feel about me dating again?"

"I would feel fine, Greg," Genia says, "I don't want you to cash in on your love life. You are still a very *young* man. A pro football player and dedicated crew member. I want you to be happy in your personal life too. So let me guess. Kilo has a sister that's interested in you and you like her too? Is that it?" She smiles big as she looks from Greg Jr to Kilo.
Greg Jr smiles and says, "Yes ma'am. That's it, exactly."

"Her name is Patricia," Kilo says, "She's my younger sister. She's finishing up college at CSU. They met during Thanksgiving and she hasn't shut up bugging me about wanting to date him *since* then."

"I don't blame her," Genia says, "He's a prize."
Then she turns to Greg Jr and says, "You have my blessings. Please move

on with your life. I want you too. *Shoot*. I'm gonna be looking for a date for myself, soon too. I've been without a real man in my life for nearly two decades."

They all laugh as Kilo and Greg Jr lock elbows with Genia on both sides. They head to the exit and on out the double doors and into the courtyard. Kilo and Greg Jr walk Genia to her car, where Pac Man and Woody are waiting to trail her home. They all leave and get on with their day.

Opening time at The Spot II

Tank, Nina and their kids are just arriving at The CrewLand Mall. Tank, Nina and Jerica drop Lil Tank off at *Granny's House Daycare*. Then the 3 of them head over to open up *The Spot II*.

"It's noon and the last Friday of the year," Nina says, "The New Year's teen crowd will start pouring in by four o'clock. The staff is set, baby. Do you need me to do anything else before I head to the salon?"

"Nah," Tank says, "I'm good. I've got my second in command here with me. Ain't that right, Jerica?"

"That's right, daddy," 11 year-old Jerica says as she smiles. Tank smiles too. Then he tells Nina, "You *see*. We got the opening covered. Let us know if you need *us* to come get the salon running smoothly."

Before Nina can jab back, Tank cell phone rings. It's June. Tank answers. "What up, big June?" Tank ask as he chuckles.

But his laughing will end soon. June has called him to inform him about Rebbie's erratic scheduling. Tank can tell he will need to take this call, in his office. He tells June to hold on and places him on hold. Then he catches Nina before she leaves out of the double doors.

"Baby," Tank says to Nina, "I do need you to help Jerica with the set up. Just until I finish this phone call. It's June."

"Okay," Nina says, "Is he okay?"

"I'm not sure but I think so," Tank says, "He probably just needs to pull my ear on some things."

Nina heads back in. Her and Jerica get busy setting their club up for the 6pm *EA-Sports* tournament. Tank heads up the elevator to his office, as he takes June off hold.

"What's going on?" Tank asks.

"Man, I don't know," June says, sounding distraught. He says, "Rebbie has been keeping weird hours lately."

"Weird how?" Tank asks.

"I've been home for eleven nights," June says, "Since returning home, after our lose in Oakland on the eighteenth. She comes in late, most *every* night. And she never really has a real reason for *why* she's late."

"I know her and Jerica stay at the dance studio late, some nights," Tank tries, "I mean she's very dedicated to her craft, bro. Just like you are."

"I know," June says, "But last night, when she came home. She said she was at the dance studio. Her Navigator was there, alright. But there wasn't any other vehicles there. I got out and went to every door. I *beat* on those doors, man. I called her cell phone. Never got her. Then two hours later, she comes home. I didn't even ask where she was. She volunteered the info. She said she was at the dance studio."

"Well June," Tank says, "When she dances, sometimes she has her earplugs in. It just depends. Don't jump to conclusions, bro. This *is* Rebbie we're talking about. She was the slowest out of her girls, when it came to getting down to the good part. So I don't even wanna act like she's seeing somebody. You know?"

"I don't wanna think it *either*," June says, "But it's something *way* different about her moods lately."

"Like what?" Tank asks.

"I was talking to her, this morning," June says, "I don't even think she was listening to me. I started off talking about our game, this Sunday against the Ravens. She was just saying '*Yea.*' So I decided to see if she was even listening. I said, '*I even invited Diana to come see me play.*' And she said '*Yea. That's nice, honey.*' And she didn't even blink."

"*Damn!*" Tank yells, "Oh hell *no!* She wasn't listening to you. Did she have something else she was focusing on?"

"Her cell phone," June says, "She was *textin.* She said she was talking to her girls. But I don't believe it. I don't believe that shit at *all.*"

"That would throw me for a loop too, man," Tank says, "I don't even know what to suggest."

"Can you see if she was textin Nina?" June asks.

Tank doesn't want to do that. Not at all. He doesn't know if he'll find out Rebbie was or she wasn't. And he doesn't want to be the 1 to know it. If she wasn't. He decides to stall June out. He's going to try something else.

"I'm gonna see what I can find out," Tank says, "You be patient. Give me time to check something's out. Alright? And I'll get back at ya. I just need you to focus on this last game of the season, on Sunday man. This is no big deal. You'll see. Calm down and stay focused. Alright?"

"Alright, cuz," June says, "I'll try."

Tank says, "I'll get back with you as soon as I can look at a few angles. Alright?"

"Alright, cuz," June says reluctantly, "I'll c-ya."

"In a minute, cousin."

This conversation with big June has Tank feeling confused but antsy too. He needs a release. An idea hits him. He hangs up with June and calls Ajay immediately. He's so focused on his call to Ajay. That he doesn't even notice when Nina walks into his office. Ajay answers on the 2nd ring.

"What it do, man?" Ajay answers.

"Ajay. What do you know about Rebbie?" Tank asks, "I just got off the phone with June. He's thinking she's messing around. You know anything about it?"

Ajay thinks for a minute or two. He doesn't even want to go into it. Not at this very minute. He's spending quality time with his wife and kids. Though he figures Rebbie and Jarvis has picked up their meetings. He'd rather not get into a discussion about it. Not until after he's spoken with Jarvis. He's going to do that before tomorrow's game. For now, he has to stall Tank out.

"What do you mean? What do *I know* about Rebbie?" Ajay asks, trying to sound as puzzled as possible.

"Do you think she's messing around on June?" Tank asks.

Ajay knows he has to halt this conversation. He's not going to go into it, at this moment. He'll want to discuss it with Jarvis. He has to discuss it with Ebony before he'd go outside of those involved or his home. He comes up with a response that will surely get Tank to hang up and get off of his phone with any conversation about a female cheating.

He finally says, "Rebbie was the last one outta the foursome to give her man some pussy and the last one to get pregnant. You do remember that, right? That's what I know about Rebbie. She ain't the first to do shit, outta the foursome girls. So anything she does. Will have to be done by Nina, Ebony and T-baby, first. So are you asking me has my wife been messing around? Or your wife? Or T-baby? Be *damn* careful how you answer me, bro."

He pretends to be perturbed. He knows Tank will walk a fine line to keep from getting him riled up. And it works. Tank heads the other way with his questioning.

He says, "I told June. He *buggin* out. You know he's feeling antsy because *he* cheated. The elders told us not to ever cheat, once we was married. They said it would break down the trust factor. You know?"

"So you ain't trying to say Ebony's been cheating then. Right?"

"Hell *fuck* no, Ajay! *Damn!*" Tank says, "My twin ain't never been a dishonest female. She can't even see her *own* ass without you seeing it first."

Ajay has to laugh. He knew Tank wasn't going to push it, if he brought his *only* sister into the equation. Tank has to laugh too.

Then he says, "I told June to chill out. He never really even wanted Rebbie to have a job. So that might be what's really going on. I don't know. I'm just telling you what he called *me* with. And for the record. My fuckin wife ain't no dishonest woman *either*. She did open my damn eyes, a few years back. But she was in more danger with them Jake clowns. Then she was, of getting with one of em."

Tank turns to see Nina standing there, inside of his office. She looks puzzled and inquisitive, all at the same time. Tank knows he has to end his conversation with Ajay. Because if he's ever going to ask Nina about Rebbie. The time would be now.

He finishes up his call with Ajay, saying, "Well now that the most important woman in the world is in my office. I'll have to bid you farewell, bro."

"Ebony's sitting right here next to me, bro," Ajay says, "The most important woman in the world is laying against my chest. And even if it *was* two of her. They'd both be *right* here."

"Bye, Ajay!" Tank yells as he laughs again.

"Later," Ajay says, chuckling as he hangs up.

Ajay looks at Ebony. She's already aware of what the call was for and about. They'll discuss it later. It's not a priority for them, at the moment.

But it's on the front burner at The Spot II. Nina is very inquisitive. She wants to know what that phone conversation was about. So Tank and Nina are about to discuss it, right now.

"So what the hell is going on, baby?" Nina asks, "What's up?"

"That call earlier, was June," Tank says, "He thinks Rebbie's up to something. Or someone besides him."

"For *real*," Nina says, trying to act surprised.

It's not working on Tank, too well. He can tell there's something going on in his wife's mind. Because if she was insulted by what he'd just asked her. Her comment to him would've been made with a lot higher octaves in her voice. Tank gets right to the point.

"Do you know something, baby?" Tank asks.

"No I don't," she says, vying to stay bonded with her foursome girls until the end. She asks, "Is June messing around, Jeremy? Is that why he's not keeping up with Rebbie?"

"I don't know nothing about it, if he is," Tank says, "He's been straight since Rebbie caught him out by the U, awhile back. But now he's saying *she's* keeping weird hours."

"At the studio is the *only* place I've known Rebbie to be," Nina says, "And most of the time. Jerica is with her. There's no way in *hell*, she'd be messing around anyway. Rebbie wouldn't even mess around when June was doing it. *Heavily*."

"I know," Tank says, "Just look into it from your end. I don't even wanna talk about this shit, no more. Ajay asked me the right damn question. He asked me was I trying to tell him *Ebony* was cheating. Or was my wife cheating. And he mentioned T-baby too. Cause he said all three of y'all would have to do something. Before Rebbie would. And when he asked me was my wife cheating. That brought it all back home for me. I'm only concerned about my home. You know?"

"Yes," she says with a smile, "Because our home is on point. And as for as I know. So are the rest of my girls. Ajay grew up with us, just like you did. Rebbie never did *anything* first."

She laughs and so does Tank. Nina wants to drop this subject too. But she will get in touch with Rebbie, at her first salon break. She wants to know if Rebbie's years of kissing and oral sex sessions with Jarvis. Have advanced to *full on sex*. She can't wait until her first salon break. She's going to be on the phone with her girls.

Williams Accounting and Finance, CrewLand Mall

T-baby and Wes are at the office getting tax work finished. They'll be prepared and ahead of schedule for the 2006 tax season. T-baby is still reeling from all the Johnson beef information she's received via Wes. She's itching to talk to her girls about it. But Wes reminds her, it's not a topic for regular conversation.

"You have to remember," he says, "Only you and Ebony know, at this time. So you and Ebony can discuss it. But Nina and Rebbie have to be brought up on it by their husbands. That's the way it was dictated to me. And that's the way it has to be done. Just be patient. I'm sure Ebony knows. Ajay said he was going to tell her before she had the triplets. So I'm sure he's gotten it done, by now."

TIME TO SHOW-RELOADED-Time Will Reveal 6

CHAPTER 64

WHAT'S GOING ON?

Jackson Heights, Ajay and Ebony's mansion

At Ajay and Ebony's home, things are calm. Both he and Ebony wish there was no drama amongst the crew marriages. But they also know, there's something going on between Rebbie and Jarvis. Neither of them know if it's advanced to full on sex yet. But their lack of knowledge will change after the phone call, Ebony is about to receive from Gwen Rhodes. *Jarvis' wife*. Ebony's phone is ringing right now. She looks at the caller ID, then shows it to Ajay.

He says, "Just answer it and let her do most of the talking."

"I'll see what's on her mind," Ebony says, "She may bring all of the things we both have questions about. To a brighter light."

"For real," Ajay says, "I'm gonna take Ant and head to the sports complex while you take the call."

"And make sure he brings you up on *everything*. Okay?" Ebony says and smiles, as she answers her phone.

"No doubt," Ajay says as he prepares Lil Ajay for a trip to their community center and sports complex.

Before leaving, Ajay gives Ebony a kiss. Lil Ajay kisses her on the cheek. Then him and Ajay head out to the garage. Ebony gets back to her call with Gwen.

She says, "Hello there, stranger. How was Christmas?"

"Hi," Gwen says, "It wasn't *nearly* as nice as yours. I saw Ajay's film on the news. I had to call you and say congrats on the triplets. You and Ajay are *awesome*. You two are my role model couple. Always have been."

"Thanks, Gwen," she says, "It's been wonderful. I have to admit. My husband has been *on point*. I miss our personal time, though. But you *know* we'll have to take a vacation for a few weeks."

She giggles and tries to keep their conversation on a lighter note.

Gwen laughs and says, "I know it never lasted for six weeks."

Ebony laughs more and says, "It won't *this* time either. Gwen, the world knows that's my *medicine*, right there. My calm. Even *during* the storm."

They laugh hard before Gwen gets on to her reason for calling.

"I really wanna apologize again for my little sister," Gwen says, "We've got her moved far enough out, so she won't have *a lot* of chances to run into Ajay and bother him *anymore*."

"I know and that's good to know," Ebony says cautiously.

She can tell by Gwen's tone of voice, that there's a larger problem. There is much sadness and worry in her voice.

Finally Gwen says, "I wish Jarvis senior was more like Ajay. Since we moved from Jackson Heights, he's even worse with his time management."

"Gwen, he was like that in college," Ebony says and tries to laugh it off. She adds "Don't you *remember*?"

But Gwen is determined to make Ebony understand that Jarvis is more like a part-time tenant, at their home.

She says, "Jarvis hardly even comes home, Ebony. I don't know where he's spending so much time at. But I just know, it's another woman."

"Gwen, don't jump to conclusions," Ebony eases.

"I don't think I am," Gwen says, "Ebony he rarely sleeps here. When he does. He sleeps in our son's room. Or they sleep in the entertainment room. And he looks forward to going on the road. Now when the Cav's return from the road. Does Ajay sleep somewhere else, that same night or *any* night?"

"I think you know that answer," Ebony treads.

"*Exactly*," Gwen says, "Jarvis only comes to the house to get more clothes and to spend time with Jarvis junior. He barely talks to me and when he does. It's only about our son or just to make sure I'm okay *financially*."

Ebony asks, "He *is* paying the bills and taking care of his son, right?"

"Of course," Gwen says, "He pays for everything. And you know he made me stop working at CrewLand. He said it was because he needed me to spend more time at home. But now that I'm at home. He *never* is."

"But how does that mean he's cheating, Gwen?" Ebony tries.

"Because he never wants *sex*," Gwen says, "That was one thing we always agreed on. Our sex life and how plentiful it had to be. That was our staple. The main thing that we *both* agreed on. But now, it's like he's living somewhere else!"

Ebony knows about the condo that Jarvis Sr has. She also knows, Gwen doesn't know about it. She tries to take Gwen's mind into another direction.

"Gwen, do y'all argue a lot?" she asks.

"No," Gwen says, "*Never*. I argue but he never does. He just says I'm blowing things outta proportion."

"Because you might be," Ebony says, "Gwen you know how much Jarvis wants to be crew, right?"

"Yes," she says, "And so do I."

"Well he may be upset about not making it in," Ebony says. Then she adds heat for Gwen, saying, "And he might feel like it was because of you. Does he know about you and my twin, back in college?"

"No way!"

"And you're sure he doesn't know?" Ebony asks.

"He's never said anything to me about it," she says, "And I know Tank wouldn't tell him. Would he?"

"No he wouldn't," Ebony says, "I'm sure of that. But he told Nina. He told *his* wife."

"Oh my God," Gwen says, "Would she tell Jarvis?"

"No she wouldn't," Ebony says, "She would never do that. Nina is all about her husband and him being honest with her. She wouldn't try to ruin your marriage. She's fine because she knows it didn't continue."

"I need to ask you something," Gwen says suddenly.

Ebony takes a deep breathe. She hopes Gwen is not about to ask her about anything which is on the lines of Rebbie. But Gwen's on a roll.

Ebony takes a deep breath, then asks, "What do you need to ask me?"

"Are there any grown women, who take lessons at your girl's dance school?" Gwen asks, "And do you know any of them?"

"Wait. *What*?" she steers cautiously. "Dance school? What in this *world* are you getting too?"

"I just wanna know if you'll ask Rebbie, if she's seen my husband around her school," Gwen says, "Will you?"

"I will," Ebony says, "But I wanna know why you want me to ask her that? What is this about?"

"My little sister Nickeia said she has seen his vehicle over there, many times," Gwen says, "She said she's seen it parked there. Like three to four nights a week."

Ebony decides to turn this conversation in the other direction. While putting Gwen in the hot seat, at the same time. This way, Gwen will leave the dance school talk out of this conversation. And at the same time. Ebony won't be at risk of giving anything away.

Ebony asks, "Tell me what was Nickeia's reason for being over by the dance school?"

"She be out riding with girls, her age," Gwen says.

But Ebony is on a roll, this time. She says,

"You do know what's right next to Rebbie's dance school, right Gwen? My husband's sports complex and gym. You remember that. Don't you?"

"Yes," Gwen says, "She said she was riding with girlfriends, the

81

first time she saw his Benz. After that. She said she would ride through there, just to see if she saw it again. Because she knows he hardly ever comes home."

"And don't you think your little sister knows you would be okay with her riding past my man's place of business, all week. As long as you thought it was just in passing? And just to look out for a hint of something she could find out for you?"

"So Ebony. What are you saying?" Gwen asks.

"I think Nickeia is riding through there for a spotting of Anthony. And she's not gonna go through there when they're on the road. Or playing a game. *Why*? Because she knows Anthony isn't gonna be in that area *either*. I just don't believe Jarvis is hanging out at no damn dance school. I think Nickeia is playing on your worries. While at the same time. She's still stalking my husband. Now is *that* possible Gwen? You know her better than I do. Is that something she would do?"

"It is, Ebony," Gwen says, "*Damn*."

"*Right*," Ebony says, "Talk to your sister. Okay? Because no one can park in Rebbie's parking lot without a parking pass. And only members can have a pass. So is Jarvis taking dance classes?"

Gwen laughs. Which makes Ebony laugh too. Then Gwen sums it all up. She says, "I'm gonna talk to Nickeia when she gets in, tonight. Ebony I didn't even think about it, *that* way. I'm so sorry. *Again*. She probably is only riding through there. Because she knows Ajay will be there, when he's not doing game stuff."

Ebony counters, "When my husband *is* in town. He's at home. When he's in Cleveland and not at home. He's with our son and/or our crew. We have crew who hold down his sports complex. Whether he's home *or* on the road. Anthony is barely there. He's with me and our six children. Twenty out of the twenty four hours of *any* day, that he's *in* town. So tell Nickeia, if she's looking for Anthony. She'll have to come through me. Because I do his scheduling, when it's not for the Cavaliers. Do you think she'll do that?"

Gwen answers with, "No way. I bet she better not do no more dumb shit toward you nor any other crew. I think you're right. Now that I think more about it. She's riding through there. Hoping she'll spot Ajay. *Damn*."

"Exactly," Ebony says, "And I'm gonna need you to look into that. Sooner than later. From *your* end. Because if I have to look into it. It's not gonna be nice. And it will damn sho ruin any chance *either* you or Jarvis will have of getting voted into *this* crew."

With that, Gwen let's go of the talk about Rebbie's dance school. She does

TIME TO SHOW-RELOADED-Time Will Reveal 6

not want to make Ebony think about that area *anymore*. She gets on to some lighter conversation.

After several minutes, Ebony comes up with an excuse. She wants to end this call with Gwen, right now and hang up.

"I have three mouths which need to be fed *from me*," Ebony says and laughs. "I'm gonna have to get the triplets fed and start lunch for us."

With that, her and Gwen hang up and Ebony breathes a sigh of relief. She know she's going to have to get her girls on the phone now. She has to know what the *hell* is on Rebbie's mind. Or if she's lost it, *completely*. By having Jarvis meeting her *anywhere*. But him or *any man* whom she has history with, meeting her at her place of business. Is just dumb.

"I've gotta get Nina and T-baby on this phone," Ebony says to herself. "And we're calling Rebbie, *today*. She's gonna have to spill it."

Ebony gets back to her daughters. She has Lannie and Lea there, to help her. While she feeds Ariel, Arianne and April. She thinks over the talk she just had with Gwen. She knows it's possible Nickeia saw *exactly* what Gwen had told her. But Gwen's response to the scenario Ebony came up with. Is what she's going to roll with. Because as easily as Gwen had backed off the subject. Ebony knows it's very possible that a sighting of Ajay *was* the initial reason for Nickeia wandering down that street in the first place. Ebony's going to stay with that scenario. Until Gwen gives her a *real* reason to change it. For now, she's going to take care of her daughters. Once she gets a real opportunity. She'll get together with Nina, T-baby and Rebbie, so they can discuss, *the obvious*.

Allen Saul Williams Sports and Recreation Center

Ajay and Lil Ajay arrive at the sports complex. They head in and speak to Ally, Steven and Jamal. Then they head on into Ajay's office to proceed with their talk.

Inside Ajay's office, him and Lil Ajay get back to their manly conversation. They'll have to head back home for an early dinner. Before Ajay has to head to his pre-game practice. Lil Ajay has already made his father aware that he's no longer a virgin. They had that talk, the day after. Today, they discuss how significant Lil Ajay's Rioshauna and Jaylisa hook up are, to their future plans and the demise of *several* enemies.

"It seems convenient that you had *two* pieces of the crew puzzle, at your discretion, *that* night," Ajay says and smiles. "But we both know it wasn't a mishap. *Right*?"

Lil Ajay chuckles and says, "I know my crew worked that out. And the best part of it is. The ho's don't have a clue."

"For sho," Ajay says and chuckles too.

Then Lil Ajay says, "It's hard for me *not* to focus on that devil bitch, pops. Especially cause I know she'll be in the Cleveland jail, in *five* days."

"That goes for you and me both, son," Ajay says, "Her days are already counting down. Know that."

"The thing is, pops," Lil Ajay says, "Jaylisa would turn her over to us, if I wanted her too. She started off fucking Bradley. But she's been calling me everyday since Christmas. Several *times* a day."

"That's because you got that Jackson man mentality and the *magic stick*, son," Ajay says as he laughs. "Even more than that. You knocked me outta the youngest crew to fuck slot, too. I don't even know how to take that either, man. Plus you had two ho's to my one."

"It was just opportunity," Lil Ajay says and cracks up laughing. Then he adds, "But just like you told me, last year. Once you get to the pussy. There's no way you're gonna stop *getting* to it."

They both laugh hard. But they have much more conversation to have and they get right back to it.

"And just so you know," Ajay says, "Until you get Kimmie's heart. The best is still, yet to come."

"I believe you, pops," Lil Ajay says, "Before you got mama to like you and go there with you. Did you think about her, when you was with the other girls?"

"Hell yea!" Ajay says, "To be honest with you, as I always will be. The only reason *for* the other girls. Was to fine tune my sex skills. So I would know what to do with Ebony and what *not* to do. All I've ever wanted to do in my life and sex life. Is to please your mother. But son, it was on the day when you and Lannie came, that I knew what her ultimate happiness was. There's *nothing* I can ever do, that will bring her more delight than she has, every time she has a child. So there's another place where you topped me too. The *ultimate* place. In your mother's heart. And to you and your five sisters. I'll gladly take that second spot. Hell, I'm honored to be in second place when it comes to my young ones."

"That makes my day, pops," Lil Ajay says, "My mama will always be the most important female in my life. Cause I know, as long as I live in a way where I don't hurt or disappoint her. I'll be the best I can ever be."

"That makes *my* day, son," Ajay says and smiles.

Lil Ajay smiles and adds, "Mad cool. Now, before we have to head back.

Let's get back to the *necessary* satisfaction topic. How we can use all of these unnecessary girls, to get these necessary things done."

"I love how you put that, son," Ajay says and laughs. Then he adds, "I'm gonna find a way to incorporate Darlene into Angel's demise. I've just gotta find a way to tolerate her ass, in my space. I don't have a clue yet. You got something for that?"

"I know she's more than willing," Lil Ajay says, "And with Olivia, who's her niece, feeling left out, the other night. Maybe we can work from that angle."

Ajay smiles and says, "Are you willing to give her some of your time?"

"If it means getting to that devil," Lil Ajay says, "I'll give her some dick. If it gets me closer to that devil. I will. And only for that reason too. It will have to move fast, though. Because I have no interest in Olivia or Libby or whatever she likes to be called."

Ajay laughs and says, "It will. Because once Olivia feels *she's* in. She'll bitch and complain to Alana and Darlene about Jaylisa. And Alana will be in the middle. Because she has contact with Angel. And oh yea. We can call her ass, devil. It fits a lot better than Angel. That's for *damn* sho."

Lil Ajay asks, "So how will me giving Olivia time. Get Darlene time with you?"

"When Olivia gets pissed about Jaylisa still being in your life, along with her," Ajay says, "And she's complaining to her mama and aunt. I'll get Jamal to bring Darlene by here, for a meeting with me. Right here in my office. I'll figure out a way to make her think she has a chance. At the same time. I'll make sure she knows how much *devil* frustrates me."

"Oh yea, pops," Lil Ajay says and laughs. "If Darlene think she can help *you* with something. She's gonna go *all* out."

"Fuck yea," Ajay says, "She'd do devil, *herself*. If she thought it would get her some time with me. But just know. I will be having this whole discussion with Ebony. Before any type of meeting happens with Darlene involved. I'll let Ebony help me figure out how to play it. Your mama is a very brilliant woman, son. She'll have a sure win way to pull Darlene's ass in. And she'll want me to make sure Darlene *thinks* she's gonna get some time. *See*? I'll be handling my *real* business with the woman whom my life is dedicated too. Plus Ebony will know *every* single thing in the plan, before *anything* jumps off. That's how it has to go. And oh yea. I have to let your mother know about your updated sex life too. Just so you know."

"I agree with all of that, one hundred percent," Lil Ajay says with a smile. He's still smiling as he says, "I'd rather you tell mama that part,

anyway. It'll be better than for me to have to tell her. Cause I don't think I can do that."

Ajay says, "I'll handle that for you, son. That's my job. Your papa big Al will tell you that much. He did it for me. He told mama about me, back in the day and mama was glad to know that I wanted to be with Ebony, in a real way. She knew Ebony was gonna be the girl who kept me on the right mission. Crew like. You feel me?"

He smiles and says, "Yes sir. I do. My mama is a queen. All I ever wanna do is to make her proud of me. And I'm gonna do that too. Anybody in this world who hurts my mama and never made it right with her. I would wanna put something together to get rid of them. But I know that ain't gonna be you."

Lil Ajay was smiling when he said that.

Ajay smiles too and says, "Not ever again, in my life. I live for your mama. And I have the best life a man could want or need. She's my motivation. Always was. Always will be. Smile on that, son."

They're both smiling. Then Lil Ajay stops smiling and adds,

"But that devil who goes by the name of Angel, is mine. *Period*."

"I got it, son," Ajay says, "I've already let crew brothers and your mama know that you will be the one who takes the last breath of that Devil. Now, let's head back to the house. It's almost dinner time. Plus there's gonna be something else that'll brighten up your day."

"And you're not gonna tell me," Lil Ajay says while laughing. He adds, "Are you, pops? You know I'm like you, when it comes to surprises. Right?"

They are both laughing as they emerge from Ajay's office. They say, "In a minute to Ally, Steven and Jamal. They head out and hop into Ajay's 2006 Mercedes Benz 2-seater. They leave the sports complex and head home for dinner.

On the way home, Ajay tells Lil Ajay more about him and Ebony's lives in the 90's. They arrive at their estate, in a great mood.

Ebony, Lea and Lannie are nearly finished making dinner when Ajay and Lil Ajay come in. Ajay enters the house and gives Ebony a kiss, just as he always does. Their kids smile every time they see their parents kiss. Ebony hugs Lil Ajay. Then the house phone rings. Ebony answers. It's Erica on the line.

"Hey sis-in-law," Erica says.

"Hey, lil sis," Ebony says, "How are you? And how's the new pregnancy going?"

"Everything is good, girl," Erica says, "I wanted to let you know that my sibling-in-laws have just arrived. Alan and Kimmie are already asking to come to your house."

"Let me let Anthony know," Ebony says, "He'll come pick them up. So they can have dinner with us. Me, Lea and Lannie are just about done. Okay?"

"Okay," Erica says, "I'll tell them to be ready."

They hang up and Ebony informs Ajay.

"Kimmie and Alan are at Erica's," Ebony says, "She said they're already asking if they can come over here. I think they should have dinner with us. What do you think?"

"That'll work," Ajay says, "Son, come ride with me to pick up Alan and Kimmie."

"We can just get Kimmie," Lil Ajay says and laughs.

Ajay laughs too. Lannie looks at her brother and rolls her eyes. She thinks he's being unfair.

Lannie asks Lil Ajay, "So why is it okay with you for Kimmie to come. But you don't want her brother to come too? He hangs out with you everywhere else."

"I was just kidding, twin," Lil Ajay says and continues to laugh. He adds, "He needs to come. I need to keep my eyes on *him* anyway."

"You're gonna be watching Kimmie. Not him," Lannie says and giggles.

Lil Ajay doesn't offer a reply to his twin sister, on that comment. He just smiles and follows their father out the door.

Ajay and Lil Ajay head over to Erica's to pick up Alan and Kimmie for dinner. They arrive back home in 10 minutes.

When they get back inside their mansion, they see Ebony, Lea and Lannie are just about to set the dinner table. Ebony gives Alan and Kimmie a hug and a kiss. Then she asks Kimmie to help her and her daughters set the table. Kimmie accepts with a huge smile. They start to set the table.

While the females set the table, Ajay takes the 2 boys into the 2nd floor of the library, so they can have some male bonding time.

In the kitchen, Ebony is talking to the girls. She knows Lil Ajay likes Kimmie. She also knows Alan likes Lannie. She wants to get a feel for where the girls minds are, when it comes to the 2 boys. Although she knows their talk isn't going to be as full as the males upstairs. She's going to see if they ever think about Alan and Lil Ajay, when they're not around.

"So ladies," Ebony starts, "We're going to be having dinner with

guys at the table today. I know my husband is making sure they know how to carry themselves around you. I wanna make sure you little ladies know the same. Okay?"

"Yes ma'am," each of them say.

Ebony can see that they're both blushing, at her comment. But neither little girl shows a sign of anything Ebony can feed into it.

She continues. "Well ladies. We're gonna set the table up *really* nice, so the guys can join us. Is there anything in particular you two young ladies wanna ask me?"

Suddenly Lannie asks, "Is it weird for me to think Alan is cute. But I can't say it *to* him?"

"Not at all, Atlantis," Ebony says, "You're just not ready to say it to him. If that day ever comes, where you feel comfortable with saying it. Then you will. I felt the same way about your daddy, when I was little. I've always thought Anthony was a cutie pie. The thing is. He liked me, way back *then*. He liked me then, the same way he likes me now. I just wasn't as advanced in *that* way of thinking, as he was. Not yet. I wasn't able to think in the terms of relationship stuff. But once I was. I lived for my life to come to the place where it is today. Anthony is the one who showed me what real love is all about and what real admiration is too. It's because of him, that I know how to recognize real love. So Atlantis. My advice to you is to take your time. Grow at your *own* speed. Because if Alan likes you, the way your father likes me. He wouldn't want you to do or say anything you're not comfortable with. Not until you're ready too. Okay?"

"Yes ma'am," Lannie says and she smiles big.

Kimmie says, "I'm the same way as Lannie. I think Lil Anthony is the cutest boy in the world and he is so nice to me. People might think he's mean. But he's not mean to me. He told me that he wants me to call him Anthony. But he said nobody else can call him that. He just wants me to call him by his real name. All by myself. He just looks at me and smiles. All of the time."

"His daddy was the same way, Kimmie," Ebony says and smiles.

Ebony, Lannie and Kimmie smile from ear to ear. Lea is giggling. Though she doesn't really know what they're talking about. She's laughing because they're laughing. They have the table set now, as they finish up their conversation. Ebony is going to invite the guys back in.

She says, "I know they're having a talk, like ours. But theirs is probably a bit more grown up. So when we sit down at the table together. I want y'all to pay attention to how they are, with each other. And you'll know what they were talking about when they were away from you. Just watch how me

and Anthony vibe with each other. That's what I want you little ladies to demand, when you do get to the type of feelings that me and Anthony have for each other. You see. We both feel like we know there's a lot of admiration between the four of you. And like my big mama and eventually *my mama*, told me. The grown ups around you, can see it. Even when you think *we* can't."

Ebony smiles as she heads to the elevator, so she can bring Ajay, Lil Ajay and Alan Anthony back down to the dining room table.

New Year's Eve, 2005

Chill, Renee and the entire crew attend Ajay's game tonight. The crew have their own section in *Quicken Loans arena* and the crew's section is packed for tonight's game. Everyone is here except Greg Jr. He's back in Detroit. The Lions have a home game against the Pittsburgh Steelers tomorrow. There's only 1 other Cleveland crew missing, from the Cavaliers game tonight. That 1 missing member is *Patricia Thomas*. She's the new interest in Greg Jr's life. Her brother Kilo had gotten her an airline ticket to Detroit, after knowing she had the blessings of Genia Johnson. Patricia flew out with Greg Jr on yesterday. Her and Greg Jr wanted some personal time and Kilo made sure it happened.

After the Cavaliers game, which the Cav's won 97-84 against the Pistons. All of the crew stop by *Stoney's Bar-N-Grill*. Ajay and his family are here as well. They all get a bite to eat and have some fun family time. Before it's time to open the 2 clubs and allow the guest to start filing in. Chill and Tank know both clubs will be full and will have lines formed on the outsides of each. They're ready for tonight's crowd. But while they're all still seated in Stoney's, Chill has to crack a joke. Before they can get on with the rest of the night.

First he chuckles, then he says to Ajay,

"We *had* to go to the game *and* stop by here too. That way we would get a chance to see you and Ebony before this year ends."

"And we're getting to see y'all on *y'all* anniversary too," Tonya adds and giggles, "Hey now!!"

"I didn't think that would happen," Jr says and laughs.

June chimes in and adds, "That's why the Cav's scheduled a game for today. They wanted to make sure the crew would see them."

"So I take it that them being off to themselves, *all* the time....," Wes starts.

Tank finishes Wes' sentence, saying, "…..didn't just start after you moved to Cleveland, Wes."

"They've always been *missing* in action," Nina says and laughs.

They all laugh as Renee adds, "Oh yes and I'm writing this down, right now."

T-baby laughs and says, "Cousin. Tell em! You would cut us off, right now. If you wasn't in that *down* time after your delivery status. Ha? Let em know!"

"And you know it," Ebony says and laughs.

Ajay has to have a say, at this point. He laughs and adds,

"Oh we *are* gonna shut it down shortly. I just wanted to formally introduce Alan and Kimmie to big John and pops. This night belongs to *my* woman. We could break *another* record, if we could just get to the house. Y'all do know that is my *real* basketball game plan. Right?"

June laughs and adds, "Yea Ajay. We *been* knew that. Ebony brought out the *'leave it all on the hardwood'* side of you."

"I agree," Rebbie adds with more laughter.

Ajay chuckles and continues. He says, "You notice how my game stepped up after nineteen eighty nine? Now I know we won *tonight*. But hey. I've gotta get the lift back under my jump shot or coach Brown, Lebron, Jarvis and everybody else is gonna be hounding Ebony about hooking me up."

They all laugh very loud. Lil Ajay is laughing harder than all of them. He loves his dad's humor. Plus he knows he's very serious about his need to get back to the sexual side of his marriage. He decides to help his daddy out.

"I'm ready to go home, pops," he says and everybody howls with more laughter.

Ajay leans into Lil Ajay and they give each other a fist bump aka "a pound" while they smile at each other.

Still smiling and pointing to Lil Ajay, Ajay adds, "This is me, right here. To the highest degree."

Even big John and Al have to give their grandson some dap. Lil Ajay finally laughs too.

Big Al says to Ajay, "He's got some of me and John too, now. Don't act like you don't know that, son."

Ajay laughs and agrees. He says, "But it *is* time for me to get my family to *our* spot."

Everyone agrees and laughs.

It isn't long before Lil Ajay is helping Ajay to pack up the triplets, Lannie and Lea, so they can head to Jackson heights.

"It's all good, cousin," Jr says while still chuckling. "We appreciate the little time y'all shared with us."

Ajay smiles and looks over at Rebbie and June. They're both here, along with Orian and their twin boys. And even though they chimed in on the conversation and laughter. They seem more distant from each other, than ever. Ajay knows why too. But he's not going to go into it, right now. He still has to talk with Jarvis. That's going to happen before the Cavaliers road trip to Milwaukee, on the 3rd day of January. He knows Ebony still has to talk with Rebbie too. She just hasn't gotten to it yet.

Ajay gets Lil Ajay to help him get the triplet's bags out to Ebony's 2006 Escalade. He's going to warm up the SUV, before Ebony and the girls have to come out and get in. Ajay and Lil Ajay head on out to the SUV.

Just as they sit the bags inside, Ajay sees Jarvis pulling up in his Benz.

"I guess I need to have that talk, right now," Ajay says to himself.

He starts the Escalade with the remote. Then he tells Lil Ajay to let Ebony know, he'll send him back inside when he's ready for her and the girls to come out.

"Yes sir," Lil Ajay says as he heads back inside.

Before he gets to the door, Lil Ajay turns back to see Ajay walking over to Jarvis' passenger door.

Lil Ajay says, "I'm going to tell mama what you said, pops. Then I'm coming back outside to wait for you in the SUV. Is that cool?"

"*Definitely*, son," Ajay says, "Or actually. You can come sit in the backseat of Jarvis' car. I'm gonna holla at him, for a few minutes."

"Cool," Lil Ajay says because that's exactly where he wants to be.

Ajay sits down in the passenger seat and looks at Jarvis. Jarvis has a guilty look on his face immediately.

Ajay says, "I think you know what I'm about to say. Don't you, bro?"

"I know what it's about," Jarvis says, "But I don't know exactly what you're gonna say. No."

"Are you here to meet Rebbie?" Ajay asks bluntly.

"No," Jarvis says.

"So why are you here?" Ajay asks, "Just tell me the truth."

"I was coming to hang out with the crew," he answers.

"But you *did* know Rebbie was gonna be here," Ajay says, "Didn't you?"

"Yea."

"Jarvis, how far has it gone?" Ajay asks, "Tell me that part."

"It's still the same, Ajay," Jarvis says, "It hasn't advanced any farther than where it was at, the first time. And we both decided that. I don't want her to have penetration with me. While I'm still married. She isn't going too anyway. Believe it or not. For the past two months, we spend the majority of our time talking about how she's always wanted to be with a man who would just listen to her. And I do that."

By this time, Lil Ajay is getting into the back seat. He closes the door and looks at his father. Ajay glances back at him and notices Lil Ajay has a look of anger on his face.

Immediately Ajay asks, "What's up, son? You look angry. What's up with that look?"

Lil Ajay answers, "I wanna know why my mama whispered in my ear and told me to tell *you*, to tell *him* not to come inside of the bar and grill. What did he do to my mama?"

Ajay chuckles as he looks at Jarvis. Then he tells Jarvis to hang on and to not say anything else. Just listen first. Then Ajay turns his attention to Lil Ajay in the backseat.

He says, "Jarvis hasn't done a *damn* thing to your mama. My *wife*? Hell no. Or there's no way *in hell* I'd be sitting in the car with him. Just having a conversation. I would've pulled his ass *outta* this car and we'd be on the concrete, *gettin* it in. Son, that's not why your mama doesn't want him to come inside the bar and grill. I know why she told you to make sure he didn't come in. Okay?"

"Yes sir," Lil Ajay answers.

Then Ajay looks back at Jarvis and says, "Tell my son why his mama doesn't want you to go inside, right now. And don't worry. He's got a *Jackson* man's mind. He can handle anything that's said to him, in a manly way."

Jarvis looks at Ajay and asks, "You want me to tell him names too?"

"Yes," Ajay says and grins. "Tell *him* the same way you would tell me. If I came to you and said my wife didn't want you to come into any spot, at the moment. How would you respond to me?"

"Okay," Jarvis says, "Well, I know if you asked me Ajay. You would already know there was nothing I had done to your wife, to bother her. So this is what I would say to Lil Ajay."

He turns around in his seat and looks at Lil Ajay, who now has a puzzled look on his face.

Jarvis says, "Your mama just wants to make sure it's comfortable for

everybody who's inside and comfortable for me too. She knows I am very much in love with one of her best friends. But she also knows its not a good idea for me to be around that friend, in public. And while everybody else is around too. It's because her friend wouldn't know how to handle the situation with me present, as well as…" Jarvis looks at Ajay.

He doesn't feel he should say anything which will alert 6 year-old Lil Ajay as to what female or male he's referring too.

Jarvis adds, "I just think she would probably be *very* uncomfortable in that surrounding."

Lil Ajay says, "But her friend likes you too. So why would she be uncomfortable?"

Both Ajay and Jarvis look at him. They both have a look of surprise on their faces now. Ajay has to know what his son's last statement meant.

Ajay turns to Lil Ajay and asks, "What do you know about this situation, son? And you can tell me and him, at the same time."

"The friend of my mama's, that he's talking about. Is mama Rebbie," Lil Ajay says.

Ajay looks at Jarvis and shakes his head. Jarvis looks down. He's trying to figure out *how* Lil Ajay knows whom he's in love with. Ajay takes it from here.

He says, "Son, go ahead and put us both on. How do know it's Rebbie?"

"Because I always see him and mama Rebbie out by the condo's. *All* the time," Lil Ajay reveals. "When me and my boys go out there to hang out at the gee spot. I see them almost every time. I notice it, pops. In the past month or so. I've seen them out there, a lot. I don't even think Bradley and my boys noticed it. But I do. I've seen y'all going into a condo, out there. About eight times, at least. So when my mama said tell pops to tell you not to come inside. That's when I figured she knows it and she's not okay with it. But then again. She can't know it. Because that would mean my pops know y'all been out there too. And he hasn't told me about it."

"Son, is that why you was upset," Ajay asks.

"Yes sir," Lil Ajay says, "Because I thought my mama was."

Ajay says, "Well I didn't know that part. Not the part you just said. I didn't know they was meeting up regularly. So son. You knew more than me *and* your mama. I guess until your mama said that to you. You didn't think it was anything to tell me about? Is that right?"

"Yes sir," Lil Ajay says, "Not until just now. When my mama said that."

Lil Ajay looks at Jarvis and asks, "Are you and mama Rebbie hooking up?"

Ajay looks at Jarvis and says, "Be careful how you answer him."

"We're not having sex, Lil Ajay," Jarvis says, "And we never have. She's a married woman and I'm still a married man. *Technically*. But not for much longer. Rebbie just wants a man who will listen to her. A man who hears and supports what her dreams are, in life. And she knows I did that from the start of our friendship. I still listen to her now. And I will forever. That's what it's about, for us. There is no sex going on, at all. We do kiss though."

"But y'all hide it from big June and the crew?" Lil Ajay asks.

"I suppose so," Jarvis says, "Yes but we have to. Because grown ups will think it's more happening than what actually *is* happening. I'm in love with her. *That's* true and I know she cares about me, *deeply* too. But as of right now. We're just there for each other. I can tell her about my marriage and how I wanna end it, so I can get on with my *real* life. Your pops knows about that part already. But just so the both of you know. She tells me, she wants to do the same."

"Whoa," Lil Ajay says, "I knew that. I can tell by how she is when she's around big June. It's like she want a whole crowd of people around. So they don't have to be alone. They're *nothing* like my mom and pops. Big June and mama Rebbie don't even smile and look at each other, when they're together. Right now, they're just together inside because everybody else in there. But when I see her walking with big Jarvis. Both of y'all be laughing and stuff. But I'll just say it like this. As long as you don't piss off my mama or my pops. Then I ain't got no beef with you. My parents and grandparents marriages are the *truth*. I can't say too many other people have that same thing. Even in my crew. But just so you know. However my pops feel about it. He'll let you know. And I'm gonna be on his side. Whatever he tells you. The same comes from me."

"Bet," Jarvis says before he looks at Ajay.

Then he says, "Your son is a man, already. Bro, he is *way* ahead of his years. And I'll let you both know. I will never do anything that would upset either one of you. And *definitely* not misses Ebony."

Looking at Lil Ajay, Jarvis adds, "I know how precious she is to my big brother here."

Then looking at Ajay, he adds, "And Ajay, you can tell your son. I always came to you for advice. Which is what I wanted to do in this situation. But Rebbie don't want me too. Only because she don't want it to get back to her husband. She knows he'll think it's more going on, than what is."

"So it never *use* to be?" Ajay asks.

"We haven't done that since she's been married and that is the one hundred percent truth," Jarvis reveals. "However, she told me that she told her girls we still do. As late as last week. But we haven't. We haven't touched each other, in *anyway*. Besides a hug and kiss since the college days. And I wanna keep *that* truth between the three of us. *Okay?* Because she made me swear that I wouldn't reveal that. But we haven't. Rebbie wants her girls to think its more. I know it's only because she knows her marriage isn't what she wants it to be. Bro, even your son can see it. She just wants them to think she's getting fulfillment from me. That's the absolute truth."

Ajay sighs and then chuckles. He's relieved to know it *isn't* sexual. He can also see that Jarvis is very much in love with Rebbie. A man would have to be seriously in love with woman. To want to be with her and respect her wishes while not having any sexual contact. To be an NBA player with women throwing themselves at you, 24 hours a day. Sex is always available without commitment. But Jarvis would rather spend his free time with a woman whom he isn't having sex with.

"But you are getting sex somewhere, *right*?" Ajay ask and laughs.

"Oh yea," Jarvis says and chuckles, "I'm good."

Ajay asks, "But it's not with your wife. Is it, Lil bro?"

Jarvis says, "No. I'm not sexually attracted to Gwen. I haven't been, for a long time. Not only that. But I don't wanna be in that marriage no more. I've known that since shortly after we moved from out here. Rebbie knows I get my needs met. She has no problem with that. She knows I'm just bidding my time. And if we ever get to the point of being able to be in a public relationship. Then she would be my one and only."

"So you can spend time with her and have fun smiling and all of that," Lil Ajay says, "And you don't have to be having sex with her?"

"That is exactly right, nephew," Jarvis says, "Is it okay if I call you my nephew?"

"For sho," Lil Ajay says, "I feel you, Jarvis. I really do. I believe you too. My pops told me that's how he was with my mama. Before they got to that part of their relationship. I can't be mad at you. I'm not either."

"I appreciate it, nephew," Jarvis says and smiles big.

He knows that it means a lot to both Ajay and Ebony, how their kids feel about people who are in their lives. He's glad him, Ajay and Lil Ajay have just had this talk.

Then Ajay lets him know he has to go, so he can get his family home and get on with his Anniversary night.

He says, "I'm alright with you, Lil bro. And I want you to bring Lil Jarvis

95

around. Let him hang out wit Ant. It's time for him to get his crew lessons, firsthand. Alright?"

"Bet," Jarvis says.

Ajay and Lil Ajay get out of the car and Jarvis pulls away. Ajay and his son smile at each other.

Ajay says, "See how life goes, son. It doesn't matter who puts you together. You have to have what it takes to *stay* together. Do you have that with Kimmie?"

"For sho," Lil Ajay says, "I'm already about her, just smiling. She's the only person I've met who makes me wanna be in a good mood. Just by her being around."

Ajay says, "Cool. Go let our family know we can head on home. I need to hold my woman and see her smile. So I can sleep good tonight."

Lil Ajay smiles and runs back into Stoney's to get his mother and his 5 sisters. Along with Alan and Kimmie. He knows his pops has to talk to his mother tonight. So him and Alan are going to stay at uncle Eric's house. Ron Jr and Bradley will pick them up from there, to come back to the teen club. Lil Ajay also knows it will be less pressure on his pops, if he stays at Erica's. Because then, his mother won't be worrying his pops about watching out for him while Kimmie is in their home. Kimmie is going to spend the night with his twin sister Lannie. He'll know where she is and that she's safe and sound. He's just fine with that. *For now*.

Parma Heights

At Farah, Alana and Darlene's house, the mood is *questionable*. The 3 of them, along with Olivia and Shalom Wittman had gone to the Cavaliers game earlier. Shalom attended with them and came on home with them to hang out with Olivia, this New Years Eve night. Her and Olivia are going to *The Spot II* when Farah, Alana and Darlene go to *The Chill Spot*.

Olivia is in a contemplative mood since returning from the game. Because while at the game, she got what she considers the treat she's been waiting on. She got a smile out of Lil Ajay. When the game ended, Olivia went out of her way to make her way down to the Cleveland crew section. She had walked right up to Lil Ajay and spoke to him. And he actually spoke back *and* smiled. He had even smiled at her a second time and brushed his hand down her arm. Olivia tried to start a conversation with him, right then and there. But that didn't go *quite* her way. What Lil Ajay had done was. He told her to give him her cell phone number. She did that immediately. Lil

Ajay said he would call her later. That made her day. Since that action, all she's been doing is waiting to see if he's actually going to call her.

"He smiled at me," Olivia tells her mother Alana, Farah and her aunt Darlene.

"Shalom can tell y'all. I'm *so* serious. He was smiling from the time he saw me walking toward him. He hasn't had that look since Christmas night. The first night we met."

"He was smiling *big* too," Shalom adds, "And looking her up and down. He rubbed on her arm too. He had a look on his face like he was happy to see her walking toward him."

"Then I'd say your night at CrewLand should be getting back on track," Farah says with a laugh. "We're about to head that way, so we can get there and get a booth before all the New Year's Eve crowd gets there."

They hustle to get dressed. Then they head to CrewLand for the crews, New Years Eve parties.

Jackson Heights, Eric and Erica's mansion

Eric and Erica are standing in their doorway. They're watching as Lil Ajay and Alan pile into the SUV with Brandon, Bradley, Ron Jr, Jon and the boys in their crew.

"Y'all be true to it, crew," Erica yells from the front door with a smile. She adds, "And be extra careful and have a great time."

"And make it back here before sunlight!" Eric yells behind them as he smiles too.

Then he turns to Erica and says, "My crew family got the goods. I wished I had a kid's club when I was growing up. My little brother is beside himself. He's so glad our parents are letting them live with us. He gets to go to school with the young crew. He got it made, baby."

"Him and my lil nephew Ajay are starting to remind me of my brother Ajay and my brother-in-law, big Tank," Erica says and smiles. "They did everything together, when they was growing up. And they're still like that today."

"That's all good," Eric says, "I'm gonna lay my pregnant wife down, for some sleep. So I can be ready to whoop up on them Ravens tomorrow."

"Let's get to bed," Erica says with a giggle as her and Eric head to their bedroom.

Eric's oldest sibling and sister Leilenne has already left for The

Chill Spot. She has settled in with the crew, who are her age. Since Archie Jr and Brina got married, they've all settled their beefs. Nowadays, they are just trying to make sure Ashley Josetta and Archie III grow up in a healthy sibling relationship. Leilenne doesn't have a problem finding a date. She's fitting in nicely with Brina, Charlotte and the 4th generation of female crew. And she's already been chosen to be a bridesmaid in the crew's quadruple wedding in February 2006.

Jackson Heights, Big June and Rebbie's home

At Rebbie and June's house, things are rather tensed. June wants to stay in tonight and go to bed early. He has a huge game tomorrow. Along with Eric and Bruce, against the Ravens. He wants to spend a romantic night at home with his wife. But Rebbie has other plans.

"I'm going to the spot," she tells June.

"What baby?" he asks, "I won't be able to hang out tonight. I've got a game tomorrow. You know I never go out on the night before a game."

"I know," Rebbie says, "But Nina needs one of her girls to be out there with *her*. You know Ebony just had the triplets. T-baby is pregnant and rarely hangs out anymore. So who's left out of the foursome? *Me*. I'm going to get dressed. Mama took the kids home with her. So you can just rest and not have to worry about the twin boys or Orian either. It's okay. Mama's got Ashley and lil Archie too. All I'm gonna do is bring in the New Years with Nina. Then head back home. Okay?"

"I was hoping we could bring it in *together*," June tries.

"But I've already promised Nina," Rebbie says as she continues to pick out her outfit for the club.

She adds, "You know how me and my girls are when we're out. We don't like to go without, at least two of our quad there."

She giggles as she lays out a very nice ensemble on her dressing table.

"Ree, we never spend anytime together anymore," June says. "I just can't figure out which way to come at you. Did something change after our twin sons came?"

"Only that we have three kids," she says, "Instead of one."

"I'm asking you to bring in the New Year with *me*," he says, "Your husband. Is that too much to ask?"

"Brian. I gave Nina my word," she says, "And you didn't tell me you had any plans for us."

"I wanted to surprise you," he says.

"Well now you get a surprise *from* me," she says and giggles more. "At the time I was talking to Nina. All of my girls had plans for tonight. I had none. So I told her I'd come to the crew party. I'm gonna go ahead and get in this bathroom, so I can get dressed. That way I can make it there before midnight. I wanna be there for the countdown and ball drop."

She heads into the bathroom and leaves June standing in their bedroom. *Dumbfounded.*

Jackson Heights, Ajay and Ebony's mansion

Ajay and Ebony are at home together. They had planned to spend their 8th anniversary alone. Lannie and Kimmie are up in Lannie's room, along with Lea. They're already fast asleep. Ajay and Ebony have the triplets settled in and sleeping soundly, in their bassinets, in the master bedroom. As Ajay lays next to Ebony, holding her tight, he knows he has to bring her up on the conversation him and Lil Ajay had with Jarvis. He starts with that first.

"I found out Jarvis and Rebbie are not having sex," he says.

"He told you that?" Ebony asks.

"Yea," Ajay says, "He told me nothing has happened between them since Natty. He says they do kiss though. But that's as far as it goes. And he said he doesn't wanna sleep with her while he's still married. But he also said, *she* wants y'all to think that they are."

"*Really?*" Ebony asks in shock.

Ajay answers, "Yes she does. He said she wants her girls to feel like she has some fulfillment too. And *he* says. The thing she likes the most about him. Is that he listens to her when she has something to say. And I believe that."

"I know June never really considered her feelings," Ebony says, "When he's making decisions. He makes them for both of them. He always has."

"And he always kept her in the dark about his moves too," Ajay says, "I think she's unhappy but she doesn't wanna disappoint the crew."

"I wonder has she even tried to explain that to June, lately," Ebony says, "Because she use to try, all the time. He would just buy her a nice gift and go forward with whatever he wanted to do. And he would always decide for both of them. Or just for him and he expected her to just wait until he had the time for the two of them."

"That's true," Ajay says, "But Jarvis really loves her, baby. I don't

even know how to look at this situation. I mean. We grew up with June and Rebbie. We know how their relationship has been over the years. But she stayed loyal to him and faithful too. And she still is, for the most part."

"But kissing isn't acceptable in my book," Ebony says, "It's still cheating. To kiss a man or woman who's not your husband or wife. Is cheating."

"And Jarvis wants to leave Gwen," Ajay says.

"I could see that, awhile back," Ebony says, "Even in college. It was obvious, he was trying to do the right thing by her parents."

"And then they made a baby," Ajay says, "And he married her because he wanted his son to have both of his parents in the same home. But now, they are still *not* in the same home."

"She told me during that call, that he never sleeps at their house," Ebony says.

"Does she know where he's staying," Ajay asks, "Does she know about the condo?"

"No she doesn't," Ebony says as she sighs.

Ajay says, "Rebbie does."

"She's been there?"

"Yea," Ajay says, "But he says they spend their time conversing about the life *each* of them want. But she doesn't want her girls to know that she's *not* getting sex from him. Because y'all will know she's not happy in her marriage."

"Well, I'm actually happy she lied to us," Ebony says and giggles. "I just don't want her or *any* of my sisters being unfaithful. That's not what we come from."

"I agree," he says.

"But I do understand her needing someone who listens to her," she says, "Baby. It's like we both just said. June never gave her a voice."

"I agree with that too," he says, "I don't have any feelings about it, either way. I'm glad she lied about the sex continuing. But the thing is. Like I told you a few days ago. June feels like she's cheating. You know he called Tank and Tank called me."

"Yes I know," she says and laughs. Then adds, "And you got him off the phone because you didn't wanna give *nothing* away. But now that you know there's nothing to give away. Then all you have to say is you know she's not cheating. Baby, you don't have to go into it *any* further than that."

Suddenly he says, "Our son knows about them spending time together."

"He does?" she asks, "How does he know?"

"He's seen them walking around the condo grounds," Ajay tells her. "And he said they look happy."

"When did he tell you this?" she asks.

"When you sent him back out to tell Jarvis not to come inside," Ajay says, "He told us both, at the same time."
He chuckles and adds, "It was funny because Ant was looking mad as hell when he got in the backseat of Jarvis' car."

"*Mad*? Why?" she ask as she smiles.

"He thought you said that because Jarvis had made *you* mad," Ajay says and laughs. "But Jarvis explained it quickly. First, Jarvis was just trying to explain what you meant about him liking your friend. Once Ant understood why you said it. That's when he told us, he'd seen them out at the condo's. And he even said they look happy together. But June and Rebbie don't."

"Oh my God," Ebony says, "Our son is a mature minded man in a six year old's body."

"He's my junior," Ajay gloats.

"Yes he is," Ebony says, "I can see that he's *very* advanced in all areas. Not just the sexual side of things. Or the street side either. I really don't want him or you worrying about what Jarvis, Gwen, Rebbie or June are going to do with their marriages. Okay baby?"

"Oh I won't," he says quickly. He adds, "I'm concerned about this *right* here. What I'm holding. Baby it's up to them to keep their thing together. Not us."

"Exactly," she says, "We've gotten to the good part. And baby, I just wanna focus on *our* good part. If they need us or our input. We'll wait until they ask. But I'm not gonna be okay with you worrying about it or being the go-between. I know Jarvis is like a little brother to you. But still, as far as problems are concerned. It's about *us and our kids*, for me."

"And for me too," he says and smiles. Then he adds, "And I do have some more *us* things to talk about."

"Okay," she says, "Surely you have some *everything Ant* things to tell me about too. Right?"

"Right," Ajay says, "He's no longer a virgin."

"Oh my Lord," Ebony says as she shakes her head. "He had *full on* sex?"

"Yes," Ajay says as he smiles, "And he broke both of my records."

"*Anthony*," she says as she playfully shoves him away.

But he holds her tight as she continues, "I know your first time was at eight years old and Ant is only six. So I know about that record. But what's the other record?"

"When I got my first piece," he says, "It was only one girl."

She says, "Wait. Not only did my son start getting *head* at four. But now he has had *full on* sex at six with more than *one* girl?!"

"Yes."

She sits up in bed and faces him. Ajay can tell she's thrown off. But she knows Lil Ajay isn't only *her* son. He's Ajay's son too. And he's doing what the men in his family had done before him. Ebony stares at Ajay, for a few minutes. He can tell she doesn't like it but she doesn't say it. At least, not out loud. It shows in her eyes though. She clears her throat and asks, "How many girls has my six year old son had sex with?"

"Two. At a one time."

She shakes her head. Ajay knows it's his time to talk and right now. He goes for it.

"Ebony it wasn't just about the sex, for Ant. It was about setting the plan in motion for getting to devil and Old Jake Johnson."

"*What*? *How*?" she asks.

She's worried for her son's safety, automatically.

"One of the girls has a connection to Old Jake. The other one has a connecting to devil," Ajay says, "He wanted to make them both feel like they could have his time and attention. And in that way. He knows he can reel it into his plan. Simple as that."

"And devil is Angel Taylor?" Ebony asks for clarity.

"That's what her birth certificate says. But we're gonna change that," Ajay says and he isn't smiling. "The two girls he had on his first physical sex night was named Jaylisa and Rioshauna. The girl named Jaylisa is devil's step dad's daughter. She's Tony Mangrove's daughter. The man who's car Devil stole, when she caused you to go over that cliff and lose our first child. The other girl named Rioshauna has a connection to the Fields and the Watts. Do you remember those names? I told you about them. Her mother is Mallory Fields. Her aunt was the first person I killed at the chamber."

"Malaysia, Corey and Mike," Ebony says and shakes her head.

"That's the ones," he says, "And the Fields are relatives of old man Jake Johnson. And you already know about that beef. It's our crew's plan to get it over with. Before my kids are teenagers. Because I'm not gonna live my life worried about some old ass dead beat, trying to take the lives of

my children. It's bad enough that Chill and Renee have to have guards around Lil Kenny because he's at college. I'm ending that shit, Ebony. I have too."

"Ant has been going to the chamber with you," she says, "He's practicing, isn't he?"

"Yes he is," Ajay says, "And he's damn good already. Pops *and* big John can vouch for that."

"What does he know about Angel or devil," Ebony asks, "Does he know the story?"

"Oh hell yea," Ajay says, "And he says that bitch took his older sister. She took his birthright. The way he sees it, is like this. His papa Al has a big sister and so does his pops. He had one too. Before the devil took her away. Ebony, he says she is his and his only."

"Don't let anything happen to my baby," she says as her eyes start to tear up.

"I won't," he says, "I give you my word on that, baby girl. I will not out live *any* of my kids or you."

Ajay can see Ebony is becoming emotional. He wants to fix that right away. "Come here, baby," he says, "I might can't fuck you. But I can hold you."

He wraps her up in his arms and lets her cry until she falls asleep.

CHAPTER 65

THOSE WHO SURVIVE

<u>*The Chill Spot, CrewLand in Cleveland, Oh*</u>

Roo, Pam, Chaundra, Leilenne, Charlotte, Ally and Brina are all in a booth together, having a blast. They have Valene, who's at The Dirty South Chill Spot down in Atlanta, on the video screen. Both clubs are bringing in the New Year together, *on the jumbo screens*. The guest performances are top rated for both of the adult clubs and the teen spots too. In Cleveland and in Atlanta.

In the Cleveland spots, the New Year's eve artist are: *The Game, 50 Cent* and *Lil Kim*.

In the Atlanta Spots, the artist for the New Year's Eve party are: *Ludacris, Ciara, Young Jeezy, 3-6 Mafia and Young Buck*.
It's standing room only in all 4 clubs, with waiting lines outside of each.

The young crew ladies are having a blast during their video chat in both Spot II clubs. Valene wishes Ron Jr was in Atlanta with her. But she knows she'll see him for the quadruple wedding. They're both in it. This 4th generation crew has even found a guy to walk in the wedding with Leilenne and she's going to meet him tonight.

When their guys join them, they bring a guy who's in Cleveland visiting his big brother, for the holidays. His name is Wayan Matthews. He's 20 years old. He's Wayne's younger brother, who grew up in Akron. Leilenne catches his attention instantly. The guys had already told him about her and he wanted to meet her. When Leilenne spots him, she likes what she sees too. Chaundra had already told her that Kenny was bringing a guy for her to meet and hang out with. So the 2 of them wouldn't be the only ones without a date. Leilenne is so happy that her and all the crew girls are able to put all of the past behind them and be friends and crew. She's having the time of her life. Now that she has Wayan there. She's even more excited.

"I have always loved Cleveland," Leilenne says, "And now we're old enough to come in *this* club. The crew is the bomb!!"
They all laugh and agree.

June had been sitting around his house, trying to figure out away in which he could reach Rebbie mentally. He sulked for half an hour or more. But his curiosity finally got the best of him. He had gotten up and

started getting dressed, less than a hour after Rebbie left.

It's 11:30pm now and he's pulling into VIP valet parking at *The Chill Spot*. He makes his way to the elevator and heads up to VIP. Soon June arrives at the velvet rope. Renee isn't on the door and he knew she wouldn't be. Not on a major holiday because they have *elite* entertainers. Courtney, Wayne's lady, is at the velvet rope. June heads into VIP. He's looking around to see if he can see Rebbie. He doesn't. He moves through VIP, signing autographs as he goes. He's looking for his wife. He walks over to the TV screens. He's looking at every angle of the club. He doesn't see Rebbie in any of the views. Finally, he sees Nina. He sees T-baby too. They're both on the 1st floor dancing. He heads down the elevator and makes his way over to them on the dance floor. They look at him and make their way over to meet him.

Nina shouts over the music and asks, "You came out and didn't bring my girl again? Don't tell me you left Rebbie at home *alone*?"

The Spot II

Olivia and Shalom are at The Spot II and Olivia has already moved in on Lil Ajay. Tonight he's actually giving her and Shalom some of his time and attention. While Rioshauna and Jaylisa stand, just off from them and look on with frowns on their faces. Through Darlene, Farah and Alana, Olivia was made fully aware of Jaylisa's stepsister Angel and the reason she's in prison. Now Olivia has plans of using that to her advantage. She figures it will make Lil Ajay not want anything else to do with Jaylisa, as well. She's correct about that part. But as far as Lil Ajay's *real* agenda, Olivia doesn't have a clue. In Lil Ajay's plan, they're *all* apart of his plot to get Angelise Taylor aka Devil, to the chamber. While Olivia's concern is only to make sure Lil Ajay doesn't have anymore desire for Jaylisa. She could have saved that energy. But she'll learn that, much too late.

Immediately she decides to ease into a discussion of Angel with Lil Ajay. Bad choice but she goes for it.

"So Ajay. How do you know Jaylisa?" Olivia asks.

"I don't," he says as he continues playing the game, just to see how much info these girls have and how much they're going to share with him. He adds, "I don't know *any* of y'all. I just know y'all was up on my crew. Giving up the goods. Head, pussy, ass and all. But be clear. I don't ever want no ass. Okay? Now. What else do I need to know?"

"Well I heard about her stepsister," Olivia says, "Have you?"

"Her stepsister?" Lil Ajay plays along, "She's giving up some head too?"

Olivia laughs and says, "I heard that her stepsister named Angel, likes your dad."

"Oh really? She ain't got shit coming," he plays a bit more.

He adds, "My mama got that on lock. So where is she at anyway? I can let her know what's up."

"She's in prison, right now," Olivia says, "She's been in there for like ten years."

That's when Shalom joins in on the conversation.

She adds, "But she's about to come to the Cleveland jail. That's what I heard. She's getting close to her time served and being allowed to be let out early or something like that. She got a life sentence. But lately, I heard that she'll be getting out, in like a year."

"She went to prison for trying to kill your mother," Olivia says as she eggs it on.

"Well she didn't succeed," is all Lil Ajay says.

"No she didn't," Olivia says, "But I heard she still wants to get with your dad and she still wants to take your mama's place. She's always trying to get in touch with my mama. So she can ask my mama to get her connected to the big club and all. Because she wants to talk to your dad. She gets on my mama's nerves, *all* the time."

Lil Ajay steers through this part carefully. He doesn't want Olivia to stop talking about Angel. He just wants her to stay on point.

He asks, "So your mama is a friend of this Angel *person*? Is that what you're *telling* me?"

"No but Angel thinks she can *use* my mama," Olivia says, "She's always trying to call our house. But my mama keep playing her off. You know my aunt Darlene use to date your dad too. So my mama ain't gonna go against her *own* family for no dumbass jailbird."

"The only girl my pops has ever dated," Lil Ajay says, "Is my mama. I know that, for sure. He never dated nobody named Darlene. Only my mama. Be clear."

"Well okay. You're right. They didn't *date*," Olivia clarifies. "But your dad use to mess around with my aunt Darlene, when he was younger."

"He messed around with my mama too," Shalom adds, "When she was teaching school. I guess he use to like older women."

"And you're just like your dad," Olivia says and giggles.

Lil Ajay says, "I am a lot like my pops and my papa's too. On both sides.

But the only girl my pops ever dated and called his girl is my mama. Did y'all miss that part?"

Then he changes the subject. He wants to stay on the subject of Angel. He wants to know just how much these girls know about Angel and why she's in prison.

He says, "So Angel is in state prison and she's about to come to a Cleveland jail. Right?"

"Yes," both girls says.

"So what is she in prison for?" he asks, "Surely not, *just* for liking my pops."

"She tried to kill your mom," Shalom says, "That's what Libby was telling you. Angel ran your mama off the road and down a cliff. That's what my mama said."

"And your mama was pregnant when that happened," Olivia adds.

"And she lost the baby too," Shalom says as she looks at Lil Ajay with a sad look.

Lil Ajay decides to play this to the hilt. He wants the girls to think he didn't know anything about this and that he needs them to tell him more. But he wants them to get Jaylisa involved in their conversation. Only he wants them to have a bit more privacy.

He says "Where did y'all hear this shit at?"

"My mama told me about it," Shalom says.

"Mine did too," Olivia says, "And my aunt Darlene always add to those conversations too. My aunt really can't stand Angel's ass. She hates her, so much. She said she wants to kick her ass on gee pee."

"Do Jaylisa know about this?" he asks, "Because she didn't tell me nothing about it."

"I'm sure she does," Olivia says in a gloating tone. She adds, "All she wanted to do when you came to the condo, was to get with you. But she didn't tell you about her family history and how her family had something to do with killing apart of your family."

Ajay feels the time is now to make their move to a more private area. He wants to get these girls together and open. He wants to know just how much each of them know about Angel. While at the same time. Letting them think they are the ones who are alerting him.

"Let's go up to the VIP," Lil Ajay says, "Bring Jaylisa up there too. I'm going to go get a booth. I'll add y'all names at the rope. All four of y'all, so bring Rioshauna too. I need to get to the bottom of this and see if any of y'all are really my friends. Or what the fuck y'all are up too."

Lil Ajay storms off, as if he's upset. He heads to the elevator. He's going up to the 3rd floor of the teen club to get his VIP booth. He's going to leave the 4 girls names with Ally, who's on the rope.

In the meantime, Olivia and Shalom head over to Jaylisa and Rioshauna. They let them know Lil Ajay wants to talk to all 4 of them upstairs. Both Jaylisa and Rioshauna are happy to know Lil Ajay wants them to join him.

"Well it's about time," Rioshauna says, "He was acting like he didn't even know us."

"For real," Jaylisa says, "I was wondering was he gonna talk to me. Or just ignore me, all night."

"Oh he *knows* y'all," Olivia says, "And he's about to know y'all, *even* better."

They all head to the elevator. Olivia is happy to know phase 1 of her plan, to make Jaylisa undesirable to Lil Ajay, is in effect. But before it's all said and done. Olivia as well as the other 3 girls, will know that none of them are Lil Ajay's desire. The truth is. They're all just pawns in his scheme to avenge his birthright.

The 4 girls ride the elevator to the 3rd floor. They get off and make their way over to the rope. Ally stamps their hands with the VIP pass code and let's them through the velvet rope. They soon join Lil Ajay in his booth.

Jackson Heights, Ajay and Ebony's mansion

As Ebony tosses and turns, Ajay lays in bed holding her tight. Suddenly their house phone starts to ring. Ajay looks at the caller ID, as Ebony turns around to face him and opens her eyes.
She asks, "Who's calling?"

"Yolanda," he says, "She's probably calling to get in her happy anniversary and happy new year wish before midnight."
He answers the phone. "Hello godmother," he says with a chuckles.

"Hey Ajay!" Yolanda says, "I hope I'm not calling too late. I'm in the Dirty South Chill Spot, getting my work on. I just wanted to say happy anniversary and happy new year. And I've gotta check on my God kids too."

"Thanks and happy new year to you," Ajay says. Then he tells her, "Hang on. Let me put the speakerphone on. Your girl is right here. But I'm sure you know that. Right?" He chuckles.

"That's for sho," Yolanda says, "Ain't nowhere else in this world,

that my sister *ever* wanted to be. From the first day I met her. She told me and April about you and how much she loves you. And y'all haven't done anything but added to it. It's a beautiful thing."

"Thanks, Yo-Yo," Ajay says as he continues to chuckle.

"Thank you, Yolanda," Ebony says, "I'm right here. It sounds so good to hear your voice. How are you? And happy new year!"

"Same to you, kid," Yolanda says, "I wanted to let you know. Me, David and Charles are coming with Lynn and the crew, for the big February wedding. And guess who's coming with us?"

"Well alright!" Ebony yells, "I will definitely be looking forward to that and so will my kids. Now tell me, who else is coming?"

"April's cousin. Cassandra *Black* Pittman," she says.

"I remember her!" Ebony says with excitement, "Her, Renee and Tonya kicked it together. They stayed in touch too. She was *so* cool."

"I know they did," Yolanda says, "She said she can't wait to see all of y'all again. And she can't wait to kick it with the crew, *in* Cleveland. She didn't get to meet Nina, T-baby and Rebbie because they couldn't come that year. She said she has to see the *other* awesome foursome, all together."

"That's so cool," Ebony says, "I've gotta get my girls ready. So when are y'all gonna get here?"

"February eighth," Yolanda says, "And we're gonna stay for the whole week."

"Oh yes sir!" Ebony yells with excitement, "I'm so glad you'll be here, for awhile. The last time you stayed for more than a day or two, was when you and April came for spring break."

"I know, right?!" Yolanda says, "We'll have time to get caught up. I'll get to see my God twins and take em shopping too."

" Well, y'all can stay with us," Ebony says, "All four of y'all."

"In the garage apartment," Ajay chimes in. He says, "We got a spot for the four of y'all. So y'all can party *all* y'all want too. And not have to worry about doing or saying nothing, in front of my babies. You understand me?" He chuckles because he knows Yolanda's going to laugh at him and his bossy ways. Yolanda hears him and cracks up laughing.
She says, "That's what's up, Ajay. That's perfect, boss man. I'll get to see my God twins plus Lea and the new triplets too. *Everyday.* Plus I'll have my man there with me. And apart of April will there with all of us. Black is bringing stuff for the twins, on April's behalf. She's got stuff for all six babies. Just know that. Ebony, it's gonna be perfect. I'm good."

"Me too," Ebony says, "I can't wait to see you."

"Same here," Yolanda says, "I gotta get back to work. You know it's new years at our dirty south chill spot too. And we got Luda, Ciara, Jeezy, three six and Young Buck. Girl, these people are banana's in here."

"All the clubs are connected by video tonight. Right?" Ebony asks.

"Yes. It's so nice," Yolanda says, "We can all party together. Jb and big Chill are geniuses. Ron and Carolyn are here with all of our Houston crew too."

"And two of their sons are spending the holidays with us," Ajay says as they laugh. He adds, "This crew shit feels global, damn near."

"It is," Yolanda says, "Now I'm gonna stop cock blocking. Because I know y'all trying to push that waiting period after childbirth, outta the way."

"Not yet," Ebony says and laughs, "They just made a week old."

"Yea. We got two more days," Ajay says and laughs.

"Two more weeks, at the most," Yolanda says while laughing too. She adds, "I know it won't last. Ah man. I love you guys and I will see you all soon."

They're all still cracking up laughing as they prepare to say their goodbyes. They exchange, "*I love you's*." Then they hang up.

Ebony and Ajay get back to their 8th anniversary conversation.

"I'm so excited that she's coming," Ebony says, "And that she's bringing Black, to visit us too. This new year is going to be even better than the last one."

"It will," Ajay says, "Once we get back to the sex."

They laugh more, while kissing a lot. Ajay has to hold himself back. His dick is extra hard and he knows he can't have his pussy tonight.

"Happy eighth anniversary, baby," he says, "And happy new year."

"Happy eighth anniversary to you too, baby," she says, "And another year of happiness with the man I love more than life. And Anthony. I love you more, *every* year."

"I love you so much, Ebony," he says, "Thank you so much for saving my life. Over and over."

"It's been my pleasure," she says.

They kiss again. Then they wrap back up in each others arms, so they can get a nap in before the triplets next feeding time.

CrewLand Mall, The Chill Spot VIP parking lot

June is very upset by now. He storms out of the club and into the VIP parking lot. He's calling Rebbie's cell phone, over and over. She's not answering his calls. Nina and T-baby has followed June to the parking lot. They're trying to calm him down.

"June, calm down," Nina says, "She's okay. I'm sure she's okay."

"She said she was coming to kick it with you!" June yells, "She said T-baby and Ebony wasn't coming out and you wanted her to come so you would have one of your girls with you! *She lied*. Now where is she, Nina?!" While June is calling Rebbie and yelling at Nina. Rebbie is texting T-baby. She's at the condo with Jarvis. Her and T-baby are coming up with a way for Rebbie to get back to a safe place before June leaves that parking lot. It's going to be nearly impossible to pull this off without any drama for Rebbie. But T-baby and Nina are on the case. *#TimeWillReveal*

The Chill Spot II, Teen VIP

Lil Ajay watches as Olivia, Rioshauna, Jaylisa and Shalom make their way over to his booth. He has his game face on. The ladies sit down and Olivia starts talking immediately.

She says, "Jaylisa. You went all down on Ajay. But you didn't bother to tell him your family member is in prison for fucking with *his* family."

"*What*?!" Jaylisa yells. "Why you wanna lie on me, Libby? What the fuck are you talking about? You're a *damn* lie."

Lil Ajay decides to remain quiet and let these ho's argue it out. He wants to see what surfaces from their conversation. He sits there with an *"I'm bored with this shit,"* look on his face. He looks from 1 girl to the other while their voices get louder and louder, still. It's obvious they're trying to prove to him, who's more loyal to him. He thinks its rather amusing. Olivia goes back at Jaylisa.

"How the fuck am *I* a liar?!" Olivia asks, "Ain't that Angel bitch, your half sister?!"

"Of course, that's her half sister!" Shalom chimes in, "And I know she's not about to say she didn't know she was in prison!" Jaylisa says, "Yea I know she's in prison! But if she went to prison for messing with Ajay's family! Then his family is *my* damn family too!" Lil Ajay looks at Jaylisa. He figures her family gave her the wrong end of the prison story. He knows he'll have to work her, a different way. He's now trying to figure out a way to get Rioshauna's family discussed while he continues listening.

"How the fuck is *his* family, *your* family?!" Olivia asks.
She's all out of patience and ready to go for broke. Especially with that last comment from Jaylisa. A comment which Olivia thinks could possibly make Lil Ajay feel like Jaylisa is closer to him than Olivia can ever be. The next statement throws Olivia for loop.

Rioshauna asks, "How are you gonna act like you're on his side, Libby? When his family can't stand yours? And I don't have to scream to get my point across."

"For real," Jaylisa jumps in, "His uncle can't stand *your* mama. She tried to say Ajay's uncle was your *damn* daddy. Knowing Ajay's uncle was and still is, in love with Ajay's auntie Nina. Why don't we talk about that shit? And you're the bitch. Not me."

"That's a lie," Olivia says, "Your stepsister tried to kill his mother. Don't try to change the shit *now*."

"How is car theft, fucking wit *his* family?" Jaylisa asks, "It was my daddy's car that she stole!"

Lil Ajay wants to stop it right there. He figures Jaylisa's family hasn't told her the real reason Angel is in prison. And he doesn't want her to find it out. Not right here.

"Y'all gotta shut the fuck up," Lil Ajay says calmly, yet they can tell he's perturbed.

"Ajay. All I'm trying to do is to get the truth outta this crazy ass girl," Olivia says.

"Right after you learn what the truth is," Jaylisa responds back.

"Did y'all hear what the fuck I said?" Lil Ajay says and this time he looks into their eyes. He adds, "I can't stand all of this loud ass screaming and shit. It's time for y'all to vacate my table. Take this ghetto shit somewhere else."

"We're sorry, Ajay," Rioshauna says, "I didn't want it to get outta hand, like this. I promise. I'll make sure they calm down."

"Then you can stay here," Lil Ajay says, "The rest of y'all. *Scram*." He knows that will ease all the tension between the girls, right now. And because they want to stay in his presence. They'll calm it down. Shalom, Olivia and Jaylisa wants him to say they can stay too. But he hasn't yet. He has only invited Rioshauna to stay, at this point. He's looking at Rioshauna and smiling. She's smiling back. She knows she was with him on Christmas night. She's hoping he chooses her for New Year's eve night too.

Suddenly he says, "They're about to do the countdown. Rioshauna and Shalom. Y'all come with me."

TIME TO SHOW-RELOADED-Time Will Reveal 6

The 2 girls get up and follow Lil Ajay to the elevator and head down to the main floor for the New Years countdown. Leaving Olivia and Jaylisa in the booth alone.

Midnight at The Chill Spot VIP parking/Rebbie Wilson's Dance Hall

June is still in the VIP parking and he's still in an accusation rage. Nina is doing a great job keeping him in place. While T-baby stays in text mode with Rebbie. T-baby knows Rebbie has left the condo's and is headed to her dance studio. June hasn't stopped calling her cell phone, every 5 minutes. But Rebbie still isn't ready to answer him. Chill and Renee have joined them in the parking lot, by now. Chill wants them all to calm down and bring it back inside.

He says, "We done all missed the countdown to the new year. June, why don't you calm down, crew? I know Rebbie's okay. She's okay, dude. Come on back inside."

"She told me she was coming up here to hang out with Nina," June says, "Nina is here and she ain't even seen her nor have she talked to her."

"That's not true," Nina says, "I never said I didn't talk to Ree."

"Then where is she?" June asks.

T-baby has made Nina aware of Rebbie's movement. They're trying to give her time to get to her dance school before they alert June.

Rebbie has managed to make it to her dance studio, park in the back and go into her office. She sends T-baby another text to let her know she has made it. T-baby's smiles as she reads the text. Then she turns to June. She knows she has to sale this to him.

She says, "June, Rebbie needed some time alone. You do remember she use to have lots of it, not so long ago. She's been so depressed."

Nina adds, "She told me and T-baby she wanted to bring in the new year, in peace and quiet."

"Where is she?" June asks and this time, he's genuinely concerned.

"Come on, June," Nina says, "We'll ride with you. She's at her studio."

Renee says, "You see that, June? You did all of this carrying on and didn't even think to check by there first?"

Nina and T-baby know Renee isn't fully aware of what's happened. They'll bring her up on it later. Chill does what he's always had to do, as the leader of their generation. He gets them back to crew mode quickly.

He says, "Okay. Y'all drive on over there and check on Rebbie. And June. I

113

suggest you go there in calm mode. If Rebbie felt she needed to be alone. Then you going over there yelling, will not help matters turn out positive for you. Not *one* bit. Can you calm down and just listen to her? Can you do that, for a change? I mean without some guilt on your mind?"

June says, "Yes. I just wanna make sure she's okay. Alright?"

"Cool," Chill says, "Y'all get at me once y'all get there. Let me know everything's cool. Renee and I are gonna get back inside and keep the work force going smoothly. See ya."

"In a minute," Nina, T-baby and June say as they head over to his 2006 Acura Legend.

They drive over to the dance studio. Rebbie's 2006 Navigator is parked in the back, in the owners lot. T-baby and Nina know they have to play this up and they do.

"Are you satisfied, June?" Nina asks.

"You did all of that damn shouting," T-baby adds, "And all the time. Rebbie was right here in her place of calm. I know you feel crazy, don't you?"

"She didn't tell me she was coming over here," is all June can say.

"Probably because she knew you would fuss, June," Nina says.

T-baby cuts in and says, "Look. We're here now. Let's go check on my girl."

The 3 of them get out and head inside. They find Rebbie sitting on the main floor of her dance studio. She's in tears and she makes it clear, she doesn't want to be bothered. T-baby had come up with that excuse for Rebbie to use while they were still texting each other. June rushes over to where Rebbie is sitting in a yoga position. She has her face covered with both hands. It's obvious she's crying. While June feels she's upset about something he hasn't done. Yet she didn't bother to remind him. When the real reason for Rebbie's tears is. She didn't want to leave Jarvis. She had plans to stay with him until the CrewLand clubs closed. But right now, all she's trying to do is get June away from her studio. So she can figure out what her next move is going to be. June thinks he can make her feel better.

He says, "Baby what's wrong? Please don't cry. Let's head home. I promise I'll do whatever I can to make sure you feel better."

"I'm not ready to leave yet," Rebbie says through sobs.

"Rebbie, please baby. *Please*. Just let me get you home," June says, "Okay? You'll feel okay. Once you're in a spot that's comfortable. Your home."

"No Brian," she says, "I wanna be by myself. Leave me alone. I

want to be left alone. Nina and T-baby. That means y'all too. I wanna be alone!!"

"Okay sis," Nina says, "We'll leave. As long as we know you're okay. That's what we all wanted to know."

"I am okay," Rebbie answers, "Just please. Leave me to myself."

"I'm not just gonna leave you here and go home," June says, "You're gonna get up from here and come with me. Come on, baby."

"I am not going anywhere!" Rebbie yells, "Leave me be!! Right now!!"

T-baby and Nina step in because they know if they don't. Rebbie is going to go for broke. They don't want that to happen. And especially not right here and right now.

"June let's go and leave her alone," T-baby says, "She wants some time alone and that's what we're going to give her."

"Yes June," Nina adds, "Lets let her be. Come on. Let's go."

"Y'all just want me to leave my wife here alone?" June asks. "I'm not feeling that, at all. I want her to be where she's safe."

"I am safe, Brian," Rebbie says, "Please! Just leave me be! Now!"

"Let's go, June," T-baby says again. "We have to respect her wishes."

Nina adds, "That's true. If and when she needs to talk. I am very sure that three of the four people she would start with, are right here now. We *are* her girls and you're her husband, June. If she doesn't wanna talk right now. Then we all have to respect that. Can you agree?"

"I don't wanna leave her here alone," June says, "That's not a manly thing to do."

"So you don't wanna respect her wishes?" T-baby asks June.

She knows she's going to have to open his eyes to his *"my way or no way"* methods of harnessing their entire relationship. It's starting to remind her of the days she was with Richie Rich.

June says, "I'm worried about her being down here by herself."

"But that's what she asked for, June," Nina says, "You will need to respect that, crew. Come on."

Nina and T-baby start to move slowly away from Rebbie. They're calling June to accompany them. He hasn't moved yet. Rebbie can't take it anymore.

She says, "You can either leave with them. Or I'll leave you here and find somewhere to go. to have things the way I want them right now. Can you hear me?"

June sees a look in her eyes that he's never seen before. He can tell she's having a lot of emotions. He can also tell that she isn't in the mood to have him around her. He finally submits to her wishes.

"Okay baby," he says, "I'll leave with your girls. But just know. That is not what I feel is best or safest for you."

"Go rest up for your game, Brian," Rebbie says and turns her back to all 3 of them.

Nina and T-baby grab June on each side and escorts him back out to his vehicle. They get in. June starts up and they pull away.

Nina and T-baby don't say anything as he drives them back to The Spot, where their men are. This drama filled evening will have to go on, for now. Because Rebbie did not back down. And for once in their entire lives. Nina and T-baby witnessed June have to submit to something which Rebbie demanded. This is definitely a New Year. *Already*. For June, nothing is going to be settled tonight. Not at Rebbie's dance school.

At The Spot II, nothing will be settled for Olivia and Jaylisa either. Not as far as time with Lil Ajay is concerned. He's long gone with Rioshauna and Shalom. While the 2 of them remain at The Chill Spot II.

Happy Early morning, New Year's Day 2006!

At this point, the crew just needs to make it into this new year, as one. For Rebbie and June, 2006 is going to be a very revealing year. As for Lil Ajay, he is well on his way. He's already on the right path to getting his wishes met. He has taken Rioshauna and Shalom with him to Greg Jr's condo, for this early New Year's day. He's going to have sex with both of them. *Together*. But in the coming weeks, he wants to get information out of Rioshauna about her relatives. And he already has a plan to do, just that. He knows the work with Jaylisa is already on the right path. Because she's going to do whatever she feels she has to do, to get back into having alone time with him. January 2nd will be a big day for the Cleveland crew.

Tomorrow is the 1st day of school in the Cleveland area. Alan Anthony and Kimmie will start school with Lil Ajay, Lannie and the crew school kids.

Genia Johnson's part of the crew plan will kick off tomorrow. The 2nd day of the New Year. Her fake argument with Tonya and Renee will happen then too. That argument will make the news. From there, Pac Man and the guys will be their connection. Tonya and Renee want to make sure

116

Genia doesn't get lonely while they play out this plan to get to Old Jake. So the 2 of them, along with Chill and Jr, introduced Genia to their head of security David Jacobson, at the New Year's eve party last night. They have a dinner date set up for this week.

Also tomorrow, January 2, 2006 is the day of the fake argument. The newest *CrewLand Mall* strip will have it's grand opening too. Big John and Pearl's office for *CrewLand Trucking* is already opened and functioning. It's the CrewLand office which Pac Man, Joe, Dre and Woody work out of. The next new business which will open this week is *GPS (Greg, Paul, Sam) Construction company*. It's the initials for Greg Sr, the deceased big Paul who was Chill's father and also big Sam. Who is the father of Jan, Kim and Sam Jr. Though Paul has been deceased for 27 years. Greg Sr and Sam Sr wanted to make sure he's memorialized through their business. The 3 of them learned to build things together as young boys. The GPS idea came much later. When the electronic map system device for cars, came about in the 90's.

This strip mall will hold an office for Jan's Pediatric Clinic, as well as an attorney's office for Kim and Chaundra. Wheeler and his wife Trina Yvette will have a spot in the law office as well. The pediatric and law offices will come on by the winter of 2006 or early 2007. There are 10 offices total with 4 designated already. There will still be 6 empty office spaces left for future crew business ventures.

Today is Sunday, New years day 2006. It's a busy day for the Cleveland crew. Greg Jr and the Lions lose their game against the Steelers. They end their season with a 5-11 record. Greg Jr's season is over but his love life has perked up again. Him and Patricia are going to spend New Year's night in Detroit. They'll fly back to Cleveland tomorrow, for the CrewLand grand opening.

June, Eric, Bruce and the Browns win their game against the Ravens. But the Browns season is over as well, at 6-10. June is still wondering if he'll be able to settle things with Rebbie. She didn't come home last night. Nor did she attend the game today.

Eric is looking forward to becoming a father this year. Erica is pregnant and due in late July 2006. But there are 3 babies due before Eric and Erica's baby is expected. Arthur and Michelle are due in May. T-baby and Wes are due in June while Jan and Rob's 2nd child is due in early July 2006.

There will also be more crew initiated in 2006. Three females and

one male. Chill and Renee's daughter, Destiny Jalene Shante' Payne will turn 13 years old on July 5, 2006. Jr and Tonya's older son, Brad III is her crew man by birth. Ron and Carolyn's son, Jonathan Banks will turn 13 on September 22, 2006. He's going to date Tank and Nina's daughter, Jerica. She won't be 13 until 2007. Jonathan is going to wait for her and be her crew date at her coming out party. Ron and Carolyn are going to move their son Jonathan to Cleveland to live with Chill and Renee. That way, the crew can guide him and Jerica's relationship. An Atlanta young lady and the *oldest* Aaliyah in the crew, Aaliyah Hamilton will turn 13 years old on August 30, 2006. Her and Rich III are already talking on their cell phones daily. He's 2 years younger than she is but that doesn't matter at all. Not when it comes to the crew family. The crew monarchs and matriarchs are going to make sure they're able to date. Once Aaliyah turns 13, her uncle Ced and aunt Bre are going to let her live with Jan and Rob, when they move back to Cleveland in late 2006. That's when Jan plans to open her pediatric office at CrewLand mall. Their son Rob Jr, who turned 6 years old today, is already living in Cleveland and starting the winter semester of school tomorrow, with the Cleveland crew. The last crew inductee for 2006 is *extra* special for Renee. It's her niece and Wes' daughter, T-baby's stepdaughter Jada Renee Stewart. She will turn 13 on November 21, 2006. She shares that birthday with her aunt Renee. She's 3½ years older than Lil Jb but their relationship has already been arranged. Which is a good thing. Because they stay in contact, same as Aaliyah and Rich III. Lil Jb has moved to Cleveland already. Aaliyah and Jonathan will be moving to Cleveland soon. This crew is planning to go on in the same format as the crew's before them.

June played a great game today but he was still very distracted. He was trying to digest the fact that he wasn't able to get Rebbie to come home with him, from her dance studio, last night. He didn't sleep hardly any. He was dialing her cell phone, all morning and right up until game time. He had even rode back to her studio where her SUV was still parked. He banged on the doors and the windows too. But she never answered. That's because she was no longer there. Rebbie didn't want to talk to June about why she was crying. She wanted to talk to Jarvis, some more. But she had to break it up quickly because June had shown up at The Spot, looking for her. That's the reason Rebbie was crying when they *did* find her at her dance studio. She wanted to tell June, she needed her space. A separation. But Jarvis had asked her to promise that she wouldn't do that. Not until

they had the blessings of the crew. He told her that advice had come from Ajay and Lil Ajay too. So Rebbie didn't go for it when she was interrupted by June. She knows she still isn't ready to have that talk yet. She wants the crew's blessings, as much as Jarvis does. She hasn't figured out what she would tell June was her reason for not wanting to spend free time with him. But when June, Nina and T-baby left her. Jarvis came to pick her up, so she could stay at his condo. As soon as they got there and got inside, Jarvis had given Rebbie a key. Now she can stay there, even when he's on his road trips with the Cavaliers. He saw that she was in turmoil and he wanted her to relax. He filled his Jacuzzi tub and told her that warm bath was just for her. Jarvis remembered from their years at Natty, how much Rebbie loved to soak in a warm bubble bath whenever she was stressed out. So he accommodated her. Rebbie enjoyed her bath and a good sleep. Which lasted until nearly noon. Jarvis didn't disturb her. He only made sure there was a meal there when she rose. After Rebbie woke up and ate, she headed to her home in Jackson Heights. She knew June wouldn't be there when she arrived. Because she was watching his game on TV. He was at Brown's stadium finishing up another losing for the season. But now that the game is over. She knows he'll be home soon. And he will still be demanding a talk. *No doubt*. And he'll think he can calm and soothe her and have sex too.

Within the next half hour, June arrives back at home. He is *indeed* ready to talk. But Rebbie still isn't ready. Needless to say, she doesn't want sex either. June doesn't know why she's so distant from him. But he's still convinced that she's spending her time with another man. He *is* correct with that summation. Yet she isn't having sex, like he'd done to her. June wants to ask her. But he just hasn't found a way to bring it up yet. Nor does he have any idea whom the other man is. He remembers the advice from big Chill. Chill had advised him not to say or do anything which would make Rebbie more stressed. June gave Chill his word. So far, he's sticking to it. But it will only be a matter of time, before he has to press Rebbie for more information. For now, they'll just float around each other. They have to get their minds in parent mode. Their twin boys, Brian III and Brent will be 3 months old in 5 days. January 5, 2006. But tomorrow is the first day of school for Orian and the crew kids. June and Rebbie's marriage problems will be put on hold for at least another day.

Cleveland Schools spring semester, January 2, 2006

TIME TO SHOW-RELOADED-Time Will Reveal 6

Today is the first day of school in Cleveland, Atlanta and Houston. There are lots of crew kids hitting the school trail today.

Down in Houston, Ronald Banks Jr starts his last semester of senior high school. He's certain to graduate in May 2006. While down in Atlanta, his girlfriend Valene Hamilton is going into the spring semester of 10th grade. Kilo's son, KeJuan Thomas Jr is finishing his 9th grade year at the same high school as Valene. KeJuan Jr is the boyfriend of Stoney's daughter, Chastity aka CJ. Chastity is in 8th grade, down in Atlanta. While in Cleveland, her first cousin Brad III is in 8th at Abe Lincoln Middle school. Destiny Payne is at Abe Lincoln too. She's in 7th grade and Brad III is her boyfriend. Their parents are best friends and their fathers Chill and Jr, wouldn't have it any other way. Renee and Tonya always wanted them to date *and* marry. They just wanted them to be high school age, before they became a couple. Destiny and Brad III didn't wait. They mirror both sets of their parents, when it comes to them getting together, at a young age.

Jada Stewart is the in 6th grade at Beachwood. While Aaliyah Hamilton is a 6th grader, down in Atlanta. Jerica is in 5th grade. Her future boyfriend Jonathan Banks is in the 5th grade, in Houston. Jonathan will be moving in with Chill and Renee, this summer. Rich III is in 4th grade and already playing football for the 6th grade team. Jb III is in Cleveland already. He starts 3rd grade at Beachwood, along with his crew. Him and Orian will be in the same class. Jb III is living with his uncle Tank and aunt Nina. Mama Jo and mama Pearl are just happy to have him in Cleveland. Where they can see him daily. He was home schooled through the 1st half of 3rd grade. So this is his first year going to a public school. But the crew expects him to adjust, very well. Lil Jb is just excited to be in Cleveland with his cousins and crew, who are close to *his* age.

Alan Anthony and Jarvis Jr are in 2nd grade at Beachwood elementary. Jarvis Sr brings his son to Jackson Heights to catch the bus with the crew kids. Lil Ajay, Lannie and Ashanti are in 1st grade. Lil Ajay feels like a school pro, by now. He adjusted in kindergarten, last year. He didn't like school to begin with. But this spring semester, he's excited. Because Kimmie is in Kindergarten at Beachwood elementary, this year. Richanda Williams, Rich III's stepsister is in Kimmie's class.

Rob Jr is in Kindergarten at Beachwood too. He's already good friends with June and Rebbie daughter Orian, who's in the 3rd grade. Jr and Tonya's younger son Donovan is in the same Kindergarten class with Rob Jr. They're already crew strong and ready to push through. Just as all of their parents had done it. Their crew will be the largest, *too date*.

TIME TO SHOW-RELOADED-Time Will Reveal 6

The youngest crew kids are going to *Granny's House Preschool*. Lil Tank, Aaliyah Jackson aka Lea, Ashley Josetta and Archie III are all enrolled. Bre and Ced have a nanny for Cedric Jr, down in Atlanta. While the James' twin boys are at *Granny's House* too. But the newest crew additions, the 8 and 7 day old triplets; Ariel, Arianne and April are still at home with Ebony and Ajay.

Beachwood Elementary, 1st day of school

The first day back at school seems promising for Lil Ajay. He's already instructed Rob Jr and Donovan to keep an eye on Kimmie.

"And make sure don't nobody fuck wit her," Lil Ajay says, "Cause if they do. I'm gonna fuck em up."

"Already," Rob Jr cosigns him.

However, with Rob Jr and Donovan in a separate class than Kimmie. They don't know about her troubles which start on her 1st day at Beachwood. 1 of her classmates starts to tease her on day 1. His name is Dillon Parker. Dillon calls Kimmie a *Jap*, only because she has slanted eyes.

"I'm *half* Japanese," Kimmie tries to tell him. "My eyes are suppose to be like this."

"You half blind Jap," Dillon says and cracks up laughing.

Kimmie tries to move away from him and ignore him. But they sit in ABC order. Her last name is McNair. His is Parker. He's on the row next to her and sitting right next to her, in class. He's relentless. Kimmie has a hard time focusing on the teacher. Richaunda is in her class too. But her last name is Williams. She sits 3 rows over and in the back of the class. She's not even aware of what's going on. But Dillon is on a roll. A roll he will continue for the next 2 weeks. Until Lil Ajay finds out. And it will end, *that* day. But for the next 2 weeks, Kimmie just takes it in stride. She's very happy when the school day ends and she's happy that Dillon doesn't ride her bus. Because she won't be teased as she rides to *Big Mama's House Aftercare*. She gets on the bus and Lil Ajay sits next to her. That's when she can finally smile. Lil Ajay smiles back. He watches Lannie as Alan sits next to her. She smiles but she doesn't look at him. Lil Ajay is fine with that too.

CrewLand Mall

It's preparation time for the grand opening of crew business number 28, *GPS Construction company*. The official opening is today at

121

6pm. The crew are doing the final preparations as their kids are finishing up their 1st day back at school.

Greg Jr and Patricia have made it back from Detroit. Greg Jr wanted to be there to support his father's business venture. Patricia is going to be their receptionist.

"I'm excited about working for your dad," Patricia says and smiles.

"Him and my mama are happy too," Greg Jr says as he smiles back. "They're gonna ask you *all kinds* of questions. So be ready for it. They're so happy to see me smiling again."

"I'm glad to be apart of that smile," Patricia says, "You had every right to be sad, baby. You lost your girlfriend, *suddenly*. That wasn't even a whole year ago."

"Then Hurricane Katrina took family from you," he says, "But it sent you to me."
They smile and kiss each other.

"Alright. Let's get some work done," Renee says to Greg Jr and Patricia as she giggles.
Her and Tonya are setting up the podium where Greg Sr, Sam Sr and Chill will speak. Chill is going to speak on behalf of his deceased father. The local news will be on hand to cover the opening event. Which is convenient for the plan the crew wants broadcasted. Genia and Jacobson arrive together. Her, Renee and Tonya have gone over their lines for the fake argument. They're all ready to go.

Once the ceremony ends and the reporters are doing separate interviews, Renee steps to Genia.
She yells, "Why have you been lying on my crew and our businesses?!"

"For real! Tell her, Renee!" Tonya yells, even louder,
"Why are you even here for this opening! Especially since you think we're the reason your husband and daughter got killed!"

"Y'all need to own up to it!" Genia yells back, "Every damn day! Y'all was allowing that murderous bitch to hang around here and meet up with my husband!"

"We had nothing to do with who Matt met up with here, Genia! Or anywhere else, woman!" Renee yells.
Tonya adds, "As a matter of fact, we never liked him meeting women at our places of business! And we told him not too! And it was me who stopped him from meeting women in our shops! He had to find somewhere else to do his laundry! So get that straight, Genia!"

"Oh that's what you say now!" Genia yells back, "I know better!"

This is the point where Chill and Jr step in. They have to play their role of calming the women down.

"Hold on a minute, ladies," Chill says, "We're *live* here. This is not good for business."

"He's right, ladies," Jr says, "Let's get y'all inside. *Please*. So y'all can talk this out."

"I don't wanna talk about this shit, no more!" Renee yells, "She can leave!"

"Exactly!" Tonya yells, "If our business was so bad for your family, as you're claiming! With that *ghetto girl vibe*! Then *leave!*"

"I am leaving!" Genia responds, "I'd rather be alone in Cleveland! Then to be around anybody who helped my husband to mess over me! And got my *only* child killed!"

With that, Genia storms off. Dre and Woody are already in her car, with deeply tinted windows. She jumps in on the passenger side and they drive away. When they turn out of *CrewLand's* main exit and onto the highway. They all laugh. They know Jacobson will follow them soon.

Back in the CrewLand courtyard, Chill excuses himself from the reporters and takes Renee into the Chill Spot. Jr grabs Tonya and they follow Renee and Chill. No sooner than they get inside the main offices, the private lines are ringing while they crack up laughing too.

"That was award *winning*," Tonya says.

"It *was*," Renee says, "And this is Woody calling now."

Chill says, "That's Genia. On *cue*."

Still laughing, Renee answers the phone to Genia, who's laughing *so* hard.

"Renee," Genia says, "Did we pull it off or what?"

"We *did*," Renee says and giggles. "Those reporters are still outside trying to get more of the story. My husband and Junior are about to go back outside *right* now. So they can do the public response. Be ready, okay? Cause they'll be coming by *your* address before long."

"I'm *so* ready," Genia says, "And we'll let y'all know when those others folks contact me too."

"Oh definitely," Renee says, "And it won't be long."

"But please make sure David and me can still date while this is playing out," Genia says and continues to laugh.

"That's a bet!" Renee says, "Jacobson is already setting up his meeting with you. As a matter of fact. He's doing it right now. Joe and Pac Man will get him to you. Okay?"

"Okay," Genia says, "Love you, little sister."

"Love you too, big sister," Renee says, "See ya."
"In a minute," Genia responds and they hang up.

Cavalier's Heading to Milwaukee, January 3, 2006

Ajay and Jarvis are preparing for a road trip to Milwaukee. They're leaving out today, the 3rd of January. This is the first time Ajay has ever felt like his mentality is not completely focused on a game. The game is tomorrow, January 4, 2006. But Ajay's mind is on Cleveland and the return of Angelise Taylor. And though Angel and her folk's may not have known the actual date, she would be transferred. The crew certainly did. Their _Department of Corrections hook up_ had already given Chill the heads up. Angel is due to be transferred to a local jail in Parma, in the very early morning. Ajay wishes she was getting out on the streets so he could get that burden in his life, over with. _Without_ having to go through the phone calling sequence. He remembers when the phone calls started at The Spot. It was when his twins were first born. He'd gone by The Spot to visit with Chill while Ebony got some much needed rest. On that day, he told Angel that all he wanted was for her to be gone for good. He also made her aware that if she was ever close enough to his family. He would make sure that it happened. Over these last 6 and half years, all the senior crew males have advised him to never say anything threatening to Angel, over the airwaves again. Because that could be used against him when she does get taken out. Ajay knows it will be hard not to state his truest feelings, when hearing the sound of her voice. But he has agreed to put his best effort forward to make this plan work. Chill reminded him of how well it worked, back when they went to Philly and brought Angel and Alana back to be arrested. Ajay didn't fail to remind Chill that him and Ebony went to jail on that same night, as well.

But today, Ajay has his priorities in order. His wife and kids are the most important _beings_ in his life. And with that, he knows he can find the tolerance he'll need to get through the _set up_ phone calls with _Devil_. He's going to make sure his son is focused as well. But he's sure Lil Ajay is just as ready as he is, to rid the world of the waste named Angelise Taylor. He's taking Lil Ajay to the chamber before his flight. Because he knows his son is just as anxious as he is, about the next day.

"So how are you feeling, son," Ajay asks as they are heading to _Shaker Heights_.

"Ready," is Lil Ajay's response.

"So am I," Ajay says, "The plan has already been kicked off for Old Jake."

"I saw the argument on the news," Lil Ajay says and smiles. "We was watching it and it looked *real*. But I knew it wasn't."

Ajay says, "Nah. They practiced that shit for a week. I know Old Jake will send somebody at her. And most likely, before the week is even close to being over."

"Rioshauna is his grand niece," Lil Ajay says, "On her mama's side. Old man Jake and her grandmother are sister and brother."

"Right," Ajay says.

"Her grandmother was a Johnson before she married Rioshauna's grandfather," Lil Ajay says, "And even though her daddy is a Watts and a deadbeat too. He still works with old man Jake."

"Yea," Ajay says, "Those families have been linked since my days as a young boy. I told you that story, right?"

"I know you took out two of her uncles on her daddy side," Lil Ajay says, "And her aunt, on her mama side."

"That's a fact," Ajay says, "Now tell me what plans have you thought up for the ones that are still here? I really wanna hear it."

"I wanna get all of em, pops," Lil Ajay says, "And Rioshauna. She would sale them out *for me*. I can feel that already."

"Tell me what's up."

"She's mad at her daddy," Lil Ajay says, "Because he's a deadbeat. Plus he beats on her mama. He did it all the time and he still do it. She said she wishes *she* could kill him."

"Wow," Ajay says, "You've been on it, ha?"

"Yes sir," he says, "She wants to date me. But you know that answer. The thing is. I can use that."

"What you got for it?" Ajay asks.

"I'm gonna make her think I'm liking her. But I'm not sure about her loyalty," he says, "You know you already schooled me on that loyalty game. But I'm gonna just play it up until I can get her daddy to react. I'm not gonna let him meet me though. Not unless it's time to move. She already knows she can't talk about me to *nobody*. I told her I would make her happy. But *only* if she knows how to keep *our* situation on the low. What I told her was. I can't let it get back to my mom and pops that I'm dating a girl as old as her."

"And she bought that, of course," Ajay says.

"She did," he says, "And Arthur's wife Michelle. She wants to get

at Alana, from way back. I'm thinking we can get uncle Tank and Michelle to bring Alana out in the opening. Then use Alana as a way to get Tim and them, who moved farther east."

"To get them back *this* way, ha?" Ajay says and smiles. "I think we can get rid of both sides *and* use them to do each other. Your mama and I had this talk already. Ebony was the only one who could approve any communications I would *have* to have with Devil or Darlene. And she did. So I'm gonna get Darlene to meet me at the gym or the chill spot. But not until we've got it *all* together. After this road trip is done. It should be enough time to have everything set to where it can run smoothly."

"I agree," Lil Ajay says, "Then get it over with, once and for all. Pops, I want it all done before I even get close to Kimmie. I want all of this mess *gone*. I don't want her to *ever* have to go through what my mama went through. And I *know* Old Jake will have a mark on her, in no time."

"Indeed," Ajay says, "He'll want to do away with any chance of a Jackson man having lifelong happiness. It's just straight up stupid, how that old ass man can hold hate for so long. I feel like apart of it is just jealousy. Jealous because my grandfather's had love and he never did. He was buying pussy as a young man. And he's still buying favors now."

"That *is* stupid," Lil Ajay says, "If his hate is all about my great grandfathers not taking care of his bills. Then why, when he get some money, he wasted it?"

"Because he was never responsible," Ajay says, "But we are. I'll be back on the fifth. I'll be home until the eleventh. On the eleventh, the Cav's will start a twelve day road trip. I'm gonna need you to take care of the house and our family while I'm gone."

"Okay pops," Lil Ajay says, "No problem."

"I know Kimmie's at school with you now," Ajay says.

"Fasho," Lil Ajay answers and smiles. He adds, "We sit together on the bus, to and from CrewLand. It's cool."

"Son you're gonna feel the need to protect her from others at school, alright?"

Lil Ajay answers, "Alright. I already do and I will."

"Oh I know you will," Ajay says and laughs. "I just need you to make sure it's something we can win, *afterwards*. Because I will not tolerate my son being expelled from school. So you just be sure that it's protection for Kimmie or your twin sister. Before you unleash on *anybody*. It must be a winnable case after you win the damn fight."

Ajay laughs and so does Lil Ajay.

Lil Ajay adds, "I'll win both. I just hope nobody messes with either one of them or my crew. *Period*. Because I know I'll be in it. Especially the first two. I'll bring it for them."

Ajay arrives at the home where he'd grown up. Big Al and Big John are standing on their connected driveways. Ajay is still smiling at his son's comment.

He smiles more and says, "I know that's right, son. And now we're about to get in this pre-chamber practice and sharpen our skills on these Jake and Devil bull's-eyes. Your grandfathers put some bull's-eye posters in their jointed tool shed. Let's do this, son."

Big Al and John meet them, as they open their car doors. This isn't the Chamber. Lil Ajay will get to that. For now, they have a makeshift place for him to show his stuff. They all head inside of the shed to sharpen their shooting skills.

Atlanta

Lynn and Julie Von Reese are getting together for lunch today. Lynn wants an update on how things have been going with Julie.

"What's up, Julie?" Lynn asks.

"It's good," Julie says, "Money's good. I can't complain. So what's on your mind?"

"Heard anymore on that James *Bulldog* Taylor situation?" Lynn asks.

"Not a word," Julie says, "I do know that his cousin Angel is suppose to be moving to a Cleveland jail. I'm gonna get added to her visitor's list. So I can see what I can find out."

"Yes. She's being moved before early morning," Lynn says, "Crew wants to know what she's planning and how she's talking, these days. And that's exactly what I was gonna request from you."

"I'm already on it," Julie says, "Like I told the police, word for word. *'James left me without even as much as a text message. I called his phone for weeks. He didn't bother to answer me. Nor did he respond to the many voicemails, I'd left him. He dropped me without even telling me. I'm so glad I wasn't dumb enough to fall for his lies about wanting to be with me. I feel he only used me to stalk Ebony and the crew family. I told James that I'd known you since sixth grade. And I feel like that's the only reason he stayed in touch with me. But once we went out to The Chill Spot nightclub and he got familiar with the scene. He never even called me again.'* Now Lynn, that is

127

still my story and I'm sticking to it. And I still have all of my phone records from his ass too. To support the claims which I have."

"You still got it down, word for word too. Don't you?" Lynn asks and smiles.

"Yes I do," Julie says, "I know he's not coming back, girlfriend. That sweet arsenic took his lame ass, *right* on outta this *real* world. And permanently into that dream world he was already living in."
They both laugh.

Then Lynn says, "And I think it's a great idea to get added to Angel's visitor's list. I might want her ass to eat some arsenic too. We already got a few people who can serve it to her."

"Well now," Julie says as she bats her eyelashes. "You do know I can take care of that little task too."

"You might get that job, girlfriend," Lynn says as they both laugh. They dig into their lunch while having some lighter conversation.

"Has Ebony called her lawyer about this Angel move?"

"He called her, this morning," Lynn says, "Wheeler is always on time. He's just giving Ajay time to settle his nerves. But *trust* me. Every moment of Angel's Cleveland jail time life. We *will* have documented. My brother and Ebony will know what she's going to do, before she does it. Just like her move to the Cleveland jail. She won't know until in the morning, that she's being moved *in* the morning. But Ajay and Ebony know it already. It's gonna get done, Julie. Trust me."

"Just let me know what you need me to do," Julie says, "Because the sooner we can get that whole saga over. The sooner I can go on the *real* payroll. And stop getting paid under the table."
They laugh hard and consume their lunch.

Cleveland, Genia's home

Joe and Pac Man arrive at Genia's home to commence with the upgrades. Jacobson is already there. He had spent his first night with Genia. Now he and Genia are all aglow as Joe and Pac Man back into the driveway and park. They have arrived in 1 of John and Pearl's moving trucks from *CrewLand Trucking*. They're going to be moving Genia's old furniture out, 1 room at a time. 1 day at a time. They'll replace her entire home with new furniture, after the painting and floors are redone. This is her gift from the crew. Jacobson and Genia have the 1st guestroom ready to haul when they open the front door for Pac Man and Joe to enter.

Jacobson isn't allowing himself to be seen by anyone, from the outside. Not just yet. He's not only here as Genia's date. He's also here as her security. To protect her from anything Old Jake Johnson may try.

Joe and Pac Man are inside now. The 2 of them and Jacobson get started loading the 1st guest room's furniture into the truck. But before they can get the 1st room of furniture moved and replaced. Genia's house phone starts to ring. She looks at the caller ID.

"Guys," she says before answering, "This is the call we all knew would come. And this isn't even the first time. My role is to never answer to them without witnesses and the recorder going."

On the caller ID it reads, '*Brice Johnson.*' Brice Johnson is the youngest male of Jake Johnson's siblings and he's a grandfather. He's Rioshauna's grandfather, to be more precise. From this call, Jacobson wants to get some taped conversation started. Because the sooner they can start this. The sooner the crew can get to Old Jake Johnson and cancel his contract.

"Answer it, Genia," Jacobson tells her as he puts his listening device in his ear and starts the recorder.

"Hello," Genia says as she answers the phone.

"Well hello there, long lost family," Brice Johnson says, "Haven't heard from you since Matt and Kelly was killed."

"I know," Genia says, "I've just been dealing with it in my own way. Its been really hard on me. And over these years, with Matt always being absent when I needed assistance. I've gotten use to having to deal with hard things on my own."

"You know you've got family over here on this side of town. Don't you?" Brice asks, "We're not somebody who will put you and those you love in danger of losing your lives. Not like those CrewLand bastards did to you. We saw you on the news. Jake told me, we had to reach out to you and be here for you. That's what we did and we're going to offer it now too."

Going into character, Genia says, "Yes. And I'm happy you reached out. I was so mad. I just had to go out there and speak my mind. It's done now and I'm back to being me. Lonely is good, sometimes. I learned that from my time away from Matt."

Brice jumps on that lonely comment immediately.

He says, "Well you're not alone, Genia. You have *real* family on this side of town. You know Matt and Kelly was our blood relatives. We already don't get along with those crew assholes. So them getting our family murdered. Didn't do nothing but deepen that wound."

"Deepen that wound?" Genia asks, intentionally sounding clueless.

"What are you talking about, deepen that wound? I'm lost. What wound?"

"Genia we haven't fucked with that family for decades," Brice says, "I can tell you more about it, in person. We need to meet up so we can talk. My oldest brother, who's name is Jake, wants to meet with you. *Very soon.*"

"Meet with me about what?" Genia asks, still playing clueless.

"History. And we'll talk about all of that when we meet," Brice says, "What does your schedule look like, this week?"

Genia knows she has to stall. She wants to make sure the crew has something in place for any contact she has to have with the Jake Johnson click.

She says, "Let me check my schedule and call you right back. Is this going to make things dangerous for me? I need to know that, first and foremost. I mean. If they know I'm meeting with you? Will that put me in danger? Do they not get along with y'all too?"

"They don't like us because we don't deal with folks who don't believe in helping the next man, who looks like them," Brice says bitterly.

"That doesn't sound like them at all," Genia says, "But of course. Matt and Kelly had more contact with them, then I did."

"And now Matt and Kelly are dead," Brice digs in. He adds, "And you'll be dead next. If you don't protect yourself. We don't wanna see the same thing happen to you, Genia. That's all I'm saying here."

Genia knows she has to make this contact happen. She wants to make sure Jacobson has all of this conversation recorded too.

She says, "Let me check my appointments and get back to you. Is this a good number to call you on?"

"Yes it is," Brice says, "This is my cell number. Call me as soon as possible. I want this meeting to happen, *this* week. Okay?"

"Okay," Genia says.

Jacobson motions for her to tell him, she'll call him back before the end of the day.

Genia continues, "I'll call you back before dinner time. Is that okay?"

"That's perfect," Brice says, "We can grab a meal. I'll have a restaurant picked out, by the time you call me back."

"Okay," Genia says, "That'll be just fine. But I need to let you know that I will need a ride too. I don't drive much and I don't really know the city that well. Not for driving, that is. I barely know the east side. I don't know the west side at all."

Brice says, "That's not a problem. We'll arrange a ride for you too."

"Okay," she says, "I'll call you back today and let you know what I need to make this meeting happen."

"I look forward to it," Brice says, "Take care and I'll talk to you, later today."

"Okay."

"Bye bye," Brice says.

"Bye." Genia says and hangs up.

After the call is done. Jacobson alerts Chill and Jr, who lets Genia know to make the meeting place, *The Landmark restaurant.*

"That's the halfway point," Chill says, "We've already got security and look outs set up, for your protection. Dre and Woody will come and drive you."

"Okay," Genia says, "But is he going to be taken out today? I need to know what to expect."

"Not today," Chill says, "We must first make him comfortable with you. We're not going for just one at a time. We want the whole click. It's time to rid my crew of this beef. Which has been around longer than I've been alive. We're going start with him and his income source. And move from there."

"I'll do my part, Lil brother," Genia says, "So long as we can get Farah, eventually."

"We haven't forgotten that you wanna beat her ass, Genia," Chill says and laughs.

"I wanna bury her ass too, Chill," Genia says.

"We'll pencil that in, for the future," Chills says and they smile

Then they hang up.

[continuing from where "The Making of AJAY- "Every Man" ends!]

TIME TO SHOW-RELOADED-Time Will Reveal 6

CHAPTER   66

THE NEW WORLD ORDER

Ebony and Ajay have survived their sexual hiatus. They had replenished Ajay's fix on January 20th while he was on his road trip in Utah. After a lose to Golden State, Ebony was waiting for Ajay in his suite in Utah. She was wearing a new lingerie set which Ajay had purchased and given to her for her birthday/Christmas day, 2005. Along with the lingerie gift, he'd told her that whenever it was okay for him to do what comes natural for him. To just put that set on. Ebony was wearing the lingerie set in Utah. Ajay went in as soon as he walked into his hotel suite. It took them all night and 4 sessions of hot sex, to get them back to normal behavior. They're back to their lovemaking and Ajay's team is back to the winning side of their record column as well. The Cavaliers had beat Utah, then arrived back in Cleveland Ohio, 2 days later.

Lil Ajay has survived his 1st school fight. He had beat up that boy named Dillon Parker at school, 2 days ago. Dillon was still teasing and making fun of Kimmie and Lil Ajay got it over with. Though Alan Anthony and his class arrived late to the lunch line, Alan has already vowed to get Dillon again. Just for the simple fact that he was bothering his baby sister. Alan and Lil Ajay will work on setting something up so they can kick his ass, *away* from the school grounds. The best part? Lil Ajay wasn't expelled from school, so he knows his pops isn't disappointed in him. That means his actions were *"crew like"* which for Lil Ajay, makes it even more joyful.

Today is January 22, 2006. This is the 1st day official day which Lil Ajay will get to visit, *The Chamber*. Ajay has told him a lot about it. But until today, he's been doing his practice shooting out at his grandfathers tool shed in Shaker Heights. That will end today. Ajay is driving Lil Ajay to Shaker Heights. But *only* to meet up with big Al and big John. Big John will drive all 4 of them to the Chamber, in his Cadillac. They'll get to see what a great shot Lil Ajay has already become at 6 years old.

Lil Ajay's 1st official visit to The Chamber

They've only been at *"The Chamber"* for 30 minutes. But Ajay, big Al and big John are already impressed with Lil Ajay's shooting capabilities. Lil Ajay is a natural and he's hitting targets more precise than Ajay did when he first got to come to the chamber. Before long, Alan Anthony will join them too. But now that Lil Ajay's chamber test is done. They can focus

head first on removing those stumbling blocks known as Angelise Taylor, Old Jake Johnson and The Johnson's beef.

June and Rebbie's marriage has made it into the new year. But June is even more unsettled than ever. Since New Year's Eve, Rebbie has started to spend entire nights away from home. June feels like she's having a full on affair but he has no proof. While the Cavalier's were on the road. Rebbie stayed at Jarvis' condo, 7 of those 11 nights and went in to her dance studio from there. When June would show up at her studio to question her. Rebbie would have Chill, Jr or 1 of the fathers, already there to escort him away. She's still not in the mood to explain anything to him. She just lets him know that she isn't cheating on him, like he did to her. She leaves it at that, each time.

Crew meeting at Jacobson's home
Genia had her first lunch meeting at *The Landmark*, January 10, 2006. Not only did Brice Johnson come. But so did Jacob Denard Johnson, Sr aka *Old Jake*. They had a second lunch meeting yesterday, the 21st of January. That meeting was *very* revealing for Genia. Not only did Old Jake admit to wanting the entire crew family dead. But he revealed that he's also seeking ways *and* people, to insist him with getting it done. Genia had to get that back to Chill immediately. She wants him to know, Old Jake's group wants her help in setting up the crew. She needs to know how and what Chill and the crew needs her to do, to make it look real to Old Jake.

Genia and Jacobson are at Jacobson's home today. They have a face-to-face meeting with Chill and the crew. Mostly males but Renee and Tonya are here too. It's time to put some things in motion, now that Old Jake has asked Genia for assistance, in trade for them being family to her. Genia wants to do whatever the crew needs her to do, to get rid of *this* beef. After their Chamber meeting was done, Ajay, big Al and big John joins the meeting at Jacobson's home, bringing Lil Ajay along with them.

"So crew men, ladies and *Miss* Genia," Chill says, "This meeting is to make sure everybody is updated on the latest. Getting to old man Jake is *going* to happen. But it will not be easy, as we already know. Well Miss Genia here had lunch with them again yesterday. She now knows what crew has always known. Old man Jake's plans haven't changed at all."

"And he wants *Miss* Genia to assist them," Jr says.
Tonya adds, "Genia was still *legally* married to Matt when he was killed. But she wanna be called *miss*. Not *misses*. Just wanted to be clear on why

133

Chill and my husband are *emphasizing* the *Miss*, before they say Genia."
They all laugh and shake their heads in agreement. They have no problems
with honoring Genia's request. Jacobson agrees with, "*Definitely*."
Chill continues, "Poppa Jones and Papa Brown have made a connection
and set up travel plans which will assist us greatly."
Chill leans the floor over to the senior crew men.
Papa Jackson Brown says, "Our generation has arranged for Jeb Baker
junior, Jessie Mae Johnson-Baker and Albert Johnson to come to the states
to visit us, while we delete this madness for good. Are all of you familiar
with those three names?"

"I am," June says quickly. "Those are *my* in-laws. The first two are
Rebbie's grandparents on mama Rena Lynn Baker-Wilson's side."

"And Albert is Albert Johnson," Tank adds, "He's the son of Jake
Jr, whom our second generation got rid of out by that same Landmark
restaurant. Back when our crew was just being brought into the full pack."

"Yep and he's always been on Misses Jessie Mae's side too," Ajay
says, "She's Old Jake Johnson's sister. And Jeb junior is the son of the Ace,
mister Jeb Baker senior. The man who opened the *equality* doors for our
first generation of this crew."

"Yea," Wes says, "And during my initiation into this crew business.
I learned Old Jake turned on misses Bertha for dating and then *marrying*
Jeb Baker junior. Only because he was Jeb senior's son and because he was
white."

"That's a fact," papa Joshua says, "And the bigoted white folks of
that time, was threatening Old Jake's ass to undo that union."

"But that wasn't doable," poppa Jones says, "And just as we
always raised all of our kids to know. All white people are not bigoted. In
our young days, a lot of them spoke out *and* marched with us too. That
doesn't happen in these days though. Not too much. But Jeb senior was the
truth. He despised how some from his race carried on during the history of
the United States. And he was determined to change it."

"He adored Jessie Mae more than her own brother did," papa
Charles adds. "He supported his son's relationship with her and he made it
possible for them to move to Europe. So their relationship could flourish
without having to deal with the bigotries here. Europe is where Rena Baker
was born."

"Rena moved to the states in the early seventies," papa Jackson
Brown says, "Just in time to walk with Archie senior, in Brad senior and
Debbie's wedding. Albert Johnson attended that wedding, despite how his

big brother, Jacob Denard Johnson senior felt about his attendance."

"And mister Albert Johnson was always on the side of our crew," Lil Ajay says suddenly. "That's the reason he moved overseas. Because he didn't want to be involved in anything that went against our crew. Not even for his own family."

Suddenly all of the adults start to applaud and cheer on behalf of Lil Ajay.

"Good job, big Ajay," papa Jackson Brown says, "That's your future right there and he's on point. I expect every male in this family to know our history. I'm the oldest living crew member. I was born in nineteen thirty three. I will be seventy three years old, this year. So for me and my generation. All we want to see is that our names and our wishes will carry on. Lil Ajay is on it. That makes me *very* proud. Ajay I'm so glad that my wife Pearline and Percy's wife Eloise could see it, way back then."

Everybody laughs as poppa Percy adds, "Yes indeed they did. And if me and Jackson wanted to have any good loving in our households. We had to see it too and go along with whatever they said."

The laughter continues as poppa adds, "And you all can see how big this family has become, right?"

Papa Joshua says, "We kept our homes happy and we was made happy in them too."

The applause continues. Then they get back to the meetings discussion.

Sam Sr says, "Our crew knows me and my sister Sandy have always been good at finding out who are true owners of property. We got copies of the deeds to the property that Old Jake has spread his no good family on, for all of these years."

"I've been waiting on this report, Sam," big Al says, "What you got?"

"That property was left to Jessie Mae Johnson, now Baker, in their parents Last Will and Testament," Sam Sr says, "The land that all those haters in Old Jake's posse lives on. Is legally Jessie Mae's property."

"This sounds like *The Color Purple*," Arthur says and laughs.

Tank chimes in, "Arthur has always got a good joke!"

The entire room is laughing hard at Arthur and Tank. But they all agree with what Arthur said.

"It does seem like a *fixing* of history," Jacobson says as he laughs.

While laughing, Ajay adds, "It *is* a fixing of history and the future too."

"Correct," Jr adds and brings the meeting back to order.

Chill says, "Jeb junior, Misses Jessie Mae and Albert will be here just in time for the quadruple wedding, in less than a month."

"And they'll get to see their oldest grandson, Shannon *The Reaper* Wilson get married," Renee says with a smile.

"And they'll also get to see all of their great grandbabies too," Tonya says, "Ashanti, Ashley Josetta and Archie the third!"

"In *person*," big John says.

Archie Sr adds, "Yes. Instead of just pictures and videos. Because they have seen the grandchildren, in person. But that was way back in the days. Its time to bring them home for good. Rena would love that, so much."

"That's going to happen and it'll be great," Sam Sr says, "They're coming for the wedding and to visit for awhile. Our mission is to get them to *stay* stateside. They don't have to run anymore. Mixed couples aren't so abnormal, *these* days."

Greg Sr adds, "They already own land here. So there's no reason why they *shouldn't* be here. That land Old Jake lives on and supplies roofs for his posse on. Is Bertha's land. It's time for her to have what's hers."

Chill says, "And spread this crew all over Cleveland. Not just on the east side. My pops biggest dream was to make sure that the city of Cleveland looked like Crewland, to the world. He made sure I knew that black people are natural builders and accomplishers. Not niggers but Black. The very same mentality which built this stolen land which is known to the world as the United States of America."

June says, "Yet it's the most divided thing I've known, in my entire life."

"Not much united about it," Tank says, "That's the truth."

Eric adds, "And the change which is about to come in the next two years? Will put the bigoted face of the United States on the world's doorstep. We will have a black president, real soon. *Senator Barack Obama* is going to run. I can feel it."

Tank says, "I know that's right. And political heads like mister Jeb Junior, misses Jessie Mae and mister Albert need to be here and active too. And before all of this other stuff gets going. My thirty first birthday is in *three* days! The January events will take place Saturday, the twenty eighth and they will be here for all of it!"

"They're coming for my *home game* against the Phoenix Suns on Sunday, Tank," Ajay says and cracks up laughing. "Not for your birthday. They're just coming early. Don't get it twisted."

They both crack up laughing and everybody laughs with them. It's time to wrap up the Johnson beef part of the meeting until the Europe group arrives in less than 48 hours. It is now time for this meetings attention to be turned to getting on with the latest plans for the demise of Angelise Taylor.

Lil Ajay will have a lot to add to this part of the meeting. Chill retakes the floor.

He says, "Okay. The Johnson beef plans are processing great and Miss Ida Mae Graves will bring it all the way home. Now, next issue. Angel Taylor.."

"Devil Taylor," Lil Ajay cuts in and everybody laughs.

Then Chill rewords his statement. With a smile, he says,

"Okay. *Devil* Taylor is now an inmate in the Parma jail. She was moved in there eighteen days ago. According to attorney Wheeler, she has another year to do and her sentence will be complete."

They all laugh. Tank and June give Lil Ajay some dap too. Ajay just smiles.

"I got word from Lynn, in Atlanta," Renee says, "Her and Julie Von Reese have already touched up on the base for Julie Von Reese's part. For a crew refresher on the name. Julie Von Reese is the lady who put up with James Bulldog Taylor's fake crap, just to learn what she could and deliver that info to Lynn."

Ajay says, "James the bullshit Taylor was more like it."

"Word," Tank and June say simultaneously.

"Yes," Renee agrees, "And Julie got rid of that B S in record time. For this Devil mission. She will be getting added to her visitor's list."

"That way we won't have to wait until we can get some info out of Alana," Tonya says.

"Or Darlene," Renee adds.

Chill says, "We have several angles for Devil. Those just named. As well as Tank pulling Alana back into play. Ajay pulling Darlene back into play. And yes, Nina and Ebony have already given their permission."

Everybody laughs and Chill continues.

He says, "But Lil Ajay has a play on both of these missions. Johnson and Devil. Lil Ajay, you can give us your updates."

Lil Ajay sits up proudly. He's been waiting on this day since he's been old enough to understand the meaning of beef. It's his turn to speak.

"This is something I'm proud to be apart of," Lil Ajay starts.

He says, "I have access to Jaylisa, who is the stepsister of Devil. I have access to Rioshauna, who is the great granddaughter of Old Jake Johnson. To make it work out. I also have a link to two of their street friends, Shalom and Olivia. At this point, like I told my pops. I don't want neither one of them in my life but they *wanna* be in my life. That's an advantage for me. I'm gonna work them against each other, all the way. I already got Jaylisa to sign up on the Devil's guest list. Her request went in with Devil's mama, so I know she'll get approved. If it ever comes down to a time when we

need to know where those are that we need to get rid of. I know I can get that info out of either one of those four *thangs*."

"Work it, Lil Ajay," big Al says proudly.

"All the way to the graveyard," big John adds with the same pride. Then he adds, "And he beat Ajay's *first* Chamber scores today."

"He's knocking off *all* of my records," Ajay adds proudly. "From his first times to his first shots. Crew remember this. His legacy *is* to top my reign and he will."

Lil Ajay adds, "There's one more thing I wanna say so my pops will know I'm wit him all the way."

"What is it, son?" Ajay asks.

Lil Ajay looks Ajay in his eyes.

He says, "After seeing how these *thangs* act about getting attention from our crew. Plus I know that's what made Old Jake and Devil wanna be included. Pops I feel like you're still the best key to bringing this devil to the forefront. And since I know mama is okay with it, so long as she gets gone. Then I'm putting my all into it to help my crew get rid of this pain. Both for the crew and *especially*, for my mama, in the name of my crew and my big sister, who never got to be born. I know I've got big shoes to fill, behind you, pops. And for my big papa's Al and John and great grandfathers too. And I'm so ready."

They all cheer loud. It's the same way they use to do it when Chill's crew was coming up and the crew before them. They feel confident that their crew fight and accomplishments will go on, well into the future. If today wasn't a school day, all males and females would be at this meeting. But that full meeting will come soon. They will *all* be together to discuss this as a whole, when the quadruple wedding takes place. It's going to be a great event. This 2006 crew are just starting heat up.

From Europe to the United States of America!

It's January 24, 2006. Mr & Mrs Jeb {Jessie Mae} Baker Jr and Albert Johnson's flight arrives at Cleveland Hopkins International airport, at 10pm. Papa, Poppa, big mama, mama Rena, big Archie, Rebbie, June, Corey and his partner Bobby White plus Chill and big Al are *all* there to pick them up. It doesn't take long before they enter into the airport from the plane.

Jessie Mae yells, ""Wow! Look at the crowd that came to pick us up!"

She smiles as they all speak and hug each other, then move along to baggage claim to gather their luggage.

On the way to baggage claim, Jeb Jr smiles and says, "I feel like royalty."

"We *are*," Albert Johnson says, "They even brought along the young brothers who can relate to my social stress issues."

They all laugh because they know he's speaking of Corey and Bobby.

Corey says, "You went through things that me and Bobby will never have to deal with. I feel like I should be thanking you for paving the way for us to be open about *our* sexual preferences these days."

"Amen to that," Bobby says, "Because now we know what category those whack minds are under. The republican liars."

"They're just trying to keep it hush-hush so they can continue to hide their own skeletons," Jeb Jr says.

"Yes but there's no closet that damn big," Albert adds.

They all laugh and agree as they arrive at baggage claim. They collect all of their luggage and head to the vehicles which are parked curbside.

As they load up, Tank has something humorous to add.

While laughing, he says, "I made Ajay aware that y'all came for my birthday tomorrow and not for his next home game after tonight. The Cav's next home game against the Phoenix Suns is still five days away. My birthday is in two hours."

Jessie Mae giggles and says, "Oh yes indeed, mister Tank. We had to make it here in time for the biggest event! Plus we already know Ajay and the Cavaliers beat the Pacers. We got that update as soon as we landed and was taxiing in."

Everybody laughs. Tank has to play up that he's keeping the conversation about him *only*.

He says, "I'm gonna break it to Ajay *gently*."

They all laugh again as they load up and head for CrewLand mall. The rest of the crew attended the Cav's game. As soon as it was over, they headed straight to CrewLand mall. They want to make sure and be there waiting at *The Crew's House of Soul Food,* when the European crew arrives.

Parma. January 27, 2006

Farah's house is jumping *this* Friday evening. Farah's entire household is having a good day, according to *their* standards. Everyone but Alana, that is. But the good news the others received, leaves Alana hopeful for another shot with Tank. Olivia has already received a call from Lil Ajay. He wants her to meet him tonight at The Spot II. She's *very* excited. She has already called Shalom to make sure she's going to be ready to go to

the teen club with her. But Olivia isn't the only 1 who got a crew call today.

Both Darlene and Farah has gotten word about a future crew connection as well. Chill and Ajay sent word through Darlene's son Jamal. Him and Holly, his fiancée are out in Parma visiting. He knows Chill will be calling him soon and he knows it's about a mission. Jamal is loyal to the crew and so is Holly. Chill told Jamal to make sure Darlene and Farah are told that him and Ajay will need to speak with both of them, very soon. Jamal has done his part. Alana is the only one left out of today's excitement. But she's already setting her mind into overdrive.

"If all three of y'all can hook up with crew," Alana says, "Then I know my chances are good. I *work* for crew. I told Tank happy birthday at his party, night before last. He smiled and said thank you. So it's time for me to see where I can take this Tank thing, *this* time."

"I'm so excited and I can't even stop smiling," Farah says.
She wants to know more from Jamal about exactly what they said.
Jamal says, "He just asked me to get both of y'all phone numbers. They'll call y'all with the details and all."

"Now son," Darlene says, "Please tell me, you went on and passed my cell number to Ajay. You did, didn't you?"

"Yes and I gave Farah's number to Chill," Jamal says, "The Cav's are in Indiana tonight. So most likely it won't be tonight, when Ajay calls."
Holly cuts in and says, "I just hope y'all don't mess up anything *this* time. Because we work for them and we don't wanna lose our jobs."

"I know I'm not gonna mess up," Darlene says with laughter.
"I've been wanting some Ajay time for more than a decade. I will be on my best behavior. I can promise y'all that. I will be ready *whenever* he calls."
Farah chimes in and says, "And I will too. *Shoot.* No way in hell I'd mess this chance up either."

"Me either," Olivia says.
Just then, the house phone starts ringing. Alana already has a clue as to who's calling. It's the 1 person who can call the house phone *only*. She picks up the cordless phone.

"Hello," she says then waits for the pre-recorded message to play out.
She already knows it's Angel. Her mother Angela had already told her that Angel would have phone privileges by today. And to expect a call from her before she has to go in to work. The recording is done.
"Hey Angel!" Alana says, trying to sound more excited than she really is.

"What's up, friend?" Angel says, filled with laughter. "I'm just up

140

the road from you now, girl! It's time to get it popping, home girl!!"

"I heard you got here on the fourth," Angel says, "You had to wait *this* long to be able to use the phone?"

"Three weeks," Angels says, "It'll be three weeks by three in the morning. Plus I had to get my call list approved. But I have to let you know the best part of this phone call thing."

"What's up?" Alana asks, eager to hear what she says.

"I got approved to have your workplace, The *Spot*, on my call log," Angel says, giggling uncontrollable.

"What?!! For *real*?!!" Alana asks in disbelief.

"I wouldn't lie about that, girlfriend," Angel says, "And I was told that Ajay and Chill approved it!"

Alana feels there has to be a huge worm in this mix. She knows her aunt Darlene and Farah are each going to get phone calls from Ajay and Chill. Plus her daughter Olivia has already been called to meet Ajay's son tonight. Alana wonders why hasn't she been included, so far. She can't give away the news about Olivia, Farah or Darlene. Because Angel is on the other side of that match and so is Jaylisa, her stepsister. Alana decides to play it up for herself.

She says, "Well if you're back on the map. I needs to be back on it too. Are you gonna hook me up? And you already know *who* I want!"

Angel says, "You know I'll do what I can. I just can't wait to hear his voice. I'm gonna ask him to add his name to my visitor's list. That way, this final year won't seem so long."

"Do you think he will?" Alana asks.

"I think so," Angel says, "If he approved for me to call him at the club. Then why not?"

"I agree," Alana says, still shocked by the sudden openness of the crew.

Angel goes on about her visitors list. She lets Alana know that her usual family members are on it.

"And I added you too," Angel says, "Do you remember the white girl Julie? She use to date my cousin Bulldog?"

"Yea. Barely."

Angels says, "But you do remember her. Because you thought she was trying to get close to the crew and you was mad cause they didn't treat her, a white girl, the way they treated us. *Anyway.* She moved to Atlanta after Bulldog died. She told my mama she couldn't stand being around Cleveland without him. I guess she really cared about him. He didn't give a shit about

141

her though. And we *both* knew that. He just needed a date so he could go into the crew club and peek things out. But anyway. She's suppose to be in Cleveland for the big crew wedding. That's what my mama said. And she's gonna come visit me while she's in town."

"I hear that," Alana says, "Your mama told me that Jaylisa signed up to visit you too."

"Yep," Alana says, "She's on the list too. I should have a lot of visitors now that I'm close to home. Do you think Michelle and Tameka will visit me?"

"If Ajay visits you," Alana says, "Then tell him to make them come and see you too. I miss their two faced asses though. For real I do."
Angel says, "Me too. My call got a minute left. I'm bout to get ready to watch Ajay's game on TV. I'm in town now. So I know these inmates will be watching the home team without it costing me anything."

"Alright girl," Alana says. She laughs as she continues. She says, "Remember our phone schedule and make sure you have some good news for me when you call me back. From your side or mine. And hopefully mine will be *soon!*"
They laugh and soon, the phone disconnects.

Alana puts the cordless phone down. She's hopeful now. She looks at Darlene. The look on Darlene's face isn't a joyful one.

"Just remember who has the best shot at hooking you up, niece," Darlene says, "I didn't kill that man's unborn child. *That* bitch did."
Olivia adds, "That's true, mama. When I came at Jaylisa with that in front of Ajay junior, the other night. He didn't seem like he knew that part. He walked off and left me *and* Jaylisa in the VIP booth alone. That's why I was so glad that he called me today."

"They've got a good point, Alana," Farah cosigns. She adds, "Ajay would give Darlene a chance before he would give Angel one. I think that's a set up. I can't prove it. But I've been around this crew long enough to know, they have juice like no one else I know. I have to say it. I agree with Libby and Darlene, on this one. The best chance is *under* your roof."

"Y'all probably right," Alana says, "Well let's watch the game first. Then we can head on out to *CrewLand* for a *crew* night!"

"Oh I'm definitely watching the game," Darlene says, "Because I feel like Ajay is gonna have a great game tonight. And if he does. He will be doing press box afterwards. I always watch for that. Now I have a new glare in my eyes."
They all grab some food from the kitchen and sprawl out over the sectional

in the living room. Darlene turns on the pre-game show and they all settle in to watch the Cavalier's and Pacers game.

The Cavaliers' beat the Pacers by four, in Indiana. Ajay had an awesome game, along with Lebron James. They were interviewed together after the win. While on TV, Ajay was sure to announce that he would be attending his family's January event, tomorrow night. Not only did he do it to give *The Chill Spot* a national plug. He also knows Darlene is watching and she'll be at the club. But Darlene wasn't the reason for his nationwide camera action. He did it for Angel. He knows she was watching from her Parma Jailhouse residence. He has to make sure she knows when he'll be at the club. That's the very reason she was given the new phone number too. He knows she's going to call. Ajay is more than ready. It's time to set *"Crew Work"* in motion. The killing of Angel Taylor has never left his mind since 1992. The day she caused Ebony's accident and killed their unborn child. He knows the sooner he can reel Angel in. The sooner he can able his son Lil Ajay of his birthright.

The news reporter congratulates Ajay and Lebron on the Cav's victory and new winning streak.

"We're on a four game winning streak since that lose to Golden State," Ajay says.

Lebron has to crack on him, *live*. Lebron says, "Yes and again, I'd like to thank misses Ebony Jackson for giving Ajay his game back."

The reporter laughs with Ajay and Lebron before releasing them to the locker room.

On the way to the locker room, Ajay has to give Lebron props.

He says, "I told you, Bron. My wife is my motivation *and* my game plan. As long as she holds me. I can't miss."

They crack up laughing as they enter their locker room.

They shower up quickly and get dressed. They have a flight to Cleveland, in less than an hour.

Lebron says, "Now let's get you on back to the house so you can get your potion before Sunday's game. The Phoenix Suns will be in our home. We must send them back with a lose."

"I'm going home to make love, Bron," Ajay says.

Lebron smiles and says, "That's a triple double from you on Sunday, then. Good deal."

They head out with their entire team who are all laughing with them, by now. They're heading to the airport within 10 minutes. Ajay can't wait to get home to Ebony. She'd sent him a text message while he was showering.

That text told him she was ready for some *daddy* time. He's sending her a text right now, saying, *"Daddy is ready for you all the time."*

The Chill Spot
Rebbie is at The Chill Spot with Nina and T-baby tonight. June is here too. She knows Jarvis will be here as well. He will be coming soon. Him and Ajay's team flight has just landed at Cleveland Hopkins international Airport. Jarvis just sent her a text saying, *"I'm on the home runway."* Rebbie's reply, *"I'll see you soon. And yes, he's here. ☺"*

The arrival of the Cavalier's team flight has just been announced on the club's PA. Nina and T-baby know they have to have a talk with Rebbie. Ebony told them to call her from Renee's office and put it on speaker. Tank and Wes are here with Nina and T-baby. Nina knows they'll have to get to that talk before the players start to arrive at the club. She looks at T-baby. T-baby just gives her a nod.

Then she turns to Wes and says, "I need to take a break, baby. I'm in my second trimester with our baby. So I have to take breaks when I'm at the club, so I can put my feet up. I'll be in Renee's office."

"By all means, baby," Wes says, "I want you to be comfortable, as much as possible. Do you want me to go with you?"

"No baby. You enjoy Tank and June's company. Some male bonding time," she says while laughing. She adds, "I'm gonna get Nina and Ree Ree to go with me. We can have some girl time. *All* at the same time." Wes laughs and gives her a kiss.

As she stands, she looks at Nina. Nina already know that's their signal. That's when she tells Tank they need some girl time. Tank already knows Rebbie has an issue they need to discuss. Wes knows it too. They're both okay with it. Wes and Tank let June know the ladies need some girl time. But as usual, June isn't as supportive as Tank and Wes are. Tank isn't going to stand for it and he cuts right through it.

He says, "Come on, Cuz. You *can't* be thinking from the crew end, right now. Let these ladies have some girl time. I'm sure you know this by now. But that has always been their way of figuring out *how* to give us *our* loving *correctly*. I'm down wit it. How bout you, Wes?"

"I'm definitely down for that," Wes answers and laughs before adding, "Bye baby and ladies."

They all laugh. Even June has to laugh with them. He decides to go along with the suggestion but he adds,

"Let's walk them to the management hallway. Just so we know they got

there unobstructed. Y'all know we've got the sexiest ladies in the nation. These guys be praying that they can catch them alone."

Tank and Wes go along with June to walk Nina, T-baby and Rebbie up the VIP hallway. The ladies excuse them from there and the guys head back to their designated area.

Nina, T-baby and Rebbie dip into Renee's office. They have to get the latest update on Rebbie. They haven't had a chance to talk about that night at her studio dance club either. They plan to get to all of it tonight. They know June isn't aware of as much as they are. But they still need an update on Rebbie's situation with Jarvis. Like, how far has it gone, *too date*. That's going down tonight. Now that they are inside Renee's office with the door closed and their husbands have gone back to VIP, Nina takes the floor. She says, "First, let's get a comfortable seating position for T-baby."

T-baby says, "First things first, before I even sit down."

T-baby goes behind Renee's desk and picks up the phone. She dials Ebony's cell phone and puts her on speakerphone, while Nina tells Rebbie to have a seat.

While smiling, Nina says, "It's time for one of those *old time* Awesome Foursome talks. We all *got* to get on the same page, Ree. We can't carry you, if we don't know what's going on."

Ebony answers by the 2nd ring. She hears what Nina just said and she chimes in.

"Her and Jarvis are still into each other," Ebony says from the speaker. *"But they're still platonic. No sex has happened with them at all. That's how I wanna believe it."*

"Well has it, Rebbie?" T-baby asks. "It's time to tell the truth."

"Sort of," is all Rebbie says.

"What sort?" Nina asks.

"The same source that T-baby had with Craig in his car, out at the U," Rebbie says in 1 breath.

"So he ate you out?" Ebony asks.

"Yes," Rebbie says, "A few times. It started again on New Year's Eve before Brian showed up here and I had to leave and go to my studio."

"Rebbie!" Ebony yells. *"On New Year's eve night, my anniversary night, Jarvis had just told Anthony and Ant y'all hadn't been active in years. But it did not start that night in Cincinnati when you saw June go into the hotel with Diana Keyes. It didn't start until nineteen ninety nine. After Jarvis and Gwen was living right across the street from me. Y'all were both married, then. And to my understanding. That was the first and last time. So are you*

ready to be straight up with us? Because we understand your grief as well as anybody else. We will always have each others backs. As long as we are being crew and honoring the ladies before us. So tell us the truth, Rebbie!"

"Don't Rebbie me," Rebbie says and smiles. "It was the most sensuous time I've ever had. It was real y'all. Jarvis loves me. I know he does. I'm just trying to figure out if I can love him back."

"He's married Rebbie and so are you," T-baby adds.

"Not for long," Ebony says as she sighs.

Nina knows about the call Ebony received from Jarvis' wife. She brings that into the conversation.

"Ebony have you told Ree about the conversation you had with Gwen?" Nina asks.

"Not yet," Ebony says, *"But I will now. As long as we have time to get it in without an interruption on y'all end."*

"Wes and Tank got June secured," T-baby adds and they all laugh.

"Okay cool," Nina says, "Let us all hear it at the same time, Eb."

"Wait," T-baby says, "Is Ajay coming to the club first. Or is he heading straight home?"

They all laugh because they know why T-baby inquired about Ajay's destination. Nina answers that for T-baby.

Nina says, "Everybody who saw his post interview, knows he *ain't* coming to the club until tomorrow night. Including devil Angel's ass."

They all laugh good on that comment. Ebony confirms Nina's comment. Then she goes on to tell them about her conversation with Gwen Rhodes, 2 days before the New Year. She makes sure they are aware of Nickeia Russell, Gwen's sister, making many trips passed Rebbie's dance studio too. And she lets them know, Nickeia told Gwen that she has seen Jarvis' vehicle there, several times.

"Oh wow," Rebbie says, *"That* little bitch. She probably wasn't even looking for Jarvis when she came through there. It's right next door to the recreation center. *Ajay's* recreation center. And we all know Nickeia's past with going after Ajay."

"Hell yeah," T-baby says, "Every since the Natty days, actually."

Nina adds, "Uh huh."

Ebony continues, *"Yes. We all know about her dreams which shall be a nightmare if she ever tries anything again. But that scenario is exactly what I used to throw Gwen off from sniffing around there, herself. But the reason for Nickeia going through there is probably not far from the truth, foursome. Her first trip through there was looking for a chance to see if Anthony was there.*

But she probably saw Jarvis' vehicle on that trip and just went from there. Now she can dream about my man. But Nickeia will wake up dead if she tries anything which is disrespectful to me."

"I *hear* ya, cousin!" T-baby shrills. "And we know you can take a fool out the game."

"*I've had my moments*," Ebony says as she giggles. "*But Nickeia did see her brother-in-law's vehicle. Almost every time she drove through there.*"

"So Rebbie. The studio is off limits, sister girl," Nina says as she bats her eyes and smiles.

"We've never done anything *out of hand* at the studio anyway," Rebbie says.

"Where are y'all kicking it at?" Nina says, "Because I hope it's somewhere no one knows about."

"Me too," T-baby says, "And Ree. There needs to be an end to it. Or to somebody. For real."

"He has one of those Condo's that I own," Rebbie says and smiles. She adds, "Gwen knows nothing about it. He's on the opposite side of where Greg junior's condo is too, T-baby. So your brother won't even see us unless he puts a girl on that side."

"But that won't happen because he's got a new girl," Nina says, "And with Kelly's mom's blessings."

"Yes he does," T-baby says, "Kilo's sister Patricia Thomas and I really like her too. Just like I loved Kelly. She is crew material, *fasho*."

"So see," Rebbie says, "We got that covered, *true's*."

"*Not quite, true sister girl*," Ebony interjects.

Nina jumps in and asks, "What do mean, Ebony?"

"*Ant knows about you and Jarvis*," she says.

"Lil Ajay??!!" Rebbie asks, "I know he done been to Greg's condo but how does he see us?"

"*Because he be walking on the far side*," Ebony says carefully. She know she's going to have to let her girls know that her 6 year old son is no longer a virgin.

"Wait a minute," Nina says, "Now I know Greg junior's condo is *their* crew's little jump off spot. Like Chill's and The U was, for us."

"Yes but *how* and *why* is he able to see Rebbie?" T-baby asks, "A mile away?"

"*Some of the time, he goes walking around so he can get away from some of the….*" Ebony pauses.

"Come on wit it, Ebony," Nina urges. "First of all. I know he done

147

got head already. He *is* my brother's son. But if he's avoiding a girl. That means...."

"*That means he's gone all the way and he doesn't want that girl in his presence anymore*," Ebony says, "*Until he needs her, in order to put a plan in action*."

"That *is* Ajay warmed over," Rebbie says and laughs. She adds, "We're gonna get on with my stuff. But I have to know. Has he gone all the way?"

"*Yes. He has*," Ebony says.

Rebbie, Nina and T-baby scream, shout and laugh too. Neither of them or shocked or surprised. They want more details but Ebony cuts them short.

"*No way am I gonna go on*," Ebony says, "*That's for the males in my household. If y'all hear more. It will come from your husbands*."

"Yes," Nina says, "That's a *crew for life* rule."

"True," T-baby says and Rebbie agrees.

T-baby adds, "Lil Rich is getting head and I know it won't be much longer before he gets all the way into somebody. But his crew girl and the girl he likes is Aaliyah Hamilton. Ced's little niece."

"*Is that why he always goes to Atlanta to visit Bre, Jan and Lynn on every school break?*" Ebony asks while giggling.

"You know it is," T-baby says and laughs too.

"She's crew. *Not* a crew thang," Nina says and laughs. She adds, "So it's all good. Ron Banks son Jonathan and my Jerica are an item. But y'all already know that part."

"Yes and she'll be thirteen next year," T-baby says, "*God*, how time flies."

Rebbie says, "The crew has already matched up Orian and Rob junior for when their time comes. And I'm already nervous."

"*We're on the other side of it now, girls*," Ebony adds and laughs too. She says, "*We're gonna get to see how we made our mama's get gray strands of hair too. And I'm on the mama Jo side of it. I've got five girls*."

"With Ajay as their daddy," Nina says, "So they will not be out of bounds until they're thirty five."

They all laugh more as Nina adds, "That's a male Jackson thing. Ajay is just like daddy. It's gonna be some dead boys *every* year, if *any* of my nieces get hurt or cry about a boy bothering them. I already know that's covered!"

They continue to laugh but Rebbie is thinking about the fact that Lil Ajay has seen her and Jarvis together. She has to hear more. She gets right back to that discussion.

She asks, "Ebony. I know Ajay and how he has always been with being one who knows not to expose anyone from the crew. Even if they need to be exposed."

"Like Rich and June needed to be and wasn't," T-baby adds.

Rebbie agrees and continues, "So tell me. Can I count on Lil Ajay being the same way?"

"*Who is he just like, Rebbie?*" Ebony asks as she giggles.

"His daddy!!" Rebbie, T-baby and Nina say simultaneously.

They all laugh hard before getting back to the conversation about Rebbie and Jarvis. And Lil Ajay's conversation with his daddy and Jarvis.

Ebony says, "*Rebbie, the reason I haven't bugged you about this. Is because I know you're happy when you're with Jarvis. Ant said that to his daddy and Jarvis. It was on the night of our eighth anniversary. After we beat the Pistons. Y'all remember when I sent Ant back outside of Stoney's. He told me Anthony was about to talk to Jarvis. So I knew Jarvis was outside. I wanted them to keep him out there. At least, until we left. Because I didn't even wanna see what might happen with Rebbie, June and Jarvis, in one place. It was on that night that Ant told his daddy and Jarvis that he'd seen you and him walking out at the Condo's.*"

Nina says, "Oh wow."

"And he said we looked happy together?" Rebbie asks.

Ebony says, "*Yes and he also said you looked happy when you was with Jarvis and you don't look the same way when you're with big June.*"

"Out of the mouths of babe's," T-baby says.

"He has a man's mind," Nina says, "And he's trapped in a boy's body. Mama use to always say that about Ajay. She said that's how my daddy would explain all of Ajay's actions."

"*The same way Anthony explains Ant's actions to me,*" Ebony says. "*He is very mature. It's scary. So scary. But at the same time. I think back to how I viewed Anthony when we was still in the single digits, age wise. I always saw him like he was big Chill's age. And I'm trying to view my son in that way now. Because it's gonna be that way. He doesn't think nor does he see the world, like a six year old boy.*"

Nina says, "That's true. Me and Lynn was talking about that, last night. Lil Jb is ahead of his time too. Both of those boys have Jackson and Brown blood. They're gonna be major, in their coming of age years."

Rebbie agrees. Then she adds, "I wish we had text messages when we was teens. It has been very convenient in my situation."

"And it was convenient on that night when you had to be at the

dance studio when June was at the club, looking for you too," Nina says.

"So true," Rebbie answers and smiles.

T-baby asks, "But do y'all text, *even* when you're in the house or near June?"

"Yes we do," Rebbie says.

Nina says, "And you make him think it's one of us. Don't you?"

"Yes," Rebbie says and smiles.

Ebony says, *"You've gotta be more careful, Ree Ree. That just might be what gets you caught up."*

"Caught up with what?!" June asks in a loud voice.

He'd just come back up and barged into the office. Tank and Wes aren't far behind him. They tried to convince him to let the ladies have their girl time. But June wasn't patient at all. He had to have his eyes on Rebbie, in order for him to feel comfortable.

Immediately, the ladies wonder just how much did he hear. Nina, T-baby nor Rebbie have a quick response for June. But Ebony comes through with a gem when she says, *"She's worried about how she's going to react from the mother's side of this crew family. When her daughter gets to the dating side. Just as I am. Because Ant is already following in Anthony's footsteps. For us, it's our first time seeing how the males in this crew attract women. So now that there are three males in the office. Maybe y'all can bring us up on that side of things."*

Tank *certainly* doesn't want to participate in this conversation. He's ready to clear the room right now.

He says, "Male crew discussions *only*! Let us get back to the club party! Twin get off the phone. Ajay should be pulling through the security gate, right about now. Goodnight!"

He laughs as he disconnects the call. He turns to Nina and adds,

"Now can we go celebrate with our team, baby? We did win again tonight! Let's go!"

Nina chimes in, "He's right ladies. We've been in mother mode for too long tonight. Let's go get out awesome foursome on. Because I know Ebony's *way* ahead of us!"

They all laugh and head back to their VIP section.

Jackson Heights, Ajay and Ebony's Estate

Ebony is relaxing in bed when Ajay walks in, smiling. He gives her a hug and a long kiss.

"How's my game plan holder doing?" he asks and they both laugh. Ebony says, "I'm doing fine. And I have a plan brewing for the Suns game on Sunday."

"Ummm. I can't wait to feel and get *all* in that game plan either, baby," he says with a seductive smile. He adds, "Let me go look in on Lannie and Lea. I'll be right back. Don't you move a muscle, baby girl. The triplets are just gonna have to hear daddy fuck mama, *real* good tonight."

Ebony smiles and says, "It's only been thirty four and thirty three days since they left mama's womb. They're use to daddy's work, by now. After all, you was working when they got ready to come. They won't even twitch in their bassinets. Let alone, *wake* up. They won't be like Ant was when he caught us in the Jacuzzi, back in the day."

They both giggle hard. Then Ajay kisses her passionately.

He leans into her ear and whispers, "That's good to know because your one and only dick is extra hard and taking a new game plan, *ready*."

She smiles and says, "Yes and the pussy that's got you glued to love. Is gonna do her best to soften him up enough to get some rest."

"*Shit!*" he shrieks and blushes hard.

That's something he has *rarely* done in their nearly 19 year relationship. *Blush*. He likes that comment from his, *"baby girl."* He bends back down to her and gives her a very heated kiss. Then as he heads out to go check on his 2 oldest daughters, he yells, "I'll be back in a New York minute! I'll have to make this daddy time up to Lannie and Lea in the morning! Personal time is calling my name!"

Ebony lays back on their bed giggling as she disrobes. She knows there is no bed gear allowed for her. Not when she's past the postpartum period. And certainly, not when Ajay is at home.

Greg Jr's Condo. CrewLand Luxury Suites and Condo's

Lil Ajay is ready to add fire to *his* crew plan. He's already had all the head and pussy he can deal with, for tonight. Unless he gets some action toward handling the crew beef. At this point, he's ready to see who's the most down for him, out of these 4 *thangs*. He's already made Olivia's night. He let her suck and fuck him too. But she had to share him with Jaylisa. He thought about making them do each other but he doesn't really want them to get along. Not *that* well. Not yet. He made their fuck session more like a contest. He told them he was going to see who did him *best*. And whichever 1 of them was the best. Would get the other girl's time in the future.

Both Olivia and Jaylisa put on quite a show. Physically, Lil Ajay is tired now. But mentally, he's in overdrive. He's ready to work a plan to kick off the demise of *devil Angel* and Old Jake.

Rioshauna, Jaylisa, Shalom and Olivia are in the living room with him and his crew brothers. There are only 6 crew guys here tonight. Lil Ajay, Kilo Jr, Brad III, Rich III, Jb III & Alan Anthony. This almost makes the girls feel like they're couples. It's never been less than 2 guys to each thang, in their past hook ups. But soon, Lil Ajay brings Rioshauna into the bedroom alone. He wants to get more details on where her father Draper Watts is, *daily*.

He asks, "What's up with your dad lately? Is he still dogging you out?"

"The same thing," Rioshauna says, "He called my mama today and said he was coming by her apartment tomorrow."

"Maybe he's coming to spend some time with you," Lil Ajay tries.

She says, "More like, to get some pussy and some money. He don't do shit but use my mama."

Lil Ajay cringes. He hates a foul mouth girl. But he just grins and bares it. The mission tonight is *much* too important to focus on etiquette. Especially to someone he won't have in his company for life. He simply smiles.

He says, "I can see that sucking a good dick ain't the *only* fire that comes outta that mouth, ha?"

She catches that he didn't like her cursing. She apologizes immediately.

"I'm sorry," she says, "It just makes me *so* angry to see my mama crying all the time. And she always cries when he comes around her."

"How would you fix that?" Lil Ajay asks, "Do you ever think about that?"

"I would bust all the windows outta his Caddy truck," she says as tears form in her eyes. She adds, "He loves that truck, more than he do me. I can ask him for money for school clothes and all he gives me is like twenty dollars. But he put more than ten thousand dollars worth of tires, rims and stereo equipment on and in that damn truck."

"Wow!" Lil Ajay says, "He must be paid, ha?"

"He has an *okay* job," she says, "But he sells dope for grandpa Jake. Old Jake *is* my grandpa on my *mama* side. And *he* won't even make my daddy do one thing right. By me *or* by my mama. It's bad."

"I bet his truck is a boss whip, ha" Lil Ajay says, hoping she has pictures of it.

Preferably a backend shot with the license plate exposed and he's in luck. She has pictures of it in her cell phone photos. She shows them to him.

All views. Lil Ajay comes to life *instantly*. He has to think of a good way to get those pictures into *his* phone now, so he can get them to Ajay.

"I want a truck like that!" he starts with major excitement in his voice. He asks, "That's a two thousand and six. Ain't it?"

"Yep," she says, "He just got it for Christmas."

He says, "Send those pics to me, if you don't mind. I got a plan for me and you to have some time for *just* us. This is what I'm gonna do. I wanna show my mama what kind of truck I want. How much you wanna bet, I can get a truck like that? And I'm not even old enough to drive it yet. But you'll be sixteen *way* before me. You'll drive me around. Want you?"

"Hell yea I would!" she says with excitement, as she wipes away her tears and starts to smile.

Immediately she text the pictures to his phone as she continues to talk. Lil Ajay looks at the pictures. He pulls the back view photo to large. He can read the license plate very well. He likes that he's gotten what he wanted from this *thang*. Information which brings Old Jake into view. He smiles.

"You really do like that truck, ha?" she asks.

"More than you'll ever know," he says.

Then he changes the subject.

He says, "Why don't you give me some more head? I'm riled up again now. Seeing my dream truck, done turned me on. I wanna be in a good mood so I can get my plan together on how to get us a ride. You'll be sixteen in two and a half years. I'll have it extra hooked up by then. Better than your daddy, who dogs you out. And don't you give me no excuses when I call you to be my damn driver and my damn girl everyday either."

"I won't," she says from his lower end.

He reminds her, "And remember. We can't tell nobody about this. Not your girls nor my boys. And definitely not our parents. Okay?"

"Okay baby," she tries.

"Call me Ajay," he says, "That makes me feel like a man."

"Okay Ajay," Rioshauna says as she takes his dick to her throat.

"I love your head, Rio," he says which sends nausea chills through his body and nearly to his stomach.

But he handles it. That last comment works on Rioshauna, to the max. She lays her phone on the bed. Then she grabs his nearly 8 inch dick with both hands and starts to suck him off *royally*.

While she's working on him, he picks up her phone. First he deletes any traces of the send to his phone. Then he goes to her contacts. He sends her great grandpa Old Jake, her father Draper Watts and her mother

Mallory Fields info, to *his* phone. He deletes those traces too. He looks at her working him. He smiles and says,
"Rio this is one of the best nights of my life."
She goes all in on that comment. While he lays back and gets ready to cum.

Ajay and Ebony's Estate, Jackson Heights

Ajay has made it back to the bedroom where Ebony lays naked and underneath the covers. His eyes are peering at her, as he picks up the remote to their home entertainment system.
He asks, "Do you remember saying this to me, earlier tonight before the Jersey game?"
He switches it to CD and clicks play. The first song starts.
Mariah Carey. We Belong Together.
First he smiles at her and she smiles back.
He says, "We've got some good history with M.C."
"A real *vision of love*," she says while smiling. She adds, "And I can see it so clear, baby. We *definitely* belong together. Mariah is right."
He sucks in his air as he slides under the covers with her while looking at her naked body. He rubs across her tummy which is almost back to it's original flat status.
He says, "I wanna see all of this tonight, baby girl. I know you can see how hard your dick is. *Right*?"
"Yes I can," she moans as his hand moves up to her chest.
He rubs on her full breast.
She whispers, "Do you still like my breast?"
He's still whispering, as he says, "Hell yea. Henny and Penny will always be loved by me, *Ebony*. I still think about when *these* breast was all I had. That is, once you finally trusted me to touch em. That was long before you was ready for sex though. I went to bed *so* many nights with my dick as hard as it is right now. But that shit is over. This body is ready and it's calling me."
He lifts the covers so she can see his dick. He's looks into her eyes. Then he lets his eyes drift down her body and licks his lips. She smiles. His hand goes back to her breast.
He says, "It was all of those years I spent on these, that made these babies grow into the healthy samples they are today."
She's smiling. He's rubbing and playing with her breast and her tender nipples. She moans as she keeps eye contact with him. There is something *so* sensuous about watching him, watch her while he anticipates *sexing* her.

154

He says, "I know they're tender, baby. And I know I can't suck on these sweet nipples, *too* hard."

"Not unless you want the triplets *first* A-M feeding," she says and they both giggle.

He says, "No way. I would never take a feeding from my babies. Or my baby girl either. Ebony for each of your three pregnancies, I noticed something that I have to give my kids credit for *again*."

"What's that?" she ask as she smiles.

He says, "The growth of your breast. My babies milk made these beautiful breast, even bigger and *softer* than I could. And these nipples too. *Wow!* They look so good. They've always made my mouth water."

She cracks up laughing and says, "You've said that *a lot* more since Ant and Lannie came into this world. I'm just glad you still like them. I was thinking they would go soggy right after my first pregnancy."

"Nah they didn't," he says, "Give big mama credit for that."

"Yes," Ebony says, "Because she told me to be sure and breast feed *all* of my kids. She said that would keep my breast firm. Or as firm as possible until I get old. Then they'll go south."

They both laugh but Ajay has to get right back to the sex talk. His vision of her breast isn't going to allow his mind to focus on anything else. Unless it's an emergency situation. To be an emergency which would pull him away from sexing his wife? It would have to be 1 of their kids and that's not the case. So he stays on the subject of her ample breast.

He says, "I know I can't have the nipples tonight, baby. I know I can't suck on em. Not hard anyway. But I'm gonna lick the hell out of em. Do you hear me?"

"Yes baby," she whispers, already feeling erotic from his touch.

He says, "But I'll share these pretty nipples with my babies. My babies *only*. But the rest of this fine and sexy ass package is mine. *All* mine."

He begins licking and lightly sucking on her tender nipples and breast. She moans.

"Ohhhh! I miss you *all* the time, Anthony," she squeals, "What I said before the game came directly from my heart. I wanna make sure you know. I meant *every* word of it. I am so addicted to you. Every time you touch me.........., it seems like something *brand* new. You've always been like a really good drug to me. Since day one. And like you said to me years ago, about your addiction. I *never* wanna be rehabilitated either."

They both smile. Then they kiss long and hard. He runs his hand down her body and finds her throbbing clitoris. He rubs it gently. She breathes

heavier with slight moans. He pushes his index finger inside of her pussy and starts to kiss her aggressively.

After the kiss, he says, "I still remember when I couldn't even put my fingers in here, without you panicking."

"Yes and you got me passed that problem too," she whispers while still kissing his lips.

Then she grabs and holds his head with both hands, while they trade tongues with each other. It's heating up quickly. That's normal for their sex lives. But Ajay always finds a way to make each session a little bit different. Ebony is loving the precursor to the lovemaking, she's about to receive. While still tongue kissing him, she grabs his braids and tangles her fingers in them. She kisses him even harder. Finally they release lips. He goes to her chin and then her neck. She's still holding his braids. She knows he's about to head south and she wants to taste him too. She's going to ask him if she can suck him to pleasure land. He had said she couldn't, not as long as she's nursing. But he did let her suck his dick in Utah, a week ago. Not since then though. She's gotten her pussy eaten, at least once everyday, since then. Unless he was on a road trip. She wants to request of him that she get to do a dick sucking, once per week too. And see if he'll allow her to orally please him. He certainly pleases her with his tongue and his 15 inch dick, on a daily basis. She's got to try it. At least.

What can it hurt to ask?

She says, "Baby."

"Huh," he grunts and he kisses her belly button.

"I wanna taste you too," she tries.

He doesn't answer. He just continues to head south. She rubs through his braids again. She tries again.

"I want some sixty nine action," she says, "It was *so* good in Utah. I wanna taste you again baby. *Please*?"

He pauses and looks up at her.

"Please, baby," she pleads.

He doesn't say anything. He's just staring at her. She doesn't know if he's lost patience with her already. Or if he's waiting on her to make a move. As Mariah Carey sings on, she decides to make her move.

She starts to scoot her body around. She continues until they're laying across the bed, side by side, in opposite directions. He's still watching her. She slides her face toward his crotch. He's just watching her. She's not sure what his stare means. She remembers him telling her that him

156

receiving head from her, makes him feel vulnerable. But that's only more motivation for her to go through with it. She's always tried to find a way to take some of the growl out of his beast of a dick. She's determined to make this play. If he doesn't want her to taste him. Then he's going to have to stop her. She goes for broke.

She reaches out and grabs his dick. *Her dick*! She moves all the way in. She places her mouth on it and gives it a sweet kiss. He moans but he's still watching her. She opens her mouth and takes his dick in between her lips. She starts to suck on him. He moans again.

Suddenly he reaches for her legs. He grabs them with force and spreads them apart. He dives in and grabs her clitoris between his lips.

"Oooohhh baby!!" she yells from the sensation of his cool lips on her pussy. She whispers, "Yes Anthony, baby. I wanna make you feel as good as you always make me feel."

"Do your thing, baby," he says, "I know you got a supply for my *Tre'* already stored in the fridge. Right?"
She whispers, "Yes I do, baby. I pumped enough milk for two days."

"Then let's suck and fuck each others brains out, baby," he whispers. "I've gotta give you what you want. No matter what it is. As long as it makes you feel good and shows me what you got for me."

"Mmmm."
She takes him to her throat. He gasps for air as he gets back to licking her sweet pussy. She's sucking and licking. He's licking, sucking and sticking his tongue as far into her pussy as he can get it. They're enjoying each other to the fullest right now. She's moaning a lot. He's gasping and grunting a lot. They're getting to the good part.

Mariah's song is on repeat. As it begins again, she can feel his body tensing up. She knows her body is *already* tensed. She can feel her climax inching up but her goal is to make him cum *first*. This 69 action has become a, *"who can make the other one cum first"* contest. She realizes it now. That has always been Ajay's way. He wants all that she's got but he never wants to feel like she's doing him, better than he's doing her. He told her that would make him think she would get bored with him and his sex. She knows that's an impossibility though. Because his sex is never the same and it's always *damn* good.

"It's so fuckin good, baby," he says, in an almost loud voice. "Suck yo dick, baby. Oh yea!!"

"Ooooo," she wails, "I'm about to cum, baby. I want yours. I want it. I want it now!!"

"Go get it!" he orders, "Because this sweet nectar is right here."
So true! No sooner than he says it. She starts to moan *very* loud. She's still sucking on him as she cums. She's moaning while taking his dick to her throat. He's loving this move 100%. She spawning out of control and still sucking him.

"Ooooo! Oooohhh!" she yells, "I'm cumin!!! Oh God!! Yes!"
She starts sucking on him ravishingly. Licking on him and slurping him too, with all of her might. She wants him to have his payday along with her. She can feel his dick throbbing in her mouth. She knows *this* throb. Her pussy is both familiar and addicted to it. Ajay's nut is on the way. He might let it go, now that he's made her cum first. She's super wet and she's still sucking and moaning. He reaches to his southern end and puts his powerful hand behind her head. He's now guiding her head as she sucks him to his destination. He knows it's going to be a massive one. And oh yes it is! It's finally here!!!

"Oh baby! *Shit*!!" he blurts out. In a loud voice, he says, "Aahhh, baby girl! Baby girl! This shit feels *soooo* good! *Damn*!!"
He's cumin. She's still cumin too. Their bedroom or anywhere else where they have sex is orgasm heaven. And they haven't even started to fuck yet.

The 2nd play of Mariah's song is coming to a close. Ajay grabs the remote. He wants to play another song. Next on deck:
Unpredictable. Jamie Foxx.

Still in their same position after their 69 action, they both lay and pant. Just trying to catch up to their breath. Ebony looks at him. He's looking at her. Suddenly he smiles because he knows she's going to make a comment on the song.
She says, "Now that fits us since the kids came. Do you agree?"

"That fits *you*, baby," he says and chuckles. He adds, "It fits you to a *tee*, tonight. You just went all out, didn't you? You *took* some of yo dick tonight, baby. If I wasn't in love with you. I'd file a damn police report."
She giggles and says, "It felt like it was *willing* to be had by me. I didn't take it. It was right there. I can't always leave him out of the mix. Our private parts are suppose to be equal. Ain't that right?"
He says, "Say what *our* private parts names are."
She cracks up laughing but she doesn't answer him. She just smiles. He laughs too as he turns her around to get his dick closer to her pussy. He stops his laugh almost instantly. Then his face turns very serious. She knows he wants her to answer him. She's still shy about saying the names of their sex parts to him. It gets him more aroused. In her opinion, he doesn't

need anymore motivation to fuck her. She doesn't want to push it too far either. But he's still watching her.

He says, "You still can't say those words in front of me? You and your girls talk about it all the time. So tell *me*."

He's looking into her eyes impatiently.

Suddenly he sticks his finger back inside of her pussy. The sensation makes her jump.

That's when he asks, "What is this?"

"Your pussy," she mumbles and he can barely hear her.

"I didn't hear you. Say it a little bit louder."

"That's your pussy," she says and blushes.

He reaches down and grabs his dick.

He asks, "And what's this?"

She smiles shyly. She knows this name is still going to be a hard 1 for her to say to him. Even though his dick is and always has been, her 1 and only. But he's still watching her. It seems as though he's running out of patience too. He's still holding his dick in 1 hand. He starts to play inside of her pussy with fingers from his other hand. She's slowing around. She's hoping he'll give her a pass but that's not going to happen and she should know that already. He tries again.

He asks, "What is this?"

"Yo dick," she barely mumbles.

"I gotta hear you, baby," he says. "Louder please."

"It's your dick," she says and she feels weird, all of sudden.

He says, "So I have a pussy and a dick?"

"No," she says and smiles.

"So which one is mine?" he asks.

She points to her pussy. He shakes his head and says,

"Nah. Talk to me, baby girl. Which one is mine?"

"My pussy is yours," she says plainly.

He's not smiling at all anymore. He wants her to get pass this mark tonight.

He says, "Finish it up. Who's dick is this?"

"Mine," she says.

He says, "Say it."

She pauses for a few seconds. She has to find a way to get off of this cliff. Because if she doesn't answer him, he's going to use *her dick* to battle it out with *his pussy*. And for all 18 years of their relationship, she's known she won't be on the winning end of that battle.

"Your dick is mine," she says.

Now he feels like he has to coax her. He says,
"Say…, that's my dick. Just like that."
> "That's my dick," she repeats after him.
> "Say it again."
> "That's my dick," she says again.
He asks, "And do you want it?"
> "Yes."
> "Tell me you want it," he says.
> "I want my dick," she finally says.
> "I want my pussy too," he says, "Can you hear that?"
She's lost. She knows it's about something sexual. Another 1 of his *"way in"* gestures. But she has no clue of what he's speaking on. She know he's going to bring her all the way along. *Soon.* So she asks, "Hear what?"
> "Can't you hear your dick calling you? It didn't have to call you to go into your mouth," he says arrogantly. "So why don't you rush yo dick on up into my pussy? Why don't you do that? Ha? Tell me that."
She smiles and says, "I just thought we was taking time to catch our breath, baby. That's all."
He smiles and says, "Are you stalling on me? I think I know what your plan was, Ebony."
She looks at him and cautiously asks, "What plan are you talking about?"
He asks, "Do you think you can wear me out by sucking me off? Was that your plan, baby?"
He chuckles. She smiles and shakes her head.
Damn. He knows I'm still scared of that big dick!

She knows he's going to wear her ass out in this next session. But she has to save face, at least.
She says, "I *can* never and *will* never wear you out. I know that already."
> "Then it's time for an answer, sweetheart," he says and smiles.
He adds, "Because your dick is calling you."
Then he whispers, "And my pussy is calling me, baby."
Ebony has to get in her last win of this *sexcapade*.
She whispers back, "And only you can answer your pussy, Anthony."
With that, he rams his dick into her already wet pussy and goes straight toward the bottom. She yelps as he knew she would.
He asks, "Oh and by the way. I can't be daddy to you, no more?"
> "Yes. Yes." she says quickly.
She's trying to catch her breath and plead her case, at the same time.

If there's a need too. Ajay loves it when she calls him daddy. But tonight, she's been calling him baby, all night. Now she wonders if he's perturbed by her not calling him by his very masculine, pet name. So she gathers herself. He's on his knees with 1 of her legs propped up on each of his shoulder. He's looking down into her eyes and slowing grinding into her. She tries to talk to him. While whispering in her mildest voice, she asks,

"Are you upset at me for not calling you daddy?"

"Do you think I am?" he asks.

"I don't know?" she says as she breathes out each time he pushes inside of her.

"No I'm not upset at all," he says as he pushes his dick into her, on pace. He adds, "I just didn't know it was gonna be two changes from you on the same night."

She doesn't respond because she's not sure if he's being truthful about not being upset. She knows her man. If and whenever he has something to settle with her. He always does it in this situation. A *sex* battle. One she has never won and she's not going to win it tonight either.

He says, "Do you have anymore changes for me?"

"No I don't," she says, "I promise."

He chuckles as he continues to fuck her. He can see a certain fear in her eyes right now. She knows her man, so she knows when it comes to sex, he's the supplier to her. He's the giver and she's the taker. It's not like he doesn't appreciate her wanting to please him fully. Because he does. But he knows what her game plan was tonight. He decides to let her know it now. He pulls her legs down and lays them to either side of him. He stretches out and lays on top of her. The entire time, he's staring into her eyes. He knows she's fragile right now and he doesn't want her to cry. Not from fear nor sadness. So he places his head on her shoulder so he can whisper in her ear.

He whispers, "Baby what was you trying to do? Even it up? Huh? Take some of the spark outta yo dick?"

She already knows not to even try lying to him because he knows her, as well as she knows herself. So she decides to be honest. He's still fucking her while she tries to tell him what her mission was during their erotic oral sex session.

She says, "I was trying to give my dick some pre-game."

He stops fucking and cracks up laughing. She smiles because she knows he thinks she's being dishonest.

Still chuckling, he says, "Some pre-game ha? What was that about? What was the mission? Tell it baby."

"I was trying to take it down just a little bit, daddy," she says, "I wanted to be able to handle it better than I ever have."

He starts to fuck again. He's holding her hips and pulling her in the motion which pleases him. He raises up while still pumping and looks into her eyes. He says, "Baby your dick is always one hundred percent for you. It don't matter if I get a nut. Once it's hard again. It's gonna go even harder. You see. The first nut is the fastest one. It's the quickest and softest one."

He kisses her aggressively. Then he adds,

"And my pussy knows your dick the best. It's wet and *squeezing* him tight. Always accommodating to me. So if you *ever* expect me to half fuck you. I'll just tell you right now. That shit is not *ever* gonna happen. Okay?"

"Okay," she says while breathing harder.

He pauses quickly and grabs the music remote. He looks down at her. He wants to see her reaction to this next song.

He says, "Whenever I can't explain it in words. I just try to take you back to the very first time you allowed me to kiss you."

He presses the switch button to bring up a new song. She smiles. It's not a new song to them or their love for each other. It's older than both their love and them. The 3rd song:

Voyage To Atlantis. The Isley Brothers.

He looks at her and smiles too. From this point, there's no more discussion needed. He pulls her into his arms. She holds him very tight. She knows it's about to be a storm. *The norm*. The sex play of her *entire* life. A man who wants to make sure she's left wondering can she ever top him when the topic is bodily pleasure.

He's grinding now and she's just holding on. His kisses are wild but she's loving it. She always has. She knows she always will because when it comes to sex for him. It's all about pleasing her. Always has been. Tonight she knows for his mission, it always will be. She holds on. He's working it out. His needs his aggressions, his love and his joy. All of those things are in 1 place. Inside of her.

"Ooooo this shit feels soooo good Ebony," he moans, "You don't have to change a damn thing. Do you hear me?"

"Yes!"

He's banging her now. He wants his pussy in the way, *he* wants it. *Innocent*. Waiting to be schooled and then cooled by him. How could she have forgotten *that* part. He's raising up on his knees and pulling her ass to him. He's aiming for the bottom. She's screaming because whether it's his pussy or hers. It's not big enough for this dick which is large enough to be split

between 2 men. As the Isley Brother's sing, *"I'll always come back to you."* She's at his mercy and in her mind and her heart, there's no other place for her. He's lightening his stroke because he knows she has some nectar that wants to spring. He's in coaching mode now.

"Come here, baby girl," he says, "Come on to daddy."
She arches her back and let's her sweet juices flow.

"Oooooooohhh dad-ddeeee!!! Oh God!! Mmmmmm!"

"Get that shit!" he demands, "Wet my sweet pussy! Wet it! Wet it! Come here!"
She's out there again. A place that's very familiar to her. It's ecstasy and it always looks *ever* so beautiful when she arrives. Ajay is kissing her down her body while still pumping his huge dick into her. He's visited her neck, her nipples, her shoulders and her ears too.

"Oooooooohhh Yeesssss!"
She's screaming in pleasure and that's turning Ajay on more than even dick sucking could. He's on the edge of spraying his juices.
He says, "Can I wet it, baby? Huh?"

"Ooooo Yes daddy! Wet me! Pleezzzzzzzzzzzeee!"
That's the *winning* game plan right now. Ajay throws his head back and lets it flow.

"Aaaaaaggghhhh! Fuck! Ooooo shhhhiiiittt! Ebony, bayybeee!"
They're squeezing each other so tight, not even air can get between them. He grinds to a slow pace as the Isley's song begins again. Ebony has her usual tears and no energy but she's fine. She's well satisfied as usual. She's holding onto Ajay. He's her man. *Hers only.* Her husband. Her first and *forever* love. She looks at him as they both breathe very hard. She smiles. He smiles back.
He whispers, "You're grown for real now, baby girl. I fucked you good and hard and you're still awake."
They crack up laughing and continue holding each other tight. They kiss and listen to the song which they shared their 1st dance on when she first allowed him to touch her. He wanted to teach her how to slow dance, that day in his room at mama Jo and big Al's house. It was also 1 of the 1st songs they danced to as husband and wife.

He pulls up from a tongue kiss and looks into her eyes. She's looking at him too.
He says, "I love you, baby girl. I love you so much. I'm a blessed man."

"I love you, daddy," she says and smiles, "And yes, you heard me correctly. I said *daddy*. You still have the upper hand after eighteen years.

And I'm cool with always losing our sex games. So long as you're winning them and fully satisfied with them."

"Oh I am *indeed*," he responds in his sexiest voice, that he knows she loves.

"I love it when you win," she whispers, "It's what I fell in love with. Keep winning. This is home for me."

With that, he pulls her back in close to him and they kiss hard again. Then they lay in each others arms and reminisce while listening to the #1 song of their nearly 2 decade long relationship.

Voyage To Atlantis by The Isley Brothers.

TIME TO SHOW-RELOADED-Time Will Reveal 6

CHAPTER 67

GIVING UNTO YOUR YOUNG

It's before sun up, Saturday morning. January 28, 2006 is a huge event day at CrewLand mall. They have crew birthdays to celebrate.

Tank turned 31 years old, 3 days ago. Bruce turned 28 on New Years Day. Bruce, Kim and the entire Cleveland Browns team have been looking forward to this official *CrewLand* party so they can do it up big. Jb, Tank and Ebony's baby brother Jesse turned 25 on the 7th of this month. Ron Banks Jr turned 18 and he's looking forward to being apart of the crew celebration. He has loved and been included since he was 2 years old. Back in 1990 when his father Ron and mother Carolyn became crew, down in Houston Texas. Valene Hamilton, his girlfriend from Atlanta by way of New York city is in town to celebrate with him.

The juvenile crew have birthdays as well. Rob Jr turned 6 on New Years Day. Lil Ajay's main interest, Kimora "Kimmie" McNair turned 6 on the 20th of January. This is her 1st CrewLand party. Lil Ajay wants to make sure she enjoys it *royally*. She's been smiling at him since he beat up Dillon for teasing her at school. Since that fight, Kimmie's parents sent Lil Ajay an open invitation to visit Chicago, anytime he wants to come.

Arthur's son, DeMarcus Tremaine Owens will be 11 years old on January 31st. He was the ring bearer in Tank and Nina's wedding back in 1996 when he was almost 14 months old. His mother was an Air Force officer who was stationed at *Wright-Patterson Air Force Base* in Dayton Ohio. Her and Arthur met when she was on leave with some of her female Air Force buddies. They came to Cleveland on their vacation with plans to go to *The Chill Spot*. They had heard about the spot from a guy in their squadron. The guy had met Lynn in basic training. She told him all about the mall her crew owns in Cleveland. DeMarcus' mother's name was Captain Janice Roberts. Her and Arthur met at The Chill Spot on her first night in town. That meeting turned into a week long encounter. She had gotten her divorce and was looking for a stress reliever. A man who wasn't trying to stay in her life. Arthur *"Money Shot"* Owens was *that* guy. Captain Janice headed back to Dayton, not knowing she would have to find Arthur again, sooner than later. She found out she was pregnant, 3 months later. Her divorce had been final for 7 months and she knew her ex-husband wasn't the father. And though she had no intentions of contacting Arthur, ever again. The pregnancy made it a must. She let Arthur know about the pregnancy and that she wanted their child to have his last name.

She also told Arthur she didn't want any child support from him. But she did want the child to know his father. Arthur was okay with his child knowing him. But as far as no child support, he wasn't okay with that part. On the last day of January in 1994, Janice gave birth to DeMarcus. Arthur went to Dayton to see his son born. It was on DeMarcus' day of birth that Janice told Arthur if anything were to happen to her. She wanted him to take custody. Arthur was certainly okay with that. Being the man that Arthur is, he still sent monthly support. He sent videos, pictures and gifts too. Captain Janice brought DeMarcus to visit after he turned a year old. That's how he got added to Nina and Tank's wedding. Arthur made sure Janice kept an up-to-date camera so she could send him current pictures and videos. That way he could keep up with his son's progress. Arthur sent pictures and video's of him and the crew, all along. DeMarcus wasn't living in Dayton. He'd lived with his maternal side of the family, in Oklahoma City because his mother was an Officer. And in the US Air Force, being a single female parent was frowned upon. However Janice was allowed to add him as her dependent. Arthur and Janice kept in touch. Michelle met Janice, once Michelle became apart of Arthur's daily life. Michelle and Janice got along just fine too. But December 2005 brought about a change for young DeMarcus Owens.

Captain Janice Roberts was killed in Afghanistan while serving on an elite mission. In her Last Will, she left everything to DeMarcus. With a request that his father have custody of him. DeMarcus was sad about losing his mother but he's excited to know he would live with his father. He always enjoyed the video's and pictures of his father and the crew. Now he has the chance to be here with them and be a member too. Thanks to his father, whom he's admired and respected since the start. He already has a crew title. Plus Chill and Ajay set him and Orian, June and Rebbie's daughter, to be a crew couple when the time comes. Orian will be 9 years old in May. So this crew will *not* end any decade soon.

There are no crew babies due this month but there will be some crew births throughout 2006. The first due date is May 26, 2006. Arthur and Michelle. This is Michelle's 1st child but Arthur has DeMarcus, who's already living with them. They're still living in Chill and Renee's old home, across the street from big John and big Al. Ebony and Ajay's childhood homes. But Arthur is having a home built in Jackson Heights, on Payne's Lane. It will be ready for occupancy by the end of March, 2006.

"I'm happy you're here, son," Arthur says to DeMarcus.

He adds, "I know our father/son relationship has been distant for most of

your life. But that's all changed now. Are you okay with living here?"

"Yes I am, dad," DeMarcus says, "I always asked mama to let me come and stay with you. She told me if anything happened to her. I would."

"Well you're at home for now," Arthur says and laughs. He adds, "But we have a new home that'll be ready before your little sibling is born."

"I know," DeMarcus says, "I like to go to Jackson Heights already. CrewLand park is awesome. Plus all the males my age, live out there. They already said I'm gonna be in the crew with them. We gonna ball like crew players."

He laughs and so does Arthur and Michelle.

Michelle says, "You have your daddy's sense of humor, son. I'm so glad you're here with us. You're gonna be a *great* big brother by the end of May. And we'll know whether it's a boy or a girl, next month."

"I hope it's a boy," DeMarcus says, "I want a brother first. Then I want a sister."

"Ah hold on, son," Arthur says, "Let's take our time. You're trying to turn me into Ajay *already*? He's got major money to go along with his big family."

DeMarcus laughs and says, "Him and misses Ebony got six kids. Y'all gotta work fast if y'all gonna catch up with them."

They laugh hard as Michelle gives him a hug. She's looking forward to new motherhood and being a mother to DeMarcus too.

She says, "I don't know if we can catch up with them, Marcus."

"Hell nah," Arthur says, "Because they ain't done. And if Ajay decides to retire soon. They're gonna add to that total."

DeMarcus says, "They got a mansion now. Too many more kids and they're gonna need a shoe to live in. Like that Lil old lady rhyme."

They laugh again as Michelle adds, "Trust me. With the money those two make. They can build a *real* big shoe if they want too."

They laugh it up as they continue taking photo's at The Spot II.

Michelle is in a *trust* spot with the crew, these days. She's paid her dues and she's in on getting rid of Angel and Alana, for good. Lil Ajay is working a foolproof plan at this moment. Michelle and Tameka will play a major role in the demise of Angelise *"Angel but lives like the devil"* Taylor. Alana, Darlene, Farah and Olivia can go as well. If the timing is right.

There are no Crew anniversaries in January. Brandon James and Charlotte Coleman will change that with love, before long. But they won't be the very *next* nuptials for the Cleveland Crew. The next crew wedding will be quadrupled on February 14, 2006. *Valentine's Day*. The 4 couples of

the biggest crew wedding too date, are as follows:
1. *Shannon "Reaper" Wilson* to *Brittany Neon James.*
2. *Kenneth Ramon Payne, Jr* to *Chaundra Ann Coleman.*
3. *Jessie Lee Brown* to *Ruthie Nakia Williams.*
4. *Samuel Logan, Jr* to *Pamela Darius Jackson.*

Crew Gear and *Crew Styles II* already have the dresses made. The tuxedo's are ready to go too. Between both stores, they do it all nowadays. No longer do they have to use a tux rental shop. *CrewLand Mall can handle it all. The Crew's House of Soul Food* along with *Stoney's Bar n Grill* will provide all of the foods from the 4-way bridal shower, bachelor party, rehearsal dinner and the huge reception too. Rich's brother Corey Grey stays onboard and attentive to crew business. He introduced 3 unique cuisine dishes since he's been with *Crew's House of Soul Food.* He earned shares in the restaurant for his adage to the menu. Corey, Bobby White and Tameka had planned to live in Chill and Renee's Shaker Heights home when Arthur and Michelle move to Jackson Heights in March. But that will change. Tameka isn't far from having her own share of Crew's House, as well. At present, she's the head server and does all scheduling for the entire servers staff.

Crew Cuts I and *Crew Styles II* will handle all hair styles and cuts. *Crew Smokes & Drinks* will handle the liquor. Rebbie has set the 4 brides bridal shower at the largest meeting room of *CrewLand Suites and Condo's.* The Bachelor party location is secret as usual. And as usual, the brides-to-be are trying to find out where it will be held. *The Chill Spot* and *The Chill Spot II* is where the after parties will be. But the huge reception will be held at Ajay's business spot, *The Allen Saul Williams Sports and Recreation Center and Complex.* Ajay will have a meeting with Darlene planned and executed, prior to this big wedding date.

Cheston *"Stoney"* Coleman's memorial was held at the December celebration. He was killed on December 26, 1990. *15 years ago.* There's a death to honor at the January event as well. Paul Payne Jr, big Chill's father, who was injured in a car accident caused by Old Jake Johnson's team, died January 31, 1988. Chill's mother, Willamena Wright-Payne was killed in a car accident in 1979, which was meant for her husband Paul. She died in that accident. Her death will be honored in March. March 17th will be 27 years since she was killed.

Ajay and Ebony's Estate, Jackson Heights

It's 5AM. Ebony is up feeding the triplets while Ajay still lays in

bed. He's waiting on her to come back and lay down. That's when they hear the side door charm buzz. It's Lil Ajay coming in from his male crew night. Ebony glances over at Ajay. He knows that look already.

Ebony says, "A six year old coming home at five o'clock in the morning is not going to be okay with me."

"I'll go talk to him right now," Ajay says and smiles.

With a sigh, Ebony says, "I know. You're just gonna tell him, he should just spend the night."

Ajay laughs as he heads to the 2nd floor library. He wants to let his son know that was a *"real crew move"* he'd made earlier.

Ajay knows his son's reasons for being out late. It was to gain Rioshauna's full trust. Ebony doesn't know it but Ajay and Lil Ajay have been in contact with each other since before midnight. They always text each other with updates. Or in Lil Ajay's case, just to check in with his pops. Lil Ajay had already sent the photo's of Draper Watts SUV to Ajay's phone. Ajay has them and he's about to get that Old Jake Johnson *demise* ball rolling *today*.

Lil Ajay is seated in his chair, in the library. Ajay walks in and gives Lil Ajay a hug and a pound, first thing.

"That was an awesome move, son," Ajay says, "You're a soldier. For real. And you are *definitely* my son."

Lil Ajay smiles and says, "Thanks pops. It just seemed like the thing to do. She said she had pictures. I told her I wanted to show them to my mama so I can get a truck like that. I told her, *she* was gonna be able to get a license before me. So she would have to drive me around in it."

Ajay cracks up laughing before saying, "And I'll get you a caddy truck and put your name on the plates too. Just let me know if she starts to fall back and you need some spice for your plan."

"I will do, pops," Lil Ajay says and laughs. Then he asks, "So what's the next move for the pics?"

"I'm emailing Arthur, right now," Ajay says while he's on his laptop which is assessable to crew men *only*.

He sends the photo's to Arthur and request that he get in touch with Jacobson for all location information.

His message to Arthur. *"It's time to reel Old Jake in."*

Arthur responds immediately. *"All good. Jacobson is here to secure the closing of the spots. If he's wit it. (which I'm sure he is.) We can run these before we head home. I'll get back before tonight's party set up time. See ya."*

Ajay's salutation. *"In a minute."*

After that's handled, Ajay and Lil Ajay talk about his night out and how the action went down.

"I kicked it with Rioshauna, most of the time," Lil Ajay says, "I want her to feel like she can trust me. I told her from now on, I don't want her hanging with the other three girls. Not if she's gonna get with me."

"And that way," Ajay says, "You can start the run on Jaylisa, Olivia and Shalom. Correct?"

"That's the plan," Lil Ajay says and they give each other another hug, another pound and this conversation is done.

June and Rebbie's Estate, Jackson Heights

It's been quite tense in this household. Long before the birth of their twin son's on October 6, 2005, changes were already visible. Their twin sons, Brian James III and Brent James will turn 4 months old in 9 days. That would be a big cause for celebration in a happy home. But Rebbie and June's relationship *and* marriage has been on the rocks for years. It just hasn't been discussed by them. Not yet. Only because talking is something Rebbie isn't interested in doing with her husband anymore.

It officially started back when Rebbie caught June at the *University [The U]* apartment of Diana Keyes. His situation with Diana had been off and on since his years at UC. Prior to her attendance at UC, Rebbie got wind that her man wasn't being truthful. It was 1 night during 1 of their many long distance phone conversations where June was obstructed by something or someone else, the entire time. Feeling as though something wasn't right with her, *then* boyfriend. Rebbie left in Ebony's car and headed directly down hwy 71 to Cincinnati. When she arrived, she didn't find June at their campus home. In an upset temper, she set out driving around Cincinnati. It was *then* that she saw June's vehicle parked and him jumping into a car with another woman. Rebbie followed them and ended up in the parking lot of a hotel. She watched as June and that woman went inside. After that, Rebbie sat in Ebony's car alone. She was upset and crying. She didn't know Diana. Not by name. Not then. But she would learn of her a *very* short time later. It was on that same night at that hotel, that she was rescued.

Jarvis Rhodes came out to try and find her. He found Ebony's car in the hotel parking lot. Rebbie was still inside of it and very upset. Jarvis stayed with her to calm her down. He listened to her grief and wiped her tears away for hours. It was on *that* night that Rebbie and Jarvis found

170

their connection. That connection never left. They shared their first kiss on that same night. But they didn't take it any farther. Not on that night nor during the entire 3 years while they were students together at UC. They didn't proceed until *years* later. It was after both Rebbie and Jarvis were already married to the same man and woman that they were dating *during* college. Brian *"Big June"* James and Gwendolyn Russell. It was long after college. It was after the upscale neighborhood of *Jackson Heights* was built. And after Jarvis and Gwen had been allowed to build a home there. They moved into Jackson Heights in 1998. Rebbie and Jarvis took their acquaintance to 1 of the physical nature in late 1999. They experienced oral sex at a luxury hotel in downtown Cleveland. That was during the seasonal holidays between Thanksgiving and Christmas of 1999.

With only 4 days left in January 2006, Jarvis and Rebbie still share kissing and groping during their alone time. But sexually, they still have only that 1 instance of sex. *Oral sex*. That evening, they served each other and thoroughly enjoyed it. They have plans of adding to it very soon. Only neither of them want to be still married to June and Gwen when it happens. Jarvis already did the paperwork to start *his* divorce. It hasn't been filed because he wants to make sure Gwen is aware of his plans before it's documented in court. He's not concerned about Gwen's feelings. This move is about their son, Jarvis Jr. Jarvis Sr's plans are to have his divorce papers on file by Monday January 30, 2006. He invited Gwen to tonight's crew celebration. He asked if he could use the 3rd floor boardroom and Chill granted him that. That's when Jarvis will tell Gwen, he wants a divorce.

The word of the divorce has already gotten to a few of the guys in the crew by 7am. Ajay, Chill, Jr and June know about it. Ajay was the 1st guy Jarvis told. Of course, that was after he told Rebbie. Jarvis shared it with Chill and Jr at the Cavaliers game win celebration, last night. He let them know that was the *real* reason he needed a private space for the conversation. Just after Jr learned of it. He was meeting with June, for last minute preparations for the CrewLand January party. Jr and June's meeting had to be away from Tank to keep some parts of it as a surprise. Jr told June what Jarvis' request was about. That's when June found out. But he knows nothing about Rebbie's involvement with Jarvis. June was always cool with Jarvis in college and because Ajay was and still is cool with Jarvis. June's feelings will most likely change, *this* year. Because Rebbie has plans of taking the same actions as Jarvis. She's just trying to wait until after February 14th and the Crew's big quadruple Valentines Day wedding is complete. *Time Will Reveal*

171

As for today, Rebbie is just bidding her time. She just has to be calm and nonchalant. She'll simply go through the motions just to get to the evening. Then it'll be club time and she's certainly going out. Her dance school is closed for today to prepare for the big crew party.

Her and June's 8 year-old daughter Orian is excited to have breakfast with her *entire* family at the table. It's been awhile. June had always blamed his reasons for being away so much, on his professional football career. That was used back when he was having rendezvous too. By 2002, Rebbie was no longer complaining about his mischief. By then, she was looking forward to a rendezvous of her own. As for today, she just wants to get through this morning without another disagreement, argument or sex before it's time to leave. June is hoping for some alone time with her. Since they didn't have sex when they made it home from their club. It seems he hasn't been able to figure out a way to bring up a good conversation. Rebbie is quiet too. Finally, 8 year-old Orian starts a conversation.

"Daddy I helped mommy cook breakfast," Orian says excitedly.

"You *did*?!" June asks in surprise. He adds, "It smells so good. I miss having meals with you, your mama and your brothers too."

"I do too, daddy and so does mommy," Orian tries, "That's why she wanted me to help her cook. So we could have a good talk. She's not crying anymore either."

Rebbie tries not to look shocked after that comment. She didn't expect her daughter to tell that part. But June sees this as an opportunity to get a conversation going with his wife.

"You were upset about something, baby?" June asks Rebbie.

"No. It was just my allergies," Rebbie lies.

She knows Jarvis has made the move to be with her, *publicly*. She wants to be with Jarvis too. That's what has her upset.

June continues, "Are the allergies okay now?"

"Yea. Somewhat," Rebbie answers.

"I'm glad to hear that," he says, "You know I don't want anybody in my family to be sick. Not you, Orian nor our twin boys."

"I'm okay," Rebbie says, "I'm use to them by now. I'll be okay. Once we finish breakfast. I'll be on my way to help set up for the January party."

She's inhaling her breakfast quickly. She wants the time at their breakfast table to end, sooner than later. She has no desire to be around June anymore. She even loathes the idea of her husband trying to be inclusive, all of a sudden. He hasn't been that way for nearly their *entire* relationship. He

has always put the guys crew plans and *thangs*, first and foremost. But now that it would be convenient for her, it's no surprise that he's finally decided to change. Now he wants to spend time with her but she doesn't have that desire anymore. And she hasn't really felt true love for June since Jarvis moved into their lives at a crew induction level. She's wanted Jarvis since their 1st encounter in the hotel parking lot. It's also been that same amount of time since she's had no desire for her husband. The only thing she's trying to figure out, is how she's going to tell June she no longer wants to be monogamous with him. In accordance with the females in this crew. There can only be *1 man* in their lives, at a time. Rebbie wants Jarvis to be that man. She's just got to figure out how to remove June. She wants to spare their 3 children's feelings though and that is her *only* concern.

Ajay and Ebony's Estate

Ajay and Lil Ajay are still in the upstairs library. Ajay sent a text to Chill and Tank while he was emailing the photo's to Arthur. 2 hours have passed. It's 7am when Arthur hits him back with info.
Arthur's email: *"Jacobson and I just finished closing up. Should we wait here with the keys?"*
Ajay's response: *"Absolutely. Is Chill and Tank still out there?"*
Arthur's reply: *"They're coming in the door now. They're looking for you."*
Ajay's reply: "Me and my son are on the way."
Ajay shuts down his laptop and tells Lil Ajay to wash up and prepare for a ride to CrewLand.
He adds, "I know I don't have to tell you but I'm going too anyway. Look in on Lannie and Lea. Bring them back down with you when you come to my room to give your mom a good morning greeting. See ya."
Lil Ajay smiles and says, "In a minute, pops."
He heads out to him and his sisters floor of the mansion. Ajay heads down stairs and back to his master suite.

CrewLand mall, The Chill Spot in Chill's office

Chill, Jacobson, Arthur, Tank, Jr and Ajay are all gathered. Lil Ajay and Jr's son Brad III are here too. It's 9am. Tonight is the big CrewLand party and all they have left to do is open the doors. This meeting is about the information on Draper Watts' Caddy SUV and Angel's demise.
"Thirteen Fifty Seven , Warren road," Chill says, "Lakewood."

"That's the address that Draper Watts' Cadillac SRX is registered to," Arthur adds.

"And that's Old Jake's *current* property," Jr says.

"One of them, yes," Ajay says, "But ain't this a new one?"

"The newest one," Jr says, "*His* address though. Not a teammate."

"For years, all of his teams property has been in his name," Tank says, "We got a lot of those addresses too. Which is good."

"But this new one *is* his," Ajay says, "Tell me I'm correct."

"You are correct," Chill says, "Because this one wasn't on our list *until* right now. And this isn't where Draper lives. Nor is it where Mallory Fields lives either. And she's Old Jake's granddaughter."

"So wait a minute," Lil Ajay says. "Rioshauna's daddy is using her great grandpa on her *mama's* side, address to register his vehicle?"

"That's right, son," Ajay says, "This info you brought to your crew is *huge*. This is Old Jake's quarters. This is where *he* lives."

"I agree," Tank says, "Because we already got the addresses for the rest of the team. The ones who would matter and who would hide him."

"So this guy Draper," Jacobson starts, "He's definitely on *team Jake*. He has to be *all* the way in, if he can use his home address."

"That's probably where he sleeps too," Jr says, "Because I've already learned of how ill he treats Mallory. And Jake's ass don't check him on *none* of that shit either. Why not?"

"He's a street dude," Brad III says, "I know he supplies powder."

"We was doing that in the eighties," Jr says and they all laugh.
Tank adds, "They're still two decades behind our crew's progress. I'm not even shocked."

"True," Arthur says, "But what is Draper's worth to Old Jake? Besides washing money and storage for his stash?"

"He's muscle," Chill says, "He packs heat and runs with a street gang. He's got gang members on his payroll."

"So he knows about the beef with us, by now," Jr says.

"And if he was in anyway about the business," Tank says, "Then he would *have* to be interested in knowing any connection he could have to our crew."

"Yea but he's a deadbeat dad," Ajay says, "He's not hands on with his daughter. According to her words to Ant. He's all about himself. So there's no way he'd find out through her."
Lil Ajay adds, "Plus Rio already knows not to tell nobody about me. Or it's a wrap. Draper don't spend no time with her and she can't stand him. Plus

he makes her mama cry. Either by hitting her or just treating her like shit. Rio is the one who gave me the pictures of his truck."

Ajay adds, "My son told her, he wanted the pictures so he could show them to his mama. And he was gonna get Ebony to buy him the same truck. So whenever this girl Rio get a license. She'd be able to drive him around in it."

Tank cracks up laughing. Before he says, "That's damn sho *yo* seed, Ajay!"

"Game like a boss," Jacobson says and laughs too.

"She's dumb too," Brad III says, "Mama Ebony got a *Escalade*. That's all the Caddy trucks she's *ever* had! He got a S-R-X. That's the baby of the caddy bunch. Rio is spawned out on Lil Ajay. She's gonna be extra dumb. To dumb to even think, *why would he be swooning over my daddy truck when his mama and daddy is rich?*"

They all crack up laughing again. Lil Ajay thinks it's hilarious and he has to comment.

He says, "But crew brother. If she ever brings that up to me. I'm just gonna say it ain't yo daddy's truck that turns me on. It's you."

They all laugh hard. Lil Ajay adds,

"Besides, just know that my mama is always gonna have the best of the best. Her and my sisters will always ride in style. Right, pops?"

"Damn straight," Ajay says and continues to laugh.

"Amen, nephew," Tank says and chuckles even more. Then he says, "But back to Draper. He's a pusher, a gang member and a deadbeat. I can definitely understand how he would fit in with Old Jake. But what is Draper's real worth to Old Jake? Getting to us?"

"That's the piece of this puzzle I've been researching," Chill says. "I thought that from day one, when his great-granddaughter came popping up at the spot two. But that's not the angle. Because Old Jake would've made Draper increase his visits with her, if that were so. And Lil Ajay would know that already because Rio would surely tell him. It's about the street money he makes and the guns and gang shit, he's apart of. That's what glues Old Jake. Jake sees him as muscle."

"Gotta be," Arthur says, "And since he's seen by Jake, as holding the reigns. He can fuck over his granddaughter, anyway he wants too."

"So long as Jake is getting paid," Ajay says, "He don't give a damn *how* a woman is being treated. His sister fell in love with the son of the most powerful white man in Ohio, Jeb Baker senior. Old Jake disowned her over pressure from racist assholes. That old piece of shit ain't changed a bit."

"Not in the least bit," Jr says.

"So when can we do him in?" Lil Ajay asks.

Brad III adds, "Hell yea. When can we take both of them to the chamber. It's time for *our* crew to get it in!"

Chill's crew smiles and gives dap to both Brad III and Lil Ajay. They know they're ready for the next phase and Chill's generation don't plan to make them wait, too long to get it done and over with.

Before they can wrap up the meeting, the main phone is ringing. Chill looks down at the caller ID. Then he looks directly at Ajay.

He says, "Right on cue, Ajay. It's the devil."

"Oh hell yea," Ajay says, "Hook her ass up."

Lil Ajay dawns a glowing smile. He knows that's Angelise Taylor calling. She's trying to make a connection to his pops. This day is *definitely* going his way.

Chill says, "Okay. I'm about to take the call. Who all will talk?"

"I know I want too," Lil Ajay says quickly.

"Me and my son," Ajay says as Chill answers the phone.

"The Chill Spot," Chill says.

Then he holds on while the jail house monitors speech is played. It takes another minute before Angel is put through.

"Hello." Chill says.

"Hi this is Angel. First I wanna say thank you so much for taking my call and allowing me to have your number on my call list," she says in 1 breath.

"You're welcome," Chill says, "How can I help you?"

"I would really like to know if I can call back tonight," Angel says, "And if you will ask Ajay if he'll talk to me, when I call. I know he's gonna be there. I watched the Indiana game last night and I heard him say he would be at the crew party celebration. I just need you to ask him if he'll talk to me. Will you do that?"

"You wanna speak to Ajay?" Chill asks.

It's taking all of his strength, not to laugh out loud.

"I *really* do," Angel says, "I wanna talk to Ajay more than anything else. I really wanna apologize to him and let him know how much I regret ever doing anything to hurt him."

"Well as it just so happens, Angel Taylor," Chill says, "Ajay isn't that far away from me. As a matter of fact. He's sitting right here. Would you like me to give him the phone?"

Angel says, "Oh please do. *Yes*. I hope he'll take it. Please ask him to take the phone."

Chill says, "Hold on."

He puts the phone on silent so he can get his laugh out. Ajay isn't laughing or smiling. He's all business, at the moment.

He says, "Tell her I said I'll talk to her with the speaker on. That's the only way. But y'all just know. She is only to hear me, Chill and Ant. Okay?"

Everybody agrees and Chill takes the phone off silent. He relays the message to Angel.

She says, "That's fine if you put it on speaker. I'll talk to him, anyway I can. No problem."

Chill flips to speakerphone and lays the receiver back down.

Ajay says, "It's on speaker now. What do you have to say to me?"

"I'm sorry, Ajay," Angel says as tears come immediately.

She continues, "I never wanted to hurt you. I promise I didn't. I love you, so much and I lost my mind. I will never hurt you or anyone you love again. I just wanna be able to make it up to you. Please tell me what it is I can do to fix this."

You can die, bitch!

Ajay's thoughts came straight from his truest feelings. But he's not going to say that out loud. Not just yet.

He says, "The best thing you can do is *prove* what you're saying. I would have to believe you. And after what you did. That's gonna be kinda hard. Surely you can feel where I'm coming from. Right?"

"I can understand that, Ajay," Angel says, "I really do. That's why I'm asking you. What is it that I can do to get your forgiveness? I'll do it. *Please.* Just let me know. The worst thing I did in my life was to hurt you and your family."

"The love of my life," Ajay says, "That's who you hurt, *physically.* The only woman I've ever loved and still love, even *stronger* today. That's gonna be very hard for me to live down."

Angel is still crying real tears. She wants Ajay's forgiveness. Something she will *never* have. But he's got to make her think there's a way to get it. He has to give her something to keep her ass in view, on his killing scope.

He says, "I'll tell you what, Angel Taylor. You actually took the little girl who would've been my first child. You took her before she was born. But my first born is sitting here with me. Maybe he has an idea. Because to be honest. I really don't."

"I would love to talk to him, Ajay," she says.

Lil Ajay clears his throat. He has waited all of his life, for this opportunity.

177

He wants to make the best of it. At the same time, he wants his father to see that he's more than ready to handle the responsibility of getting Angel to *The Chamber*.

Lil Ajay says, "Hello. My name is Anthony junior. Call me, Lil Ajay."

"Hi Lil Ajay," Angel says, "You are just as handsome as your dad."

"I know," Lil Ajay says dryly.

It takes strength from every guy in the office not to laugh out loud. Lil Ajay is very impressive already.

Angel asks, "Can you tell me something I can do to get forgiveness from your daddy?"

"Yes," he says.

Ajay holds his breath. He doesn't want his son to blow this encounter. But he has faith in him, so he doesn't intervene.

"What is it?" Angel asks, "All I need for you to do is to let me know what I have to do. Whatever it is in this *world* that I can do to show how sorry I am for hurting your dad and your mom too. I will do it. Tell me and I'll do it."

Lil Ajay looks at his father. He gives him the most confident look Ajay has ever seen on him. Ajay knows he's got this, so he sits back in his chair.

Angel repeats, "Just let me know what you want me to do."

"I want you to be my friend," Lil Ajay says, "That's where it's gonna have to start. If you can make me like you as a friend. Then you might be able to get my pops to forgive you. Because I'm *way* more angry than he is. Because of you, I don't have an older sister. Just like my pops, his pops and every male on my pops side. That was my oldest sister and because of you, I'm the oldest living child in my family. Which means I have a lot of responsibilities. So if you want my pops to *ever* believe that you can be forgiven by him. Then first, you will have to impress me. I wanna know do you think you can do that?"

"I will," Angel says, "I'll do it. You are *so* smart. You're six years old and you are *so* smart. Smarter than people, five times older than you."

"I have a question for you," Lil Ajay says. "You will need to answer it before we can keep talking. Here's the question. Are you ready for it?"

"Yes," Angel replies.

Lil Ajay asks, "Am I smarter than you? Tell me that."

Angel says, "I think you just might be. But I'm gonna work hard to impress you though. Just let me know what you want me to do next. I wanna make

sure you're okay with whatever I do, when it comes to trying to be friends with your daddy. I mean that, with all my heart."

Lil Ajay says, "The next time you call. I want you to call for *me* and not for my pops, from now on. I'm not gonna be okay with you doing anything else that can hurt my mama. So all of your calls have to be for me. My pops will make sure I'm able to talk to you. But don't call for my pops until I can call you *my* friend *first*. Are you wit that?"

"Sure, Lil Ajay," she says and smiles. "Just let me know when I should call again."

"Tomorrow evening," Lil Ajay says, "After my pops home game is over. We play the Phoenix Suns at one o'clock. So call at five o'clock. My pops will work that out with big Chill to have me here to talk to you. Now I need to know will you be able to do that?"

"I sure will," Angel says.

"Okay. You got one minute left," he says, "So it's time to go, for today. I'll talk to you tomorrow."

"Okay, Lil Ajay," Angels says, "I love you, little man."

"You'll have to work on that too," Lil Ajay says, "It's gonna take a long time before I'll ever be able to believe that. Work on it. Okay?"

"Okay," Angel says.

The line goes dead.

Ajay and all of the guys are quiet for another few seconds. The grown men are very impressed with how Lil Ajay handled that call with Angel Taylor. None of the grownups are more impressed than Brad III. He comes over to Lil Ajay instantly.

He says, "Give me a damn pound, crew. You are the man."

Him and Lil Ajay give each other a pound and a hug too, while Ajay and the men in the room just smile proudly.

Then Ajay says, "Chill I need to forward her calls to my home phone. We'll be flying outta here at nine, heading to North Carolina for that Bobcats game. I gotta get my loving in before I jet out. No way in hell am I gonna put my game plan loving on hold for *that* bitch! And it needs to be done and over by five."

"I got it," Chill says, "If her ass don't call by four thirty. I'll let her know the call will need to wait until Friday, the third. That's when you and the Cav's will be back for two home games. From the fourth through the sixth. We can roll from that. Let's get to the next task."

They move on to the next issue on the crew table. That's when Lil Ajay asks,

"While we're here. Can we go ahead and schedule the meeting with Darlene and my pops?"

Again with pride, Ajay asks, "How about we make that and the party for Olivia, on the same night? Alana has already asked junior if she can have it at CrewLand mall. I think it would be best to do both on the same night."

Tank chuckles and says, "So long as I don't have to be a direct part of *any* of it. Except for making money. It's cool with me because the party for a sixteen year old will have to be held at the spot two."

"True," Jacobson says, "This could be major advancement for both of the nemesis' too."

Arthur says, "Alana is a big part of getting all of the above, *again*. Tank you're the main asset to move that bitch. *Still*."

"I know and that's the shit I don't like," Tank says.

Chill says, "Alana is a definite link to Angel Taylor."

"Old Jake too," Jr says, "Through her daughter and through Angel. Because there's one more thing I wanna add to this mix. Old Jake has been putting money on Angel's book since she first went in."

"Yep and Draper Watts was added to her visitors list, once she was moved back here," Jacobson says.

"Because he's been fucking her," Brad III adds. He asks, "Y'all don't know about that yet? Kenny junior sent that to me on my crew email, 2 days ago. He said one of his high school classmates put him up on that. Kenny junior's classmate have folks that live out there by Angel's mama. He said Draper comes out there to visit, about twice a month."

Chill says, "I got that email too. I was gonna bring that up next. I'm so pleased that our next generations are keeping this shit in view. I'll share the idea of an all in one plan today. Once we get all the cards on the table."

Tank says, "It damn sho sounds like an all in one."

"And Tank you're a big part of what we need to glue them all together," Arthur says, "Michelle is the other half of that glue. She can get to Alana. Her and Tameka both. Michelle is wit it. Her plus Corey can get Tameka to play her part. Michelle and Cory are the best two people who can surely get Tameka to come onboard. Them *and* the senior generation."

"Because Alana wants to be friends with Michelle and Tameka again," Ajay says, "So she can get into the crew family, the way they are. Cousin Corey will get in on coaxing Tameka. I know he will."

"If Rich was still living," Chill says, "This would be his link. From the male side, that is. But his half brother Corey is a great second link."

"Him and Tameka are still buddies and roommates," Jr says.

Ajay says, "Corey will make it happen. He's crew, all the way. The first generation had him to go to the airport when the Europe crew arrived. That told me all I needed to know. Chill I know you agree with me about Corey being ready to move shit for this crew. Right?"

"I agree one hundred percent," Chill says, "Corey is true. All he ever wanted was family and acceptance of his lifestyle. This crew has grown a lot *because* of Corey. I can remember when I wasn't open to accepting the gay lifestyle. But that changed completely when Corey came into this family. He is the truth. He opened all of our eyes and hearts too. Because we now know that it doesn't matter what your sexual preferences are. All that matters is that he's true to us."

"And he most certainly is that," Jr adds, "He came into this circle seeking his brother. His brother wasn't in his right mind to show Corey the acceptance that he should have. But he was battling himself, truth be told. Not Corey."

Ajay says, "That's a fact. So Corey is crew. And as crew, he's gonna do what's needed to secure things for crew. He's got my confidence and vote."

"Same here," Chill says, "We're all in agreement. Corey will assist Michelle in bringing Tameka along."

Moving farther, Tanks says, "So we do the party at the spot two for Olivia. That'll bring Alana and Farah out. Darlene will come for the meeting with Ajay, if nothing else. What are we gonna do to get at the Old Jake side of this triangle?"

"Genia can assist with that part," Jacobson says, "They're always trying to get her to look at them as family. We'll need something separate for Old Jake's side of this. Something on the adult side of things. Something which will deal with the deaths of Matt and Kelly."

"And we'll have to go outside CrewLand properties for that," Ajay says, "Because ain't no way that old ass fart is coming to CrewLand. He'll know it's a setup."

Chill says, "That's true but we *can* move something out in Parma to attract Jake. That's the halfway point between CrewLand and Lakewood. And we've already flown in his long lost relatives from Europe."

"Misses Jessie Mae Johnson-Baker, Mister Jeb Baker junior and Mister Albert Johnson are already here," Tank says.

Ajay adds, "And Mama Rena is already assisting us with keeping their arrival low key. Until the time is right."

"We can hold the remembrance event for May thirtieth," Arthur says, "That'll be the one year anniversary of Matt and Kelly's deaths."

"That will be to *attract* Old Jake if he's still alive," Chill says.

Jr says, "And the next event could be in August. The thirteenth is Michelle and Money Shot's, one year wedding anniversary. Plus the baby will surely be born by then."

"And that will attract Angel," Chill says, "Because Michelle and Tameka are the glue that will get Angel's ass to show up there. Other than the Ajay's. We can make it work smoothly with Michelle and Tameka. Have them to get their reconnection with Alana together soon. Arthur will get Michelle rolling on that, as soon as possible."

Tank says, "So the first move is the twelfth of February. The second move will be May thirtieth. The third move will be August thirteenth."

"Correct," Chill says, "I think that's a great set up."

"Cosign," Jr says, "Chill and I will contact Alana and Darlene, *right now*. We'll let them know about the party approval and the meeting with Ajay on the party date. Alana will share this with Angel and Angel will tell Alana about her talk with Ajay and Lil Ajay, for damn sure."

Chill concludes, "Oh hell yea they will! This crew ball will roll smoothly from there."

The crew guys have unhitched the plan to rid themselves of a generational scab. Old Jake Johnson is the age of papa Brown's crew. But he is still yet to outgrow his 4 decade long beef with the Cleveland crew. Ridding their family of this 1 person has been a goal Chill set as a preteen. Chill, Jr and Stoney vowed to end this beef during their reign. But Stoney was murdered in 1990 on the day after Christmas, from a plot executed by Old Jake. Losing Stoney only made Chill's crew more vengeful about this 40 year old beef. To the 3rd generation of crew, Old Jake Johnson's death is the only thing that will assure them all that Stoney is resting in peace. That promise was made to Stoney before he was rushed to surgery, that early morning after Christmas. Bre made that promise to him while she was begging him to stay strong and fight to stay alive. Stoney didn't make it. But his crew's promise to him, all during his lifetime, most certainly will.

Chill says, "Stoney has been gone for fifteen years and thirty three days. It is our job to make sure he can rest in peace."

"And we damn well will," Arthur says, "I miss my brother. He brought me *in* this crew. From day one I felt like I owed him my life. I'm willing to give mine to get him that closure."

"Agreed!" The other men say.

"Agreed!" says Lil Ajay and Brad III.

Tank says, "In three days, it'll be eighteen years since big Paul died. I know

we'll be honoring him tomorrow night. Chill, bro....I miss your pops. I know you do too. I did a lot of my growing up at big Paul's house."

"Cosign," Ajay says as Jr and Arthur agrees.

Chill says, "We will surely honor him. I miss him too. I'm gonna get Old Jake's ass out of this game before my pops will be resting twenty years though. That motherfucker is the reason my pops is gone. I must get that over with."

"Agreed," They all say.

Then Brad III raises his hand and stands up. He has something else he wants to add to the Stoney and big Paul's, peaceful rest comment.

He says, "I'm looking forward to it. My pops was nineteen years old when big Stoney got killed and my mama was pregnant with me. I'm fourteen years old now. I gave my word to my pops that I would do what I have to do to make *sure* big Stoney gets peace before I reach nineteen. That's the age my pops was when big Stoney was taken away. I'm the head of the four and a half generation of this powerful crew and I'm ready. I'm willing and I'm able to do whatever's needed to bring peace to my first cousin CJ. She was in auntie Breanna's stomach when her daddy was taken away from us. She never even got to meet her pops. I'm bringing peace to her *and* to my girl Destiny too. Because I know her pops, big Chill here, was one of the two who they wanted to hit *first*. Big Ajay was the other one. That's because of what their fathers and grandfathers did and stood for. I'm just gonna get this on outta the way right now. I'll make the *fuckin* news if I have too, to protect my family. *My crew*. My word is bond."

"That's *my* son," Jr says proudly.

Jr gives Brad III a pound and a tight embrace. That's the way the crew guys show each other love and respect. 1 by 1, each man does the same to Brad III and Lil Ajay too.

Then Chill adds, "I'm proud as fuck of your crew *already*, Brad three!"

They all chuckle.

Tank adds, "This crew will never cease. Just know that shit!"

"Amen," Ajay says as he looks at Lil Ajay. Then he says, "Son you already got this ball rolling. Let's head home."

With that, the meeting is adjourned. Chill sets a 2nd meeting for tomorrow, after the Cavaliers home game. They'll go over the demise of old Jake, Angel and whomever else needs to go. The men know without a doubt, all of their sons are ready to handle business and personal. The crew are ready and very well aware that the best way to bring on a *New World Order* is by *Giving Unto Your Young*. The crew is 4 generations deep and are still as

strong as they were from the start. Ready to take on any problems their families are faced with and get them solved or eliminated. That's crew style 101!
Roll on Crew!

Parma

It's been 1 hour since the crew meeting ended. Angel gets to use the phone again. She has to call Alana and tell her about her call to Ajay and Lil Ajay, an hour ago. She tried to call 20 minutes earlier but the call wasn't answered. That's because Alana and Darlene was on a call with Jr and Chill, getting their verification of Olivia's party at The Spot Two. And Darlene's private meeting with Ajay and maybe even Lil Ajay during that same event day. But Angel has to talk to Alana. She's trying the call again and this time, it's answered.

"Hello," Darlene says.
She turns to Alana and says, "Oh this is for, *just* you. The jail house speech is playing. It's the murderous bitch convict of the century. This is definitely for you."
Alana smiles and takes the phone.
"Hello," Alana says.
Angel yells, "What's up?!"
"Damn! You sound excited as *hell*," Alana says, "And yes *indeed*, I am too! And I gotta tell you why."
"I am excited as hell," Angel says very excitedly. She adds, "That's why I had to call you, Alana. This is a damn good day, home girl. I called you so I could tell *you* why!"
Alana cuts in and says, "Let me go first, Angel. Because *trust* me. Mine is the *business* of the day. Listen to this. I got a call from big Chill and Junior today. That's why we couldn't answer your call when you was trying to call me, earlier. Guess where my baby girl Libby will be having her sixteenth birthday party?"
"Where?" Angel asks. Then she guesses the ultimate. She says, "The Chill Spot!"
"Close," Alana says while laughing. She adds, "The Spot two. She's not old enough to have it at the adult club yet. But you know I told you about the under age club that the crew opened in ninety seven. Right?"
"Yes and I've heard so much about it from Jaylisa," Angel says. "I know her, Libby and their age group *lives* in there!"

184

"Hell yeah they do," Alana says, "But the crew is the bomb shit, girl. It made my day when they called me and told me that."

Then Darlene yells from the background.

She says, "They made my damn day too! Make sure you add that part, niece! Let that inmate know about the meeting that's set up for me *during* my grand niece's party! And that meeting is with the *sexiest* man in the world! The man *that* convict on the phone wishes she could have!"

Angel can hear Darlene being braggadocios. She isn't fond of Darlene at all. Or vice versa. The reasons for both of their hate of each other is obvious. Both of them are still longing to be the affection of Anthony Devante "*Ajay*" Jackson, Sr. Darlene is laying it on thick though. Angel hasn't even gotten to her good news yet because Darlene has to get hers in and make sure Angel hears it.

Then Angel asks Alana,

"What kinda meeting is that old ass hag bitch having?"

Alana giggles but she checks Angel quickly, saying, "Don't hate on my Tee Tee, homie."

Darlene hears Alana's response and comes straight to the phone. She puts her hand out for the phone but Alana is slow to hand it over. So Darlene switches it to speakerphone and dares Alana to undo it.

Then Darlene says, "If you got something to say to me, bitch. Say it now while this phone is on speaker so I can hear you."

Angel responds with, "No problem, bitch. What I asked was. What kinda meeting is that old ass hag bitch having? Can you hear me now bitch?!"

Alana cringes slightly and looks at Darlene. Alana knows her aunt isn't going to back down. Darlene comes right back at Angel.

She says, "Well murderous jailhouse bitch. I have a meeting with Ajay on the same night of Libby's party. Ajay requested the meeting and he said to make sure I can be there. Because he *really* needs to see me in a damn good way. A *damn* good way. Do yo worthless ass hear me *now*, convict?"

Angel's response is, "I just got off the phone with Ajay *and* Lil Ajay and they want me to call them back tomorrow. *And* they are both on my visitors list too. Do you get any visits? Hell no! And yo old ass is in the *free* world."

Darlene is taken back with that comment. She loathes this news about Ajay and his son speaking to Angel on the phone. But yet, it was Chill and Jr who called her with the news of *her* meeting. Ajay didn't even do it *himself*. But she has to respond to Angel and put her back in second place.

Darlene says, "My meeting is in *person*. No prison guards and monitoring. It is a *private* meeting."

She can't end there. She has to add a lie or 2, just to cure her own anger, hurt and temporary disappointment at knowing Angel will have contact with Ajay as well. Darlene spews more.

"We *will* be meeting three nights per week, up until *that* meeting. And the same afterwards," she lies. She continues, saying, "Now how many personal visits do *you* have on schedule, convict?"

Darlene is laughing now because she can tell Angel is stuck. Angel hasn't given a response yet. But she's about to do just that.

With an even bigger lie, Angel responds with, "They're both coming to visit me, in two days, old bitch. So you see? He wants to see me *so bad* that he's coming to the jailhouse to see me. *Before* he sees you. And he's bringing his son to meet me too. For your info, old hag. Today, his son made me promise that I would be his friend. Not only Ajay's friend but *Lil* Ajay's friend too! So tell me, senior citizen. Why do you have to wait until a celebration for your family to meet up with Ajay for the first time?! And in a public place! Oh and will your meeting be like mine? Ajay *and* his junior? Hell no! So you ain't got the upper hand, trick. You old hag bitch!"

Darlene has to add more to her future meeting with Ajay. She can't be outdone by convict ass, *Devil* Taylor. Darlene goes further into her own lie.

She says, "This is our third meeting, convict. I wasn't even suppose to share this information with *no* one. But I done let you push me to it, with all of your dumb ass talk. So I'm so sorry to ruin your day. *Not*! There you go, convict. And don't worry. I'll tell Ajay tonight at the January celebration. We'll see each other tonight too. Will you be there?"

Darlene giggles and continues, "Hell no you won't be there. You've got time to do. But you can find you another, you murderous bitch. Because Ajay has someone to fill his down time. Every since you got locked up, dummy. Oh yes and you do know he became a new father on Christmas Eve and Christmas day. And I'm the pussy he came back too, while his misses was on a maternity hiatus. So tell me. When is the last time you had that sweet dick, convict?"

Darlene is on a role as she adds, "Oh wait. You've been getting pussy fucked for the last decade *plus*. Shut the fuck up and keep my name out of your killer ass mouth!"

Angel is quiet. Alana is just stunned as she stands there quietly too. She knows her aunt Darlene made up a lot of that spill. But at this point, Alana is wondering if Angel's admission about her phone call with Ajay and Lil Ajay is the truth as well. The only thing Alana knows is true, is what she told Angel about her phone call, Olivia's party and Darlene's February

12th meeting. Before Alana can cut Darlene and Angel's bum rush off, the line goes dead. Angel's 15 minutes is over. Alana looks at Darlene and shakes her head. She starts to look doubtful.

She says, "Auntie you went off on Angel. Where did you get all of that stuff you was telling her?"

Darlene continues the lie, she started with Angel. She doesn't trust her niece with knowing she made it all up. She decides to add more to that lie.

"When I was on the phone with junior and Chill for my part of the call," Darlene says, "That's what they told me to do if I had contact from Angel. Make up shit to make sure she understands that Ajay isn't interested in her, in a sexual way. He would be interested in me, before her. Because she killed his child and almost killed his woman. So I was just telling her what I was told to say to her. But in my own way, of course. And hell yeah, I enjoyed the hell out of it too."

With that said, Darlene heads back to her bedroom to pick out what she will be wearing to the crew party tonight. She has a huge smile on her face. She knows she's got the upper hand on both Angel and Alana, at this point. That's good enough for now.

Farah is just waking up. She'd gotten wasted at The Crew Spot last night. She heard the very end of Darlene and Alana's conversation. She has to be brought up on what transpired while she was recovering.

"Alana, what all did I miss?" Farah asks.

Alana says, "Come on in the kitchen and get some coffee, buddy. I've gotta fill you in on the phone conversations of the morning."

They head into the kitchen to talk.

T-baby and Wes' Estate, Jackson Heights

T-baby was slow to rise today. With a baby due in June, a few weeks after Michelle, she's dealing with daily morning sickness as well. But she's up now and done in the bathroom, just as her cell phone starts to ring. It's Rebbie calling her.

"Good morning, foursome sister," T-baby says very jubilantly. "Are you still at home?"

Rebbie whispers, "Yes I am and I'm looking for a way out. Are you finally awake? I've been calling you since _I_ was at breakfast, three hours ago."

"I was laid out, Ree," T-baby says as she giggles. She adds, "This morning sickness is _way_ worse than it was with Lil Richie Rich. It's after ten now, though and my stomach is _finally_ settled. What's up with you?"

Rebbie continues, whispering, "I need an excuse to get up outta here."
She adds, "I need you to *need* me for something. *Anything!*"
T-baby giggles more. Then she asks, "Are you meeting Jarvis?"

"I wish," Rebbie says, "But not *this* morning. I just wanna get out of *this* house. Mama and mama Brenda are headed this way to pick Orian and the twins. Brian thinks we're gonna have the whole day to ourselves, before it's time to head to the celebration. I don't want a day alone with him, T-baby. So tell me you need me."
Rebbie giggles. T-baby can't help but laugh at that remark. But before she can respond to Rebbie, Wes walks back into the room. He sees that she's awake. He gives her a kiss.
Then he says, "Good morning, baby. I'm glad to see you're up and dressed for the day."

"Hey baby," T-baby says, "Yes. I'm up and feeling like half the day is already gone. Did you, Richie and Jada have breakfast yet?"

"Of course we did," Wes says and smiles. He adds, "And we all cooked it together. We made enough for you, baby. We left your plate in the microwave. Would you like me to bring it to you?"

"Thanks baby. But I'm about to head to the kitchen," she says, "But thank you, so much. What would I do without you."

"Get stalked by me," he says and they both laugh, then kiss again.
As they head to the kitchen, Wes says, "Lil Rich and Jada are out there in the park with their crew. And *more* than ready to get to their crew party. That's all they talked about during breakfast."

"I know they are," T-baby says and laughs. She adds, "And so are we. Right?"
Wes says, "Yes indeed, baby." He laughs and starts to sing *Snoop Dogg*.
"It ain't nuttin but a crew thing. Baby."
T-baby giggles and says, "I've got Rebbie on the phone. She's about to head over here. You know us *awesome foursome* ladies *gotta* get together on our crew party swag and gear."
Wes laughs again and says, "I *do* know that. I can't wait to see how sexy you're gonna be. I wonder if I'll be able to stay at the event for longer than a couple of hours."

"Now you already know we're *definitely* gonna get it in, baby," T-baby says with a seductive smile.

"Thank you, Lord," he says peeking at the ceiling. He adds, "While y'all do that. I'll get the adult males together, so we can start getting these kids to *The Spot Two*. I've gotta pop in on Chill, at his office too.

He's gotta bring me up on the new crew plans. Then my big sis Renee wants to see me too. So as you can already see. This is gonna be a *very* long day. And it's looking like it's gonna be an even *longer* night."

"*Crew weekend* is in affect," T-baby says and giggles. She adds, "And the best part about The Spot Two events. Is us *mothers* don't have to dress the younger kids before they go."

"That's an even *huger* help for us fathers when *we're* in charge of them too," Wes says and laughs. "Their celebration will be all day. They're gonna be dressed by Crew Gear before their evening party begins. So they can go as they are."

"Absolutely," T-baby says, "You drive careful, baby. I'm gonna get back to Rebbie and this call. I love you."

"I love you too," Wes says and they kiss again. He reminds her, saying, "Call me if you need me for *anything*."

"Let me repeat this part," T-baby says while smiling. "I'm getting some of that before the celebrations starts. Just reiterating my *needs*."

"I'm all in, baby," Wes says quickly.

They kiss again and he heads out to the garage. T-baby gets back to her call with Rebbie.

She says, "Well come on over, Rebbie. We got the house to ourselves. I know big Arch and big Brian are getting your kids, *any* second. Come on now. Before you start feeling trapped and end up saying something you'll regret later."

"I'm already heading across the street," Rebbie says and laughs. "While you and Wes was talking. I was telling my husband I had to go check on you because you're having a bad morning and Wes has to leave. Timed it just right too. Because Wes is pulling over to the park to scoop up the kids. I'm headed to your kitchen door."

They giggle and hang up.

Rebbie walks into T-baby's kitchen and breathes a sigh of relief. Then they both crack up laughing again.

Immediately T-baby says, "Crew sis. You've gotta find a medium. In all of our lives, I've never known you to be this volatile, foursome sis. You are not unpredictable to me, Nina and Ebony. We know what's up. But I *do* know June is on edge. He's been talking to *all* of the men about your distance. Something has got to be settled and soon."

"It will be, T-baby," Rebbie says calmly. "I'm gonna leave him. My mind is made up."

"Oh wow," T-baby says, "You've made up your mind, huh?"

Rebbie says, "I have. All these years I've cried and prayed and begged him to be honest and faithful. But that last time was the last straw. I never got over it and I have to be real with myself. I'm filing for divorce, sis. I'm gonna wait until after the big Valentines Day wedding. And Jarvis is filing his *Monday*. He's already had his papers drawn up. Plus he has a meeting scheduled with Gwen during tonight's celebration. T-baby, we wanna be able to go *all* the way with each other. And you know there's no way in hell I'm gonna be owing to *two* men. I want Jarvis and he wants me. You're the first person I'm telling this too, besides Jarvis and my mama."

"What did mama Rena say?"

"Before the twins came, she told me to be absolutely sure before I did anything," Rebbie says, "But y'all know what it's been like for me, with Brian. I have to keep it real. The *only* reason it lasted this long, is because I got pregnant with the twins. That's when me and Jarvis backed off of each other. Well,... *he* did. But I never wanted too. I wanted my foursome sisters to *think* I was with him, all the way. Like I said. I wanted to be and I still want to be. But Jarvis is going to respect the crew rules, so I respected *his* wishes. I told him that you, Ebony and Nina know that part already. But did y'all know Jarvis got his own condo during that time?"

T-baby says, "I had no idea until we talked in Renee's office."

Rebbie says, "Before he bought it. He told me he wasn't gonna stay with Gwen. She's gonna find *that* out tonight. And Brian has less than a month before I tell him."

"Rebbie I hear you and I really hate it, so much," T-baby says. "But sister. I've been there. I know exactly how you're feeling. It took two men in my life, for me to find the man *for* life. Richard and I wouldn't have made it and he knew that. That's why he tried to take me to the grave with him, when he took his own life. I miss him, for Lil Rich's sake. But Wes is wonderful. Lil Rich loves him like a father, so we are both blessed. All I can say is, you have to do what your heart tells you. You've got my support. I know Nina, Ebony and all of the crew females will support you. I feel like the men will too. They know how we were raised and they know how rough it's been for you, with June. I got you, Rebbie."

Rebbie smiles and hugs T-baby.

She says, "Thank you so much, awesome foursome sister. I haven't figured out how I'm gonna tell Brian yet. But I'll have it ironed out in a few days. And then, like I said earlier. Brian will know before February ends."

Suddenly T-baby says, "Rebbie we've *got* to get Nina and Ebony in on this conversation."

Rebbie says, "Let me call Nina. You call Ebony and let's see if can we meet up while the kids are gone. *Wait*. Are the triplets gonna be leaving Ebony at home for the first time, today?"

"I think so," T-baby says and giggles. She adds, "That is, if Ebony don't change her mind. All the granny's are suppose to get their grandkids today. Let's call her and Nina and see what's up."

They get Nina and Ebony on the phone. Within minutes, Rebbie, T-baby, Jerica and Nina are headed to Ebony's Estate. They all need to have a foursome talk. It's going down today. It's something they haven't had a chance to do in *quite* awhile. When all 4 of them get together to talk through any problems or changes, they're dealing with. They're going to have some Awesome Foursome time on this day. Just the 4 of them. Like it was, back in their premarital days.

Parma

"Wow," Farah says, "Things are turning up for everybody, ha?"

Alana says, "Yes it is, girlfriend. And it's about damn time."

Alana has just finished bringing Farah up on their upcoming connections with the crew which had just come into play today.

"Do you believe Ajay *really* talked to Angel?" Farah asks.

"Yes I do," Alana says. She adds, "She wouldn't make that up, Farah. She's knows I would go straight to CrewLand mall and ask around, if I thought it was a lie. And she knows if she lies about something like that. It would piss Ajay off. That's the last thing she wants to do, at this point."

Farah says, "For real. But I can't believe he talked to her. Plus he had *fine ass* Chill to call you guys and set up a meeting for him *with Darlene*. Libby is having her sixteenth birthday party at crew property too. I love it."

"It's on and popping, Philly sister!" Alana yells and giggles.

Farah says, "So what do I get out of this deal? And you too?"

"You know who I want. That shit ain't changed," Alana says.

"Same with me," Farah says, "Maybe it's gonna come together for us too. Feels like it's been forever since I could even get close to Chill. I'm gonna do my part. *Whatever* it is. And y'all better include me, *friend*."

Alana says, "I needs to be fitted in too. Darlene has a meeting with the dick she wants. So we best play it smooth with her. Then maybe she'll work to get us to Chill and Tank. But we damn sho can't show no love to Angel. Not in front of Darlene because she'll leave our asses hanging."

"I'll do whatever it takes," Farah promises.

CHAPTER 68

THE PAST REVISITED

Rebbie, T-baby, Nina and Jerica are at Ebony's house when Jo and Pearl arrive to pick up all 5 of Ebony and Ajay's daughter's plus Jerica too. *The Awesome Foursome* will have sit down and chat time as soon as their kids are gone with their grandmothers.

Pearl says, "Let's get our six granddaughter's loaded up, Jo. So we can get on up outta here before Ebony tries to change the plans."

Jo laughs as she agrees and says, "Amen. Y'all come on, Nina. You, T-baby, Rebbie and Ebony. Help us get these six princesses in my extra large van so we can be on our way."

"Cool," Nina says and giggles.

Pearl adds, "We have these extra large *and* lavish vans now, Jo. We're balling hard, crew sister."

"Oh you are *so* correct, Pearl," Jo says and laughs. She adds, "Our sons and husbands got us living like the queens we are. You *heard* me?"

All the ladies are laughing hard as they load the 6 girls into Jo's van. Ebony has to say something behind Jo and Pearl's comments though.

"Our mom's are sounding like they're headed to the hip-hop Chill Spot," she says. "Maybe my Tre' needs to stay home. Lannie and Lea can stay home too. Our daughters are not allowed at the club."

"Mama *please*," Lannie says, "We wanna go. Tell her, Lea."

"I wan go with my nana's," Lea says. "Please mommy."

Pearl says, "Oh y'all *are* going, sweethearts. Your daddy has already said me and your nana Jo can bring y'all to the spot two with *us*. And he said your mama cannot go and she cannot stop y'all from going."

Then Pearl turns to Ebony and says, "Are you gonna go against what your dear husband asked us to do?"

"I plead the fifth," Ebony says while smiling shyly.

They all laugh. Even Lannie, Lea and Jerica laugh too. The girls are loaded up now. Then Jo and Pearl hop in. Jo starts up the van and soon, they're on their way out of Jackson Heights.

Ebony, Nina, T-baby and Rebbie head back into Ebony and Ajay's home. They go straight to the parlor/breakfast nook combo area and get comfortable. Nina, T-baby and Rebbie have to make sure Ebony is going to be okay. Now that her girls are gone.

"Ebony are you gonna make it?" Nina asks with a smile.

Ebony says, "I don't know yet. This is only the second time my Tre has been

away from me. Other than when I went I went to Utah, so me and Anthony could end that sex hiatus. The question is, are *they* gonna make it."

"They'll make it," T-baby says quickly. She adds, "They've got *both of* their granny's. Plus all of the other grandmother's and great-grandmother's are at our *CrewLand* mall waiting for them to arrive."

"They'll go from one set of arms to the next," Rebbie says.

"For the first *three* hours, at least," Nina adds and they all laugh. She adds, "But Ebony is gonna be just fine. She's been here before. The hardest time to let your baby go away from you for the first time. Is when it's the first baby or babies. We've all gone though that first time motherhood release stage. But after that. It's not as hard. Right Ebony?"

"I'll get back to you on that," Ebony says and they all laugh again. Then Ebony says, "But we do have some pressing things to get too, sisters. And now that we have our alone time. Let's do this. *Rebbie*. Crew sister, we're gonna lay it all on the table today."

"Amen," Nina says, "We've gotta know how to hold you down, girl. In *advance*."

"Ahead of time. In advance. However you call it," T-baby says, "That's what we were just talking about when she came by the house."

Nina says, "What we've got to do is get this story down pact. *Together*. Because we don't want another incident like that night at the chill spot, when June showed up going off like a deranged man."

"He blew up for *real*," T-baby says and laughs. Then she adds, "*Big* time."

Rebbie says, "I had to leave Jarvis' spot and haul ass to my own spot. Then pretend I'd been there *stressing* the whole time."

"I remember that," Ebony says, "I got the whole recall of it by phone. But we have to get this whole situation to a better place, Rebbie. Are you gonna remove June from your life as a husband?"

"I am," Rebbie answers, "I've been unhappy for a long time and y'all know that already."

Ebony says, "So while we're all together. I want you to tell us. What is it about Jarvis that fits?"

Rebbie says, "First and foremost. He *listens* to me. Something Brian senior has never really done. And he still don't. Not unless I shut down on him. But me and Jarvis spend hours together, just talking. About everything and anything. I can discuss my dreams with him and he listens and encourages me to go for it. *Whatever* it is that I wanna do. Brian has never done that for me. With Brian, it's always been about what's convenient for him."

"So he's still not supportive of your dreams?" Nina asks.

T-baby cuts in and says, "Nina, you mean to ask. Is he still not supportive of her *true* dreams. Right?"

"Well, yea," Nina says, "Are things for you, still the *same* way?"

Rebbie says, "*Yes*. Crew sisters, all 3 of you know it's still the same. Brian wants me to be a housewife. *Only*. He wants me to stay stuck in the house. So I'll be lost to what's going on out here in the world. And in the past, y'all know I tried that. Then I would always find out he was fucking off with some bitch. Time and time again. But after I caught him at The U, at Diana Keyes apartment. I never got over that. Not when it comes to trusting him, I didn't. Trust has always been a key thing with all of us. And for me, trust is the first thing I'd have to have to be sexually aroused."

Nina and Ebony have a very sincere look on their faces. They know in order for Rebbie to get in the mood for sex. She has to feel secure. T-baby and Rebbie have already had this discussion too.

"Tell them the rest of it, Rebbie," T-baby says, "All of it."

Rebbie clears her throat, sighs and then starts again.

She says, "I'm not attracted to Brian in anyway. *Anymore*."

"Sexually *either*?" Nina asks.

"No I am not," Rebbie says, "No way. If I could have sex with a man I don't trust. I would fuck anybody. And y'all know that ain't about to happen. I don't trust Brian, after all of the times I've caught him in lies. Even back when T-baby caught Rich fucking off. Brian knew the whole thing because he was out there with him. Damn *near* this whole time that we've been husband and wife. What worth does that say he has for me? None! That's the main reason I know I have to move on. I haven't been hot for Brian, in *years*. The times we've had sex, I faked my way through it. I *cannot* live the rest of my days like this. My mind won't even let me be turned on to him. No playing games and pretending that I am. That's why I know we can't make it, as husband and wife. Because sex is very important to me."

"That's huge," Ebony says sadly. She adds, "Anthony already knows that. I love my husband because he keeps me informed on the guys talk and the male side of thing in this crew. Anthony and Jarvis talk all the time, as we all know. Anthony saw this coming, a *long* time ago. I have to say. Rebbie, I do understand that part where you said you cannot live the rest of your days not sexually satisfied. I am *totally* addicted to Anthony and the world knows that. If I was to lose my memory. I do believe Anthony could fuck me *right* back into knowing who the hell I am."

They all giggle hard at that comment. Nina, T-baby and Rebbie have to agree with Ebony, on that point.

"If you come down with Alzheimer's or dementia," Nina adds, "Ajay will have you locked up in this damn house for seven days and nights, *straight*. Around the clock. After that week on lockdown. You'll come up outta here with a teenage mind."

They crack up laughing as Nina continues.

She says, "You'll be remembering every damn thing that's happened since you was two years old."

They share a huge laugh. Ebony agrees with Nina. Then T-baby adds to it.

She says, "That's the truth! Hell yea! But y'all, come on *now*. Ebony *is* right. We *all* have to admit that part too. Sex is and has *always* been a very important part of *all* of our lives, from day one. Thanks to Renee, Tonya, Bre and Jan, we knew how to demand what we wanted from our man. And because of our mothers, grandmothers and aunts. We knew how we had to be treated and how we had to carry ourselves in order to get the respect we was raised to demand."

"And we all did that," Nina says.

"Amen," Ebony adds.

"Exactly," Rebbie says, "Sex is *very* important and so is honesty. Being *faithful* to your spouse, that's *everything*. Sex can't be good if you don't believe you're the only woman your husband is having sex with."

"True that!" Nina yells and they all agree.

Ebony says, "Sex is like mega money in this household. I don't even have to prove that to anybody in our crew. Do I?"

"No you don't and true that too!" Nina yells.

Then she screams, "I remember when you gave Ajay some sex coupons, Ebony!"

They howl with laughter as Rebbie adds, "You *sure* did! You gave Ajay fifty two coupons. One for every week of the year!"

"You did do that, cousin!" T-baby adds, "As if *y'all* asses needed *any* sex promises!"

"Word," Rebbie says. While still laughing, she adds, "Now you gave Ajay those coupons on y'all one year anniversary. New Year's Eve was eight years, you and Ajay have been married. I just wanna know. Did y'all use those coupons and do you still give him coupons?"

Ebony is laughing very hard when she answers with,

"Hell yes we used those coupons and they didn't last the *whole* year. The meaning of those coupons was for him to get sex, *more* than once per day.

Now I do believe all three of y'all know this. Me and my husband have sex *more* than once per day. And we just brought triplets into this world, thirty six and thirty five days ago. *Shit.* We *still* got days to make up for after my Christmas post-partum."

T-baby laughs and says, "Ah hell yea! We know that already. I wanna know how long did it take for him to redeem those fifty two coupons? Just tell me that."

"One month!" Nina says while laughing. She adds, "It's *true.* Gone and admit it Ebony. Ajay told Jeremy about it. He got those coupons on their one year anniversary. They went into affect on January first, nineteen ninety nine. By the week before Easter, all fifty two of them damn coupons was spent! And the thing is. Ajay was still playing and living in Miami during that time!"

"And we all know Lil Ajay and Lannie came by July of that year," Rebbie says as they all continue to laugh.

Cracking up laughing, T-baby says, "And Lil Ajay and Lannie came *early!*"

"That was because they was tired of getting their heads beat up by their father's fourteen!" Nina screams.

Still laughing, Ebony cuts in and says, "Correction! It use to be fourteen and a half! It is all the way fifteen now!"

By now they're laid all out all over the parlor furniture. They're laughing uncontrollably. It takes them another 5 minutes to get all this laughter out. But Ebony isn't done.

She adds, "I have to admit it *and* tell it like it was and *still* is. Those first anniversary gifts was a little bit of everything. But we used those coupons in *record* time. That's the truth and I ain't complaining. Know that! Do y'all remember that *Tupac* picture? That's in our home office. And that wall picture of Anthony? It *still* hangs on my side of our bedroom."

Nina says, "And wait a minute. Didn't he give you ten grand in cash on y'all one year anniversary too?"

"Ah, *yes*," Ebony says while smiling and batting her eyes. She adds, "And I've never spent a dime of it. So it's now worth eighty two grand."

Nina gives Ebony a high five and says, "Oh hell yes! That's ten grand for each member of y'all household. With some left for the next."

"Or one thousand each for these spoiled ass Pekinese, Ike and Tina," T-baby says as she rubs Tina's back. Then she adds, "Y'all gonna have to add another ten thousand for that son that the whole crew *knows* y'all are planning to make, in due time."

"For real," Ebony says, "I do wanna break that Jackson mold of

the one son per family trend. Because I will never forget, *that* bitch ass Angel fucked us outta the *'first child is a girl'* side of the Jackson tradition. So me and Anthony have got to break new ground."

Rebbie says, "Oh yes and her demon ass is back in Cleveland too. Still in jail but back in Cleveland. And let me just add this. Cleveland is where her ass is gonna die at too. Our crew will *have* to help get our hands on her."

"Amen," Nina says. Then turning to Ebony, she says, "Ebony I know you got some news to share on that bitch. Don't you?"

Ebony says, "Yes I do. Ant is already reeling her in. Our son is very smart. Y'all know that part. But he is Anthony on steroids, mind wise."

"Oh he's got game *fasho*," Nina says, "That's all Jeremy could tell me about their meeting. *And* that he *might* have to reel Alana's ass in again too."

"Yes Nina," Rebbie says, "Tank will take one for the crew."

T-baby says, "I feel like the guys are gonna give Angel's ass to us though. Do y'all feel that?"

Ebony cuts in and says, "Certainly. That's one bitch I could kill in fifty different ways. It's because of her that I know what hate *really* means. I've had the experience of taking a life. Y'all know about mister wrong ass, Raymond White. I was fearful when I was in his company, that day at the chamber. Still when Ajay and Chill made me go back to that night when he was trying to rape me. I found my nerves. But I had experienced taking life before that night. That's something y'all don't know about."

"*What*?" Nina asks, "You've done it again since Raymond?"

"Tell us, Ebony," T-baby says.

Rebbie adds, "Right now. I wanna know. I see a look in your eyes, sister. It's like fire too. Who was it and when did it go down?"

Ebony says, "I killed someone before Raymond."

"You did?!!" All 3 of them scream.

"Yes," Ebony says, "And just so y'all know. This cannot leave this room. There was four other witnesses to it and only two of them are still alive. One of them died when the car he was in with four other crew fathers, got shot up and he went to intensive care."

"That was Chill's daddy, big Paul," Rebbie says.

T-baby adds, "That was right after Christmas of eighty seven and he died on the last day of January in eighty eight. That was a sad time."

"It was," Ebony says, "It really was. But big Paul was a witness to the other person that I killed. Nina, so was your pops."

"Oh wow!" is all Nina can say.

197

Ebony continues, "Yes he was. Chill was the third person. Neal Palmer was the maggot I killed."

"I thought Chill killed him," Nina says, "I thought him and big Paul was fighting and Chill got the gun and shot him."

"That's the story the father's came up with, after it went done," Ebony says, "But that's not what happened. Not at all."

"Will you tell us what happened?" Rebbie asks.

Ebony says, "Sure but y'all can't tell anybody. Even if they already know. You are *not* to tell what I'm about to tell you. Y'all know the crew rules. An elder can bring up news or your husband. Then and only then, can it be discussed."

"Truth," T-baby says, "That's how our crew business stays in the family. I'm cool with that."

"So am I," Nina says and Rebbie agrees with her and T-baby.

Then Ebony says, "Y'all remember the Palmer's that use to live on the other side of us. He was at big Paul's house when I went to get Chill to play basketball. He fondled me."

"What!!!" they scream angrily.

Ebony says, "Yes but let me finish telling you. Chill was in the shower. Big Al and big Paul was gone to get liquor for the card party they was getting ready to host. I went inside looking for Chill. That's when Neal, who was in their kitchen, called me in there. Long story short. He started touching me. I got upset, of course. When he heard Chill exiting the upstairs bathroom, he stopped and tried to tell me to keep it as our secret. I was crying when I ran upstairs and found Chill. Right away, Chill knew I wasn't comfortable. Neal followed me up those stairs and kept trying to tell me to keep it a secret, before Chill opened his bedroom door for me. But Chill took me into his room, closed the door and calmed me down. That's when I told him what Neal had just done. Chill headed down those stairs and confronted him. They started to fight. That part was true. But Chill was fighting him. Not big Paul. Chill was fighting him because he had molested me. But Neal started to get the best of Chill. Big Paul and big Al wasn't back from the store yet. I was so scared that Neal would beat Chill to sleep. And then, he was gonna be toughing me again. I remembered where big Paul kept his guns at. So I went a got one of them. I was gonna give it to Chill but Neal had Chill on the floor, on his back and he just kept punching him. Like Chill was a grown man. When Neal looked up and saw me standing there. It scared me even worse because I saw a look in his eyes that told me. He wasn't no good. And that he would hurt me again, if he got the chance too.

He punched Chill again and I saw blood spurt out of Chill's nose. That's when I shot Neal. I thought he was gonna kill Chill. I had to get Neal off of him. But when I shot Neal, he fell over and off of Chill. But he didn't die. He was screaming in pain though. That's when Chill got back on top of him and started beating him with everything he had. By that time, big Paul and big Al was coming in from the store. They had heard the shot from the driveway and they saw me standing there with the gun. They saw Chill still beating Neal and both of them was all bloody. At first, I think they thought I had shot Neal because him and Chill was fighting. But once they got Chill off of Neal, Chill told them why he was fighting him. That's when big Paul and big Al finished his ass off. They beat him to sleep and then chocked him to death. After that, that's when they came up with the story about saying that Chill did it. Chill agreed to it, for two reasons. One was because neither of those fathers wanted it known that I had been abused in that way. And two, because Chill would go to Juvenile Detention and not Jail. And it would let anybody else who was thinking about fucking with Chill. Know to think twice. Chill wanted to go to juvenile hall because he said he wanted to protect my virtue. They all did. And an the day that was happening to me. Anthony was having his first sexual intercourse with Marsha Robinson. Do y'all remember her?"

"Yes," Rebbie says.

"Miss Lou's niece," Nina adds. "She liked Ajay for a long time."

"But he never liked her," T-baby says, "I remember that whore. Richard fucked her, later on down the line."

"So did Brian," Rebbie says.

"Jeremy did too," Nina says, "All the guys in our crew had her. Except for Chill and Stoney. But I didn't even know Ajay had fucked her."

"He did," Ebony says, "He was the first one from our crew, who had her. Like many of those ho's, we all know. But she wanted to be his girl and he wasn't going for that. The reason I mentioned that, was to make this point and help y'all to understand why Anthony is so faithful to me now."

"Tell us, cousin," T-baby pleads.

Ebony continues, "He got his first pussy on the same day I was being molested. And then, he was with that devil ass Angel on that night when Raymond tried to rape me. Anthony told me that was the only sign from God that he needed, to know that he was suppose to be next to me, at every possible moment. Protecting me from any harm and protecting the pussy that was born to be, *all* his."

"Ah, I love that," Nina says as she tears up. She adds, "I hope

that don't sound wrong. But y'all, my brother spoke from his heart when he told Ebony that. Because he put all of those ho's to the side when he knew Ebony was all his and our parents was all for it too."

"I agree with Nina," Rebbie says.

"Me too," T-baby adds, "Ajay was teaching Richard, June and Tank, the whole time. He always tried to make them get on the same page he was on. Tank got it. Richard never did and it seems like June got it but too late."

Ebony says, "I suppose so. But the craziest part about all of it was. I had forgotten all about that whole thing with Neal. I had blocked it from my memory or something. I just know that whenever Anthony and me got to the sexual part and he would try to put his fingers inside of me. I would push him away. *Every time.* I didn't know why finger fucking gave me the creeps. But in nineteen ninety seven before we even got to our wedding date. He got me to remember that whole incident with Neal. It was because of the affect it had on me, every time he tried to put his finger in me. Anthony knew something was wrong. I had blocked that whole thing out. But because of Anthony's love for me and him always wanting me to be comfortable with him. And to always know I was safe with him. He brought that memory back to me. He helped me to remember it. I remembered it after I shot and killed mister wrong. But I still hadn't told Anthony about it. Rebbie, I revealed that part about Neal to Anthony on the same night that Orian was born."

Tearfully Rebbie says, "Oh Ebony. Sister I am so sorry to know that shit happened to you. Twice in your life, an asshole tried to touch you when you didn't wanna be touched. I remember when you and Ajay went to spend the night at the Fillmore Hotel downtown. I thought you might've been sad because we all had babies and you didn't have one yet. And only because bitch ass devil had made you lose yours."

"Oh my God," Nina says with tears still rolling down her face too. She says, "I had no idea. I know my daddy has always been very protective of you. Just like you was our *real* sister and *his* daughter. We always use to say you was extra spoiled. More than any of us. But Lynn would always say it was because daddy knew he wanted you to be Ajay's girl. Which is true too. But Ebony, sis I didn't know."

"Me either," T-baby adds and she's crying hard tears too.

She adds, "Cousin you've been through a lot of shit. And you started going through yours before we was even in double digits, age wise. And Ajay knows it all. Don't he?"

"Yes he does," Ebony says, "After I shot Raymond, the Neal part started coming back to me that same night when I was at the motel with Anthony. In room *one eleven*, like always. But it wasn't until the night Orian was born, that it *all* came back. I told Anthony that same night. Then he got on the phone with big Al and Chill. And Nina, your daddy knew I had finally remembered what Neal did to me and that I had told Anthony. Him and Chill told Anthony that night, that they still wasn't going to speak a word of it. And all they wanted him to do was to continue with his plan of making sure I was his and his only. And protected in every way. I've been fine every since that disclosure to Anthony. Finger fucking and all. We gets it all in now, baby."

She has to laugh. She wants her girls to stop crying and relax. She let's them know that she's over all of the sadness in her life.

"Anthony seen to it," she says, "Now I need for y'all to cheer up. I'm *fine*. I promise. Hell I was like six year's old when that happened. I'm thirty years old now and loved more than life, by my one and only. Plus six precious children too. Now let's get some more girl talk in. I just wanted y'all to know that y'all wasn't and aren't the only one's who went through tough times. Or in Rebbie's case. Still going through tough times."

"I *really* wanna kill Angel's ass *now*," Nina says.

"Fuck yea," T-baby says, "My cousin had been through enough bullshit. *Way* before her *dumbass* got sprung on some dick she would never own."

"And like Nina said," Rebbie says, "I do feel like she will be our team shot. Hell it's time for us to do away with a bitch *together*. We've done damn near everything else. *Together!*"

Nina adds, "I done said I'm wit it. I'm gonna keep hinting it to Jeremy."

"I'll do the same with Wes," T-baby says.

"Here we go again," Rebbie says, "I do believe I'll be telling Jarvis, when that time comes because he's already making his move. But before we finish with the Jarvis and me, talk. I do have one more thing to reveal and it's about a meeting tonight. Jarvis is meeting with Gwen in Chill's office, during the Crew celebration. He's gonna let her know that he wants a divorce and that he's filing it on Monday."

"He ain't wasting no damn time, is he?" Nina asks with a smile.

"No he's not," T-baby says and laughs.

"Okay and when are you gonna file yours?" Ebony asks.

"February seventeenth," Rebbie says, "Three days after the biggest wedding in the history of our crew. I'm gonna let Brian know, right after

the wedding is done. Unless he pulls it out of me, sooner than that. But I plan to tell him after the quadruple wedding. Then he can have those few days to speak his mind. But he isn't gonna change mine. I want Jarvis Rhodes in my life, *all* the way."

"Y'all still haven't actually fucked, have you?" Nina asks.

"No," Rebbie says, "No penetration. No. Just that oral sex and it was *damn* good too."

"I hope for your sake, that his dick is good," T-baby says, "Because if it was me. I would *have* to have a sample before I signed my damn name." They chuckle but Nina agrees with T-baby. So does Ebony. *Somewhat.*

Ebony says, "Anthony decided and dictated exactly how my samples were going to come. He got it right, *all* the way. Because he let me make the choices. And still he only moved when he was sure I was ready to take that step. I have no complaints. I thank God for my life with the man that I've loved since he was a boy and I was a girl. I've always prayed that all of us would last. Bre, Greg junior and T-baby lost loves through death. In Greg junior's case. He lost his first love the same way his crew brother is about to lose his. Greg Junior lost Erica to Eric because he was always unfaithful. But Bre and T-baby lost their first loves to *death*. Stoney and Rich are gone and it's still hard for me to accept that part too."

"Me too," T-baby says, "But y'all know I was getting ready to divorce Richard before he took his life and tried to take mine, along with his. That's still so sad to me."

Ebony says, "I know it is. But now you've got a man who loves you to the core. Wes is awesome. Rebbie I want you to be happy. So you do what you need to do to be happy. I'll support you. We all will. T-baby's first love and marriage ended the way crew marriages usually end. *Death*. Which is the only way a crew marriage has ever *ended*. Rebbie you'll be the first crew member to actually get a divorce. As I said before. I truly understand it and I will always support you and be here for you. But as crew goes. I just hope that's not a sign of what's to come for anybody else in our family. Unless it is absolutely necessary. Do y'all agree with me?"

"Agreed," the other 3 say.

"Now it's time for some lighter conversation," Nina says, "Some fun shit. What are we gonna wear to the crew celebration? Because my man is thirty one years old and this is *his surprise* party too. So y'all know I'm gonna be *hella* sexy tonight!"

"And naked before midnight," T-baby says and they all laugh.

T-baby laughs louder and adds, "And I plan be naked *way* before then.

Me and Wes is getting it in, like we're Ebony and Ajay! Even if we have to go up in one of those Chill Spot offices. I'm pregnant, as y'all know. And it makes me so damn horny!"

They all continue to laugh as they kick back and continue to talk the way they've always done it, for their entire lives. All in and together. *Crew style*!

The Chill Spot, early afternoon in Renee's Office

Wes has finished his meeting with Chill and Jr. He heads to his big sister Renee's office to meet with her by 1pm.

"What it do, big sis?" he asks as he gives her a hug.

Renee smiles and says, "It's doing pretty good, little brother. How are you and yours?"

"We're doing *and* feeling great," he says. Then he adds, "Except for when we first wake up."

They both laugh and Renee adds, "Well its your fault. Just know that. Us women have to deal with the sickness *before* the beautiful babies get here. But we'll gladly trade that part with you men. How's that?"

"No thanks," Wes says quickly as they continue laughing.

After taking her seat behind her desk, Renee gets on to the reason for this meeting, she'd requested.

She asks, "Guess who's back in the picture. Besides those you just learned about in Kenny's office?"

"I know it better not be Paula," Wes says of his ex-wife.

Renee giggles and says, "No, you *nut*. She'd be in ICU if she showed up here, after the way she mistreated my only *true* sibling. I've got a score to settle with her ass."

Wes says, "Big sis, you would beat her ass *so* bad, she wouldn't even remember her own damn name. Much less mine. *Hey*! On second thought. Maybe we can pencil that in."

They laugh again before Wes asks, "So who's in view, sis?"

"Keno," Renee says, "The Japanese wife from the mansion in Mentor-by-the-lake."

Wes says, "When *my baby* was in ICU and Rich was dead? *That* Keno?"

"Yes."

"What the fuck does she want?" Wes asks dryly.

Renee says, "She was asking why didn't we published the letter that Rich left with her. She showed me the agreement, her and her husband had signed with Rich. It's a contract that all three of them signed, agreeing to

203

publish his life and true feelings. In the case that anything ever happened to him or his memory."

"Wait," Wes says, "That *depression* note? Sis, you've gotta be kidding me."

"I wish I was, little brother," Renee says, "But I'm serious. Rich did a Last Will type of thing and left it with them. According to Keno, he did it with *them* because he knew we would never honor him or his wishes, when it came to him being heard. She faxed it to me. Here it is. You can look at it if you wanna see it. I called you in to see me because I don't want this out. Not before T-baby knows about it. Because Keno and her folks are planning on going forward with it."

"Rich wants to make his family look bad?" Wes asks, while his face holds a puzzled look.

Renee answers, "Rich has always wanted more light than Ajay. While at the same time, he never had the correct mentality to treat any crew woman, T-baby to be more precise, like she deserved to be treated."

"Amen to that, big sis," Wes says, "But I'm thinking of what we should do, first and foremost. Before they go public. I think we need to bring Ajay and Ebony in on this. And my wife, as well."

"So we can beat Keno to the punch," Renee adds, "Yes. Because they are gonna publish this crap."

"Is it possible for us to buy them fools out?" Wes asks.

"Oh we'll certainly try that first," Renee says, "But I wanna make sure T-baby knows everything about this letter before it goes public. She was in ICU, damn near dead, when we first learned of this. It's time to tell her. Because she'd already mentioned some of the things in this letter, to me. It's time to let her know she was correct. And at the same time, it gives more pride to her and all of us, *her crew*, that she was very wise when she made the decision that she made. Back when she decided she was gonna leave him. She knew he always put other *things* before her."

"She's number one to me," Wes says, "I wish you would've let me date her, *way* back when I first saw her, big sis. If I had gotten her, back then. We wouldn't be dealing with this bullshit right now."

"I know that's right," Renee says, "But crew rules are crew rules. You're crew now, so you know the rules as well as I do. It keeps things in order and I can certainly vouch for that. That's why the crew before us, always stressed that we go after what we're good at and master it. Rich was very talented, musically. But he never focused on that part. Then he was damn good at football too. He mastered that part but because of his

insecurities when it came to Ajay. He turned to crack cocaine. As if that was going to help him prevail. But he had a go-getter for a girlfriend. T-baby has always been a go-getter. Nobody can tell you that better than Ebony. I thank God that T-baby has always been as intelligent as they come. And it wouldn't surprise me one bit, if she already knew that Rich wanted Ebony before he wanted her. That's a conversation she and I have already had too. Before Rich committed suicide and certainly before this letter. Which *I* feel he left behind to hurt his crew after he was gone. But little brother, you know T-baby is *not* slow. Not at all."

"We've had a similar discussion, many times," Wes says, "Before we got married and a few times *since* we've been man and wife. We have this in common, as you know. So I agree. It's time to make my woman aware of this depression note that Rich left as his final statements."

"Let's set it up for early next week," Renee says, "That way we can decide what offers we'll make to Keno. I don't want it public and neither does Kenny. But I do want T-baby to know that he had made plans to have Keno and her man publicize it, in the event that *we* didn't. Which means Ebony was correct when she said Rich had planned to take his life and T-baby's life, months before that shit happened. We're nipping this in the bud, *this* week."

"Let's include Claudia too," Wes says, "She was there when all of this came into view."

Renee says, "Okay. We can do that and invite mama Anna and Rich senior too. Along with you, T-baby, Chill, Ajay, Ebony and myself. We're gonna knock this out the park. *By any means necessary.*"

"Or have something to show it correctly *before* they release the shit," Wes says. Then he adds, "LaTrisha is the woman for me and I'm the man for LaTrisha. We was meant to be together. We always were and this proves it, more than anything."

"I agree." Renee says, "Rich-the-third doesn't even mention Rich, anymore. So I know you're doing a great job as his daddy. I'm so proud of you."

"I get it from you, sis," he says, "You became a mother at fourteen years old and look at you now. A college graduate and big business owner. LaTrisha will have a masters degree in May, before our baby comes. And she said she *will* march across that stage at Cleveland State. She might be taking her classes online. But she's gonna march in plain view. She's going back to the league in oh seven, for another season or two. So I don't want a *damn* thing to shadow her accomplishments. Nor bring her to the point of

feeling depressed. She's the best part of me. I'll be damned if I'll allow her to be hurt, in *anyway*."

"That's why I'm so proud of you," Renee says again. "You were correct when you said, you and T-baby are one in the same. Paula put you through similar situations as Rich did to T-baby. Paula has gone on with her life and signed over her paternity to T-baby. So it's time to let Rich rest in peace, for the last time. I know T-baby will wanna do this to protect Rich-the-third."

"And that's my reason for wanting to get it over with too," Wes says, "Rich-the-third has his mother's mentality. Thank *God*. He doesn't have any of Rich's ways. So I don't want him to be hurt nor slighted, in the least bit."

"I just wish Rich would've thought about his son and his daughter too," Renee says, "Before he requested something like this."
Wes adds, "Rich-the-third and Richaunda are very tight. They spend so much time together, as sisters and brothers are suppose to do."

"And your niece, my baby girl Destiny and her crew girls, are already trying to find a match up for Richaunda," Renee says and smiles.

"Indeed," Wes says, "They wanted to match her up with Jr and Tonya's baby boy, Donovan. But they're blood. He turns five this year and Richaunda will turn six. We'll work something out. But as far as this letter goes. We'll get it over with. *Know that*. I've gotta get to the house. I owe my woman some loving before the celebration tonight. And I'm gonna make sure she knows about this meeting before we head back this way. Okay?"

"That works for me," Renee says.
She stands and comes around her desk to give her brother another hug.
She says, "I am so glad to have you here. I can't say that enough. It feels whole, for me."

"Same here, big sis," Wes says. "See ya."
"In a minute."

Crew Cuts and Styles I

It's 4pm. Tonya and Justine are hard at work, getting the young crew ready for their 5pm event at *The Chill Spot II*. They've got all the girls nearly done when the spot officer Deloris Miles comes walking in the door.

"Hey ladies," Deloris says, "How's everybody doing today?"
Justine says, "We're crew fine, Deloris and how are you?"

"I'm doing just fine and so happy and blessed to be here," she says

with a giggle. "I'm looking forward to working these big crowds tonight."

"Good," Tonya says, "Because you know how crew do it. Always the place to be."

Deloris says, "You're right about that. This place is always packed. All the businesses, for that matter. *CrewLand* is so thorough. I brag about this place to everybody who are not in the area. Or anybody who haven't heard about it. And even when somebody ask me about it. I brag."

She giggles more. Tonya smiles but she doesn't comment. She can already see where this conversation is headed. She doesn't even get in an offer of a guess. Because Deloris' upcoming request, verifies where Tonya has already figured this conversation was heading.

Deloris says, "Some of my family are in town. They came up for tomorrow's Cavaliers game. They have been bugging me to death to ask you all if they can come to the celebration tonight. I told them I would ask as soon as I got to work. So that's why I'm here."

"I'm guessing Katrina Dobbs is one of those family members who wanna come on the property?" Tonya asks in a telling tone.

"She is," Deloris says, "She has promised me she will be on her best behavior. She's got her three sisters here with her. Along with eight others. Two nephews, two nieces and four of my cousins too."

"Well Deloris," Tonya says, "CrewLand mall *is* a public place. All paying customers *are* allowed on the property. Unless they're banned. Is Katrina still banned?"

"Not anymore," Deloris says, "Her ban ended on *Martin Luther King holiday.*"

"Less than two weeks ago?" Justine asks.

"Yes," Deloris says.

"She sure did keep up with that ending date, didn't she?" Justine asks in the same telling tone Tonya had used.

"Yes she did," Deloris says, "She loves the club and CrewLand mall, *period*. I do know that much. Each time she's been in town. She's always wanted to come but she was still banned."

Tonya asks, "Does she remember *what* got her banned?"

"And that ass whooping before that ban came?" Justine asks.

Deloris says, "Oh she definitely remembers what got her ass banned from here and so do I. She's been apologizing to me since all that mess happened. I believe she's learned her lesson. I made sure that she knows, it will be up to my bosses if she can *ever* set foot on crew property again. I wanted to check with you all first. She wasn't just going to just show up here.

I would never allow anything like that to happen. Not since I learned of what she'd done."

Tonya tells her to hang on while she makes a call to Renee. Deloris has a seat while she waits. Tonya picks up the salon's phone and calls Renee.

While Tonya is on the phone, Gwen Russell-Rhodes and Nickeia Russell walks into the shop. Justine has to let off a humorous comment.

She says, "This salon must be an information desk *and* a permission booth. Because my crew brain and bones are making me feel like there's a second request *on deck*!"

Tonya giggles while she's on the phone with Renee. Renee hears Justine and laughs too.

Renee says, "Tell Justine she's on it like a detective, over there. I'm gonna send her and Kilo a gift basket full of sex toys and Moet!"

Tonya relays the message to Justine. Justine and all who hear it, laugh hard. That's when Justine has to let Tonya and Renee in on some very good news.

She says, "Tonya I have to tell you and Renee something. But I can't share it in public. Not until the big announcement is made tonight. So can we slip into the office, Tonya? This will only take a minute."

Tonya says, "Destiny, Jerica and Jada. Y'all keep an eye on the front. We'll be right back in *one* minute. Come on Justine and talk fast."

They laugh as they head to the back.

Tonya and Renee think it's about the females who have just come into the salon. But Justine has some news to share about her, Kilo, Greg Jr and Kilo's sister, Patricia.

As soon as they're in the back office, Tonya puts the phone on speaker.

Renee asks, "Justine, what's up?"

"Y'all know KeJuan asked me to marry him, on New Year's, right?" Justine asks.

"Yes we know," Tonya says, "And?"

Justine says, "We set a date."

"Oh hell yea!" Renee yells, "When is the wedding?"

"We decided on January twentieth, two thousand seven. Less than a year from now," Justine says, "And we already plan to have young crew couple, CJ and KeJuan junior as the young bride and groom. But me and KeJuan don't plan to be the only couple getting *married* at that alter."

"Who's sharing those nuptials?" Tonya asks as she giggles.

"We want to share it with Greg junior and my sis in law, Patricia," Justine says, "That's the only reason we're giving it another year. The two

of them are so suited for each other y'all. And I know this is the love that Greg needs. And Patricia is like a school girl when he's around. A *horny* school girl!"

They laugh hard before Tonya and Renee congratulates Justine.

Renee says, "I am *so* with that, Justine. I knew you and Kilo was gonna make it. You can thank me and Kenny for that hook up. We saw that shit from the door."

They all giggle again.

Then Tonya says, "We gotta get the girls up outta here and over to the spot two. But we'll get together and have these plans ready, *way* ahead of time."

"And we will all be coaxing Patricia and Greg junior to get their wedding shoes fitted too," Renee says, "It's damn near time for me and Tonya to pass these female leader reigns on over to the next generation. And before that happens. I want *all* of my damn generation married and babied up. *Hint, hint,* Justine!"

They all laugh before Renee adds, "And tell Deloris I said, if there is *any* bullshit out of Katrina tonight. She's *fired.* I know Gwen is getting dumped tonight. So tell her she can bring Nickeia. She'll need some shoulders to cry on. Or someone else's ass for us to beat if Jarvis tells her he's leaving her for Rebbie and she jumps stupid. See y'all later, crew sisters!"

"In a minute!" Tonya and Justine yell back before the call ends.

Tonya and Justine laugh harder as they head back into the shop to disburse Renee's message.

Tonya lets Deloris know that Katrina can come as long as she's on her best behavior. She gives Gwen the same advice before Gwen even ask her if Nickeia can attend too.

Then Tonya says, "Now Justine. Let's get these pretty haired girls across the way."

With that said, Destiny, Jada and Jerica lead all of the young girls across the landing to The Spot II.

T-baby and Wes' Estate, 5pm

Wes and T-baby have just finished a *very* heated session of sex. Now they're holding each other and still breathing heavily.

Out of breath, T-baby whispers, "That was so good. As *always.*"

"Cosign," Wes whispers with even shorter breath. He adds, "You are *definitely* the best I've ever had, LaTrisha baby. I *still* wish we could've started out together. I've wanted you since the first time I laid eyes on you."

209

T-baby smiles and says, "I know and you always tell me that. I knew you wanted me, way back then."

"You remember Ajay's thirteenth birthday party," Wes says.

"When you told me, you would give up anything to be able to kiss me," she says and smiles.

He gives her a kiss. Then he says, "*Exactly*. If I could've done that, *then*. We'd be on year number ten or more, by now."

"We're over halfway through our first year as husband and wife," she says, "And I feel like I've known you *all* of my life. I'm *so* in love with you, Wesley. I am *finally* happy. With no fears and no doubts. Now I understand what me and Ebony's granny Pearline meant when she use to say, '*First impressions are the truest impressions. If you don't like them. Don't pretend you do nor attempt to change or fix them. Just be you and choose to please you. Anyone that is honest will do the same.*' And that's exactly what you was doing at Ajay's thirteenth birthday party. You was being all the way real, then and honest too. I knew you really liked me and I liked you too. You spoke your mind to me on *that* night. And baby, I was feeling you *big time*. But I was going by what we always called, *The Crew Code*. I've lived long enough to learn that the crew code is about honesty, first and foremost. It's about being whom you are, to the best of your ability. Not being someone who passes the test of somebody you *think* you're suppose to match up with *automatically*. Renee and I have had this conversation, about four or five times in our lives. And just so you know. We both felt like I should've spent Ajay's thirteenth birthday with you. But we thought we would be in trouble with the elders if I'd done that. We *all* know better now though."

She giggles and Wes cracks up laughing.

She continues, "I never really felt like I was Richard's first choice."

Wes is suddenly dazed as he stares at her. He's thinking she already knows about the depression letter which he's about to show her and talk to her about. But she doesn't.

"Whenever Richard and I would argue. He would tell me that Ebony was better than me," she says, "He wanted to be with my cousin. Nobody knows that but me. So *please* keep this between us. Because Ajay would go dig his ass up and grind his bones apart if he found out he had said shit like this. Richard was very jealous of Ajay, for *so* many reasons. His *popularity*. His street *cred*. The attention he *always* got from older women. *All* the females, for that matter. And the way he was able to fuck *any* girl that came to a crew event or get-together. The way Ajay got and kept Ebony's *undivided*

attention, was always something our crew admired. Ajay was always *very* smart and *very* take it or leave it. *Very choosy too*. That's why he has Ebony. They are two of a kind, *ethics* wise. From day one, Ajay was taught by big Al and his grandfather Al, how he was to behave as a male if he wanted to be in Ebony's life. They knew what uncle big John wanted for his only daughter. And if Ajay would've did anything the *wrong* way, when he approached Ebony. He would've had to deal with big Al. Still to this day, it would be that way. So Ajay took his time and learned what was the right way to approach my cousin. Ebony was only gonna be impressed by a male who did exactly what *her* mentality wanted. Ajay put in the work to learn what it took to get her to, *exactly* where they are right now. I loved Ajay with Ebony, from the start. Because she was very quiet. She watched and learned what she wanted to do and what she didn't wanna do. But me, Nina and Rebbie felt like we had to teach her everything that we *thought* we'd learned. She would listen to what we had to say. But she didn't let us teach her shit. She did things, *her* way. Ajay just waited for her to let him know when *she* was ready for whatever move she felt like *she* wanted to make next. Which is the absolute *perfect* way. The one code that our generation of crew vowed to is this; *'We will give unto our young, the knowledge needed. Not only to persevere. But to lead and continue with forward change. While reaching another and teaching another.'* And Wesley, I am *so* proud of the way I see Richard-the-third behaving with Aaliyah Hamilton. She's the reason he spends *every* school break in Atlanta or she comes here to visit. He told her that he's gonna wait for her as long as she wants him too. That's the same thing you said to me, at Ajay's thirteenth birthday party. You said, if I'd say I would date you, you would wait for me and move here when Renee got things together for you. Baby that was nineteen eighty seven. Now here we are. Ajay and Ebony are the happiest of all of my crew that we're together now. Ebony has always had my back. She was the one who said I should wait for you, back then. She only wanted me to be as happy as she was, then and is now. I'm there now. Thank you God for bringing Wesley Jermaine Stewart back to me."

Wes smiles. He now knows that informing his lovely wife about the letter her deceased husband left behind. Isn't going to shock her, in the least. At this very moment, he wants to get passed the letter from Richie Rich.

     He reaches down to the floor and grabs his jacket and pulls his copy of the depression letter out of his jacket pocket. Then he turns back to T-baby and says, "This is something I want you to read. This will prove to you that the feelings you had, way back then and what you *just* described

today. Shows that you was and still *are*, one hundred percent on point. I've known that since you were ten years old."

She smiles. His face holds such a very *sincere* look of confidence. He wants to relieve his love of any and all questions as to rather moving on with him wasn't the right move. He lays on his back, pulls her back into his arms and hands her the letter.

Nina and Tank's Estate, 5:30pm

Nina and Tank are in the middle of their 3rd love session of the day. The sex they started with, at the beginning of today. They went right back to as soon as they returned home. The 2nd session of this afternoon is doggy style. Tank is working his wife over very well. He's very vocal about what his wishes are too. In a very demanding voice, he says,
"Don't nobody need to come knocking on our damn door nor ringing the bell. We're gonna be fucking until it's time for us to head to the event. Or until the cows come knocking. Is that clear?"

"Oooo baby!" Nina screams in agreement. She yells, "Yes Jeremy! Oh baby! You got energy for *days!*"

"Fuck me, baby," he oozes. "I gotta feel every bit of my sweet ass pussy before I can get this nut."
He slaps Nina's butt and goes into overdrive. She's throwing it back on him to the best of her ability. But this is a session ruled by Tank. He feels a nut creeping up on him. He's doing his best to fight it off but Nina starts to talk sexy to him. She knows she's got to get him worked up so she can pull his orgasm out now. Because if he keeps up at this rate. Nina knows she won't even have enough strength left in her, to attend tonight's celebration. Which includes Tank's 31st birthday celebration too.

She starts to back it up on him. He's drilling her on each stroke. Each push. Though it's pain mixed with pleasure, Nina knows she has to keep up with his pace. She *has* to keep up. She keeps pushing back on him. He keeps grinding into her until finally, all he can do is pound her hard because his nut is right there.

"Ouwwah!" she yells from the pain of his pre-ejaculation thrust.
She screams, "Get it baby! *Damn*! Get that hard dick emptied out! *Please*!! Before you take this pussy that belongs to you, out of commission! Come here, baby! *Now!!*"
Tank unloads and he's extremely loud while doing so. His nut is out now and flowing like a stream.

Afterwards, all he can do is flop down on their bed. Nina is still lying on her stomach and breathing hard. They both need to catch up to their breath. But Nina is staring at him. She can see anger in his eyes and she's curious as to what has him so angry. She has to know why he's upset.

In a breathless whisper, she asks, "Baby what's going on? Why are you so pissed off today? I know some shit went down during that meeting at Chill's office. What's going on, Jeremy? Tell me. *Please.*"

"That bitch ass Angel called for Ajay," he whispers as he stares at the ceiling above their bed.

"*What*?!" she screams as she rolls over on her side, facing him.

"Yep," he says.

Nina says, "So *that's* what made Ebony rush us on up outta they house today. Ajay called her, just as him and Lil Ajay was leaving Chill's office. He *had* to be telling her about that bitch's call. Because Ebony said he was on his way home and they needed to have their privacy. And baby, she had the same look on her face that you have on your's, right now. I wanna know why that bitch called. What's going on, baby?"

Tank doesn't say anything. He just continues to stare at the ceiling.

Nina continues, "That bitch needs to be passed on to us, Jeremy. I know y'all putting together a plan to get rid of her ass. And her ass needs to be passed on to us. *The awesome foursome*. I know Ebony can do her. She's done a motherfucker before. *Two*, as a matter of fact. She told us about Neal Palmer, today. All this time we was thinking Chill did his ass. But Ebony said she did him. Did you know that?"

"Yep."

"My daddy knew it too," she says, "But Chill took the rap. I was looking at Ebony's eyes while she was telling us about it. It was like she was in big Paul's home, all over again. And then, in the chamber with Raymond White, when she talked on him. Shortly after that, is when Ajay called. From the time he started talking to her, Ebony was fresh outta chat mode. She was looking like she did, that night at the chamber, when she smoked that no good ass rapist for trying to rape her. So what do you think she would do if she could get her hands on Angel, in the chamber?"

"Push her fucking wig back," Tank says while he still stares at the ceiling.

"Will you put our names in the next discussion?" Nina asks. "She took the first baby from my brother and my best friend. I can do her ass in and not lose one minute of sleep. Jeremy I'll agree with whatever it takes to get that bitch put in our hands. Me, Ebony, T-baby and Rebbie. Let me,

213

T-baby and Rebbie do her ass in, for *Ebony*. *Hell*. Y'all can bring Katrina and Darlene's ass too. And you know Alana and Farah can be included. Me and my girls are just ready for all of these nothing ass bitches to get theirs and get the hell up out of *all* these crew lives."

"We'll see about making that happen," Tanks says. "You just be ready to get it over with. You hear me?"

"I'm hear you," Nina says, "And I'll do my part. I promise you."
With that, they get up and head to their master bathroom. It's time for them to get ready for tonight's festivities. Nina has to take Tank to Shaker Heights. She'll pretend she has to go by her parents home to pick up some things, she'll need at the event. Basically, she has to waste some time so it will give the rest of the entire crew time to get to The Spot and set up to surprise Tank for his birthday.

"It's my birthday week and all I feel like doing is sending these fake, nothing ass bitches to hell," Tank says.
Immediately Nina responds with, "I'll help you on that one, baby. *Word*."

Ajay and Ebony's Estate, 6:30pm

Ajay has just finished updating Ebony on today's meeting and the phone call from Angel, at Chill's office. Ebony's in a contemplative mood after hearing that her son has Angel, right where he wants her.
Ebony says, "A phone call at four tomorrow is going to be *very* unlikely. Your game is at one."

"Oh I know and I knew that, *then*," Ajay says, "It's just a set up to keep her excited. I already told Chill to play if off from where Ant left it and reschedule it, from Friday forward. That'll be the third of February. We play at home from the fourth through the sixth. Ant can get his in during that time. We discussed that before he went to spot two."

"I want her freed," Ebony says suddenly.
Ajay looks Ebony in her eyes and says, "You do, don't you?"

"Yes," she says, "And I want some closure to that other madness too. The Trina Yvette madness you was telling me about, after we all had lunch *together*?"

"Attorney Wheeler is the one to fix that one," Ajay says.

"You're going to let him hear what you recorded her saying, right?" she asks.

"Of course. But that can hold. Old Jake and devil, goes first."

"Good," she says, "I agree with the priority part. Because with
214

Trina Yvette. You won't have to say much about the recording. I heard it all. All I needed to hear, to know she wants my husband. My man. My *life*."

"All yours," Ajay agrees. "In *every* category. I told you *way* back on that early morning of July third. Your pussy is the *only* one I need and want. And it's all mine now. Ain't no *fucking way* I need to stray, Ebony. We're still coming up with new ways to please each other. Sexually and just in our daily lives. Baby, that's what has made *every* other female, who's come after me, in *life*. Want me. They want what you have but they don't even realize that it's because of you, that I'm desirable to *them*. And it ain't not *one* of those many ho's, been nowhere near, *close* to you. You don't have that to worry about. *Ever*. Not as long as you are *you*."

Ebony smiles big. She has always loved to hear Ajay say things like this. And he has always said things like this. She knows she has no reason to doubt or not believe him or in him. Because he has shown and proved it all. For *all* of their lives. She wants to make sure he knows who she wants, as far as removing the undesirables from their lives too.

She says, "I want to make sure that each and every one of those outside, *wish they could be in my place females*, get what they deserve. And I want a part in *all* of them. From Darlene to Devil. On to Katrina and Trina Yvette too. I would throw Roc in that picture but she stayed in her sensible and safe lane. However *Tim*, can be done away with, along with the others I named. And I don't even have to be apart of that one."

"Ant and myself," Ajay says with a smile, "That punk bitch is ours. He came into the picture on Old Jake's side and he was planning to try to take you, on some Raymond White type of shit. Which you and me talked on, many times since then. He came in and is going out, with Old Jake."

"Good," she says, "Get him done, daddy. Because that whole Old Jake mess has been about trying to harm our ancestors and us too. That really has to go before our children are crew."

"You have my word, baby girl," Ajay says.

She adds, "There is one more thing I want done. Something that will bring Devil closer to leaving this earth."

"What's that?"

"Recommend an earlier release date for her," she says, "I don't care what reasons y'all come up with. I want this over with, so our son can move on. And he is *our* son, Anthony. So there is no way he's gonna let this rest. I know you know that. *Correct*?"

Ajay says, "I know it. And he's ready, Ebony. And devil *will* be released early. Baby, Ant is way ahead of his age. You know that by now. Correct?"

"He's the little you," she says and smiles. She adds, "Plus he has my father and grandfathers genes. And the genes from your side too. His patience is absent when it comes to *anyone* who has hurt you and I. Me and mama Jo have been talking, for two decades. I knew what to expect. Trust me. I'm on the mother side of this now. But mama Jo is my role model when it comes to being the mother of a Jackson male. She raised a damn good one and he's all mine. I trust her way, one hundred percent. She knew Ant would wanna do away with Angel from the moment he was born. She *has* been tutoring me since the eighties."

They both laugh. Then Ajay adds, "She knew she wanted you as her *only* son's woman too. She took your side before she would take mine. And I had no problem with that."

Ebony smiles. Then she goes right back to her desires for Angel Taylor's demise.

She says, "Me, Nina, T-baby and Rebbie are gonna be at the chamber when Angel goes to meet her maker. Just make sure that's in the plan. We have talked about Angel getting what she deserves since that night at Arthur's, when I whooped her behind and then got her arrested."

"We'll make sure y'all foursome girls get to take some of her air, baby," Ajay says. He adds, "Okay?"

"Okay," she says but she knows Ajay is not done.

He says, "But Ant is gonna be the one to take that last breath. This is about his birthright. He doesn't have his older sister. We want him to be able to move on with his life and be productive and successful. Right?"

"Yes," she says, "Of course we do."

"Then this is the way we go about *giving unto our young son*," Ajay says. He adds, "Just by us having that devil's name back in daily conversation, makes each day feel like *the past revisited*. Our son wants to relieve that pressure off his mind. And I understand what he's dealing with, one hundred percent. I'll give him *whatever* he needs to relieve that pressure. My pops *and* big John did that solid for me, Tank and Jb. Ant is a natural and he's *very* intelligent in the way he's setting up, not only that devil's demise. But he's working the Old Jake's demise too."

Ebony says, "It's in his heritage, Anthony. Mama Jo brought me up on the mother's side of this. So I get it. And I understand it *completely*. I just wanna make sure one thing is *crystal* clear."

"What's that?" Ajay asks.

"My son will make it home," she says, "*Each and everyday*. That's what it will take for me to remain this good *and* free mother, wife and

business woman that I am and that you love. I will not go on if I lose *any* of our kids. And Ant is my only son. The Jackson history shows that he may be the only son that I'll have. I'd lose my mind if I lost him."

"I hear ya," Ajay says, "And you won't lose him nor our girls."

"Promise me," she says.

"I promise you that Ant will grow old, along with his sisters," Ajay says, "And they will *all* out live us. Because I'll have to die on the same day that him or one of my girls do. I got that from my pops."

"Good," Ebony says, "Y'all can carry on, as needed. To get Angel released earlier than next January. But you will keep me abreast of every move. I'm sure of that."

"I will," Ajay says. Then he adds, "But Ant said he was gonna have a brother. Did you know that?"

Ebony giggles and says, "Yes I remember that. He says it *daily*."

"I know our triplets are only a few days past a month old," Ajay says, "So I'm not gonna rush you into trying for that son. But you'll let me know when you're ready. Just like you always have."

She says, "That's a fact. But you love to practice, Anthony and all of our kids *are* gone. So our private time is on. We've talked enough for now."

"Come here, baby," Ajay whispers as he leans in for a long kiss. He adds, "We got time for a quickie before we have to head to CrewLand."

"Should I undress myself?" Ebony asks with a shy smile.

Ajay starts to remove her clothes as he picks her up off of their parlor room couch. He continues kissing her passionately, as he carries her toward their master bedroom. Then he stops suddenly.

He says, "We don't have *any* of our kids at home right now. So I'm gonna start fucking, right here in the hallway. If all we have time for is a *quickie*. Then you'd better not let me make it to our bed and lay you down."

Ebony giggles hard as they go for it, right there in the hallway outside of their bedroom.

June and Rebbie's Estate, 7:00pm

When Rebbie arrived back at home from Ebony's, she was home alone. But that changed about 20 minutes ago. Big June came back home after learning that she was here. He really wants to get close to his wife, so he goes for broke.

Rebbie is sitting on 1 of their bar stools in their den. June walks up behind her and gives her a kiss on the back of her neck.

Then he says, "I really miss you, Rebbie. I miss you, so much."
Rebbie smiles slightly but she doesn't say anything. June continues.
"I just wanna know what I can do, to make this feel like a home to you again. Please baby. Tell me what you need."
Rebbie says, "I need my space. That's what I need, more than anything. My private time and space."

"I wanna be apart of your time and space. Rebbie," June tries.
"I just wanna make sure you *know* that you're the only woman in this world I desire."
Rebbie says, "Oh it's like that *now*? Brian is it *really* like that now?"

"Yes it is," he says, "And it always has been. I learned that, a long time ago."

"It wasn't that long ago when you was still fucking around on me," she says. "You've been outside of our marriage, several times. Even after we had Orian. You do remember all of that, right?"
He says, "I do, Rebbie and I apologized for all of that. Because I was then and still am, very sorry that I hurt you. I promised you that I wasn't gonna mess up again. And I haven't."

"I never did, Brian," she counters back. "You are my first and only, as far as penetration goes. You cannot say the same thing. Even since our marriage, you can't say that. Can you?"
He shakes his head no and looks down in disappointment. He feels ashamed and guilty, still. But he didn't catch what she'd just said.
'As far as penetration goes.'
She continues, "How would it make you feel, if the tables was turned? What if I'd been fucking over you for our *entire* relationship? How would that make you feel?"

"I can't even imagine, baby," he says somberly. "That's why I feel like a damn fool for ever doing *any* of it. I had the best woman in this world, with me from day one. I wasn't being smart at all. It wasn't even crew like, to tell the truth. I did some dumb shit, along with Rich sometimes. But I can't blame Rich for my fuck ups. I'm a man. I was raised to stand up for my mistakes. *Independently*. That's what I did when you brought it to me and that's the same way I'm going to handle it now."

"You can't imagine the hurt it causes, Brian," she says, "But I sure as hell can."
He's thrown off by her language. This side of Rebbie is very new to him. He feels ashamed because this is who she has always been. He just never really gave her a voice. Her *own* voice. Now that he's looking into her eyes, he can

see that she's filled with anger. Her eyes are showing it but her voice is still very calm. He knows he has to say something to bring her back to calm, all over again.

He says, "Rebbie I have *always* loved you. I've never been in love with anybody *but* you. That's the truth. I was just doing dumb shit, back then. If I could go back and change it all. I would, Rebbie. I promise you. I would change every bit of it."

"But you can't change it, Brian," she says, "That's the problem. Neither can I and I've tried. All of those memories stayed on my mind for *years.* *Before* we got married and had Orian. Even before our twin sons were made, I was still feeling as though I was alone and wasn't appreciated. Because if I was. There's no way our relationship and marriage would have the history that they *both* have. Do you even realize that this is one of the *few* times that you have actually let me finish a damn sentence? *Do* you?"

"Yes. And I'm sorry."

"Don't be sorry, Brian," she says, "I'm tired of hearing you say you're sorry because you don't have to tell me that part. I've been the one on the receiving end of those things that you're always saying you're sorry for. I tell you what. How about you put yourself in my place. Imagine how you'd feel if I was a damn whore. A cheating ass woman. Would you be as calm as I am right now?"

"No. I know I wouldn't be," he says, "That's why I came to the decision that I had to be faithful to you and treat you the way you deserve to be treated. Right down to listening to you when you have something to say. I want you to have your career. I look at Orian and I know how I wanna see her blossom. I want her to be just like her mama. Just like you. I want her to live out her dreams. I want the same for you. I'll do anything you need me to do, to make you happy, Rebbie. Just tell me what I need to do for us to get back to where we started."

Where we *started*?" Rebbie blurts out in a doubtful tone. She adds, "We started out with you cheating on me. I'll tell you what. You can go back to that if you'd like. But it ain't no way in *hell* that I'm gonna stay around behind another route of it. I'm never going for that again. No way."

"I don't wanna cheat with *anybody*, Rebbie," he tries, "I ended all of that because I wanna spend my life with you. I've only wanted to spend my life with you since day one. That's the same way I feel today."

Rebbie can't take it anymore. Everything in her, wants to tell him that she no longer wants to be with him, *romantically*. She only wants to co-parent their 3 children. But she can't say it. Not this soon. She just wants some

peace. Some private time. Or anything that won't lead to the 2 of them talking about the 2 of them, as husband and wife. She's done with forfeiting her life and her love. They've had this husband and wife title for 9 years, 9 months and 6 days. Yet Rebbie still feels the same way she's felt since the beginning of their courtship. Like a *Love on hold!* Her oath as crew and her concerns about making her elders proud is the reason she tried to make this relationship with her first love *work*. They joined together in a double wedding ceremony with Rich and T-baby. A crew couple who was dealing with many of the same issues which led to a marriage that was on the road to ending. That's because they never *formally* joined. Not in the ways that would've made their marriage whole. Not in the ways that has flourished for all of the crew couples before them. Rebbie and T-baby have since agreed, that is the 1 thing they share. *Fitting in by living under the crew oath umbrella.* There's only 1 other couple in this crew who went beyond togetherness and found their way back to each other.

Richard Trevon Williams Sr and Anna Dionne Wilson-Williams.

The parents of Richard Trevon Williams, Jr. Richie Rich is the crew brother who took his own life, just over 3 years ago. Rebbie doesn't want to see that for June. She definitely wouldn't want Orian, Brian III and Brent James, their 3 kids, to feel that hurt. But in her heart, Rebbie knows all she is capable of doing now, is commingling with June. The love she *tried* to have for him, he didn't adore nor reciprocate. Not until now. When it's too late. And it's too late now because she's done. She's wanted to end their marriage since she found love with Jarvis. But she knows if she ask June for a divorce right now, she won't even be able to enjoy the celebration tonight. Because he's going to make her request, the topic of discussion with every male crew member during tonight's event. So for now, Rebbie knows she has to find a way to come to a truce with June. Anything that will end this conversation about rekindling because that's not going to happen. She's not interested in that. Not at all. She wants to get passed these next couple of hours, until they can get out of their house and head to CrewLand mall.

Suddenly she comes up with an idea. A way for her and June to spend this *borrowed time*. She turns around on the bar stool and faces June. She can now face him without a frown. She smiles. He smiles back.

She says, "I have an idea of what I wanna do until it's time to get ready for the celebration."

That sparks June's ears up. He smiles harder and puts a sexy look on his face. He's thinking that she's about to give him another chance to prove himself to her. But he's wrong.

He's smiling still, as he asks, "Let me know what's on your mind, baby."
She says, "I wanna watch the video's of our kids. I wanna pull out their baby books. Their journals too. The *whole* nine. Let's put our minds on the three most important people in this world to us, as parents. Is that *doable*?"
He's rather disappointed to know that *all* she wants to do with her alone time with him, is watch their kids. But he has no other choice. He should look on the bright side. At least she came up with something they will be doing *together*. It's been a long time since they've spent *any* alone time together. He figures that maybe watching the history of their kids, might just change the mood for both of them. He smiles big again.
He says, "Let's do it."
"Cool," she says and smiles.
With that, they head to their home office to pull out all of the memorabilia of their 3 children. Once they've collected it all, they head back into their main living room. Rebbie pops in the video of Orian's born day. June is still smiling. Rebbie is smiling now too.
For June, he feels this is the start of getting back to what he has learned has always been the best part of his life.
For Rebbie, she feels like she's just gotten herself some breathing room and through another uncomfortable moment with the man on her marriage certificate. She now knows she has suggested the correct thing. Because spending time watching and involving their children. Is the only thing which has kept her sane around June, since the day Orian was born. And especially now, since she has fallen in love with Jarvis Rhodes, Sr.

T-baby and Wes' Estate, 7:45pm

T-baby and Wes are still laying in their bed and still holding each other tight. She has read the depression note from her deceased 1st husband, Richie Rich and they've discussed it in full. Wes is so pleased to see that his lovely wife is still smiling.
T-baby says, "I'm not surprised by that letter, baby. That's something I've known, the whole time."
"Renee told me, she didn't think you would be shocked," Wes says. "She said y'all had similar discussions over the years."
"We have," she says, "Richard got his ass beat by Ajay, a few times when we was growing up. Everything from him scaring Ebony. To him messing with Ajay's baseball cards and private property. Which is one in the same. Baby, Richard always wanted to be better than Ajay. That's

something I figured out before we became boyfriend and girlfriend. To be honest. That day he asked me to be his girlfriend, we was having a crew dinner. He knew Ajay had a big announcement to make, about basketball. Plus he knew Ajay liked Ebony and they were already spending time together. *Innocent* time. Like playing basketball or listening to music in Ajay's room *together*. Richard just wanted to have the upper hand, for once. So he announced our courtship, at that dinner. I thought back on it after I matured. I think he was just trying to make Ebony feel like Ajay didn't really like her enough to ask her to be his girlfriend. Of course, that didn't phase Ajay nor Ebony. They were happy for us. But I always felt like I was Richard's savior from *himself*. That's how it was from day one. He did crazy things, just to get attention. Or to look like he was tough or gangster. He wanted to do bad by Ajay. But he knew he couldn't whoop Ajay. So he would do shit to piss Ebony off, trying to scare her or whatever. That got his ass kicked by Ajay, just as if he'd done something *to* Ajay, himself. To tell you the truth. Richard never stopped that shit. You remember the day he went to their house after the twins were born. Right?"

"Yes," Wes said, "I remember it well. You and I were becoming closer during that time. And he was spiraling all the way out of control. And you just said, you think that's when he started with this depression letter."

"I do," she says, "Because of the part where he wrote, '*It's time for me to teach you a lesson.*' And '*I'm gonna slap some sense into you and one day you'll thank me.*' He wrote that part before he hit Ebony and hurt my twin, nephew and niece. So he was writing this letter for more than a year, before he took his own life. I could sense that he was *too* far gone. That's why I wanted a divorce. I was his savior. I know that much. That's why he took his own life and tried to take me with him. As if that makes any sense."

"It doesn't," Wes says, "I didn't feel comfortable with him coming here, that day. Or you being alone with him and I told you that."

"You was making dinner for me, you, Lil Rich and Jada," she says and smiles. "I was so ready to divorce him and move on with you."

"I'm so glad you survived and we're here, baby," he says, "And on our way to one year, as husband and wife."

"True that," she says while still smiling. She adds, "And I'm in *real* love and finally happy. Let's get ready and go celebrate our love."
With that, they head to the shower together. It's time to do it, *crew style*.

TIME TO SHOW-RELOADED-Time Will Reveal 6

CHAPTER 69

FAMILY FIRST

The crew celebration is banging, as usual. Tank will be honored along with Bruce and Jesse aka Lil man, at *The Chill Spot*. Ron Banks Jr is being honored at *The Dirty South Chill Spot*, down in Atlanta.

DeMarcus Owens and Kimmie McNair were 2 of the guest of honor at *The Spot II* celebration earlier. Along with Robert Jenkins Jr or Lil Rob. Lil Rob flew in from Atlanta to be honored at *The Spot II*. His date for his 1st big event was Aaliyah Imani Jackson aka Lea. Ajay and Rob arranged it and they made sure they were dressed to match each other. Rob and Jan's son has already been matched up with Ajay and Ebony's 2nd born daughter, as a future crew couple. All the younger Atlanta crew flew in with Rob Jr to celebrate with their crew. The Spot II party started at 4pm, for guest arrival. The honorees were honored at 8pm and their party ended at midnight. The all-day crew celebrations have kept *CrewLand Mall* crowded since around noon.

The Chill Spot is always the place to be. Tonight is no different. Their party started at 10pm. The crew officially honored Tank, Bruce and Jesse at midnight. Many *Cavaliers* and *Brown's* players are in attendance, as usual but the Cavaliers have a 1pm game tomorrow and a 2am curfew to adhere to. Ajay is going to make sure his teammates clear out of his crew club by 1:30am and go straight to bed. He knows he'll make it. Because that's what him and Ebony are going to do.

It's 12:45am and Jarvis is bidding his time. He has spent more time in VIP with the crew and his teammates. Then he has in the booth with Gwen and Nickeia, down on the 1st floor. He's cracking jokes and *janking* with Ajay, their teammates and the crew. He's just having some relaxation time while waiting to meet with Gwen at 1am. He only wanted enough time to tell her, his plan before he has to break camp. He doesn't want her to have any extra time because he knows she'll try to plead her case. But in his opinion, she doesn't have a case. He's done with her as his wife.

Jarvis is seated with Ajay and Ebony, who's VIP den is diagonal from June and Rebbie's. Jarvis is seated in the very spot he needs to be in, to have direct eye contact with Rebbie. They're both using the view to their advantage too. While June is still, none the wiser.

Ajay is making sure Jarvis stays low key, when it comes to Rebbie. Ajay has caught the eyes she's been giving Jarvis. He knows if June was to catch 1 of the glances. Then Rebbie and Jarvis' secret love would be

exposed immediately. Ajay's plan is to keep things calm in VIP, so him and Ebony can enjoy their *usual* hands-on time, at their very 1st Chill Spot celebration *since* their triplets were born. So Ajay no longer wants to be *security*. He looks and Jarvis and asks, "Are you ready for me to get Chill on that program? Because *we* needs to give *somebody's* eyes a rest."

Jarvis chuckles first. Then he says, "I'm ready. I need to get that out the way and over with anyway. That way, I can be light as air for tomorrow's game. We gotta make sure them Suns get an El in Quicken Loans Arena. You know. So yeah bro. Let the boss man know I'm ready to head to the meeting room. I'm ready to get that weight off my shoulders."

"Word," Ajay says as he types into his table monitor and summons Chill.

It's approaching 1am when Chill makes his way to VIP. He gives recognition to all his crew and the pro sport players too. Then he makes his way over to Ajay and Ebony's den and shakes hands with Jarvis.

Chill asks, "I heard you was ready for me to come through."

"Yes indeed, Chill," Jarvis says, "I'm ready to get this meeting done and over with. I got a curfew to make."

"Damn right, he do," Ajay butts in. He adds, "And he's got fifteen minutes to get it done."

Chuckling, Chill says, "Word. Do you want me to send somebody down to get Gwen? Or would you rather me to have Renee page her?"

"Page her, please," Jarvis says. "That'll be faster. It took all I had to sit at their booth for those twenty minutes I was down there. Especially when *VIP* has the best view."

He looks over at Rebbie and smiles. She's already smiling and watching him as he stands with Chill. Chill caught their eyes, same as Ajay has been.

"I can see that it does," Chill says with another chuckle. He adds, "Take your time, man. If it's meant to be. It'll happen. I'm up on it, just so you know. Just keep letting Ajay guide you through it. Cool?"

"Definitely," Jarvis says.

Chill says, "Let's hit it."

Chill and Jarvis head to Chill's office while Chill radios Renee to get Gwen up to the 3rd floor and into the individual meeting room, *ASAP*. Jarvis is ready to inform Gwen that his divorce papers will be on record Monday, January 30, 2006. A day and half from now.

After Jarvis is gone. Ajay takes Ebony's hand and brings her to her feet. She comes straight to him and they kiss. After the kiss, Ebony puts her hand on Ajay's cheek and brings his ear down to her lips.

She whispers, "I think it's time for *all* of us to get to the dance floor before it's time to leave. We need to do something to keep Rebbie occupied. She started looking all gloomy as soon as Jarvis walked away."

"I'm noticing that too, baby," Ajay says. "Let's do this."

Him and Ebony move slowly away from their den and head toward the VIP dancing area. They stop at June and Rebbie's den, first. They tell them to come join them. June hops up quickly. Rebbie is slower to rise but she does come along. Nina, Tank, Wes and T-baby are right behind them.

"Let's go turn this muthafucka out!!" Tank yells and chuckles.

"You know it, baby!" Nina screams in cadence.

All 4 couples are giggling as they hit the dance floor. Soon, Michelle and Arthur join them. Next, Steve and Ally makes it to the VIP dance floor.

Five minutes later the floor is raided by Jr, Tonya, Chill and Renee. They bring the extra hype like this crew did it, back in the day. Back when they only had Chill and Renee's house to party in.

"This ain't nothing but a CrewLand party! That's all! That's all!"

Renee starts to chant and everybody else joins in. They're enjoying this crew time, just like they always have and will.

Next Tank and Nina yell,

"Put your right hand in the air! Put your left hand in your underwear!"

The rest join in and finish, saying,

"And just wiggle, wiggle, wiggle, wiggle, wiggle!! Just wiggle, wiggle, wiggle, wiggle, wiggle!"

The VIP is *crunk* and everyone is having a great time. Even Rebbie loosens up while dancing with June. He's all smiles.

Ajay leans over to Chill and asks, "Is the meeting in play?"

"Yessir it is," Chill answers with a chuckle and a rise in his left eyebrow. "And she was smiling when she went in."

"That's about to change," Ajay responds.

"Fasho!" is Chill's response and they both chuckle and get right back to enjoying their crew time.

It's only been 10 minutes since Jarvis went up to the meeting room. And already, KeJuan is contacting Chill.

"What's up, Kilo?" Chill answers over his radio.

Suddenly he's leaving the dance floor and heading toward the hall which leads to the meeting room area. With a *"mind occupied"* look on his face.

KeJuan radio's back, saying, "Gwen is screaming, cursing and throwing shit. I'm at the door waiting on word from you."

"I'm on my way," Chill says.

When Chill arrives at the door, he's not alone. Every member of the crew who was on the dance floor with him. Followed behind him when they saw the look on his face. Chill uses his key and opens the meeting room door.

Inside, Jarvis is calm but Gwen isn't calm. Not at all. She's very loud and very abusive with her language.

"Who is the *bitch*, Jarvis?!" Gwen yells. "You wanna leave me after all these *years*?! How the fuck can you do that?! I've been a hundred percent wit you and we *both* know, I can't say the same for you! Cause I know you've been fucking around wit-!"

Ajay cuts in and says, "Gwen. It's time to calm your voice down or you will *never* be back here. We don't mind people who are like family, using the private areas. But we have business to do here. You can either calm down and be able to leave on your own. Or stay hood and get escorted out. Which do you want?"

"Ajay, Jarvis is cheating on me and he just told me he's filing for divorce on Monday," Gwen says as she cries. "I know you know who it is, Ajay. Tell me. Let me have that much. Let me handle my shit muthafucka-"

"Hold on, Gwen," Ebony cuts in. She says, "Don't you *ever* use curse words toward my husband. He's speaking to you in a respectful manner. You will do the same. Or I will have to take it from here. Then we can do this *however* you'd like. Which do you want?"

"It can be whatever it need to be!" Nickeia chirps.

Renee had sent Erica and Kim to get her from downstairs, to try and help with calming her older sister down. It's obvious she isn't going to do any better than Gwen. Nina, T-baby and Rebbie walk over and stand in front of Nickeia and fold their arms.

Nina says, "You will have to come through me first. Make a move."

"And me second," Rebbie adds.

T-baby says, "And it ain't no way in hell you'll get passed me. Cause even with child, I can still mop this damn floor with your ass. Bring it. So you can get rolled the fuck up outta here. Don't you ever threaten my cousin nor my crew. Now act like you don't understand me. *Please*."

"Did you get that?" Nina chimes in.

"I dare you to speak, bitch," Rebbie spits.

Nickeia doesn't comment again. She eases her way around them and goes to stand by Gwen's side.

That's when Nickeia says, "Big sis. What they doing to you? Jarvis, what's up? Are you still dogging my sister out?"

Renee cuts to the chase and says, "It is time for you two to leave and stop with this *disrupting* of business. Now you can either be escorted down to your vehicle. Or I'm gonna carry you out of here. But you *are* leaving. Right now. Let's go."

"Gwen and Nickeia. You two need to follow Renee," Tonya says. "And I'm following y'all."

"So are we," Nina says as T-baby, Rebbie and Ebony agree.

From there, Renee escorts Gwen and Nickeia down the hall and to the elevator. Which takes them down to the VIP valet parking lot. Everyone from the meeting room heads down too. The females take the elevator. The men take the stairs. They meet by the valet door and exit into the parking lot.

Once they're all outside of the club, Gwen starts back with the talking or rather yelling to Jarvis.

His only response is, "I've already told you what I'm going to do. I'm done with this conversation."

To Gwen, Chill says, "I've got Wayne bringing your car around."

"And here is Courtney with your coats and all," Renee says. "Put them on. It's time to go."

The word about the disturbance had grown wings inside the club. Some of the regular guest are making their way around to the side of the club, to see what's going on in the VIP parking lot. Katrina and her buddies are now in the crowd of onlookers. Many bystanders are asking what happened. But Katrina is just enjoying this chance to be within 10 yards of Ajay. She can't stop staring at him. None of the crew are paying her any attention yet. Her aunt, officer Deloris Miles, is in on security and assisting with getting Gwen and Nickeia into their car. Gwen is still loud.

Renee tells her for the last time, "Be quiet. Get in your car and leave. That is, if you ever expect to revisit *any* part of crew businesses again. *Clear*?"

Nickeia knows she doesn't want to be banned again. So she starts to help Gwen into the car.

"I'll drive you, big sis," Nickeia says, "Let's get away from here. We don't act like this. This is beneath us. Let's go. I got you. Even if Jarvis wanna leave you hanging. Get in and let's just leave."

Gwen finally scoots into the passenger seat and Tonya closes the door. Nickeia goes around and hops into the drivers seat. Officer Miles directs them out of the parking lot and toward the exit of CrewLand Mall.

After Gwen and Nickeia are gone. It's time for Ajay, Jarvis and the rest of their teammates to make their 2am curfew. It's 1:45am.

Ajay yells, "Alright Cav's! Let's make it!"
They all head to their respective vehicles. Ajay and Ebony head toward Ajay's 2006 Mercedes-Benz convertible coup. Nina, T-baby and Rebbie are walking them to their car, along with Tank, Wes and June.

No one noticed the trash when she took it upon herself to move over and stand next to Ajay's car. Not until they make it over to it. Ajay stops in his tracks. The look on his face is a mix between anger, nausea and discomfort. The unwanted person is Katrina Dobbs. She's smiling and has her hand extended. As if she thinks she has the option of a handshake from Ajay. He's still frozen in his tracks. It's about that time when Ebony notices Katrina and starts around to Ajay's side of the car. Her girls follow her.
That's when Katrina says, "How are you, Ajay? I don't mean any harm. I just wanted to shake your hand. It's been a minute since I've been this close to you-"
Ebony cuts her short, saying, "Don't you ever say a word to my husband, *bitch*. Or you will have to deal with me. Do you understand me?"

"Say some dumb shit and get dealt with," Nina adds.

"Like a deck of cards, bitch," T-baby says.

"Fifty two pieces and two jokers," Rebbie adds, "That is what we will make out of you and these 3 bitches with you."
She's motioning to the 2 girls standing next to Katrina.

By now, Renee and Tonya spots them all and head on over to clear out these riffraff bitches too.

"Do you wanna be banned again, Katrina?" Renee asks.
Tonya is calling Officer Miles over, as she says, "If we ban you again. You will be costing your aunt *her* job. Because you nor *anyone* resembling you, will *ever* be allowed back on any of *our* property."

"Exactly," Renee says, "Now I need to know if that shit is clear to you this time, Katrina *and* Deloris?!"

"Yes, I'm sorry," Katrina says.

"Yes it's clear," Officer Deloris says. Then in a disgusted tone, she turns to Katrina and says, "Go get your *damn* coat and hat and get the fuck from down here. They only allowed you to come because *I* asked for their permission. And *this* is how you repay me?! I know you remember what I told you when I said you could come. Right?"

"Yes. I'm sorry," Katrina tries again.

"Sorry as hell is more like it," T-baby says. "Get your ass in the club, if you planning on staying here."

"And this is your *last* warning," Ebony says calmly. "Try me."

228

With that, Ebony joins Ajay, who's already warming up his car. She gets into the car and they pull away. Nina, Renee, Chill and the rest redirect the crowd which had gathered.

"If you're staying at CrewLand," Tonya says, "Then you will need to go inside the club or Stoney's. *Any* open business. But no one will remain outside. Not unless you're heading to your vehicle to head off of this property. So *move* it."

It doesn't take long before all of the spectators re-enter the club.

Ajay drives off and heads home. All of his teammates have left CrewLand too. But Ajay is still perturbed. Ebony can see it in his expression, so she's still pissed off.

"It's something about revisiting the past, that makes me yearn for the chamber, Anthony," she says calmly. "I saw the look in your eyes which I haven't seen since the night I found out what that bitch did to you. I'm fuming right now. I can't lie. It's time to add her damn name to that chamber list. Okay?"

"It's been on there," Ajay says in an almost whisper.

"Ant knows about her. Doesn't he?"

Ajay doesn't say a word. He just glances over at Ebony, for a couple of seconds. Then he puts his eyes back on the road.

"Good," she says, "Let's get home. I've got to make sure your game plan is tight for tomorrow. And it's time for me to get my loving too. The sweetest loving in this world that all those *'nowhere close to being me whores'* just can't seem to shake away from trying to get too."

Suddenly she giggles. Ajay looks over at her. He smiles. Then he chuckles.

Calmly he says, "You are my air, baby girl. You know just what to say to make me come right back to myself. And you know what to do too."

Ebony reaches over and rubs his dick.

She says, "I saw this rise when I said that last statement. That's all the confirmation I needed. You didn't even have to compliment me, just now. I know this is mine and *only* mine. Has been and will be. For life."

"Let's get on through this gate before *your* dick burst out of this suit," Ajay says and chuckles again.

"Mmmm," is all Ebony says with a shy smile, at first. Then she giggles.

They go on through the gate and speak to Officer Carl Bronson and Officer Larry Davidson. They're securing Jackson Heights tonight. Jacobson has the night off. He's at *Stoney's Bar n Grill* with Genia Johnson. They're an official couple now.

He'll be back at work tomorrow after the game ends. Ajay and Ebony speak to Bronson and Davidson. Then they head on home.

"This is our last night to have our home *all* to ourselves," Ajay says in a very sexy tone.

"In the words of *LL Cool J*," Ebony says, "*I think I'm gonna need backup*."
She laughs because she knows Ajay is going to reciprocate in kind.

"No backup," he says, "*I need love*."
They both laugh as he pulls into his garage spot and parks. Remotely, he closes the garage door back. They get out and head toward their kitchen entrance, directly from the garage. On the way, he locks his car remotely too.
Ebony giggles and asks, "Ant won't be coming back to get the keys, right?"

"He's got about four more years," Ajay says while smiling.
He adds, "Chill and pops are working on that early release you requested."

"It's time to roll all that baggage up into one ball," Ebony says.
Ajay adds, "And then *shoot* that damn ball!"
They laugh hard as they make their way to their bedroom. It's Ajay and Ebony time.

Game Day morning. Cav's vs. Suns, January 29, 2006

The Foursome are on a 4-way call, this morning. Preparing to give Michelle a call and have her to invite Tameka to today's basketball game. Ebony wants to get the ball moving on getting Angel released from her Cleveland jail stint, as early as possible. So the crew will start by showing open arms to all of her affiliates. After Ebony and Ajay pleased each other *fully*. They discussed their plan for Angel's early release, in detail. Ebony is bringing Nina, T-baby and Rebbie up on the next phase.

The first part of the phase is going to involve Michelle and Tameka. During their early morning discussion, Ajay told Ebony, he was going to leave 7 additional tickets for Michelle and Arthur. Those 7 tickets are for Tameka, Alana, Olivia, Rioshauna, Jaylisa, Darlene and Farah to be at the game and in *reserved* seats.
T-baby says, "Sounds like Ajay is ready to get that chamber move in gear. Sooner than later."

"Amen," Nina says, "Especially with Ebony saying he's got daddy and Chill going to attorney Wheeler, on a *Sunday*."

"Cause he's ready for that devil to meet her maker," Rebbie says.

Then Rebbie asks, "So how soon do y'all think she can be released?"

Ebony says, "She's scheduled to be released in the middle of next year. Two thousand seven. But we're pushing hard for an earlier release. Like this summer or no later than the fall of *this* year."

"And jus know *this*! That bitch ass devil can be pushing up daisies before me and Ebony turn thirty one years old," Nina says with a vicious tone to her voice.

Ebony adds, "*God willing*. And I have to tell y'all. After last night, I wanna add Katrina to the list."

"I *knew* it, cousin," T-baby says and laughs. She adds, "I saw it in your eyes, Ebony. You was *so* ready to whoop her ass in that parking lot."

"Just know that day is coming again," Nina says, "Before she takes her last breath. We are whooping her ass. *Seriously*, foursome. Katrina has got to go. Because her dumbass hasn't learned a damn thing from that ass whooping she got in the spot."

"After we drug her ass through The Chill Spot and left her barely conscience," Rebbie says, "She still tried to get at Ajay, last night. On the *sly*."

Nina says, "And I saw that Raymond White look in Ebony's eyes, when that bitch tried to ease up on my brother for a fucking *handshake*. Ebony, you was steaming."

"Big time," Rebbie says, "And with all of that aggression I was feeling after Gwen and Nickeia acted an ass. I was ready to whoop *all of* their asses."

"Oh it's coming, foursome," Ebony says very calmly. "As granny Pearline use to say, *'Just bid your time.'* It will be here sooner than you know. Mark my word on that. Just be ready to get it over with."

Nina says, "Damn straight. It's time to add to the mix. Let me and T-baby get on this call to Michelle. So we can let her know, we want her to get Tameka onboard for the game today. Big mama already gave her the day off from *The House of Soul Food*."

"And Michelle and Tameka can call Alana," T-baby says, "Let her know they *all* have free game tickets too."

"Oh shit. We can already count Alana and that bunch in," Rebbie says, "Just on the free tickets *alone*."

"For real," T-baby says, "And they get to sit with the crew. No way in hell are they not gonna bite this banana."

"Just make sure none of their asses are close to me and my six babies," Ebony says, "Not even close enough for conversation."

"I already know Lil Ajay ain't gonna let that happen," Nina says quickly. She adds, "My nephew will never let ho's near his mama or his sisters. He *is* Ajay, to the hundredth power."
They all giggle and agree. Then they end their call, so Nina and T-baby can call Michelle and Arthur.

Big Chill and big Al have just finished their meeting with attorney George Wheeler. Wheeler agreed to start procedures into letting the penal system know that the crew family will not have any opposition to an early release for Angelise "Angel" Taylor. Chill and big Al converse about the forward movements the crew are making, on their drive back home.
"Well that part is done and it sounds good," Chill says as him and big Al chuckle.
Then Chill asks, "So how soon do you think she'll be released?"
Big Al says, "A year early. By August, of this year. Less than eight months from today. Which is going to be plenty of time to put her goodbye together. And also, we're gonna add another goodbye or two, along with hers."
"You're speaking on the top spot fool, I'm sure," Chill says as he drives.
"Definitely," big Al says.
Their talking about the demise of Jacob Denard Johnson, Sr aka Old Jake.
Big Al continues, "Genia and Jacobson are already pulling that together very nicely. With the help of Jeb, Jessie Mae and Albert."
"Our Europe crew are *really* good at staying low key," Chill says, "They're moving very quiet. I am *so* impressed."
"Experience," big Al says, "They aren't concerned about being out front. Not at all. Not this soon. They know how to get close to Old Jake without him even knowing what to look for. They know every link."
Chill says, "I'm honored to have them here. It's been *way too* long anyway. And with Old Jake thinking they're still *abroad*. That's gotta be a plus."
"Oh it will be, fasho," big Al says and chuckles. He adds, "They're comfortable out in Jackson Heights. Holding down Greg Junior's home."
"Him and Pam stay on the go, so much," Chill says, "So that's very convenient. And when they *are* in town. They stay out at the condo. Even though there's enough room at his home, for all of them."
Big Al says, "Greg wants to make sure they feel *all* the way at home. He even has Jacobson and Genia stay there with them, three nights a week."
Chill says, "And that's the move. We had a great talk, the other night. The Baker's, Albert and Jacobson have gotten Genia, all the way on point. Big

232

Al, this demise for Old Jake is going to happen soon. I can feel it."

"And very smoothly too," big Al adds, "John and I speak with them, twice a week. This is going to be a monumental year for this crew."

"I agree with you on that monumental part, big Al," Chill says, "It's past time to get that part of this crew legacy, over and cleared. *Fully*. So all of our future crews can live their lives. Without any type of worries about retaliation from a lazy ass nigger with the truest nigger mentality I've *ever* known. And I'm a street dude. My pops schooled me on what to look for, from Jake. He was *so* on point."

Big Al says, "In two days, it will be eighteen years since one of my strongest brothers left this world. Old man Jake is eighteen years in debt to this crew. We're having our crew male bonding meeting, on Tuesday afternoon. That get together is all about big Paul. Your father is sorely missed, Chill. I wanna make sure you know that. I don't know if you really realize how much my generation truly misses your pops."

"I know," Chill says in a almost whisper, "I know. I really do."

"He's proud of you, Chill," big Al says suddenly. "I know that, for a fact. Everything he wanted you to achieve. You *have*. And you have done even more than what he wanted to you to do. Lil Kenny and all of the males will be here for big Paul's remembrance. Lil Kenny is one of the four grooms bringing it home, in a little over two weeks. So you know he's gotta get his *final* preparations for that big wedding. It's only *sixteen* days away. Jb, Rob and the men from Atlanta are coming for this big Paul event too. That includes Ron and his sons. It's *major* for our second generation of this crew, Chill. Paul was a very *huge* part of our generation's progression. And his father Paul Senior was the man who laid it down, along with the father's before my generation. I wanna make sure his only grandson knows that. Because he will make sure it stays in check, with *his* generation."

Chill says, "I agree that my pops and grandpa was huge to the crew. I can surely tell because y'all honor him *every* year, on the date he passed away. I appreciate that more than I can ever put into words. Me and Kenny talk about it *often*. He remembers pop. He was four when daddy passed away but he remembers him. Which makes it a little bearable. But I will always miss my pops. Being without him, is what made me remain on the correct crew path. Because I would never wanna leave Kenny or Destiny without their pops. Nor my love, Renee. So I'm just honored that the crew hold my father in such a high place. It means everything."

"The honor is all ours," big Al says, "We'll be at your spot by noon, on Tuesday. You don't bring *any* supplies. We got it all on the way."

They both chuckle before big Al says, "The foursome girls got that other play active, this morning, right?"

"Yes indeed," Chill says, "Renee told me right before you called. Nina and T-baby getting Michelle into her *true* crew form. And I know you already know Ajay is leaving free game tickets for the underhand's, right?"

"Yep," big Al says and chuckles. He adds, "Pulling all the strings, at once. So we can free the world of all of the bullshit that we know of."

"Bullshit which was actually created because none of those less than nothing's, could *ever* be crew worthy," Chill says as he pulls up to Al and Jo's house.

"Amen!" big Al yells and laughs.

Then Chill says, "So I guess we'd better get prepared so we can head to Quicken Loans Arena, ha?"

"Hell yeah," big Al says, "We get to miss church and watch my son ball. Gotta be the start of great week."

They both laugh hard. Then they give each other a high five and say so long. Big Al heads inside of his house. Chill drives on to Jackson Heights to pick up his family for the game.

Quicken Loans Arena

The Cavaliers won against the Phoenix Suns today. There wasn't going to be any hanging out for Ajay and Ebony. Because the Cavaliers have a flight to Charlotte, North Carolina tonight. That game is tomorrow night. Then the Cavaliers will return on the following day, just in time for Ajay and Jarvis to attend the male meeting in honor of big Paul.

Jarvis left Wheeler with pay and instructions to file his divorce papers while he's in Charlotte. Wheeler's office will handle that, for sure. Wheeler also has a meeting with the Ohio state parole board, on behalf of Angel Taylor.

Ajay and Ebony head home with their 5 daughters while Lil Ajay gets up with his crew. But this game night isn't over, for the crew's *special guest* of tonight's game.

Michelle, Arthur and Tameka are heading straight to *Stoney's Bar & Grill* for some hang time. Before leaving Quicken Loans Arena, Michelle invited Alana, Farah, Darlene, Olivia, Jaylisa, and Rioshauna to meet them there and the 6 *thangs* accepted. Nina, Rebbie and T-baby wanted to attend the hang out, so bad. But big Al and big John both told them, "Absolutely not." The fathers know it's *much* too early for that kind of a stretch.

Besides, they don't want any of the thangs to do or say something, which would get their asses kicked by the *foursome*. Because that would put this chamber move on hold again, *indefinitely*.

Arthur, Michelle and Tameka arrive at Stoney's, first. They head inside and reserve a large crew section. Within minutes, Alana and the rest arrive. They come into Stoney's all giddy and hyped up. Arthur signals for them to come on over to the booth and be seated. They do. Arthur takes down all of their food orders. He turns the order in to big Al and big John, who have arrived from the game and taken lead.

"We always got the night shift," big John says to Arthur.

"That's when it all adds up or ends for good," big Al adds as all 3 men laugh.

Arthur says, "Well my part is done, for now. I'm off to regular duties. But first. I've gotta get a picture of Michelle and Tameka with the fish, they're about to pull in."

"Dinner this summer," big John says while chuckling.

Big Al adds, "Bon a petit!"

They all chuckle as Arthur heads back over to the booth where his pregnant wife Michelle and Tameka are seated with Alana, Farah, Darlene, Olivia, Jaylisa and Rioshauna.

He says, "Okay. I got y'all orders in. I'm off to the photo booths but I wanna get a shot of all of y'all before I head out."

"Pose, ladies," Michelle says and smiles.

Arthur takes a couple of angle shots of them. He gives Michelle a sweet kiss. Then he winks his eye at Tameka. She knows that means, *she's* on. That's when Arthur heads off to get the clubs open and running. Michelle and Tameka are staying behind for some serious talk with Alana and her posse. Arthur had stressed to Tameka that she is the glue. Now it's time for her to show her stuff. Tameka knows what her best angle will be in this group. She sets in immediately.

"Alana," Tameka says, "What have you been up to?"

"Working at *The Juice*, as you know," Alana says, "I'm a fulltime mother now. This is Olivia."

"Hi," Olivia says.

"Hey Olivia," Tameka says, "I haven't seen you since you was a baby."

Olivia says, "I'll be sixteen in two weeks. I'm having my party at the spot two. How cool is *that*?!"

"That's awesome," Tameka says. She knows she has to play this up

big. She adds, "Anything the crew takes part in. Is gonna be the best. And it will be the talk of the town, for *weeks*."

"I believe you," Olivia says, "It's already the talk around school. Everybody wants to make sure they can get in. I'm feel like a superstar at MLK. It's all I've wanted since I got here."

"And it's on and *poppin* now!" Alana says, "That made my day when junior and Chill called me and told me. The crew was gonna host her birthday party. I damn near cried."

Farah cuts in and says, "She did cry. She was so happy and emotional. I'm so happy for her and Libby too."

They all laugh. Then Michelle asks, "Olivia, are you gonna introduce us to your friends? Are they coming to your party?"

"This is Jaylisa and Rioshauna," Olivia says, "I call em Jay and Rio. They'll be there, *fasho*. We had our disagreements, for a minute. But that's all been cleared up. Thanks to Ajay."

"Not father Ajay," Darlene cuts in. She adds, "Be *clear*. She is talking about *Lil* Ajay."

Farah says, "But I'm hearing he's like big Ajay, in younger years."

"There have never been *younger* years for father Ajay," Darlene says. "He has *always* been mature. I'm sure his son is from that same tree."

"From the same tree? *My* tree," big Al says and chuckles as he startles Darlene, Alana and Farah instantly.

They didn't see him walking over to their booth. Michelle and Tameka did. They just smile. Tameka breaks the quick silence.

She says, "Hey pops Al. How are you today?"

"I'm very well, Tameka," he says, "Just like you and Michelle. I see you two ladies got a crew booth *full*, over here."

"Yes we do," Michelle says, "And our Cav's won today. So we had to get some crew food in us. Before we head over to the party spots to celebrate it all off."

They all agree and laugh.

Big Al says, "I just wanted to assist Corey and Bobby with getting your food over here. Before I heard speaking on my son and my grandson. *My* tree limbs. I just wanted to make sure she knows what tree she's speaking on. So she'll speak accurately. Y'all enjoy and have a safe night."

Big Al walks off and goes back behind the counter. Big John gives him a fist bump. He didn't hear the conversation. But he saw the look on big Al's face as he was returning. It was a *"I caught that hand-off speaking on my son"* look.

"Crew men are always the talk of the town," big John says and chuckles.

Big Al chuckles with him and resumes their duties, as they prepare for the customers who are arriving.

Back at Michelle and Tameka's booth, the conversation is stalled momentarily. Darlene is worried that she angered big Al. *Ajay's father.* She remembers how she first met big Al, back in the day. When she was a substitute teacher. Michelle and Tameka know all about those days, by now. Michelle has to let Darlene off the hook so they can continue with their move, of hooking them all over again.

Michelle says, "You can breathe, Darlene. Pops Al wasn't fussing at you. He was just stating a fact. You *do* know that's Ajay's daddy and I know you do. He just heard what you said and corrected you. That's all. *Relax.*"

"I don't wanna make *him* mad," Darlene says is a whisper. She adds, "That's the *last* thing I would wanna do."

Tameka says, "Like Michelle said. He wasn't fussing. He heard his son's name and made sure you act like you know that it was *his* tree, that you was speaking on. You can't act like you didn't know Ajay's daddy before you knew Ajay. Keep it real, Darlene."

With that, Tameka and Michelle crack up laughing. Which eases the tension for Darlene. She has to smile.

Then Michelle has to get on to the real work. She says, "Alana, did you know I added my name to Angel's visitors list?"

"No," Alana says, "I never thought you would."

"Why not?" Michelle says, "I was there when it all went down. I never hated either one of you. Know that. I just don't believe in physically hurting anyone and getting away with it. Especially when they didn't do anything to you. Do you feel me?"

"I do. I agree with you on that," Darlene says as she cuts in.

Alana says, "I feel you and I agree with you too."

"But justice was served," Michelle says, "And Angel is almost done with her time. I have no beef with Angel and none of you should either. I want to make sure, all of y'all know. I don't have any. None whatsoever."

"And I don't either," Tameka adds. "Angel fell in love with a man who was never gonna be hers. We know that side of this too. If she hadn't did what she did. We all could've still been friends *and* friends with the crew too. I'm adding my name to her list, this week. Ebony's big mama told me to do it. So now. Do y'all see how real these people are? It's not just about the good dick you can get or got. They are *black pride*, for real."

"Amen," Michelle says, "But the dick is good too, *now*. Arthur is *all* good! Now let's eat and enjoy this rekindling time. We use to party like the best of them. Farah came along after Tameka and me. But Darlene was here from jump. She knows us and how we get down on the dance floor. Jaylisa is Angel's half sister. Rio is her and Olivia's friend. They're gonna have to learn from us. It's time for us, the older ladies, to be the best examples. See what I'm saying? I'm about to be a mother, myself."

"I *knew* it," Alana says, "I got word about it, at work. I get all the good info, now that I work for the crew. You look great and you're still not really showing yet."

Michelle says, "I feel pregnant though. I might now look it. But I feel it."

"You look great," Farah adds.

"Thank you," Michelle says, "I'm looking forward to being a mom. I really am. Alana is going to be an example for me now. She's been a mother for almost sixteen years."

Alana says, "I'm wit it. I'll do whatever I can. I had to learn how to do it, the right way. But I finally caught on. I have to admit. Working for the crew helps me to learn how to set better examples for Libby. I'm so glad I got the job I have. The crew elders make sure I know what I need to do. It's really cool."

"That's how crew gets down, Alana," Tameka says and smiles. She adds, "They are all about togetherness. But you have to be respectful to them, to get *their* respect. Be respectful of what or who they have and are with. Me and Michelle learned that and now look. They have *our* backs."

"But Arthur's got my front too," Michelle chirps in and they all crack up laughing again.

Then Alana turns to Tameka.

She says, "I've *really* missed you and Michelle."

"So are you ready to fix that?" Tameka asks, startling Alana.

Alana has to answer and she does.

Teary eyed, she says, "I am. I really am."

"Cool," Tameka says, "Then we'll get that done too. Now! Give me a hug. Then let's grub, so we can go get our party on."

Tameka and Alana stand up and give each other a hug. They're all giggles from there, as they dig into their plates. They keep the conversations going.

It's the goal of Michelle and Tameka to get this group of ladies comfortable, trusting and talking. The crew wants to know everything about *their* plans, as far as the crew are concerned. And the plans of anyone else they know and have access to, who are trying to get *near* the crew. And

also, how far these *thangs* are willing to go to get crew respect. Michelle and Tameka were told to find out how far these 6 thangs would go, to get crew time and attention. Tameka has already vowed to the 1st generation that she will go as far as needed, to get reciprocity for them. For Michelle, it goes much deeper than that. She has a vested interest. She's carrying a crew seed. Plus she's been itching to get even with Angel *and* Alana. It's because of *their* actions and her being around them, in the early days, that she had such a difficult time getting Arthur and the crew's trust and admittance. Being able to become Arthur's 1 and only, took even more proving. Simple because of her being around *thangs,* from the start. Tameka and Michelle are *in it to win it* now and already off to a great start too. Al and John looks on and grades them. In the last 9 years both Michelle and Tameka learned that *crew style* is a great way to move forward.

The next to walk through the doors of *Stoney's Bar & Grill,* brings a smile to the faces of Olivia, Rioshaunda and Jaylisa. It's a group of young men. Young *crew* men. Lil Ajay has just walked in with Brad III, Alan Anthony, Rich III plus Kilo Jr, who is KeJuan's son. He's in town for the private male event which is being held in 2 days, in honor of Paul Payne, Jr. Arthur's son DeMarcus is with them, as well. These 6 young crew men walk in and head straight to the counter to speak to big John and big Al.

With a cool smile, Lil Ajay asks, "What's up with my two *big* pops?"

"Looks like *you're* what's up, Lil Ajay," big John says with a chuckle. He adds, "You got the attention of all *three* of those young girls over there in that crew booth, from the time you walked in the door."

"For *real*, John," big Al says. Then turning to Lil Ajay and while chuckling, he adds, "He's right, Lil Ajay. Now, we're your *grandfathers*. You've gotta put us on, man. Tell us old men, what's up."

Lil Ajay laughs and says, "It's just crew life. It ain't me. I didn't start this whole thing. I got it from y'all. I was born into it and y'all laid it out for all of us. I gotta say thank you and thank the *lord* because I'm honored."

They all laugh more.

Then big John looks at big Al and says, "Okay, Al. So he's got that part right."

"Amen," big Al responds as all 8 of them share a laugh.

Big John asks, "What's on, for this Sunday afternoon?"

"Not much," Brad III says, "We *might* have an early run."

Rich III adds, "But other than that. We just gonna kick back and chill."

"They gotta get my feet wet," Kilo Jr says. "They said they had to school me. And I'm *so* ready."

DeMarcus adds, "And I do believe your feet wetting time is gonna happen *soon*, Kilo. Because I see three prospects."

"We'll see what we can do for you, Kilo," Brad III says. "We gotta bring you in *correctly*. That's Fasho." Then turning to Lil Ajay, he says, "You wanna work something for our newest brother?"

"I don't see why not," Lil Ajay says. He adds, "But let's get our own booth and see what they do on their own, first. I'm not going to that booth and request them. Not *even*."

Big John and big Al snicker and give each other a pound. Then big Al says, "Y'all go grab a table. We already got some grub cooking for y'all."

"Yea," big John says, "We know what y'all favorite foods are and we already got it going. Go on and take a load off. See ya."

"In a minute," All 6 say in unison.

They head over to their reserved booth which is against the far back wall. Olivia, Jaylisa and Rioshauna have been watching them, the *entire* time. Lil Ajay and the guys know it's only a matter of time before the 3 youngest thangs, make their way over to their booth.

Michelle, Tameka and the 6 thangs have finished their food and are preparing to head out.

"I'm full as a tick," Darlene says as they all laugh.

Farah says, "I am too. The food here *and* at the Crew's House restaurant is always *so* good.

"It is indeed," Alana says, "Ladies and my long lost buddies. Let's head home and get dressed for tonight. It's time to get our groove on again. Tameka and Michelle. What time are y'all hitting up the chill spot?"

"Eleven o'clock," Michelle says, "I'll be working too."

Tameka says, "I'll be there to party. I'll look for y'all when I get in there. Cool?"

"Cool," Alana says and smiles. Then she turns to Olivia.

She says, "Libby, let's go home and get dressed. We can all come back together. We just *ate*, crew style. So it's time to *party* crew style now."

Olivia says, "Me, Rio and Jay wanna stay and hang out."

"Yes we do," Rioshauna says, "Lil Ajay is here. I wanna go see what he's got going on."

Jaylisa adds, "That's the business, right there. We're going over to their booth and see what they got going on."

"Mama can y'all bring us some changing clothes, if they don't have a way to get us home?" Olivia asks.

"My daddy will make sure we all get changed," Jaylisa says. "He'll

get us to our houses to change our clothes and then bring us back to the spot two."

"That's the business," Olivia says, "Its crew style at the booth in the back. That's where we're about to be. We'll check in with y'all later."

With that, Olivia, Rioshauna and Jaylisa head toward the back booth which holds the 6 crew guys. Alana, Farah and Darlene leaves a tip and head on out to Farah's car. Michelle and Tameka walk out with them.

Alana says, "I really enjoyed this time. I can't wait to see y'all later. Y'all made my day."

"*Our* day," Farah says, "I appreciate the gesture, indeed. I wanna thank both of you. It means a lot to all of us."

Darlene says, "The young ones too. Even though their attention was taken as soon as that young crew stepped in the building."

They all laugh.

Michelle closes with, "It's all good. That's that crew magnet. We'll catch up later. I've gotta get to Arthur and see what he needs. before I head home to change."

"We'll catch up later," Tameka says, "I'm riding with Michelle. And don't forget to meet Michelle at Crew's House for dinner, on Friday. I'll be working. So I'll make sure y'all are seated in my section."

"Will do," Alana says.

Then they all say goodbye as Farah, Darlene and Alana pull away. Michelle looks at Tameka and says, "Great job. Friday is on schedule. Arthur will let us know if there's anything in *particular* that we need to bring up in that meeting. I'm proud of you."

"Thanks," Tameka says, "It's my pleasure. Let's go see what your husband needs for his studios tonight. Then we can go get dressed and get back up here, geared up for part two."

They laugh as they head over to Que Psi Phi pictures and video store.

Chill's Office, Saturday 2/4/2006

Today is Angel's call day. It's been set up since Sunday, when she'd called back hoping to talk to Lil Ajay. Ajay and Lil Ajay are here today. Ajay, Chill and Lil Ajay discuss the events of this past week, while waiting.

"That memorial for your pops, mom and grandparents was off the chain," Ajay says to Chill. "It takes me back, *every* year."

"The crew give em *mad* props, Ajay," Chill says. "If I could put it into words, I would. But I can't. I never can. It's just love. *Pure* love."

Lil Ajay says, "Both of my papa's miss your pops, *real* bad. They told me they was like brothers. I see you and my pops, the same way."

Ajay says, "We are, son. Know that."

Chill adds, "Truth." Then switching gears, Chill says, "Arthur's got that boat sailing with Michelle and Tameka."

"We discussed it at the memorial, the other day," Ajay says, "I just want them to make sure and pull it all the way together. I already told you, Chill. All them ho's can go to the chamber. I wouldn't give a fuck."

Lil Ajay says, "Me either."

"It's doable," Chill says, "If they get one peep about what the crew plan is and something gets out or in the wrong hands. Then they're gonna have to go down too. Period."

Then they discuss the newest move on Old Jake Johnson, Sr.

Chill says, "Our first generation got a damn good plan on getting to Old Jake. I'm sure you heard about the move they discussed at the memorial. It's *platinum*."

"Misses Ida Mae Graves," Ajay says with a pleasant smile. "She's gonna be the bait. From day one, we all remember that the females in the first generation saw her as good company for papa Brown. But my father-in-law and big Greg wasn't comfortable with that move. Not at first."

"But papa Brown is the *only* one who could make that decision," Chill says with a chuckle.

"Amen," Ajay says, "Now, he didn't *move* her in or nothing like that. But he said she could be his female companion, from time to time."

Still chuckling, Chill says, "And that's all she wrote. Because nobody else has any type of priority on what papa Brown decides or wants to do with his private life. If he wants female company. I don't have a problem with it. Neither does anybody else in our generation of crew. His dues are long paid, as for as our crew goes."

Ajay agrees saying, "Indeed. That's why we got her that spot in Parma."

"Papa Brown wanted to keep misses Ida Mae at a comfortable distance," Chill continues, "And that turned out to be another of many, smart ass moves on his part. As of the last 3 months, Misses Ida Mae has been going after Old Jake, for companionship. That shit is working fine."

"Dating?" Lil Ajay asks.

"Yea son," Ajay says, "Companionship is the best way to put it. Because she's not going to go any farther than papa Brown instructs her to go."

"That's smooth for an old dude," Lil Ajay says and chuckles.

Chill says, "I'm glad you see it that way, Lil Ajay. Because those are your roots. That's part of where you got your intelligence from. Using things for the best outcome and only having a female in your life, for the betterment of you. Me and your pops learned from papa Brown's generation. So you're blessed to still have him around to make sure you're being guided the correct way."

"Yes sir" Lil Ajay says, "He knows *so* much stuff. Whenever we get together, I don't even say a whole lot. I just spend that whole time listening to him and poppa Jones talk. They know *everything*."

Chills says, "The two of them and their generation have put together *nothing* but winning plans. Plans which improved things for our entire crew family. All generations since theirs."

"And your grandparents was apart of that bringing in the wins too, Chill." Ajay says.

"Oh, fasho," Chill agrees and chuckles. "And putting Old Jake to rest is the ultimate move forward, for *all* of us."

Ajay adds, "And papa Brown's new plan will go down in crew history. He's going all out on this one. Him, Poppa Jones, Logan and Wilson. They knew how to get to Jake. Send him some hope of getting pussy."

"Better than what any of us could've come up with," Chill says.

"I'm just glad I'm in *this* family," Lil Ajay says.

"We're all glad you're in this family too, Lil Ajay," Chill says and gives him a pound.

Ajay smiles proudly as he looks at his son. He's ready to introduce some additional leverage to help pull Old Jake Johnson in. Leverage from the *sexual* side. Because he knows Mrs. Ida Mae Graves would never be romantically involved with anyone. Only papa Brown would have that option and only if he wants it.

Then Ajay says, "Chill, I got an idea to bring in some younger women to cloud Old Jake's judgment from the sexual side. And pull his younger fleet in. I mentioned it, awhile back."

Ajay and Lil Ajay have had this conversation already. Lil Ajay knows exactly where his father's conversation is headed.

He steps in and asks, "Can I tell him about this part, pops?"

Ajay shakes his head affirmative.

Then Lil Ajay says, "Uncle Chill, I know you remember Nicole and Angie from back in the day. Right? They use to do *anything* my pops wanted them to do."

"Hell yea," Chill says and chuckles, "I remember them ho's."

"Pops still got them on a long leash," Lil Ajay says and laughs. Then he adds, "He got with Dre and Joe and told them, he wanted them to pull the two of them back onboard. And just so you know. Pops already cleared it with my mama."

They all laugh at that comment. But Chill already knew Ajay would *never* make a move toward *any* female from his past. Without making sure his wife and his future, Ebony approved of it *first*.

"They been outta the loop with crew for a decade," Ajay says as he chuckles. "Really they never was *in*. Not publicly. So Old Jake's posse wouldn't have a clue that they would be moving on crews behalf."

Chill says, "We can shine them on Draper. Let's start there. So we can keep his attention elsewhere, when its convenient. But we have to make sure they are *well* schooled before we move on *any* route with them."

"I'll have em all the way down," Ajay says and chuckles. Then he adds, "Ebony has already said it'll be okay."

Lil Ajay asks, "But Pops, what if the *only* reward they want is some of you? How are you gonna handle that?"

Ajay chuckles and asks, "What makes you think they'll try that, son?"

"Cause that's how ho's do it," Lil Ajay says with a chuckle of his own. He adds, "Like them three, from Sunday night. I'll just say we got Lil Kilo, *crew* baptized real good out at the condo. But I had to start em off. I knew them thangs was gonna want me to participate. So I had to break em down. After that. They did whatever I wanted them to do. So long as I kept acting like I was feeling them."

Ajay and Chill give each other and Lil Ajay a pound, on that statement. They're both familiar with that action. They all chuckle before getting back to the discussions. But Lil Ajay still wants an answer to the question he asked Ajay.

"So what if they want you to fuck em, pops?" Lil Ajay asks again. "You didn't give me no answer."

Ajay answers, "This dick belongs to Ebony Brown-Jackson. I'm sure you know that. Right son?"

Lil Ajay laughs and says, "I know it."

That's when Ajay says, "Then Angie and Nicole would have to fuck you, if they want some Ajay."

Lil Ajay laughs. Then he asks, "How do they look and how fine are they?"

Ajay and Chill crack up laughing. That makes Lil Ajay laugh too.

Then Lil Ajay says, "We'll deal wit it, pops. So long as they know they ain't getting nothing they can keep. Nor *nothing* that belongs to my mama."

"True that, son," Ajay says, "And *any* thangs that have ever been in my personal space. Knows that shit and they knew it, way back then too. Now since I made it to the NBA. The motherfuckin *world* can tell you who this dick belongs too. So we can move on along with this discussion. I'm well owned and damn proud of it."

While chuckling, Chill says, "Misses Jessie Mae has already made contact with Misses Ida Mae. They're moving forward on that Old Jake Johnson situation. Now if Draper takes interest in Nicole and Angie. We're gonna shower them with helpful funds and make sure they got ducks to spend. Just to reel him in."

"They're older than Draper too, son," Ajay says and laughs, as he looks at Lil Ajay. Then he adds, "So Draper *will* be wit it. These thangs got history on that Westside already. Angie and Nicole has history with his baby mama's dead ass cousin, who's name was Jake the third. *And* his friend Greg Harrison, who is a dead ass too."

"They're two of the three, who killed big Stoney. Right pops?" Lil Ajay asks.

"Correct," Ajay says. Then turning to Chill, Ajay says, "Chill I wanna get rid of that other bitch too. While we're doing this addition phase."

"Katrina Dobbs," Chill says instantly. Then he adds, "I already know you do and so do I. I'll just put it like this. It's on the table, Ajay. And I give you my word on that. But we're going after Old Jake and Angel, first and foremost. We can put Pac Man, Woody, Dre and Joe on that Katrina issue. Once the main targets are set in motion and rolling smoothly."

"Cool," Ajay says, "So long as I don't have to deal with her ass, in the future. The shit she pulled on me. Left me feeling off key and played, for a long damn time. I don't like that vulnerable feeling I *still* get when that bitch is present."

"I know, bro," Chill says, "And we *will* erase it, in due time. Me and Renee had this same talk with junior and Tonya. Lynn and JB was in on it too. We just talked about that bitch while we was all at the memorial. So don't think we don't know she needs to go. JB said that it's taking *everything* he has to keep Lynn from taking her ass out. Just on gee pee!"

They all chuckle. Lil Ajay likes that a lot and he has to have his point made too.

He says, "That's my big auntie, right there. She don't take shit off nobody. She's not gonna *ever* be okay wit what that ho did to my pops. Auntie Lynn ain't gonna ever be okay with *no* bitch messing with my pops *or* my mama

either. She told me about that during the same time when pops told my mama about it. It happened on that night we was all out at our house, having a party, pops. And that ho Katrina was there too. Auntie Lynn told me about it and she said, the only reason she was telling me. Was because she knew I was already smart enough to understand what she was talking about. And I was gonna be three years old in six weeks."

"And you remember it too," Chill says, "Don't you, Lil Ajay?"

"I do," Lil Ajay says with a very serious expression.

Chill adds, "Well I'm not surprised. You've got every side of those Jackson membranes."

They all laugh again. Right about then, is when the phone starts ringing. Chill looks at the caller ID. Then he looks at Ajay. He doesn't have to say a word.

"I know," Ajay says, "And if I gotta pretend to be forgiving of her ass, right now. Then you'd better let my son handle this call. Because right now. He's got the best game for that devil."

Chill smiles as he answers the phone and waits for the recording to play.

Once Angel is on the phone, he informs her that both Ajay and Lil Ajay are present. But Lil Ajay wants this call.

Angel says, "Okay! I'm just fine with that. He's my friend. Please put him on. I've missed him, so much. *Already*."

Lil Ajay takes the phone and the conversation begins.

CHAPTER 70

THE LEGACY LIVES ON

The return of Angela Graves and Nicole Griffin

Today is February 6, 2006! Much has been accomplished by the crew, in the last couple of days.

Lil Ajay completed his call with Angel in true crew fashion. He let her know that him and his pops had signed up for her visitors list. Along with Julie Von Reese and big Chill. Though Julie Von Reese will be the only one visiting her, within the week. He didn't tell her that part. What he did tell her was, he had no idea when or *if*, him or his father will get to visit her. Because his mother will be the 1 who will make that call. Angel said she understood. While Lil Ajay let her know, he didn't care if she understood or not.

She just giggled and told him, "You sure are *Lil* Ajay,"

That comment was said by her, before the call ended.

After that call, Lil Ajay had turned to his pops and said,

"She knew you, back then. Before she almost killed my mama and before she *did* kill by big sister. She just let me know all of that, in her last reply."

Ajay, Chill and Lil Ajay wrapped up their talk and went on about their day.

Mrs. Jessie Mae Johnson-Baker and Mrs. Ida Mae Graves have moved into stage 2 with Old Jake. Last night, Ida Mae had a dinner date with Old Jake at the Cleveland Marriott, out by the airport. Old Jake requested that they spend even more time with each other. They have another date planned for tomorrow night. Where Old Jake will come to Ida Mae's Parma home for dinner. Ida Mae lives in a home which the crew provided for her, a few years back. She lives in Parma, just as Farah and them do. Farah, Alana and Darlene live in north Parma. Ida Mae lives on Westlake avenue on the south side of Parma. Which is only 8.2 miles from 1357 Warren Road in Lakewood, where *Old Jake resides*.

Jessie Mae set eyes on her older brother, last night. She had to see what he looked like, after 51 years. Jessie Mae got married to Jeb Baker, Jr in 1954 when she was 17 and Jeb was 18 years old. They moved to Europe just before their birthdays in 1955. Jessie Mae is 68 years old now, 2 years younger than her brother, Old Jake. In Jessie Mae's opinion, Old Jake truly looks his age. *Old*. After last night's dinner date was over. Ida Mae and Jessie Mae met up and talked until way past midnight.

"He looks every bit of seventy and then some," Jessie Mae had said to Ida Mae.

"He does look his age," Ida Mae said and giggled. She added, "But you don't, Jessie. You don't look a day over forty."

"I suppose it's because I didn't stick around for all the bullshit, he setup and chose to live through," Jessie Mae had said.

"And it's been *decades* of him keeping up bullshit too," Ida Mae had said. "I've known Jackson Brown junior for more than three decades. And Jake has kept up *some* kind of bullshit during the entire time I've known him and the crew."

"Jackson Brown and this crew are some go-getters, as I'm sure you know by now," Jessie Mae said, "They didn't steal their mentalities neither. They inherited it. My husband's father had their backs, all the way. He had me and Jeb junior's back too. But Jake didn't. My own brother disowned me for dating a white man. It was straight out embarrassing for me, more than hurt or anything else. To have my *black* brother side with the bigots and my *white* father-in-law side with the blacks."

"Old Jake is *definitely* on that Willie Lynch side of black," Ida Mae said. "I've heard all about him and even lived through some of his bullshit with the crew, as I've already made you aware of. And trust me. Jackson Brown's wife Pearline and the crew women, *her* age, kept me informed from day one. So I'm very aware of your brother's actions. And I'm more than willing to assist Jackson with pulling his card. I'm black, *all* the damn time. *Fully* black. There is no way I could ever have real feelings for a male, like your brother. So it makes me feel even stronger just knowing that his sister is right here by my side, in this plan."

"I am," Jessie Mae said, "And I'll be here. We got the same middle name, sister. That means that all we needed was a plan to get to first base. A start. And the crew put that in motion for us. They did it very *well*. That's a natural thing for them. But now we're in the middle of this action. *Second* base. And it's flowing smoother than Lake Erie."

"And we shall see this thing all the way through to home plate," Ida Mae had said and they both giggled awhile before they headed home for bedtime.

Rebbie and June are still, just moving around each other in their home. Jarvis' divorce from Gwen was filed by Attorney Wheeler's office, 8 days ago and Gwen has been served. Jarvis and Gwen's married will end as soon as Gwen ceases with the false allegations and desperation attempts to

change Jarvis' mind. That will *not* happen. Big June's boat is on the same lake as Gwen's boat sits. Except June still hasn't been told. And he won't be. Not until about 10 days from today. Rebbie and June's communication level is still at a minimum. While Rebbie and Jarvis still talk, at least once per day. They talk in person, if the Cavaliers aren't on the road. And by phone, when the team *is* on the road. But tonight, the Cavaliers have a home game against the *Milwaukee Bucks*. All of the crew will be there as usual. And you can count Rebbie in that number of crew who will attend. Jeb Jr and Albert Jackson will be there too. While Jessie Mae and Ida Mae will remain on their Old Jake stroll. But the crew also have some more out-of-town guest coming in, prior to tonight's game.

Ebony's longtime Houston friends Yolanda and David are now apart of the Atlanta crew and married too. They will be arriving within the hour, along with Charles, who was April's man. Charles is still single and *still* missing April, both being alive and in his life. But for the crew, he's bringing along a relative of April's whom the crew met while they visited in Houston and have been longing to see again.

Cassandra "Black" Pittman of Gulfport Mississippi is on that Cleveland bound flight too. It will be touching down, *very* soon. They'll land in the city of Cleveland in time to have brunch at *Crew's House of Soul Food*. And they will certainly be attending Ajay's home game tonight. They are just 4 of Ajay's, *first time NBA game* guest. There will be 2 more.

Angela Graves and Nicole Griffin aka Angie and Nicole, from Ajay's high school days, will be at the game as well. These 2 females came into the crew picture, awhile back. Before the crew went *completely* legit. Angie was a stash girl from the Westside, who was sexually introduced into the crew by Jr. Back when Tonya had taken her final trip to visit her maternal family in Detroit. Angie was *well* deleted out of Jr's memory before Tonya returned. But Angie enjoyed that night with the crew, so much. She wanted more. She could still attend the crew parties but not as Jr's date. It wasn't going to happen with Jr, anymore and she had to accept that. So after Angie's 1 night stand with Jr. And her desire to still attend their parties in the future but not alone. She decided to find a partner to attend with her. That's when Nicole came in play. Angie had already turned her sights toward Ajay, after she laid eyes on him, 1 night at Jb's 16th birthday party. That made her deletion more convenient for Jr and the crew, as a whole. Because the crew knew Ajay wasn't going to keep Angie. Nor any other woman in his life. Not for the long haul. The crew knew Ajay was wise enough to let any outside female know, she would only be in his

presence when it was convenient for him. Because Ebony Brown was the only girl who could have his undivided attention. Both Angie and Nicole accepted and respected that rule, from day 1. The most memorable and important thing about them to Ajay, was when they came through with funds to get him to Houston to care for Ebony, after the Raymond White attack. They will certainly be Ajay's guest at tonight's game. Because Ajay has a new mission which he wants them to be apart of. Angie and Nicole has received the news and they are both *very* excited.

Dre, Joe and Pac Man made the connection with Nicole and Angie, Ajay's *thangs* from back in the day. And Nicole and Angie are more than ready to meet back up with Ajay, after all of these years.

"I've been trying to run into Ajay for a decade or more," Nicole says as she giggles. She adds, "So just to know that *he* asked you to look for us. Tells me there's a mission at hand. That only the *N* and the *A* can handle. And I have to admit. This request to be in Ajay's company again, made my damn day!"

"Mine too," Angie chimes in, "I thought Dre was on some bullshit, at first. When he told me *Ajay* wanted us to meet up. I thought he was fucking with my mind. I said *nigger* please. But then, he had that same look on his face then, that he has right now. So Nicole, that's why I told you we need to bring our asses on out here *today*."

"And be about the business that Ajay brings to you," Dre says. "If you become a problem. You will be dismissed and sent back into the abyss, as far as Ajay goes. Are we clear?"

"Yes," They both chime in.

Dre and Joe have just arrived at *CrewLand* mall and brought Angie and Nicole with them. Dre parks his Pathfinder near *Stoney's Bar & Grill*.

From his passenger seat, Joe turns to face Angie and Nicole, who are seated in the back.

He says, "Y'all remember the points we made from day one. Speak only when you're spoken to. When it comes to *any* crew member. Any generation of the crew, at that. Ajay will give y'all the details about why he requested us to bring y'all back into his life. But if you do something fucked up and sit wrong with *any* member of his crew. He will dismiss y'all asses, on *that* day. Now, Dre wants to add to this. So listen."

Dre adds, "Ajay is a happily married man, *these* days and the father of six. *That's* his priority. His only son is the oldest child. So he'll attend some of whatever meetings y'all have with Ajay. And Lil Ajay will be a *big* part of whatever the plan is that Ajay has on the table for y'all. If neither of them

mention being personal with y'all. Y'all will not mention it to them. Am I clear?"

"Very clear," Angie says, "But I pray that he mentions it."

Nicole adds, "Even if it's just for one time. For old times sake. I knew it was something *so* different about Ajay, way back then."

Angie adds, "He was always *royal* like. He didn't start shit. Unless you came wrong toward him or his crew. He didn't take shit off nobody either. I knew he would be with the very girl that he's still with today. No shock there. I just hope he'll give me another shot at feeling him. For old times sake or for whatever sake he wants to call it."

She giggles.

Dre says, "Then make sure Ajay is the one who mentions it. Clear?"

"Clear," Angie and Nicole say in unison.

Joe says, "Cool. Let's head inside Stoney's."

They all climb out of the Pathfinder. Both ladies giggle as they head into Stoney's Bar & Grill. Dre leads them in and has them to sit at the counter, on barstools. Big Al and big John speak to them and welcomes them both.

"Good morning, Angie and Nicole," big Al says, as they both speak back. Then Angie adds, "You're Ajay's father, right?"

"I am," big Al says.

"He looks just like you," Nicole says.

Big Al says, "But he's taller."

Big John chuckles, then says, "Good morning, Angie and Nicole. Welcome to Stoney's bar and grill. Would you ladies like something to eat? We don't cook this early but we'll get some food brought over from the restaurant. It's on the house today."

"Sure," Angie says, "Thank you, so much."

Big Al place menus in front of Angie and Nicole. While Corey sets up their places with silverware and ice water, then he phones *Crew's House*.

Big Al says, "Check out the menu and let Corey know what you'd like. He'll take care of you from there. He's Ajay's first cousin on his mother's side, by the way. So you two will be well taken care of. Enjoy your time at Stoney's and welcome."

With that, big Al returns to the back for his regular duties. Nicole and Angie decide what they want to eat and place their orders with Corey.

Joe and Dre are at the other end of the counter. Dre is making contact with Chill to let him know, Angie and Nicole are in place.

Chill says, "That's cool. Ajay and Lil Ajay are still in the territory. They went over by Ebony's office. I'll get at Ajay and let him know it's in play."

251

"Alright," Dre says, "Text me when y'all about to head this way."
"Cool," Chill says, "See ya."
"In a minute," Dre responds and they end the call.

Renee and Tonya have already swooped up Cassandra to roll with them during her stay in Cleveland.

"It's time to see what CrewLand has to offer," Cassandra says, "And remember crew. I want y'all to call me, *Black*. Richie Rich gave me his word, down in Houston. He's gone now, so his word is bond. Him and the crew knew then, that I'm one hundred percent black and proud of it."

"Black, it is," Tonya says with a smile as both her and Renee give Black a fist bump.
Renee says, "Black you're gonna roll with us. Our Cassah is *sue* Cassah!"
They all crack up laughing as Black responds with, "Let's get it poppin!"
All 3 of them head into Crew's House of Soul Food for a hearty breakfast.

Five minutes later, Ebony arrives with Nina, T-baby, Rebbie and Yolanda.

"What's up, Black?!!" Nina yells, "I know it's you because I've heard all about you. And it was *all good*!"

"What it do?!" Black yells back, as she give hugs to The Foursome. She adds, "Come on, Yolanda. I'll give you a hug too. Since you came in with the Awesome Foursome of CrewLand!"
They all laugh and get seated for some great conversation and excellent food.
T-baby says, "I'm glad to finally meet you. One day we're gonna get both of these Awesome Foursome clicks together and shut everything down."

"That's right," Black says, "I know the crew is gonna come to Gulfport, one of these days. And me and my sisters will make *sure* y'all have a ball. Bren, Cookie and Carrie are all doing fine. We're grown up and got *mad* responsibilities now. But y'all know the deal. We will *all*, always be as real as they fuckin come."

"True that," Rebbie says with a smile.
Tameka comes over to their tables to bring glasses of water. She speaks to everybody. Renee does the introduction of Tameka to Black.
She adds, "She's like a sister to us now, Black."

"She's all the way on the right side, then," Black says, "That's cooler than a fan. Tameka you're alright with me. You heard me? If these sisters down with you. I'm down with you too."
With a smile, Tameka says "Thanks so much. It's a pleasure to meet you.

You fit right in with these real sisters. I'm gonna go get y'all orders in."
She smiles at Black as she heads back toward the counter to turn in their food order. She sends an assistant server over to bring their beverages.

Back at the table, as their beverages are being placed in front of them, Black is still staring at Tameka. Ebony notices the stare. She smiles. Black looks at Ebony and smiles too. Then Ebony says,
"Did I notice a spark? It seems so. Tell me if I'm wrong, sister Black."
Black smiles and says, "You still don't miss a damn thang. Do you, Ajay's girl?"

"I just thought it was some attraction in y'all glances toward each other," Ebony says with a smile. She adds, "I'm definitely Anthony's girl. For life. Did I see what I thought I saw?"

"You're on it," is Black's response.
That's when Renee raises her glass of ice tea and says, "How about we do a toast for sister Black." They all raise their glasses. Renee continues, "You are our crew sister. Live your life and personal life, *however* you choose. It won't change a damn thing from our view. We are not judge nor jury. And we only execute when harm is aimed at our crew."

"Amen," Yolanda adds and they all giggle and toast.
They kick back for some great food and to catch up on conversation. That's when Black starts filling them in on a childhood friend of hers who was just killed by police officers, 2 days ago. He was killed while in the booking room of their jail, in Gulfport Mississippi. *February 4, 2006!*

"What?!" Tonya screams.

"Hell yea," Black says, "While we're all still trying to come back from the damage of hurricane Katrina. They took my homeboy in on a simple charge and now he's dead. His name was Jessie Lee Williams junior. Him and Bren, my foursome sister, grew up together in what we call *North Gulfport*. It use to be an all black neighborhood. Still is, for the most part."

"So let me get this straight," T-baby says, "Jessie wasn't already doing time? He went in the same day?"
Black says, "No he wasn't already doing time. He was taken in an *hour* before this beating shit happened. He went in for being drunk and arguing at a family function. Nothing brutal whatsoever. So basically. He was going in to sleep it off."

"So why was he beaten?" Rebbie asks.

"Because he was black," Nina interjects.

"Pretty much," Black says, "This is how it went. While Jessie was in the booking area. The pigs was making comments to him, like he was a

less than. Just jawing at him and saying what they could do to him since they had him in cuffs and custody. Jessie simply asked for a fair shot. He told them if they was gonna fight him, to take the cuffs off of him before they started the fight and give him a fair shot. Jessie was laughing when he said that shit. But from there, they went at him with full force and he was still handcuffed."

"Damn," Renee says.

Black continues, "It got a *hell* of a lot worse. They hogtied him, put a bag on his head. Filled the bag with pepper spray. Beat him some more. Kicked, punched, elbowed him. Drop kicked him. You *name* it? They did it."

"That's so fucked up," Tonya says sadly.

Black says, "Yes it is. He's dead now. At the hands of Gulfport police. And why? For being drunk at a family cookout? He was on medication and he hadn't taken his meds. That's what made him antsy at the cookout."

"And now he's dead," Ebony says, "From the hands of the police who are paid by your tax dollars. There'd better be some justice coming for Jessie."

"For real," T-baby says.

"It's being investigated by a local lawyer, I think," Yolanda says, "Right, Black?"

"Attorney Michael Crosby," Black says, "He's going after those bigoted assholes for taking Jessie's life. I'll keep y'all up on how it goes."

"Please do," Tonya says.

Black adds, "Jessie has seven children who are now left without their daddy. This shit has me consumed. I am so pissed off. I want Justice for Jessie, so I will *definitely* be on front street. My foursome sister Bren, she's on the streets daily. Getting the word back to Crosby from the streets. And to the streets from Crosby. We want them damn pigs sent to prison."

"But that's Mississippi though," Nina says, "Do you think racial justice is possible? We have crew who started out there. They left running north to get away from that same type of bigoted bullshit. On second thought. *Yes*. Justice is possible."

"That's apart of our crew legacy," T-baby adds.

"And *Justice* is a must," Rebbie says.

"Damn right, it is," Renee says, "And it better damn well happen. Lock their asses up, so some of those they done sent up, probably on bogus shit. Can whoop they're asses good."

Black says, "I would help with those ass whoopings and have his kids in those circles of inmates, who are whooping their motherfucking asses too."

"That would be *just*," Rebbie says.

"That would be *full* justice," Black adds, "That would be those bigoted mothafuckaz getting it how they live."

"True that," Tonya says.

Nina says, "I really wanna know how this racist bullshit plays out. Because for a human to go to jail and then end up killed by the police, who are suppose to serve and protect? That's like going backwards. That's the type of shit that sent our crew north. And then, once they got to a safe place here. They got justice through their offspring."

"My mama is one of those offspring," T-baby says, "And her and my uncle Sam got my grandpa Joshua and granny Sally's property back too. Grandma Sally passed away in two thousand and one. But she told me she was *so* proud of my mama and uncle. Because they got educated and went back through the system and got the land back which belonged to her and papa."

"That's justice," Black says, "And that's the same shit I need to see happen in Jessie's name."

"Keep us informed," Ebony says as she raises her ice tea glass again. She adds, "Erica is on her way to join us. And she's going to bring some great news. At least, as the United States of America goes. This is two thousand and six. But still, we deal with racism and bigotry. The same way big mama and her generation did, decades ago."

Nina adds, "Amen, Ebony. It's passed time for Justice, for just us. It's time for change."

"And we're going to do our part to make it happen," Rebbie says.

"We have been through a lot as a family," T-baby says, "But y'all know we have always pulled through whatever bullshit that came our way. *Racism. Willie Lynch* styled black faces. You name it. This crew has faced it and knocked it the fuck down. The same shall happen with anything else which comes our way. Do y'all feel me?"

"Yes we do!!" the ladies all yell in unison.

Again they all raise their glasses for a toast and continue with their great conversation.

Across CrewLand parking area, Chill, Ajay and Lil Ajay have just arrived at Stoney's Bar & Grill. Its 10am. Dre and Joe are still there, now seated in the crew booth. Angie and Nicole have just finished their meals. From the time they see Ajay come through the doors of Stoney's, they're both giddy with excitement. They've both spun around on their stools, so

they can keep their eyes on Ajay. Chill, Ajay and Lil Ajay head over to the booth and sit down with Dre and Joe. As they do, Nicole and Angie continue to watch and try to get Ajay's attention. While the 2 of them are watching Ajay. Lil Ajay is watching them.

"What's good, crew troops?" Joe asks.

Chill says, "Another day. Another dollar. Crew style."

"Word," Ajay says, "So let's get down to it. Have they been told not to come with dumb shit? Or will I need to express it?"

Lil Ajay cuts in and says, "Express it, pops. They've been watching you and giggling since we came in."

"And Lil Ajay got the dibs on em, from the door," Dre says and chuckles.

"And I already know that's natural bloodline action, for him," Joe adds and chuckles too.

Then Ajay says, "Let's get this done, so me and my son can head home. This is game day and y'all know the rest."

Chill chuckles and adds, "Yep. Nothing will get Ebony's game plan time. So let's get this phase open and moving."

"Cool," the rest of them say.

That's when they get up and all 5 of them head over to the counter. They speak to big Al and big John as they all sit down on counter stools.

Big Al says, "I've briefed these sisters on their mission already. Along with John here."

"We did the briefing, so we could save game plan time," big John adds as he looks at Ajay and they all chuckle.

Ajay says, "All good." Then he turns to Nicole and Angie. He asks, "What's up to you both?"

"Hey Ajay," they both say as they still giggle.

"Let's get this clear and out front," Ajay says, "This reunion is about business. Unfinished business. Is that clear?"

Angie says, "It's very clear, Ajay. Your father-in-law and your father have already broke it down to us. And you know we're down to help you, in anyway possible."

"We'll get on it as soon as you tell us to get started," Nicole adds with a suggestive stare.

Lil Ajay says, "Cool. Just so long as both of y'all know that's not what you're getting on. Not anytime soon anyway. Do the work first. Right, pops?"

Ajay says, "Absolutely."

"This is the little you," Angie says, pointing to Lil Ajay. She adds, "He looks just like you, Ajay."

"And it's obvious that his game is passed down too," Nicole says.

Ajay says, "Then both of you already know that no bullshit is going to be tolerated. And no personals will come your way, if you don't handle the business correctly."

"Oh we're gonna hold it down for you and the crew, Ajay," Angie says, "We give you our word."

Chill says, "Cool. It starts tonight after the game. But before you two head to the game. We're going to introduce you to misses Ida Mae Graves. She lives on the Westside, very close to y'all. She's going to carry the two of you as her grand nieces whom she found out about within the last few years."

"And she's gonna get at Old Jake," Ajay says, "Just asking him if he has any younger family members whom her nieces can meet and spend *their* time with."

Chill adds, "She's going to make Old Jake think that she's requesting young males, so y'all aren't around them so much. And interfering with *their* time together."

"And that's when we're suppose to insist that it be only one. And he *must* have some street cred and flava," Nicole says.

"Ruff neck style and banging," Angie adds, "And we aren't suppose to settle for nobody else but Draper. Or a true link to Draper."

"Word," Ajay says. Then he turns to his father big Al and his father-in-law big John. He adds, "Y'all laid it down perfectly. So I'm sure they know where my game and my sons game came from. Right?"

Big John says, "Our wives and mothers."

They all laugh before big Al adds, "We filled them in completely. They know they have to stay on point. Nothing else is even possible unless this mission is moving to *our* liking."

"And we'll let these two Ajay's know if they need to come bearing gifts for you two ladies," big John says. He adds, "And my decision will be made based on how y'all handle this mission. If you're familiar with crew style, at all. Then you already know our business has to be handled per *our* specifications. When our business ventures are handled correctly. We bring the best personal gifts known to mankind."

"Is that clear enough for you ladies?" big Al asks Nicole and Angie, while darning a very handsome smile.

"Yes it is," Angie answers and blushes.

"It's very clear," Nicole answers. She adds, "We will not let Ajay

Jackson and his son down. Nor anyone else that they call family. I give y'all my word."

"My word is bond too," Angie adds.

"Then this meeting is adjourned," Ajay says. He adds, "I'll see y'all after the game. But I have to head home and get ready for tonight's game." All 7 of the males chuckle. Then Chill says, "This meeting is a wrap." With that, they all give hugs to Nicole and Angie. Then Chill, Ajay and Lil Ajay head out the door. Right behind them are Dre and Joe, who are leading Angie and Nicole back to the Pathfinder. They're going to take them back home so they can get what they're wearing to tonight's game. Then Dre and Joe are going to bring them back to stay in a guest suite at *CrewLand Luxury Suites & Condominiums*. That is where they will dress and relax until game time.

Back to the crew ladies at *Crew's House of Soul Food*. Erica Jackson-McNair has joined the 8 of them and the conversation has gone from Jessie Williams Jr's death to presidential status.

"Senator Barack Obama is going to run for president?" Renee asks. She adds, "Erica that is the best news I've heard politically, in a long time."

"Yes he's going to run," Erica says, "And yes it *is* the best political news, in awhile. I agree with you on that. And Eric told me that the news is already buzzing around in Chicago. But the *official* announcement will be coming soon."

"I'm so hyped about that info," T-baby says.

"I am too," Ebony adds, "I'm hyped and ready to campaign for him. And I don't even have to ask our first generation how they feel about it either."

"I can't wait to hear big mama yell, Crew style!" Nina yells with excitement. She adds, "This makes my day too. I've been hoping he would step on up and get this country back in shape."

"A black president," Rebbie says, "Even though he came from a white woman, like me. He's black in this movement. Just like me. This makes my day and it can make major changes in this world."

"From the *peace* side, anyway," Tonya adds, "But y'all be ready to see bigotry, on the *front* page. Okay?"

"For real," Black says, "A black man in the white house is going to set these bigots off, *big-time*."

"And show racism worldwide," Ebony adds, "Bring it on."

They all applaud the good news. They see this as a move forward which they know the crew will fully support.

Suddenly Ebony smiles because Ajay, Chill and Lil Ajay are entering the restaurant.

"Hey baby," Ajay says as he comes straight over to Ebony and gives her a kiss while Chill does the same with Renee.

"Is Ebony the only person your big head can see in here?" Nina asks Ajay jokingly.

"Yep," Ajay says, joking back.

They all laugh and greet each other as Chill, Ajay and Lil Ajay join the 9 ladies who have finished their food.

Ajay is happy to see Black again. He says, "Welcome to CrewLand, Black. I got to get this on out here, so you'll know where my crew head is at."

"What's on your mind, Ajay?" Black asks.

Ajay says, "I've got somebody I want you to meet. You see, I've gotta find a way to keep you hanging around Cleveland. For awhile, at least. Because you are *definitely* crew material. Plus I've got some work with your name on it too."

Black says, "Well there you have it, folks. Ajay *knows* that I know and respect that Ebony is off the market. So I'm ready to hear whatever it is you have to say, Ajay."

That makes Ajay chuckle. But he likes her comment a lot. He goes on.

"I'm not gonna allow you to be without a date while you're in my city," Ajay says, "I've got somebody in mind that I think you'll dig."

"She works here," Black says and smiles.

With a surprised look, Ajay says, "As a matter of fact, she does."

"Too late, Ajay," Tonya says, "Black already passed first base."

They all laugh at that comment. Just then, Tameka arrives at their table with their check.

That's when Ebony leans into Ajay and whispers in his ear,

"They've already given each other those puppy eyes, baby. You're dead on with the idea you was about to bring. But they're already digging each other."

Ajay looks up at Tameka. He can see that her total attention is on Black and likewise.

He smiles and whispers to Ebony, "Damn. I'm slow as hell."

They both smile at each other.

Then Ajay whispers, "Crew has come all the way around. We don't deny nor discriminate."

"True," Ebony whispers back. "We'll have two same sex couples in the family before long. Then Corey and Bobby will have a female couple to party with. That's cool and equal too. Plus Erica just told us that Senator Obama is going to run for president, in two thousand and eight."

"Well *damn*," Ajay whispers, "We about to get this country to real equality for all. While putting this racism shit on the front burner. Then burn it the *fuck* up. That's damn good news, all the way around."

They smile at each other and kiss again as Lil Ajay watches them with pride. They enjoy their time at *Crew's House of Soul Food*. It isn't long before Ajay and Ebony prepare to head home.

"I have to get Anthony's game plan ready," Ebony says and she smiles shyly.

"We know," Nina says as if she's in an impatient mood, before she cracks up laughing and pumps her fist into the air.

They all have a good laugh as they prepare to head out.

Eric comes in just before they all leave. He's meeting Erica there, so they can head the medical center to see Dr. Weston. They're going in for their 2nd prenatal visit. Their baby is due in early August.

"We're coming back through to pick up Lil Ajay, Alan Anthony, Lannie and Kimmie when we finish at doctor Weston's," Erica says.

"Keep your eyes on Alan Anthony," Ajay jokes but holds a serious look on his face.

Ebony has to counter. She says, "And keep the same eyes on Ant too. Can y'all do that too?"

"The two guys are cool," Eric jokes as he gives Ajay dap.

Erica counters with, "And the girls are *crew*. We're watching them, all the way."

Renee and the rest of the females give Erica a fist bump, as they all share another laugh. Ajay and Ebony give Lil Ajay some love and they head on out to the parking lot. Ebony rode in with Nina. She's riding home with Ajay. Lil Ajay is going to catch a ride back to Jackson Heights with Erica and Eric, when they return from the medical office. For now, they drop him off at *Big Mama's House*. He wants to catch up with Alan Anthony, who's already there. Lil Ajay knows why he's hanging out there. His twin sister Lannie is there. Lil Ajay knows Kimmie is there also. The girls are there with his grandmother's, Pearl and Jo. Lil Ajay's baby triplet sisters Ariel, Arianne and April are there too. And though he knows he'll see Kimmie there. He's not going to push up on her. Not at this time. He'll just keep an eye on her. He knows he can talk to her in private later. Because he knows

TIME TO SHOW-RELOADED-Time Will Reveal 6

Kimmie and Lannie will be back in Jackson Heights, at Eric and Erica's home. So they can get ready for tonight's basketball game. He'll talk to her there.

Southwest Parma, 7203 Westlake Avenue 11pm

The Cavaliers beat the Bucks by 3 points and the Cleveland fans celebrate royally. Then they head off to CrewLand malls night spots to continue celebrating and having a good time. But Ajay and Ebony head home. Ajay has 2 road games which start in 2 nights. February 8th in Minneapolis. February 10th in DC. He'll be flying out with the Cavaliers, tomorrow afternoon.

"So you know it's about to be more game plan time for us," Ajay had said before he and Ebony extended their farewells to their crew and headed to Jackson Heights.

"What else is new?" Nina had said as she got in another joke jab with her only brother, before they all left *Quicken Loans Arena*.

Alan and Kimmie sat next to Lannie and Lil Ajay during the game. Lil Ajay made sure Kimmie got every snack and game toy, she wanted. Kimmie truly enjoyed the game. Lil Ajay enjoyed having her sitting next to him and he was a perfect little gentleman. Ebony can vouch for that. She had Lil Ajay on her right side and Lannie on her left. Alan sat to the left of Lannie. Kimmie sat to the right of Lil Ajay. The triplets had all of their laps and nearly every other member of the crew, who attended the game too. And though Angie, Nicole plus Farah's pack sat very close to the crew. Neither of them got to hold 1 of Ajay's triplets. Crew's trust wasn't going that far.

Lil Ajay and Alan left the game with *their crew* brother's, as usual. But they'll stay at Lil Ajay's home when their rendezvous' of tonight are done. Lil Ajay knew his pops wanted the mansion all to himself, for some personal time with his mother Ebony. So he's surely going to oblige his father's wishes. And he's going to take advantage of his automatic *extended hours*, late night permission too. Lil Ajay already knows his twin sister Lannie is heading home with Kimmie. His triplet sisters are staying with Nana's Jo and Pearl. So his big brother duties are done for tonight. His crew *thangs*; Olivia, Rioshauna, Jaylisa and Shalom had attended the game with Farah, Alana and Darlene. At this present moment, the *thangs* are arriving at The Spot II. And they all have hopes of being chosen crew prizes, before this night ends.

TIME TO SHOW-RELOADED-Time Will Reveal 6

In Parma, at 7203 Westlake avenue, Ida Mae and Old Jake have been having another quiet and friendly *conversation only* evening. They had watched the Cavaliers game on TV. She had to endure Old Jake's ridicule and horrible talk about Ajay and his entire crew family, for the entire game. She's sick and tired of him and that started from day 1 of this mission. She's only putting up with his BS because she's down with the crew's mission. Plus she knows the move which is schedule to happen within the hours, will be essential in assisting the crew with bringing this decades long beef to a finale. During their date, a few weeks back, Ida Mae told Old Jake about her nieces whom she was able to find a few years back. On their dates since then, Ida Mae had been asking him to help her find some younger guys whom her nieces would be attracted too. Old Jake has already told her, he would do that.

"I've got males of all ages, who are at my grasp," Old Jake had gloated. "And these nieces of yours, sounds like they got the freaky side of your genes. I'll hook them up with a real soldier. He can handle them. Plus that will take care of their demand of a street tough dude too."

"Okay," was Ida Mae's response that night.

Tonight, Ida Mae is still pleased to hear Old Jake brag on this guy, who is still unknown to her. She's just praying that it will be Draper. Because that would bring her a step closer to not having to deal with Old Jake's company anymore. The setup with Draper Watts will bring the crew's beef with Old Jake Johnson, that much closer to done and over with. Ida Mae knows they'll have company in a few minutes. Her long lost nieces *Angie* and *Nicole* will be stopping by soon. Before long, the conversation will come up of them begging her to assist them in finding a young man. Since Ida Mae was able to find a man for herself, is what they'll harp on. Angie and Nicole will emphasize that they like to share their men. So they'll need to meet a man who's tough in the streets and down for a ride or die chick. Ida Mae just has to keep the conversation going with Old Jake until they arrive.

"I'm just glad Cleveland got the win," she plays on. "I'm not that pro, on sports. Nor do I know all. So I wouldn't know who's good or bad."

"The win is good," Old Jake says, "But they be giving that Jackson fool all the damn credit. It was four other guys on that motherfucking floor. And *shit*. Lebron is the superstar. Not that nothing ass eastside nigger. Just be glad you don't know that klan of niggers, like I do."

Before Ida Mae can respond, her doorbell rings. She responds in thought as she heads to the door.

What a damn relief!!

She opens the door. Angie and Nicole stroll in and hugs Ida Mae.

"How you doing tonight, auntie?" Angie asks on cue.

"I'm doing fine," Ida Mae says. Then whispering, she says, "Better now."

They all giggle as Nicole adds, "I see that car outside. You've got company. Who you got up in here?"

On cue, Ida Mae giggles flirtatiously and says, "It's a friend of mine. And yes it's a man. Where y'all men at?"

They stroll on into the den while carrying on this baited conversation.

"We don't have no man," Angie says. Then she looks at Old Jake and adds, "But I see you do. This must be that handsome man you've been bragging about. I know it is."

"I haven't been bragging about him," Ida Mae says while smiling. "I said I met a good man. He's a good friend though."

Angie reaches out her hand to Old Jake.

She says, "I'm Angie and this is my best friend Nicole. Nice to meet you."

Old Jake shakes hands with both of them. Nicole smiles and starts to flirt.

She says, "My great aunt got her a good looking man, up in here. Where my man at? You ain't got no friends?"

"For real," Angie says, "Please tell me there's some more men in your click, who got this kind of time to spend with a woman."

"As a matter of fact, there is," Old Jake says confidently.

"Well where they at?" Angie asks, "I know it's almost midnight. But it's a week night. Hopefully one of them is still reachable."

"For real," Nicole adds, "We need to meet whoever you know. That's got spending quality time, on his mind."

Old Jake says, "I got a nephew I want y'all to meet. I've been telling Ida Mae about him....."

The door bell rings.

Old Jake continues, "....that should be him, right now. I sent him a text message and told him to drop by. After Ida Mae told me that you two sisters was going to drop in."

"We'll get it," Nicole says, as her and Angie rush to the front door.

They give each other the eye, as they get closer to the door. They know they have to play this move up huge, if it's Draper.

"I know my game," Angie whispers.

Nicole whisper back, "So do I. And we gotta get the Ajay's blessings."

"Who is it," Angie asks through the front door.

"Draper," answers the male voice on the other side of the door.

TIME TO SHOW-RELOADED-Time Will Reveal 6

Ajay and Ebony's Estate

Ajay and Ebony are just taking a break from their *game plan session.* Which they started as soon as they arrived home from the arena.

Ajay is still short winded, as he says, "That's the way to show me I'm home, baby. I'm married to the best pussy in the world. Your mind is alright too."

Ebony giggles as she snuggles up close to him. She's feeling very satisfied too, as usual.

"Our lovemaking is always good, Anthony," she whispers, "And it *has* been since day one."

He smiles and says, "I agree. It's what love is suppose to feel like. We're there, Ebony. And we've been here for a *long* time. That is what makes everything else outside of us, more feasible. Because there is no stress in my home. I love you for that and I will love you for life."

"I cosign you," she says and smiles. She adds, "If there is any such thing as a perfect life. I feel like we are very close to it."

"We will be, very soon," he says, "As soon as we get all this beef shit out of the forefront."

Then switching gears, she says, "Our Old Jake plan is unfolding well, ha?"

"Damn good," he says, "Nicole and Angie should be at Miss Ida Mae's house right now. KeJuan and Wayne on top of it. They're laying low by *The Landmark.*"

"That's the famous *midway* point of the beef," Ebony says, "I'll never forget that history you told me about. Which happened near the landmark."

He says, "Where I witnessed our fathers take an enemies life with their *bare* hands? I won't forget it either."

She says, "Wayne and KeJuan are doing this in a safe way. Right?"

"Oh yea," he says, "Dre, Joe and six of their homeboys have them in sight. And they're backing them up while they all lay low. Plus they got more than thirty guys set up from Miss Ida's house to the landmark. And then, another twenty between Miss Ida's house and Old Jake's house."

Ebony looks into his eyes. She smiles because she has realized that her crew is on point and already preparing for the Old Jake demise route. And she knows that her crew are the truth. She's still looking into his eyes.

She asks, "Baby I'm already knowing what you're about to say next. Our crew is already staking out the routes, so crew will know which will be the best route to grab Old Jake on. That's what all of this hanging out is about, isn't it? Not just about protecting our crew that's on the scene. Right?"

Ajay looks in her eyes. Then he smiles, leans in and gives her a passionate kiss.

Afterwards, he just asks, "Are you impressed with your crew?"

"Very impressed," she says, "This is awesome. It sounds like it won't be much longer before we can erase some bad history."

"Know that," Ajay says and chuckles, "You know what though? I wish my grandparents and Chill's parents *and* grandparents was still alive. So they could all see his ass go to hell."

Ebony says, "I think about all of the bad history we've had in this entire crew. And I realize Old Jake Johnson is connected to ninety nine percent of it. I know my grandfathers would do him in. I can feel that in my soul."

"We're giving papa Brown and his generation the first option," he reveals. "It's time to show every crew member after them, how much hurt that one man has caused on our families. And our first living generation is where this started. So it's only right that they get the first option of taking his last air."

"What if they don't have that in them, to do it?" Ebony asks.

Ajay says, "First of all, they *do* have it in them. That's where we got it from, baby. But I feel like if they wanna pass it down. It's gonna go to Chill. Only because Old Jake cost him dearly, over these decades. If Chill gets that star. Old Jake will leave this earth knowing that the crew legacy still lives on and he has lost the biggest and final battle."

"Yes indeed. Because baby, our legacy is pro black," Ebony says, "Our side of this beef is the side that *should* live on. Not the legacy of somebody like Old Jake. His *Willie Lynch* mentality is the very thing which has cost our race so many great leaders. To be honest. I don't care who takes his life. I just want him gone. Before our kids generation is out on their own."

"I agree with you, one hundred percent, baby," Ajay says, "I told you I wouldn't be able to rest until he was gone. As far as our kids going out of our sight, is concerned. So his death will be a final chapter of our crew hardships. It's time. And after he's gone. You know where all of my focus will go to next."

"Angel Taylor," Ebony says, "And I'm with you on that one too. Because Angel is trouble which started in *our* generation. There is no way I'm going to be okay with allowing that beef to go on for decades. No way."

"It won't," Ajay says. "Her visitors list is long now. Me and Ant will only visit her if it has something to do with getting her comfortable with us, before she walks out of there. That's not even a necessary move, right

now. Because if she's anything like she use to be. She'll be looking to find me and Ant, once she's released. The same way she use to find me while she was trying to stay hidden from you and our female crew."

"I know a female who'll to be visiting her before the quadruple wedding, "Ebony says.

"Who's that?" Ajay asks, "My big sister's link?"

"Yes," Ebony says, "Julie Von Reese. Her and the Atlanta crew will arrive day after tomorrow, for the crew wedding. Lynn has already set it straight with her. She's going to visit her on the ninth. You'll be on the road when they get here."

"I wish I'd planned for you to take this trip with me," Ajay says and laughs, "But I needs to find a way to box up your game plan action."

She laughs before Ajay adds, "But I know you're helping them prepare for all the events leading up to the wedding and the wedding too. I'll let you stay home, *this* round."

She laughs more and says, "I wish I'd known you was gonna say this. Then I would've told the crew that you was making me go on the road and I wasn't going to be able to stay here and work."

"Thanks for letting me know that," he says with a smile.

She knows he's going to make plans on taking her on the next road trip and she's fine with that. But she's going to want to take their 6 kids too. He's not going to be okay with that part. They'll get to a happy medium. But for now, they have to get some closure on this Angel situation before they can get back to their lovemaking.

Ebony says, "Julie is going to bridge a big gap for us. Because she will be in conversation with her, starting after her visit. And she's going to continue it. Even after she's gone back to Atlanta. So Lynn will have the immediate scoop."

"That's all good," Ajay says, "But Ant will have the same and he's right here with us. Angel is going to put effort into being close to him, once she's released. Because she's determined to call him daily. And she would, if she could. That's the same way she'd be, once she got out too. If I would have that much patience to wait for *her* move. But I don't have the patience to wait now. And I know I'll have less patience when she *is* released. It's okay though. Because baby, Ant is doing such a good job of pulling her in. He's building her trust *perfectly*. Because she wants him to accept her. Which he never will. We know that but his game is working well and he has this direct connection with her. Baby, that is the *only* reason he's able to be calm about everything else in his life. I *know* that feeling. And Ebony,

I know you, Nina, T-baby and Rebbie wanna do her ass in. I know that. But baby, our son wants to kill her for what she did to you. And I am not going to stand in his way."

"I know," she says, "I won't either, baby. But Anthony, me and the foursome want some of that action. We deserve it."

"I know and I'll make sure it comes around so that y'all can get some of her ass too," Ajay says, "But her final breath will be taken by our son. Because he feels like she took his birthright. His older sister. Ant wanted his life to mirror mine and all of the Jackson males before him. Angel is the reason that his pedigree is different than mine and pops and so on. He needs that closure because that will be the *only* way, we'll be able to be assured that he will have a peaceful life. That's the only way that you and I can make sure that he don't go all out, just off of frustration alone."

Ebony says, "I get it and I agree. He inherited this from you and from me too, in a way. This is the same way it went with me having to be the one to take out Raymond White. So that I could *relax* and get back to being myself and secure. I get it. I must say this. It feels good to know that, in a year or so from now. We could be completely done with the beef and danger which was hatched out years before we were even born."

"Amen," Ajay says, "Plus we'll be getting ready to put a black president in the white house."

"I know that's right," Ebony agrees and smiles. She adds, "We are going to put Barack Obama in the position of president. But I predict he's going to win it *twice*. He'll do so well, that he'll get eight years."

"I wish we could change that tenure too," Ajay says and chuckles.

Ebony laughs too and agrees, saying, "Me too. Maybe we'll be able to find a loophole within these next ten years."

"Well until then," Ajay says, "Why don't you treat me to some more of your game plan action. That makes anything else that's *positive*. Possible."

Ebony blushes as Ajay leans in for another heated kiss. He starts rubbing on her breast with 1 hand, as he moves on over and on top of her.

"I'm ready to lick every part of you again," he whispers as he looks into her eyes. "I'm addicted to you, baby."

She relaxes on her pillow. All of their kids are outside of their home and in the greatest care of their crew. This is Ajay's time and Ebony's pleasure time. And she's all in.

The Chill Spot II
267

Lil Ajay is in his usual form tonight, as his time with any crew *thangs* go. He's seated in his booth in the crew section, accompanied by the usual 4 girls who continuously bids for his time. They're seated per their importance to Lil Ajay, at this time. Rioshauna Fields, the daughter of Mallory Fields and Draper Watts is seated to his right side. Jaylisa Mangrove, Angel Taylor's stepsister is seated to his left. Olivia Casey and Shalom Wittman are seated to the outside of Rioshauna and Jaylisa. As usual, Olivia is pleading her case to be seated right next to Lil Ajay.

He smiles at her and asks, "Do you see all these posters on the walls? And all these flyers on the tables, throughout this *entire* club?"

"Yes I do," Olivia says while smiling, "The Chill Spot two is letting everybody know about my birthday party!"

"I know you're excited, Olivia," Shalom says, "You're having your big sweet sixteen party at *CrewLand*, on Saturday night!"

Olivia says, "Yes I am. I'll bring in my day from the crew club."

"Your birthday will be brought in from this club," Jaylisa says, "That's hot!"

"And it's better to have it on that Saturday night, before your birthday," Rioshauna adds, "That way we don't have to go in early. Like tonight. Because of school, the next day."

"Exactly," Olivia says. Then turning her attention to where her eyes never left. She says to Lil Ajay, "It's about to be midnight now. How long are you hanging out tonight, Ant?"

Lil Ajay says, "I don't know. Why you asking?"

Olivia smiles flirtatiously and says, "I was hoping we could get together before I have to go home."

"He's sitting next me and Jaylisa tonight," Rioshauna says, "That should tell you where his attention is, for tonight."

Jaylisa says, "Please, Rio. Don't start another argument. Ajay don't wanna hear no beefing."

Olivia goes right back at Jaylisa and the feud is underway. The 4 girls go back and forth at each other. All the while, Lil Ajay is quiet. He's not even looking at either of them. He's looking at his cell phone photo's. Admiring the pictures he'd taken of Kimmie while they were at his father's game, earlier tonight. He doesn't have plans of spending time with either of these 4 girls, this evening. He's going home within the hour, as soon as he gets the text message from his father.

TIME TO SHOW-RELOADED-Time Will Reveal 6

Chapter 71

NO MORE EXILE

It's Saturday morning, the 11th day of February. All of the crew are either in Cleveland already. Or they will be here by tomorrow night for the big crew events. The crew quadruple wedding is going down in 3 days. Tuesday, Valentines day! February 14, 2006 at Noon. All 4 of the couples are home and getting their last minute preparations ready.

The 4 crew couples are:

1: Shannon Tyreek "Da Reaper" Wilson & Brittany Neon James.
2: Kenneth Ramon "Lil Chill" Payne, Jr & Chaundra Denise Coleman.
3: Jesse Lee "Lil Man" Brown & Ruthie Nakia "Roo" Williams
4: Samuel "The Cupid" Logan & Pamela Darius Jackson

The 2nd generation of crew parents are thrilled to see their youngest offspring pledging matrimony, before either of them have become parents. Mama Jo and mama Belinda are bragging on Pam and Sam Jr. Because even though Sam Jr and Pam have been living together, across the street from Ebony and Ajay since Jarvis and Gwen had to sale and move. They still haven't made any kids. Pam always jokes about it, saying,

"It's because I live right across the street from my big brother Ajay. And Samuel never wants to make Ajay angry."

Ajay always chuckled at that comment but he never denied it.

This early morning, all of the brides-to-be are kicked back in Pam and Sam's home, as they wait to be called down to *Crew Gear* for their final bridal gown fittings. The grooms-to-be aren't far away. They're laying low at Greg Jr's home in Jackson Heights, just up the Cul-de-sac. The big crew wedding is considered the *main* event for the crew. The 16th birthday party for Olivia will start at 9pm at The Chill Spot II and it's expected to be filled to capacity. But over at The Chill Spot, there's a meeting taking place at noon. Between Ajay and Darlene.

Darlene has longed for this day to happen for a decade or more. While Ajay loathes it. But he knows it's a pertinent move he has to make, so he can add more iron to the dismissal plan which the crew have for Angel. This is a game day for Ajay, as well. So the meeting time has been moved up to noon. Black and Yolanda have come over to visit with Ebony and the kids while Ajay heads to his noon meeting. Before leaving, Ajay brings Ebony to the kitchen door with him.

He asks, "Are you still okay with this meeting?"

"Yes baby," she says, "I know what it's about. It's time for her to

have a role in this riddance plan which is *long* overdue. But she's thinking it's more, I'm sure. Or she's hoping it is. Just be calm, Anthony. I guarantee you. You can get her to do *anything* you need done. So go all the way in, on her. Play on her feelings for you, if that's what it takes. I want her as a potential suspect because when Angel is taken out. I want there to be enough flare ups between the two of them, to warrant reason for her to be investigated. Along with Nicole, Angie and the rest of that *outside* wishing well."

She giggles which makes Ajay chuckle. Without a doubt, he knows his wife trusts him, 100%. Even if he's around a female who's from his past. He knows that she knows, *she* and her only, is his present and future. To Ajay, that means everything.

He says, "The audio *and* video will be running. If you wanna go over it...."

"I don't need to," she says, cutting him off, "Not unless she says something *you* want me to hear. I already know she's gonna ask for my dick and I already know your answer. Anything else which will get her in line for this mission, is *allowed*. Okay?"

Ajay is flattered and stunned, at the same time. But now, he has to notify her of a sudden occurrence which her last statement just caused.

He says, "When you said *dick*, he jumped to attention. Shouldn't we calm him down before I leave?"

She smiles and says, "If we had more time, I'd say yes. But I know all you'll need to do is think about whom you're about to meet with. My jewel will lay down and probably crawl up too."

They both laugh. Then give each other a soothing hug and kiss.

Ajay heads to the garage and Ebony heads back to the den to kick back with Black and Yolanda.

"What's up to my Houston and Gulfport crew?" Ebony asks as she takes her seat.

"Enjoying the hell outta Cleveland," Black answers.

"For real," Yolanda says.

"Renee and Tonya pulled out all the stops for me," Black says. "And now that Lynn, Bre and Jan done made it here. I figured I'd better get by here and see these babies again. In case I don't get another extra hour before flight time."

They all laugh before Ebony says, "That's how crew gets it in, Black and Yolanda. Y'all are family. So we don't hold back. Seeing the two of y'all has put April on my mind, big time. I miss her even more when I see y'all."

"I miss her everyday," Yolanda says, "Nobody has been able to fill

that void. She was the best friend anybody could have. She's sorely missed."
All 3 of them are about to get misty eyed, so Ebony decides on a way to keep their hang out time, cordial and uplifting.
She says, "I pulled out some things that I know y'all will remember. I made copies for both of you. Me and my foursome sister's already got them. The two of you have to be included too."
    "Cool," Black says, "What's up? Let me see the goods."
They laugh as Ebony digs into the box which she had brought out and sat in the Den before the 2 of them arrived.
She says, "First, I want each one of y'all to have one of these pictures."
She hands each of them a picture of her, Yolanda and April which they had taken when Ebony, Yolanda and April was in the 8th grade, down in Houston.
    "Oh!!" Yolanda yells, "I love it! I remember when we took this. It was when we was getting our plans together to kick Shuntay, Sonya and Tina's ass. And stank ass Raymond White too."
    "April called her aunt Bren and told her all about that whole damn drama," Black says, "And Bren was itching for our foursome to go to Houston to beat them ho's asses, *for* April."
They all laugh as Yolanda bats her eyes and says, "Oh. We got that done."
    "Yes we did," Ebony adds, "Fourth lunch break."
    "I remember Ebony got even *more* pissed off because the staff broke it up," Yolanda says and laughs. She adds, "Because we had just started to get it in, *equally*."
    "April told me them three ho's tried to jump on Ebony, when she was by herself," Black says, "Ray put them up to it. April said you and her came tearing up the boardwalk and grabbed 1 each. And all 3 of y'all went to town, fair fight style."
They all giggle again as Ebony adds, "Truth. But the teachers came out, a few minutes after we had it evened up and they broke it up. *Man*! I was turning red. And I'm *dark* skinned. That don't happen often. But that day. Whoa!"
    "I'll put this picture where I can see it, *everyday*," Yolanda says.
Black adds, "I will too and I know I'll be making Bren a copy. I wouldn't be shocked if April already gave her a copy. She got pictures of y'all three and she is stingy as hell with even letting her foursome sisters *look* at em."
    "'Cause she knows y'all might steal some," Yolanda says as they all laugh again and agree with her.
Black says, "Her aunt Bren told me, April loved being friends with y'all

two. She treasured y'all, so much. And Ebony, her aunt Bren gave me a couple of things that she feels you should have back. She said April wanted your oldest daughter Lannie, her goddaughter, to have them. But April never wanted to mail it because it would've gotten damaged. So there was no way Bren was going to mail them either."

Black reaches into a handbag she'd brought with her and pulls out Ebony's bridal bouquet and a diary. Ebony and Yolanda both start to tear up.

"That's Ebony's bridal bouquet that April caught," Yolanda says through tears.

"And her diary that only me and Yolanda was allowed to read," Ebony adds as she wipes away tears.

They take a few minutes to gather themselves as they all look at the mementos and cherish them.

Then Ebony says, "I will truly save this for Lannie's wedding day. And this diary is going into her safe, *with* this bouquet. I'll have one of these sit down talks with Lannie, very soon. Now I must let y'all know. I have two more pictures for each of you."

She pulls out the second picture. It's of her, April, Yolanda, Nina, T-baby and Rebbie. *The sensational 6!* They had taken this picture at *Crew's House of Soul Food* in April 1998. When April and Yolanda came to visit for spring break. The 3rd picture she shares with them is of April, holding Lil Ajay and Lannie on the day of their christening.

Ebony tells Black and Yolanda, "I put one of each of these pictures into April's casket before the ushers made us leave the cemetery. I told April, 'I will never forget you'. They closed her casket and ushered us all away."

All 3 of them are in tears now as they sit quietly and reminisce about the great moments they shared with *April Leshay Bradley.*

The Chill Spot. Big Chill's office @ 12 noon

That day is finally here and it's time for Ajay to meet with Darlene. Darlene had shown up early. Crew brother Wayne Matthews' longtime girlfriend and now fiancée, Courtney Freeman had greeted Darlene at the side door. Courtney led Darlene to the waiting room on the 3rd floor, to wait until Ajay arrived.

Ajay arrives at 11:50am and goes straight up to Chill's office to greet him.

"What's up, bro?" Ajay asks as they give each other a pound.

"It's all good and crew like, Lil bro," Chill says with a chuckle. He

adds, "She's already here and in the waiting room. Just make it boil, crew."

"No shit," Ajay says, "Turn the audio and video on. I don't wanna have to repeat nothing I say to her in this meeting, a second time. I can't act *that* damn well."

Chill continues to chuckle as he starts the TV monitors. Then he radio's Courtney and let's her know to bring Darlene to his office.

"Okay, boss man Chill," Courtney says while smiling. She adds, "I'm going to get her, right now. I'll ring the buzzer when we arrive at your door."

"Ajay will open it with the remote," Chill says, "Bring her into my parlor. Ajay will come get her from there and escort her back into my office. You stay with her until Ajay comes to get her."

"In a minute," Courtney says.

"See ya," Chill salutes back. Then he turns to Ajay and says, It's all yours, *mentally*. I'll be in Renee's office if *physically* becomes needed."

"Word," Ajay says.

Chill heads to Renee's office from their connecting back doors. That leaves Ajay all alone and waiting for Courtney and Darlene to arrive.

It's been less than 2 minutes. The buzzer sounds. Ajay remotely unlocks the door. Courtney enters with Darlene and instructs her to have a seat. She does. Another minute later, Ajay comes into the parlor. He says, "Good afternoon ladies."

"Hey crew," Courtney says.

"Good Afternoon, Ajay," Darlene says and it's obvious that she's both nervous and excited.

"Follow me," Ajay says to Darlene.

"Of course," Darlene answers as she stands and approaches Ajay.

"Do you need anything else from me, big Ajay?" Courtney asks.

"You're good," Ajay responds, "But I'll radio for you, if I need anything. Cool?"

"In a minute," Courtney says and heads back out the door.

Ajay turns to Darlene and says, "We're gonna meet in Chill's office. It's through this door."

He opens the office door and steps inside of it. Then he holds it open so Darlene can enter.

"Thanks," she says.

"Have a seat in one of the black chairs in front of the desk," Ajay says as he heads around the desk and sits in Chill's King chair. Then he

says, "Let's get this started. First off. Is there anything you need to ask or add before we start?"

"I have to say how excited I am to finally see you, face-to-face again," she says, "And I just want you to know that I'm here for you. In anyway that would allow us to be friends, at least. I've really missed our conversations, Ajay. More than I can even express."

He knows he needs to get her wide open, *mentally*. So he plays the game as only *he* can. Along those same lines as he'd done with Angie and Nicole. He looks directly into her eyes and says,

"Well I do have a game tonight. But we're talking now. So let it out. Before we get to why I scheduled this meeting."

"Is it possible that we can have *regular* meetings?" Darlene asks, "Just to talk. If that's all it can be. But I want to be able to talk to you and just hear your words again. That's what I've wanted to say since…"

She pauses. Then she smiles and says, "It's been fifteen years, one month and three weeks since I've talked to you, in person."

Ajay wants her to move on a bit faster. He can tell that she's turned on. He also knows that he's not. But he's on a mission and he knows he's going to need her full participation. He's going to dig deep so he can get her wide open.

He says, "I know. The last time we talked was three days before Christmas, nineteen ninety. But we're here now. Is it hard for you to talk to me now?"

"I have to admit," she says, "I *am* nervous. I don't understand it, myself. But I don't want to do nor say nothing that will ruin it."

He goes in and asks, "What is it that you *really* want from me?"

"Some of your personal time," she admits.

"Then that's gonna depend on how this meeting goes," Ajay says while starring into her eyes.

"Oh my God," she says as she nearly looses her breath. Finally she adds, "Let's move forward. I'm here for you, Ajay. I just wanna make sure you know that."

"Cool," he says. Then he asks, "I've heard that you have beef with Angel. Is that true?"

She says, "The beef I have with her. Number one is about what she did to hurt you and how she almost left you without the only female that you've ever *truly* loved. Plus she took the life of your child before it could even be born. I can't even imagine how much pain that caused Ebony and you. But to be honest. I wanted to whoop her ass. And I did whoop my nieces ass, just off gee pee. Because she was really tight with her, back in those days."

Ajay knows Alana and Angel still have phone conversations. But he's not going to bring that up. He doesn't even want Darlene to bring it up. So he switches gears.

He says, "Just invite me to that ass kicking, if it ever happens."

"I'll do it for you, Ajay," she says suddenly, "I truly will."

"Okay," he says, "I'll take you up on that. Lord knows that would be the first thing I'd wanna do from the day she gets released. But you know that would make national news."

"I don't want you getting caught up on no charges. Not for that nothing ass, piece of trash," Darlene says, "Let me do it from you. I'd be honored, Ajay. I really would. I just want you to know that I've never stopped feeling you. Nor feeling *for* you. So if there's something I can do to get any kind of personal time and attention with you. I'll do it."

"Wow," Ajay says, "I'm impressed. I'm writing that shit down too. I'm taking notes on this meeting. It's why I wanted to meet with you. To see if you're still down."

She cuts in and says, "I am. Have you seen me in another relationship? No you have not." She laughs and adds, "I'm smart enough to know when the best come my way. I wish it would've been something I could've done to keep you as a part of my life. And definitely my bed."

"I'll tell you what, Darlene," he says, using the most provocative voice that he can fake. He says, "We're going to have more meetings. I've got to see if you're real about this. And I have a question for you."

"What's the question?" she asks, "Bring it on."

He asks, "I wanna know, are you familiar with Officer Miles? One of our security guards?"

"She's the only female," she says, "I've seen her. But I don't know her. I will tell you that I am familiar with her niece. That boy built one that always seems to cross the line with you. I guess every woman in this world wants to be close to you."

Ajay didn't expect Darlene to have information about Katrina Dobbs. But she does. He's impressed again.

He asks, "How do you know about her?"

"I've seen her getting out of line with you, a couple of times," Darlene says. "One time it was inside of this club. On this very floor too. That was some years ago. But she did that shit again, recently. New Year's eve night, I think it was. I was downstairs in the parking lot but I stayed back out of the way. I always do. So I can see you and not impose on you, at the same time. And I was here when that other one happened too. I wasn't

allowed on the third floor. But Alana gave me the scoop. She was working here, by then. It was on that night when T-baby's team won the title and the crew had them a celebration party. I saw when Katrina was taken outside. Or rolled out, actually. Alana told me that your sister Nina plus Rebbie and T-baby had whooped her ass good. Ebony was pregnant then, so I know why she wasn't involved, *that* night. But the other three must've laid her out. Cause everybody witnessed when the mobile medic had to roll her ass up outta here."

She giggles which makes Ajay chuckle too. But he's going to stick to the course.

He says, "Now that's an ass that truly needs to be whooped again. I wanna tell you something about that territory invader."

He leans in and let's Darlene know that this isn't even a story that he likes to share. He tells her that she isn't allowed to discuss any of this. Nor anything else they talk about. Not in this meeting or any other meeting.

"Or there can't be anymore meetings. Am I clear?"

"Yes you are clear," she says, "I will not lose your trust. I don't give a damn who gets mad. I will not make you angry. I give you my word."

That gives him a bright idea.

He says, "If it comes down to it and your housemates or anybody else wanna know what our meetings be about. Tell them we didn't talk. Tell them we fucked."

"I can *say* that?!!" Darlene ask in excitement, as she blushes.

Ajay says, "You was gonna get around to asking me for some dick, anyway. So just go ahead and say you're getting it already. That way, you can shut them up. And at the same time. That will keep them from asking you about the business we're talking about. And when it gets out that you're fucking me. I'll bet you that'll make both Angel *and* Katrina's ass wanna fight you. So that'll be bait to get you, just that much closer to whooping their asses, if they come incorrect."

"Ajay," she blushes and adds, "I cannot believe you just gave me permission to *say* I'm sexing you again."

"Did that make your day?" he asks, sporting a very sexy look on his face.

"And sweetened my dreams too," she says and giggles.

He says, "Then roll with it. But this is what I was gonna tell you about Katrina. When I was in college. She actually took advantage of me while I was passed out. I don't share this story with nobody but my wife, my family and crew. So if you share this. This will be our last meeting. Am I clear?"

"Yes you are," she answers.

"I was passed out after she put a *Mickey* in my drink," he says, "And she had sex with me. I don't even know how many times. Or if it really happened because I was passed out. I guess my dick gets hard when I'm out cold and dreaming about Ebony. I have no idea what all she did. This happened at a party we had at our mansion, down at UC. The year that Tank, Rich and June was freshman. She was a sophomore, same as me. I thought she was into females based on how she looked. But that's what she did to me. So I want you to know this one thing. I appreciate you. Because you live in my city and you attend all crew events at our businesses. And in all the time I've known you. You never disrespected my space, like that. I don't even know what all she did. But for me. She's on the same damn page as Angel Taylor. Does that make sense to you?"

"Ajay, I'll get with her ass as soon as I see her in Cleveland again," Darlene says. "Because I want you as bad as the next woman. But that is something I would never do. And you know that. Or I hope you do."

"I remember when I lived with you," he says, "If I didn't want none. You left me the fuck alone. So I believe you. I just wanted to make sure you know that this meeting is real for me. If you want me to know how much you wanna fuck with me. Then you'll have to be willing to step up, if any other woman gets out of her place when it comes to me. Because I belong to Ebony. You do understand that, correct?"

"I definitely do, Ajay," she says, "And I have respected that since that night she came back home from Houston, to visit. That was the last night I had a conversation with you. So yes, Ajay. I understand *exactly* what you mean. I will not cross *any* lines. I promise you that. And as for Angel and Katrina. Just make it possible for me to get face-to-face with them, *whenever* it's possible. I'll go in on both of them ho's and I won't say shit about why I'm doing it. You'll know why and that's all that matters to me. And I'm not gonna say or do nothing that will upset your wife either. I'm sure you wouldn't want that to happen and neither do I. Because history has already shown everybody that something like that, will shut the door on me. Okay?"

He says, "Okay. Darlene I'm just starting to see this side of you. I'm very impressed."

"That makes my day," she says, "This meeting made my day. I just wanna say this and I hope it's not disrespectful, in any kind of way."

"What is it?" he asks, already knowing she wants something sexual. She says, "The next time I see Katrina. I'm going in. And when Angel's ass

gets out and starts stalking you again. I'll kick her ass into next year. I'd do it, just to please you. I'm offering my services to you. All of my services, by the way."

He knew this was coming. He looks into her eyes and tries to make it seem as though he's feeling her.

Then he asks, "Be specific, Darlene. What type of payment do you want for your services?"

She says, "I'll whoop both of them bitches asses, for you. If you'll just let me taste that fourteen inch, chocolate dick again. And maybe ride it too."

"Deal," he says, shocking her once again. He adds, "As I said before. You can say you're getting some, already. I have no problem with that. And we're gonna meet *many* times. I'll let you know when the next meeting will be. And my son will be at the next one. I don't hide shit from him. But as far as my chocolate dick being payment? You'll have to earn that pay. There won't be none of this dick for you. Until you prove to me that you're really down for me. Do you understand me?"

"I do, Ajay," she says. "I'll do it. You have my word. The last time I had some of your dick. I was twenty four years old. I'll be thirty nine years old in sixteen more days. February the twenty seventh. And Ajay, I already know that you are *well* worth the wait. I won't let you down this time. I promise you that."

"Cool," he says, "Now this is a game day for me. So we'll end this meeting. But I'm leaving tickets for you and your group. Your son Jamal already gets tickets for him and Holly. They'll be there too. But there'll be six tickets in *your name*, this time. You want have to wait for a ticket to come through Alana, by way of Michelle. Alright?"

"All good," she says while smiling. She adds, "Can I ask you for a hug before we leave outta here?"

He doesn't answer her. He just gets up from his seat, walks around the desk and gives her a hug. She holds on very tight. Before she can even say it, he says, "It won't go any further than this, today. So don't ask me. I'll let you know when."

He looks down into her eyes, then he asks, "You do understand what I said earlier about *how* you can obtain that type of payment. Right?"

"Oh yes," she says in the sexiest voice she can muster up. She adds, "Ajay I understand you completely."

"Okay," he says, "Let's go. I've gotta run."

After that last statement from Ajay, they head out of Chill's office. It looks to Darlene like Chill just happened to be heading up the hallway

when they opened his office door. She doesn't know that he heard their *entire* meeting.

Chill says, "Meeting wrap up time, Ajay. You've got a game plan session and you've gotta get to it."

"Word," Ajay says, knowing Chill is referring to Ebony's time.

Chill adds, "I've got some lunch tickets for Darlene. She can head on over to Crew's House and Tameka will hook her up. Ajay, you head on out. You won't be a minute late for game plan. Not when you're at the Chill Spot, prior. I ain't having that."

They all laugh. Darlene doesn't know the joke is really on her. Chill knows Ajay just wants to get home so he can make love to Ebony before game time. That's his favorite ritual. The crew knows that. Doesn't matter if no one else does.

"I'm out," Ajay says and just like that, he's out of Darlene's sight again.

The Parma Mix

Olivia's birthday party is in full swing before the Cavaliers game ends. But Olivia's grand entrance is planned for after the game. She attends the game on 1 of Darlene's *6 tickets*. Darlene tells Olivia that the ticket is only 1 of several gifts she'll be giving her, courtesy of Ajay. She had shared the story with her roommates, as soon as she'd gotten home. Now Alana and Farah are still reeling from her, *Ajay news*. They can't believe Darlene had sex with Ajay at their meeting today. But with Darlene now having 6 special guest tickets. They can't help but believe every word she'd said.

Angie and Nicole are attending at the game too. Just like every Cavalier supporter, they wanted a win but that didn't happen tonight. The game is over and the 2 of them are about to meet up with their new fuck mate, Draper Watts. Since these 3 met at Ida Mae's house, a few nights ago, they've been together every single night since. They're leaving Q arena. Nicole drives while Angie calls Draper, who answers on the 2nd ring.

"What's good?" Draper asks in a sexy voice.

"Not shit. Besides me and my side kick," Angie says. She adds, "How is that sweet dick hanging tonight?"

"It's getting hard at the sound of your voice," Draper says.

Angie says, "Damn good timing too. We're both done with our business for tonight. We'll be stopping by auntie Ida's in a little bit."

"Do she need y'all to drop by there?" Draper asks.

Angie says, "We always check on her before we get in the wind. You do remember that we're long lost relatives. I told you that part. Well me and Nicole really love her and it made our lives better, just to know we have an elder that lives close enough for us to see everyday. She's very special to us, Draper. She *will* be turning seventy years old, this year. We don't wanna miss one moment with her."

"She's sixty nine, right now," Draper says, "Which is exactly where I'm trying to get to with my *cougars*."

Angie giggles and shares his comment with Nicole, who laughs too. Before yelling, "These cougars done turned your young ass out already!"

Draper tells Angie, "Tell her she's right. I'm feeling y'all action, like a *muafucka*. For real."

"We only got you by seven years, cub," Angie says to Draper as they all giggle. Angie adds, "We ain't no cougars yet. But we'll let you call us that. So long as you can keep making us roar."

"I got it for y'all," he says, "My dick is throbbing, right now. When are we hooking up?"

"Meet us at auntie Ida's crib," Angie says, "And we'll roll out from there. You'd better have your juices ready to boil over too. I needs to get this orgasm off my chest."

"Bring it," Draper says, "I'll be there in ten minutes. Be ready."

"Cool," Angie says, "We'll see you there."

They hang up. Angie and Nicole share another giggle. Then Nicole says, "He's already hooked and don't even know the mission."

"For real," Angie says, "His dick makes half of Ajay's. And that's the dick I want some more of. I bullshit you *not*. But you already know that shit. Hell, you're longing for it too."

"True," Nicole adds, "All we gotta do is show him how real we are, with this crew love. And helping the crew get rid of this riff raff, is as *real* as it gets. Then, Ajay's dick is our payment."

"And we *will* earn our payday fucks," Angie says, "That's for damn sure. While this old man out here thinking he's got aunt Ida's attention. He's gonna fall into crew hands, *real* soon. She ain't even fucking him. He's just happy to have the attention of a good ass woman."

"And she *is* a good woman," Nicole says, "And I meant what I said to her. After this crew hit is done. I'm keeping her in my life."

"I am too," Angie says, "She's on the good side of the crew. That says it all."

They arrive at Ida Mae's house, pulls into her snow plowed driveway and

parks. Before they can turn off their vehicle and get out. Draper pulls up next to them and parks on the double driveway too. He hops out and opens Nicole's door for her. He leans down into the door.

Directly to Angie on the passenger side, he says, "Don't open your door. I'm gonna open your door for you. Let me help the driving cougar get out, first. Then I'll be to yo side."

They all laugh as he proceeds. Within minutes, they're all outside of the cars. They lockup and head inside to visit with Ida Mae.

They all notice Old Jake isn't here tonight. Draper is the only one who's not in the know. Angie and Nicole already knew he wasn't going to be here. But they know he's suppose to be coming by to pick up Ida Mae for a hotel room night. The plan goes as such:

Ida Mae told Old Jake that she's ready to take their relationship to the next level. She said she wants to have sex with him. But not at her home nor his. Because she doesn't want to be disturbed by his friends or her *nieces*. She told Old Jake, she wanted to go back to the first place where they met and had dinner together. *The Cleveland Airport Marriot hotel* on W. 150th street. Old Jake committed to that invite *instantly*. He told Ida Mae, he had to run his gambling ring until about 1am and clear all the bets on the Cavaliers game, before he could leave his camp. He's going to pick Ida Mae up at home and they'll drive to the hotel to spend the night. Angie and Nicole will chill out at Ida Mae's house until the crew plan wraps up. Draper Watts will be folded into the crew's wrap, same as Old Jake will be.

CrewLand Luxury Suites and Condominiums

Officer Jacobson is off tonight. He attended the game with Genia. They are now visiting with Jessie Mae, Jeb Baker Jr and Albert Johnson at the CrewLand suites. Papa Brown, Poppa Jones and big mama are here. Mama Rena and big Archie are here too. This is yet another crew mission meeting night. The ENTIRE crew plan to get to Old Jake is laying out, *very* well. Tonight they're going over the last phase to make sure it's fool proof. Then they'll meet with the entire crew and bring them on into the *day of reckoning for Old Jake Johnson*. Before they can get into their crew discussion, Genia has some recent news which she wants to share.

"Guess who I talked to, today?" Genia says as Jacobson smiles. He already knows the news she's about to share with the crew.

"Hopefully that greedy bastard," Poppa Jones says and chuckles. Genia giggles and says, "It sure was. He saw the news about the inheritance

I received due to the deaths of my husband and daughter. He fell for it. Just like you said he would, papa Brown. He truly is a loather."

"If you look up loather in the dictionary," Albert Johnson says, "You'll see his damn picture. He always tried to live off other peoples benefits and hard work."

"We know that, *very* well," papa Brown says and chuckles too.
Jeb Jr smiles and adds, "Jessie and I know it, *just* as well."

"Truly," Jessie Mae says, "He's the very reason Jeb and I left America. He didn't want us to date. But he was always trying to get Jeb and his father to buy his friendship."

"There was no way that would've *ever* happened," Jeb Jr says. "He just couldn't get that part. My father was a true businessman and he was always about helping the next man, who was willing to do his *own* work. Jake Johnson doesn't fit into *either* one of those categories."

"He only fits into the users and N word categories," big mama says.
Big Archie says, "And he will be very well fitted into a coffin, real soon."

"It's time to rid the world of that nigger," papa Brown says, "And that's a fitting noun for *him*. It's a damn shame that he's lived this long, when his actions caused the deaths of *real* blacks. My crew and my family. I will see him take his last breath."

"And he'll have his last breath before another one of *our* crew leaves this world," Poppa Jones adds.

"He truly thinks that the money y'all set up for Genia, came from insurance policies from Matt and Kelly," Jacobson says, "As if he would be a beneficiary to *any* of it."

"That's nothing new to us," Albert Johnson says, "I'm thirty eight years old. And y'all know I left the states before I turned twenty. I was never gonna fit in with my grandfather or my father or my younger brother either. My father and brother are dead because of my grandfather and his bullshit. I tried to warn them but they called me stupid and queer. Only because I wasn't gonna beef with y'all and because I've known I was gay since before I was double digit in age. So I had to deal with hatred from my own family. Who *always* taught hate about this family. But my grand-aunt Jessie Mae and me. We learned what true love is. She learned it first and got the hell away from them. I was the only family member that she stayed in touch with and I know why."

"Because you're real," Jessie Mae says, "And I wanted to save your life. I didn't give a damn about the rest because they could care less about me. This same crew that my brother was conspiring to kill. Are the

very ones who helped Jeb and me to take care of our daughter, sitting right there." She's pointing to Rena. She continues, "Before father-in-law Jeb passed away. This crew and him, took care of us. All the way in Europe. And Albert, this crew are the ones who paid for your airline trip to Europe. I'd never told you that, until right now."

"You told me enough to make me loyal to them," Albert says, "From the day you said you wished y'all shared blood and you wasn't gonna be whole until y'all was connected *by* blood. I've been loyal to them." Big Archie says, "That happened and her name is Rebbie." They all laugh as big Archie chuckles, then adds. "My daughter and the rest of me and Rena's kids, will live out their lives in peace and harmony. This decades long bullshit *will* end before this winter does."

"And it's about damn time," Poppa Jones says.

"That works for me too," Rena says, "My kids *and* crew comes first. Always has and always will. My father is white. My mother is black. I'm both and I'm proud of it. Old Jake and those on that hatred side, I've never met and I've never wanted to meet. So his death will be no lose to me. Grandpa Jeb made sure I knew where he wanted me to be and grow from. And I'm here. The crew are my life. And *for* life. My vote has been cast in agreement to get rid of Old Jake since the seventies."

They all laugh and continue with more conversation. They're expecting a call from big Al and big John, shortly after midnight.

Ajay and Ebony's Estate! Midnight

Ebony is in *"comfort Anthony"* mode for more than 1 reason, this early morning of February 12, 2006. The Cavaliers lost to the Warriors again. Tonight's lose was by 8 points and their 2nd lose in the last 2 games. But tonight's lose was at *Quicken Loans Arena*, their own home. Ebony knows she'll have to bring that "Utah" hotel rhythm, from a few weeks ago, before he's going to rest fully. Ajay is already not liking the fact that he has to butter up Darlene. That's in order to add another step into making sure when Angel is released, the crew are in a position to have several options of taking her final breath. Plus add in the fact that the "Old Jake" mission is in forward movement, at this very moment. Ebony knows his mind is in several places, other than their bedroom. She has to change that, at once.

Lil Ajay is at Olivia's party. Lannie and Kimmie are in Lannie's room. Lea is in her own room. All 3 of them are already asleep. The triplets are resting in their bassinets, very near their parents bed as usual.

Now that Ebony and Ajay are in their California King sized bed, Ebony's mind is on 1 thing and 1 thing only. Soothing her man's mind and keeping him focused. The next game will be at home, on the night before the Valentine's Day, Quadruple wedding. The Cavaliers will play the Spurs, 2/13/2006. She knows a win is all Ajay wants in the next game. Also, she knows with all that's going on with crew, *this* week, the Old Jake mission is at the forefront of Ajay's mind. He knows it has to be a success in order to set up their next *erase* mission. Which is Angel Taylor.

"I want you to hold me so we can have one of our real talks, baby," Ebony says as she cuddles up next to him.

Ajay puts his arms around her and kisses her forehead. Then Ebony rests her head on his chest. He plays in her hair as he stares at the ceiling.

He asks, "Am I holding you right?"

"Yes," she says, "And I want you to relax. You can talk to me about *whatever's* on your mind. I don't want your focus *outside* of our home and our kids. So let's talk it out. Because I want your mind on making love to me, like usual. I can't share my love time with stress. Because that wouldn't even be my husband's way."

"I know, baby," he says, "I just need to get that text or call from Chill or pops, before I can relax."

"Anthony," she says, "Both grandfathers Brown and Jones and the rest of the first generation of crew are at CrewLand condo's, right now. I know Old Jake will belong to them before we fall asleep. When have you ever known our oldest crew to put time into *anything* and it didn't work?"

He has to chuckle after that comment. Because Ebony has just made a great point.

He says, "You're right, baby. Our first generation always hit's the mark. I'm just so use to being in the play out mix. I'm just feeling like I have to be present, for it to go smoothly."

"You've got some *smoothing* to do at home," she says and smiles. She adds, "I want you *game* ready, by tomorrow night. Because when they capture Old Jake. He's gonna belong to the *entire* crew. He will not take his last breath until every crew member, who wants a piece. Get a piece."

While smiling, he says, "You're right again. I'll chill on that part. But my mission to vet Darlene…," he shakes his head negatively.

Ebony looks into his eyes and smiles, before she says, "I know, Anthony. I know you're not comfortable being in her company. But I have to remind you of something and this should help you to understand how sincere I've always been about you and me."

"Oh wow," he says, "What is it, baby?"

"Carl, Craig, Tim and Justin."

Ajay cracks up laughing. He knows where this is going and he has to let Ebony say her peace.

He says, "Go on."

"I know you remember when me, Nina, T-baby and Rebbie had to milk them in, for a crew mission," she says.

"Yes."

"And we didn't get to complete it," she says, "But two of them are dead and the other two split town after their two friends deaths. I had to be apart of getting them to show up and you didn't like that at all. Did you?"

"Sure didn't," Ajay says, "And I know I voiced that to you, all the way from college."

They both giggle before Ebony says, "I'm glad the other two left. Baby, it ended for me when you got shot," she says sadly. "I didn't wanna be around Tim, even before I knew they were apart of Old Jake's team. But when I saw you get hit, when those guns was going off. I stopped breathing. That is the scariest I've been in my whole life. Including that night when Raymond tried to rape me. Just know that your meetings with Darlene is *crew* work. That's all it is. I know she's not on Old Jake's team or any other team that would wanna harm you. She just hopes she can get some of this."

She reaches down and grabs his dick. Then continues, "She'd do *anything* in this world to be near you. I'm not worried about Darlene. Not in the least bit. Because you have to think about me, to have sex on your mind."

"You damn right," he interrupts.

She giggles and says, "I know that, Anthony. So I want you to relax. During one of your meetings with her. You might have to let her rub on you."

"*What*! Ebony."

She says, "I'm not suggesting that you should and I already know you're not going to suggest that she do. But what if Angel was out right now and Darlene was the only one who knew where she was? And she asked you to let her earn some of her pay. She would wanna touch you and give you some head. I know that already. So would you be willing to do that if she had a direct link to Angel and we didn't?"

"Hell no," he says, "I would tell her to bring me to where that devil is at. And I'd say, after I see her. Then I'll let her do me. But in reality. I would capture both of them. I would head straight to the chamber and try to wait for Ant and the crew to get there. But if y'all take too long. I would just kill em both."

"And you know that's the same thing I would've done to Tim," she says, "If he had tried to touch me in *any* kind of way. My mind and body was and still is, for you only. That's what helped me to survive Raymond and Tim. I was smart enough to trick Raymond White when he kidnapped me and took me to the park. I knew he would've had to kill me, in order to have me. But I wasn't ready to leave you alone for the rest of your life. I had to come back to you in the same sexual condition that I left you with. And that's exactly how I was, when we saw each other again. Penetrated by you only. My love for you is what made me use my mind and I got home safe. Anthony, your mind is one hundred times more street life than mine. So I'm not the least bit worried about you being around Darlene or any other female. Just like you wasn't worried about me being around Tim, with thoughts of actually liking him. You were just worried about him pulling a sudden move that I wouldn't be prepared for. I wasn't prepared for Raymond White either. But look what happened to him. And when the time was right. I finished him. I'm so relieved that Darlene, Angel nor any other woman can out muscle you. Because they would try to take it. I know that already. I just want you to think about my situations with Tim and with Raymond. *Now.* Did I survive without being ruined?"

"You did baby," he says, "In both situations."

She says, "And so will you. This is about mentality, baby. And your mind is worth more money than we'll make in a lifetime. And we're rich *now*."

They both giggle and she adds, "You are Anthony Devante' Jackson Senior. Darlene couldn't handle your mind when you wasn't a senior. I have no doubts that you'll play this Darlene game *superb*. That's who you are, baby. And that mind of yours is what tore down every little security wall I had. Because my heart knew that you would give it your blood, if it ran out. Do you get what I'm trying to say to you?"

He gives her a very passionate kiss. Then he says, "Yes. I know what you're saying. You trust me, *completely*. Ebony that means everything to me."

"Because *I* mean everything to you," she says with a smile. "I trust you, baby. No doubts and no worries. This is a mission to remove from this world, *anyone* who did not fight to keep our very first child in this world and breathing. Handle your business, daddy." She smiles sexy.

Ebony has brought her man and his attention back to her and their bedroom. She can see that look in his eyes which automatically makes her nipples hard and her clitoris throb too. Ajay is in the mood for her. So he's back to normal. She can relax now because he's taking charge for the rest of the time they're awake.

"Your fourteen and half is calling your name," he says as he starts to kiss on her face and neck.

Ebony whispers, "My fifteen, that is. And I am *definitely* going to answer." From there, Ajay goes in. For *his* mind is now on Ebony and *Ebony only.* He'll get info on that *Old Jake Abduction* after he's tasted and drenched the sweet pussy his wife carries for him. It's *daddy Ajay* and *Baby Girl* time *now.*

Parma, Ohio

KeJuan, Dre, Joe and Pac Man are on their crew duty tonight. All 4 of them are in Parma, at different stakeout locations. Each 1 of the 4, have 4 guys with them. These extra 16 males are Dre and Joe's posse from west Cleveland. All 25 guys are now staked out and waiting to grab Old Jake and Draper Watts. Their orders are to bring them to *The Crew Chamber.*

Big Al and big John are mobile phone connected with all 4 of the teams. Big Al and big John have their locations on their video set up too. Which is located in the back office of *Stoney's Bar & Grill.* The 4 stakeout teams, 4 locations are set up as such: The KeJuan team is located on Westlake Avenue, which is Ida Mae's street. The Dre team is located on Warren Road, which is where Old Jake's home is located. The Joe team is stationed on Ridge Road. This is the long route Old Jake would sometimes travel when going to Ida Mae's house. Just in case he thought someone was trailing him. The Pac Man team is on Triskett Road which is the shortest cut to W. 150th street. That's where the *Cleveland Airport Marriott* or Old Jake and Ida Mae's hotel spot is located.

Suddenly, Dre signals the fathers at Stoney's to let them know Old Jake is in motion.

"He's leaving his house," Dre says.

Big Al says, "Stay put until we hit you back."

5 minutes later, Joe signals to let big Al and big John know Old Jake is coming down Ridge Road.

Big John says, "Cool. He's heading to miss Ida's to pick her up. Stay put and wait for your signal."

10 minutes later, KeJuan signals in to Stoney's. He has spotted Old Jake traveling up Westlake Avenue. He's been told to hold until Old Jake stops and picks up Ida Mae. Ida Mae will lead him on the route of capture.

Angie, Nicole, Draper and Ida Mae are still at Ida Mae's home when the phone rings.

Ida Mae answers in her sexiest voice, whispering, "Hello."

"Hey there, baby," Old Jake says, "I'm pulling up now."

Ida Mae says, "Okay. I'm on my way out. Did you remember to bring that package I left at your house? It has my sex pills and lingerie in it. I wanna get hot tonight."

Old Jake says, "*Damn*. It's sitting right inside the door of my house. I was in such a damn hurry to get to my pussy night. That I walked out and left it. Hurry up. We'll swing back by there to get it."

"Okay," Ida Mae says, "Here I come."

They hang up. She turns to Angie and Nicole.

She says, "Y'all better not mess up my house. Y'all can stay here while I'm out for the night. But you'd better clean up behind yourselves. Got it?"

"We got it, auntie," Angie says while giggling. She adds, "You go on and enjoy yourself. We'll see you soon."

"We want you to get to your mission with no worries," Nicole adds. "So you don't have to worry about your house being messed up. If we get *too* bold. We'll find us a hotel spot too."

All 4 of them laugh including Draper. But he's still clueless. He has no idea what's about to happen to him nor Old Jake.

Ida Mae hops into the car with Old Jake and he heads back toward his house. KeJuan signals to Stoney's. He let's them know that Old Jake is on Triskett road, heading back toward his home.

Within minutes, Pac Man signals to Stoney's that he can see Old Jake coming up Triskett Road.

Big John says, "Pull in front of him and pause at the stop sign."

That's when Pac Man notices that Joe and his team are *directly* behind Old Jake. Pac Man pulls out in front of Old Jake. When he gets to the stop sign, he stops. No other traffic's coming from either way. It's just Pac Man and his team in the front vehicle. Old Jake and Ida Mae in the 2nd vehicle. Joe and his team in the last vehicle. This is when Joe and 2 of his team hops out and moves swiftly to Old Jake's vehicle from the rear, with weapons drawn. Pac Man does the same from the front, while his 3 team members secure their vehicle. Ida Mae starts to scream. That's her part of the crew plan too. Suddenly Old Jake clicks the doors locked. Ida Mae unlocks her door immediately. Joe opens it, pulls Ida Mae out and jumps in. He places his barrel next to Old Jake's head and says, "Unlock the *fuckin* doors."

Old Jake does. That's when Pac man snatches the driver's door open. Joe pulls Old Jake toward the passenger seat. His 2 teammates jump in the back and pull Old Jake into the backseat. Pac Man takes the wheel. Joe stays passenger. Ida Mae hurries to get to Joe's car, which is still behind Old

Jakes car. Joe's last team member gets Ida Mae seated. While in the front vehicle, Pac Man's passenger team member is already in the drivers seat of the front vehicle. The other 3 are still inside the vehicle, as well. Old Jake is captured and each visual direction is secure. *No witnesses*. It's time to move.

All 3 vehicles pull away. From Pac Man's lead vehicle, 1 of his team members takes the mobile phone which Al and John are still connected on.

"We got him," The team member says.

Big Al says, "Pac man will take lead. Smooth driving. All the way east."

They keep the tracking on Pac Man and Joe's vehicles. It's time to get KeJuan and Dre on the 2nd part of the mission. Big Al starts communication with KeJuan and Dre. He says, "Move in. The ladies know the drill."

KeJuan and Dre head straight to Ida Mae's house and pull into the driveway behind Nicole and Draper's vehicles. They can hear the music playing which is their signal. Dre sends a text to Angie. A minute later, the side door opens. That's entrance into the kitchen. KeJuan and Dre bring 2 of their team members with them. 6 guys going in to snatch Draper. While 4 remain outside to secure the perimeter and keep the vehicles running.

KeJuan and Dre find Draper butt naked on the living room floor. He was about to have sex with Nicole and Angie again. Or so he thought. Nicole grabs his clothes. While KeJuan, Dre and the 4 team members grab Draper, knock him out cold and roll him up in a rug they'd brought in. Nicole search the pockets of Draper's pants and finds the keys to his Caddy SRX and KeJuan says, "Hand those to Dre. We rolling."

"Cool," Dre says, "I'm driving his Caddy with two of my team. My other two will drive my vehicle back."

KeJuan says, "Draper will go into the hatch of my Expedition. Three of my team will guard him. My final member will ride up front with me. Great job, ladies. Lock up miss Ida Mae's house and head to CrewLand."

"Got it," The girls say.

KeJuan, Dre and their 4 team members head out and load Draper into the back of KeJuan's vehicle. He's still out cold and will not be awakened until they get out on the road. Very calm and smoothly, they all start up the 3 vehicles and hit the highway.

KeJuan goes mobile to Stoney's and says, "Got second."

Big Al says, "Head in and pull to the back of *Que Psi Phi Store*. We'll meet in the stock room."

"See ya," KeJuan says.

"In a minute," big John says.

They end the mobile and video completely but leave the tracking on.

CHAPTER 72

BREAKING THE CYCLE

Ajay and Ebony's master bedroom

It's 3am at Jackson's manor. Lil Ajay has been home for an hour. With Kimmie as a house guest, Olivia's birthday party couldn't hold his attention for more than an hour. Lil Ajay left after Olivia's grand entrance. He wished her a happy birthday and left an hour after she arrived. Once he got home. He took a look at their home monitor cameras before going into his room. He wanted to make sure Kimmie was sleeping soundly. After seeing that she was, he went straight to bed.

In the master suite, Ajay's text alert goes off. He's laying snug with Ebony, after their hour long session of lovemaking. But he's still awake. Ebony has been snoozing since she heard their door chime and knew that her son was home and safe. Hearing his text alert, Ajay raises up to grab his phone. That's when Ebony wakes up. Before he even grabs the phone, Ebony says, "I told you. The first generations time always pays dividends." They both smile as Ajay grabs his phone. He has a text message from his father, big Al. The text reads:

'I just had to make sure you get some good sleep for the rest of the night. My grandson didn't wanna be nowhere else but home and we both know why. [hint: Joanna and Baby Girl status. {smile}. Son, I feel like my pops has risen from the dead. And trust me, big Ant. He's chuckling. Now go to sleep and kick the shit outta them Spurs, tomorrow night!! ☺'

Ajay smiles and allows Ebony to read the text message. She smiles too. She repeats, "I told you. *Dividends.*"

"I gotta taste my sweet pussy again," he says and slides south.

CrewLand Luxury Suites and Condominiums, 2AM

Big John just finished a phone call to his father and letting him know the mission is in over drive, bound for East Euclid and that crew owned, beef ending building in the cul-de-sac. They hang up.

"It's time to roll," papa Brown says, "The beginning of the end of this fifty year old bullshit is starting, *this* early morning. Crew team. The Chamber. Let's go."

Papa Brown, Jeb Baker Jr, Jessie Mae, Albert Johnson, Poppa Jones and

big mama head out to Poppa Jones' van. Big Archie and mama Rena hop into their car, along with Jacobson and Genia, who sit in the back seat. Both vehicles start up and pull away, heading to the chamber.

CrewLand's Que Psi Phi Pictures and Video store, 2:30AM

Big John and big Al left Corey and his partner Bobby White in charge at Stoney's Bar & Grill and headed to Que Psi Phi. Arthur meets them at the back door of his store and let's them in. They're seated in the stockroom, waiting for KeJuan aka Kilo, Dre and their teams to roll in with Draper Watts, in tow. They have an order for Draper Watts to fill. The 3 of them are watching the CrewLand security screens which cover every business in their CrewLand mall.

"Their turning into CrewLand," Arthur says.

"As soon as KeJuan backs up the back door," big Al says, "We'll roll this trolley out, secure the package and roll it in here. It's early Sunday morning. He should be able to contact the final two lessees."

Turning to Arthur, big John says, "Tim and Justin. We need to get them on this chamber run too. Me and Al have been wanting to pull the plug on Tim's bitch ass since nineteen ninety two."

"He wanted to rape John's daughter, my *only* daughter in law," big Al snorts, "And it was because of him, that my *only* son was shot. That less than ass motherfucker has *been* due for a chamber trip. Let's get this shit over with, *this* week."

"Tim and Justin are the stash brothers for Draper," big John says, "They live out in Madison. Draper has taken that trip, many times. East on I ninety, would take about forty five minutes. But once Kilo brings him in here. He's gonna contact their asses. See where they are. It's Saturday night. Club night for that generation. At least, the *less than* types. We know where they frequent too."

"That *up* culture, in Mentor," big Al adds, "Let's roll this bitch ass nigger in here and get this shit moving."

Kilo and Dre just backed up to the stock room entrance door. Arthur opens it.

Within minutes, they have Draper inside and chained to that same bench. Which was the last seat for Farah's man, Marvin Huntley. Farah's boyfriend from Philly, lost his air on that *same* night. Draper Watts might last until the weekend. Only because the entire crew, by time organized shifts, will take part in the demise of Draper, Tim, Justin and Old Jake.

The Chamber

Papa Brown and his van load have arrived, along with big Archie and his car load. Pac Man, Joe and their teams was already inside with Old Jake chained to the rafters.

"It's been a long time," papa Jackson Brown says to Old Jake, as he strolls in. He adds, "I know you remember me. Don't you, Jake?"

"If you remember me," Old Jake says, "You know I remember you too. Why are you doing this to me?"

"It had your name on it," Poppa Jones says, "Your name was on those chains you're hanging from. Just like it was on the tab for those of our crew, who's lives were taken. You saw fit to take them away from us."

"But they're in heaven, if there is one," Papa Brown says, "And my wife Pearline is there with them. She's gone, Old Jake. And no. You didn't have anything to do with taking her. Not physically. But all of your bullshit since those years of changes in this country, aided in the stress which she kept built up. And that stress is what caused her life to end."

Big mama says, "She was my best friend and I miss her. She and I talked about all the beef and bullshit that was caused by you, *many* times. Both long distance calls and even after me and my man Percy, moved back here. In every crew members mind, the stress from the unnecessary bullshit done by you, is what caused her to leave."

Big Archie says, "And you will go too. Only you'll be in hell and nowhere near those crew angels, who are floating above us right now."

"My mother, father, my grandfather and both of my grandmothers are floating around us in this chamber, right now."

All of the crew and Old Jake look toward the voice that just made that last comment. It's Kenneth Ramon Payne Sr aka Big Chill. He left Jr in charge of The Chill Spot because he *had* to be apart of Old Jake' first night at the crew's chamber of justice.

"Come on forward, Chill," papa Brown says.

Chill walks toward Old Jake. He's holding a Billy club in his right hand. He walks into the demolition square which Old Jake hangs above.

Chill says, "Lower his ass. I want him to look me *directly* in my face. And if he has any balls. He will."

Pac Man and Joe releases the chain pulley and lowers Old Jake, so that he's eye to eye with big Chill.

"Oh my," Old Jake says, chuckling, "All those you just mentioned. They saw me since you saw them. So you know my wrath, don't you?"

TIME TO SHOW-RELOADED-Time Will Reveal 6

KeJuan and his team of 4 are seated in his Expedition, in the parking lot of Toth Place nightspot in Mentor. They have driven Draper Watts to the club where Tim and Justin frequent on Saturday nights. Big John and big Al trailed them in Draper's Caddy SRX. It's being used as a mission vehicle. That idea came from Dre since he apprehended it in Parma. Dre and his teams members are here too. They're now in 1 of their street mission vans. They have 4 vans now. But the 1 their in tonight, is the same van which they used back when they did the fake kidnapping of Matt. And the same 1 they used for the *real* kidnapping of Marvin Huntley. Dre and his team are parked right next to the Caddy SRX, waiting for Tim and Justin to come out to the Caddy thinking they're meeting up with Draper. Arthur left his store keys in big Al and big John's possession. His part of the mission is complete for tonight. When they all left the Que Phi Psi, Arthur headed back to The Chill Spot to assist Jr and Tonya. While Chill left to go handle a historic part of this crew mission at the crew chamber.

From inside of the Expedition, KeJuan shows Draper Watts that he still holds his cell phone.

He says, "These niggers we need to get at. Is inside that club, right there. Now…, you do remember what I've said to you since we left Parma. Do you wanna live?"

"Yes man. Please," Draper says in fear.

"You will need to call your stash brothers," KeJuan says.

"Is this about *drugs*?" Draper asks as he trembles. He adds, "Dude, y'all can have my *whole* stash. I'll get you some more, if you want me too. All I have to do is call big Jake. He holds the grove. That's where I get mine from. Please, brother. We can work this out. I swear to you. I won't even remember none of this."

KeJuan thinks about what big John and big Al said to them, before him, Dre, Joe and Pac Man headed to Parma.

Big Al and big John's words:

"Grab dude and bring him in. Once he's in east Cleveland. We'll use him to get Justin and Tim back in Cleveland. They're his stash brothers. So their contact info is in his phone. He's gonna think this is about drugs. Until he sees the crew whom he knows is crew. So make it like it's about a bad drug deal and he'll call them. To make sure he does. Tell him you'll sweeten the deal."

Then KeJuan says, "Call your stash brothers. If you've got enough to

replace this deal gone bad. Then we can let you get on back to your sex night with them ho's you had at that crib, we snatched you from. Let's get this deal sealed up. So you can get back to your jimmy action. I'm sure they done called the cops by now. And if our work starts to look like it's gonna be interfered with. I'm gonna go ahead and do your ass in. Then go back and wax them ho's too. Here's your phone. What's it gonna be?"

Draper makes a call to Tim's cell phone. He answers on the 1st ring. Draper tells him, he's in the parking lot. He needs to do a pick up.

"Cool," Tim says, "Me and Justin bout to come out now. You in the Caddy? Or one of big Jake's rides?"

"SRX," Draper says with hand gestured instructions from KeJuan.

"On our way," Tim says and they hang up.

Tim and Justin head out of the club and head straight to Draper's Caddy truck. Only Draper is the Expedition, they passed. From the Expedition, Draper can now see Tim and Justin as they approach his SRX. They approach the passenger and rear passenger doors. Just as always, they're prepared for Draper to pop the locks of his deeply tinted vehicle, so they can hop in and roll out. But the doors that open are the slide doors of the van next to it. Dre and his team bounce on Tim and Justin immediately.

Within a minute, the have them subdued and inside the mission van. That's when guns are drawn. Tim and Justin surrender completely. Dre's team cuffs them in place. Dre puts it in drive and heads out. KeJuan and big John leave out behind them. They're all headed to the chamber.

CrewLand. 4AM

It's closing time for The Chill Spot. Stoney's Bar & Grill will close in an hour. All crew from The Chill Spot head over to Stoney's to make sure they can close at 5:00am, promptly.

The Chamber

Chill didn't respond to Old Jake's question. He wanted to hold off until big Al and big John got here. After that question from Old Jake, papa Brown took the floor and had Old Jake raised back up to the ceiling. They haven't allowed him to see their surprises yet. Jessie Mae, Jeb Jr, Albert and Rena are here. But they're in the bedroom, hidden out of view. Where they can see and hear everything said on the killing floor. Big Archie is standing next to Chill, who's phone rings instantly. With that, Chill signals big Archie, Jacobson, Joe and Pac Man and they all head toward the back

of the chamber to reopen the boat garage door. They stand off to the side. That's when the van, the Caddy SRX and the Expedition drives in and parks. They close the large opening back. Then they assists KeJuan, Dre and their teams with getting Draper, Tim and Justin chained and hoisted into mid air. Right next to Old Jake. Then Chill goes back to the killing room floor and has Old Jake lowered again.

"So you asked me if I'm familiar with your wrath," Chill says. "I feel you know that answer already. But I'm gonna humor you. I'll treat it like that question was your last will and testament. I have some names for you. *One*. Edwina Destiny Flowers-Payne. My *Fraternal* grandmother. Death date. March eleventh. Nineteen seventy seven. *Two*. Margaret Renee Wright. My *Maternal* grandmother. Death date. She was killed exactly 6 months later on September eleventh. Nineteen seventy seven. *Three*. Willamena Wright-Payne. My *mother*. Death date. March seventeenth. Nineteen seventy nine. *Four*. Paul Payne Junior. My *father*. Death date. January thirty first. Nineteen eighty eight. *Five*. Cheston Wayne "Stoney" Coleman. My brother from another mother and father. And my best friend in this world, too date. Death date. December twenty sixth. Nineteen ninety. That's the wrath of yours, I'm familiar with Old Jake. My grandfather Paul Payne Senior. My *Fraternal* grandfather. Died before all of them, on October seventeenth. Nineteen seventy one. You didn't cause that one. But you wanted to and you wished you had. That is the reason you took the lives of the first five that I named. *So*. Does that make you proud?"

"They supported those assholes who was cheating me outta my earnings," Old Jake tries.

"That's a lie."

That statement comes from the voice of a man heading toward the killing floor, from the front hallway. Old Jake can't see his face. It's a man's voice but he can't see him yet. Finally that man gets to the killing floor and stands right next to Chill.

"When the fuck did you get to walk free?" Old Jake asks.

He's talking to Stoney's father, Chester Lee. Who was released from the California Federal prison on yesterday. And flown straight to Cleveland with and by business mogul Bert Parkwood and attorney George Wheeler.

"I've been walking free since that day I took the wrap for killing your son and first namesake, Jacob Denard Johnson Junior," Chester Lee says with a chuckle.

"Took the wrap, my ass," Old Jake says, "You killed him and a life sentence was given to you. You was never suppose to be allowed to get out o

jail. You didn't give my son another chance and the penal system wasn't suppose to give you one either. But let me guess. Y'all bought y'all way into the penal system and the laws of the land too. Is that it?"

"No," big Al says as he approaches the floor, "That's not it."

Big John approaches with Al and adds, "That's not it, at all. He did some time that he was never suppose to get."

"But he took the wrap for me and my crew brother, right here," big Al says as he points to big John. He continues, "Your real hatred was for *my* father, Allen Devante' Jackson Senior. And his best friend, Paul Payne Senior. And my father-in-law, Allen Saul Williams. Yet you never got to take the lives of those three men. *Real* men. *Strong* men. You did get a few of ours, over these decades."

"Those five who were named by Chill," big John says, "Are the ones you took. Yet the ones of yours we took, is in the hundreds. And to this motherfuckin day, you haven't learned shit. You were never equal to us. Nor were you a match for us. Fool, that's the reason you came to Al and Chill's *father's*. To get on good. But your nigger mentality could never fit in. We are *black* people. We don't sell out our own, for *any* reason. You will though. Like these three young men hanging next to you. Some more sheep, led to slaughter by your lazy, less than a black man ass."

Big Al starts again, "You caused hundreds of your team to die because you didn't want to do your own damn work. You wanted to kill the loves, the families and the kids of the three men I just named. I am Allen Devante' Jackson Junior. I choked the life out of your son."

"While I was splitting his worthless head open," big John says, "I cut his ears off and drew your name on his forehead *and* his back, with my knife. Remember when Chester Lee couldn't even tell the courts any of the particulars about what injuries your son had? Of course, you do. It's because he wasn't involved in it. He was ten yards away from us. Kicking asses and taking names."

"And taking lives too," Chester says and chuckles, "I took many of em out that day. Just not the one I got the time for. But the problem I have with you now. Is that you took my *only* son. Simply because you couldn't get to the sons and grandsons of the three men, Al named. And my crew came right back and got those three ass holes who took my son."

"And still, your dumb and selfish ass, *still* did not stop," Jessie Mae says.

She has emerged from the bedroom. With her is Jeb Jr, Albert and mama Rena. This surprise for Old Jake, assures him that his death date is near.

Jeb Baker Sr had told Old Jake, way back in the beginning of this madness. Jeb Sr had said, *"If you ever lay eyes on your sister again and she's still with my son. You will meet your maker, very soon after that visual."*
Old Jake cannot speak. He has no come back for his own sister. Not at this very minute.
Jessie Mae continues, "You never had the type of love in your life, that I found with Jeb. I didn't give a shit what his *race* was. He treated me royal. Like I was a princess."

"That's what you were to me and now, you're a queen," Jeb Jr says. Then turning to Old Jake, he says, "My father could've had you killed in the fifties, for all the bullshit that you was bringing to him about me and your sister. And about him being white. But what you never realized is this. If my father was in *anyway* like those racist assholes who was allowing you to stay alive to bring drama to Jessie? Then he could have killed you in broad daylight, in front of the busiest section of Cleveland. And he would never have gotten *any* time. Simply because that's how things were, when it came down to black and white. My father never liked that discrimination type of shit. His life was filled with ways to get rid of it. To treat people the way they treated him. The most fucked up thing about it. Black people treated my father with respect. And white people tried to disrespect him because he gave out equal treatment. He treated you the same way he treated me. Yet, you had a problem with him because your sister liked me."

"I loved you then and I still do, to this day," Jessie Mae says, "It is *so* much stronger now. Because you and your family treated me better than my own did. Even before you came into my life, Jake here was an asshole to me." Turning to Old Jake, she adds, "You was trying to pimp me out to *any* male that you knew. Our parents were killed by those same mentalities of people whom you went along with, just to try to pull down father Jeb and the black families in this crew. They all looked out for me and Jeb. *All* of them. And because of them. We made it. We moved abroad and became parents. This is our daughter. Her name is Rena. Rena Baker Wilson."

"My wife," big Archie says to Old Jake, "And let me let you know this. If you say one thing disrespectful to her. You will die *way* before whenever my crew initially planned for it to happen."

"She's beautiful," Old Jake finally says. "She *is* mixed. I can see that. But she has more advantages because she can pass for white."

"Shut up, dumbass," mama Rena says, "That is the very reason I never cared it I *ever* met you. You are an embarrassment to my mother and father. To my husband and this crew family, you are a waste. My kids will

never have to lay eyes on you, after today . And for that. I thank *God*! You have never been added to any genealogical chart nor any family tree of mine. That will not change. And just so you know. My vote went in first, for you to go *directly* to hell. And as quick as possible. Hello and goodbye."

"Just so you know," Albert starts, "I'm still gay and I'm still proud of who I am and of my life. And just like my first cousin Rena. I loathed you. I wish you wasn't kin to me. And I'm ready for you to go on to hell too. That's where you've been, for all of my life. So I just wanna say it like Nino Brown from New Jack City. *See ya. I wouldn't wanna be ya!*"
Everyone in the room laughs. All except the 4 who are hanging from the rafters. Old Jake, Draper, Tim and Justin are going to die before the quadruple wedding which is tomorrow.

The sun is rising now. Those who plan to attend church today, are preparing to leave. Chill isn't 1 of them. Him, KeJuan, Dre, Joe, Pac Man and their teams are staying put. So is Chester Lee. Chill is waiting on 1 person to show up before these 4 are sent to meet their maker. Kenneth Ramon Payne Jr is due to arrive by 6am. Ten minutes from now. He's 1 of the grooms, for tomorrow. But today, he's the son of big Chill and the grandson and great-grandson of those killed by Old Jake. He has to be present before Old Jake takes his last breath.

Kenny Jr arrives at 6am, on the dot. He brought his fiancée Chaundra Denise Coleman, along with him. She will become his wife at the quadruple wedding tomorrow at noon. Chaundra is very excited. Not only because she's marrying the only love of her life. But also, she's about to see her father again for the first time since she was 5 years old.

Chill meets them at the door and walks them to the killing floor, where Chester and the rest are. Chill, Chester and the 4 teams are already prepared to do torture. They were just waiting for Kenny Jr to arrive.

"Chaundra, it is *so* good to see you in person again," Chester says. "I've enjoyed all of the mail, you and Charlotte sent to me over the years. You're still just as beautiful as you were, the day that I left."
Surprised and in tears already, all Chaundra can say is, "I missed you, daddy. I missed you so much. I didn't know you was gonna be here."

"Well of *course*," Chester says, "I have to give my daughter away tomorrow. I've missed you too, baby. It's been almost twenty years since I seen you in person. You hadn't long turned five years old when I was sent to prison. Charlotte was two. When she turned three, November of eighty six. I had served only six months of that life sentence. Your brother sent me picture of you both." Then pointing up at Old Jake, as he hangs from

chains, Chester says, "Up until he was killed by that old asshole, hanging right up there. But I still got pictures from the father of this young man that you're about to marry. Brother Chill and his crew made sure I got up-to-date looks of you and your sister, after Cheston was killed. And since your stepfather Jason came into your life. He's made sure that I got pictures too. Plus copies of you and Charlotte's report cards, certificates and all. So the only thing I missed was seeing your faces in person. Today, I can do that."

Chaundra is overcome with tears of joy. All she can do is hang onto her father and cry. She keeps looking into his eyes and then burying her head on his chest. She's at a lost for words. Chester inquires about Charlotte.

He asks, "Is your baby sister in town yet? I know she's in your wedding."

Kenny Jr answers him, saying, "Brandon is bringing her now. They just parked outside. Charlotte is gonna be overcome, just like my baby is. Cause they didn't know you was gonna be here. We wanted them to be surprised."

"You've been a good man to my daughter, Lil Chill," Chester says, "I already know your daddy done told you all about me. Because he told me all about you."

Chester and Kenny Jr chuckle as Chill looks on and smiles.

Kenny Jr says, "You know he did. You and my grandpa Paul was best friends. So I already know you're crew to your heart and as real as they come. So I want to make sure you know. I will take *very* good care of your daughter, right here. She's been my only girl. My first and only girlfriend. It took me awhile to convince her. But since she's gotten to know my crew and how the men are. She knows it's all about her, as for as love, affection and attention goes. She just finished college in December. I won't get my degree until a year from now. She's got me by two years."

"But you're man enough, son," Chester says as him and Chill give each other a pound and both of them chuckle hard.

Then Chill says, "He'll graduate before he turns pro. He could've went into the draft after his freshman year. But Renee wasn't having it."

"She wants him to get his college degree," Chester says, "That's a queen. She knows what's important. I'm honored the meet you again, Lil Kenny. You was a baby boy when I got sentenced. But I knew you had the qualities of a leader because your papa Paul Payne Junior, was *no* joke. Solid man. Hearing about his death from prison." he shakes his head. Then he continues, "It assured me that this old bastard hanging right here. Had to go and he will leave this world, right here in this chamber. The *legendary* chamber. I was here when we got possession of this building. He's the reason we bought this place and set it up to do, just what's done here."

Chill says, "So it's only justified that we drain his blood. Right here in the building that he inspired my grandfather's crew to buy and open up. Let's get started. Other crew will be in and out, during the day. But let's be clear. All of these maggots will be dead and disposed of, before my son and your daughter are man and wife."

"True that," Kenny Jr says.

Then he turns to greet Brandon and Charlotte as they're head to the killing floor to meet them.

"Oh my God!!!!" Charlotte screams as she runs straight to Chester and jumps into his arms. She continues screaming, "Daddy! It's you! I'm so glad to see you! Chaundra's getting married tomorrow! I know you're gonna give her away! Right, daddy?!"

While laughing and hugging Charlotte, Chester says, "I am. I most certainly am. And I'm gonna be here to see my future son-in-law Brandon, graduate high school in three months. Then I'll be ready to give you away to him. Whenever he's ready to take on that job, fulltime."

He gives Brandon a handshake and a hug.

He adds, "You're going to the NBA like Ajay did, ha?"

"Oh yes sir," Brandon says, "I'm going to college first. Charlotte can tell y'all where I'm signing at. Nobody knows but her."

"And I'm gonna wait until after the wedding," Charlotte says, "This is Chaundra, Britt, Roo and Pam's time to shine."

"We got to finish college first," Brandon says, "Then once I go to the NBA. We're getting married and Charlotte is gonna be a nurse. She's already studying for it at Cleveland State. But next fall, we'll both be heading off to college. And like I said, she'll tell you where."

They all laugh. Then it's time to start the torturing session for the 4 less than black fools, who still hang from the rafters.

"We're the first shift," Chill says, "Big Chester? Do you think your two daughters want in on this?"

"I do," Chaundra says, "It was Old Jake's fault that my daddy has been gone for twenty years. If he wouldn't have ever started this beef. My daddy would've still been here and my big brother would still be alive. Give me some mace. I wanna blind his old butt, if nothing else."

"Me too," Charlotte says, "Big Chill, this ain't our first time seeing this building. Did you know that?"

Chill looks at Kenny Jr and Brandon, shakes his head and chuckles.

Then he says, "Y'all crew just moves shit *too* fast. The females don't suppose to be out here, until … Oh well fuck it. Kenny your mama came out

here early too." He chuckles hard. Then he adds, "But she was living with us. So daddy said she had to know the drills."

"And she knows them too," Chaundra says.

"She sure does," Charlotte agrees. She adds, "Sister Renee and all the big sisters have been teaching us the crew game, since day one. I got my mace. Let me at him."

KeJuan aka Kilo, Dre, Joe and Pac Man pulls the levee and lowers Old Jake, Tim, Justin and Draper to the floor. Then they tighten the gag rags which have been tied throw their mouths and knotted behind their heads. That way, they're top teeth and bottom teeth will show when the pain hits them. Chaundra and Charlotte start to mace all 4 of them while all 24 of the males grab their Billy clubs. It's a time to kill. *Crew Style.*

Chill & Renee's Estate, Jackson Heights

It's 8am on this Sunday Morning. February 12, 2006. All of the crew's out of town family are in town and settled in, by now. Big Al's sister Jessica Jackson-Layton is here. She's resting at Jo and big Al's home. She didn't bring her husband Dr. Jonathan Layton, on this trip. Her son Terrell and his wife Christina are staying at Ajay and Ebony's home, along with Yolanda and David.

Jb, Jr and Ced are at the chamber. So are Rob, Wayne and Arthur. They brought Charles to the chamber with them. The chamber action is well into the 2nd shift of torture. And none of the 1st shift vacated the premises because none of them wanted to leave until Old Jake was dead and *nearly* buried. The crew's death team will continue increasing in numbers, throughout the day. Until all 4 of their enemies, cease to have breath.

Renee, Tonya and Black are at Renee and Chill's home. They're kicked back and ready for some conversation. With them are the Atlanta female crew; Jan, Bre, Lynn and Julie Von Reese.

"So ladies," Renee says, "As we all know. We'll have us a trip to the chamber today."

"Yes we *will*," Lynn says, "I can wait to pluck that old bastard who has lived *all* of these years, as a thorn in our side. Even before those of us in *this* damn room was even born."

"That old asshole took my first love," Bre says, "I have been waiting for this day since December the twenty sixth. Nineteen ninety. I *gots* to stab his ass for every year that Stoney's been gone. I don't care if the first stab kills him. I'm going in!"

"That maggot *gots* to die," Jan says, "Do y'all realize how damn long it's been since Old Jake has been a thorn to our crew?"

"Since the 2nd generation of crew was still single," Tonya says.

Black says, "I have to let y'all know. I'm honored just for y'all to bring me in this crew camp. Renee and Tonya brought me up on all the history. Now I hate that motherfucker, the same way. How the fuck did he live this long? Sending all his fools after the crew. And they're *long* dead and buried. They ain't even stanking, no more."

They all laugh. Black is always humorous but she's very real about human rights too. And she's definitely gangster to the core.

"I feel honored too, Black," Julie says, "I've been feeling that honor for some *years* now."

"Since nineteen ninety nine," Tonya says.

Jokingly and while referencing Prince's famous song, "1999", Lynn sings, *"Whoops! James "The Bulldog" Taylor, party was over, Oops he's outta time!"*

"Julie that was a smooth ass move you did," Jan says while still laughing at Lynn's song.

Bre adds, "She poisoned the hell outta that *little* dangling dick ass *scrub*."

They all laugh hard. Then Julie continues.

"Doing away with him was so easy," she says. Then laughing, she adds, "Lynn told me the reason I was able to have been in his life and not even be labeled as a suspect. It's because I'm white."

Lynn yells, "That's it! I'm telling you! That's why they never hounded you, sister girl!"

Julie giggles and says, "Whatever. I feel it's because he was worthless. But anyway. From the first day Lynn brought me into this family business. I've been waiting to get to this point of seeing the crew remove Old Jake Johnson. And let's not forget our near future statistic. The next crew chamber resident. Because that move is just as necessary as removing Old Jake. And I know y'all already know whom it is that I'm speaking on."

"Deviled ass Angel," Lynn says and they all laugh again.

"I wanna come back for that bitch's home going," Black says.

"You know you in," Renee says, "We're gonna keep you posted."

"And we will make sure you get to join us at the killing field too," Bre says, "The same way you're going with us today. "

"You will damn sho be going to Angel's home going," Tonya says. "Because you and Julie are crew family now. You're in there."

Jan says, "For damn sho. But now Julie. Tell me what that bitch talked

about on your visit with her, on Thursday. I can't wait to start stacking building blocks on this shit."

"Yes," Tonya says, "That's what this early morning chat is about. Julie's visit with Angel."

Bre says, "What the fuck was she talking about? Lil Ajay, I'll bet you."

Julie says, "We did discuss her phone calls with Ajay and Lil Ajay. It was so weird to me, though. Because *now*, she's sounding like she wants to fuck Ajay and his son too."

"I wouldn't doubt it, one bit," Renee says. "The Ajay's are the crew's trump cards."

Lynn says, "*Indeed*. That bitch has it *bad* for my brother. She's a hundred times worse than Darlene, Angie, Nicole or Anita. Hell, even Raquel had it bad for Ajay. But didn't not one of them other ho's try no shit, like Angel did."

"The bitch ran Ebony of a cliff," Renee says somberly, as she reminisces on that awful day in 1994. She adds, "I wanted Angel's ass to die, instead of going to prison. I wished she'd had a good lawyer. One that would've represented her to the point of her not getting that sentence."

Jan says, "I know exactly what you mean. Me and Ajay discussed Angel's death while we was freshman at UC. Taking her ass out the game was on Ajay's mind the whole time we was at the University of Cincinnati."

"And it hasn't changed," Renee says, "Chill talks to me about it, at least once a month. Trust me. Ajay has not and will not live that down."

"And Lil Ajay is even more determined than Ajay is," Lynn says. "He is Ajay, *reborn*. But only Lil Ajay has less patience for bullshit than Ajay did."

Black adds, "He just wants to get all the bullshit out the way. That's what he was born to do. He's the fourth generation of this crew. Nothing would shock me, about him."

"For real," Julie agrees.

Then Lynn says, "There is one other person in chains, out there where we're about to head too,…that my brother is going to demand that him and my nephew Lil Ajay, get to take air from."

"Tim Murphy," Bre says.

"Oh hell yea," Jan says, "That punk bitch was the one who started that shit at the U, on the day Ajay got shot. *Hell* yea. Ajay probably already put that demand in."

"And Chill and the first two generations of crew will oblige him," Tonya says.

Bre says, "Trust and believe that. It's about what's owed to him. Justice, on his terms. That is one crew rule that I love. My sisters remember my equal rights act in nineteen ninety one. I know you do."

"For sho," Renee says, "Danny Washington."

Tonya adds, "The last one of those three nothing ass bastards who killed Stoney, that was still alive for more than a few days *after* killing Stoney."

"And only because he was still in the hospital," Jan says, "From where Stoney shot his ass."

Lynn says, "In the fucking head too. And his ass didn't die from Stoney's two shots."

"But I finished his ass on off," Bre says, "I rode with the males in our crew. They did do away with his girl, who was there. *Shit*. They was *wanting* there to be other motherfuckers in that house."

They all giggle and Black says, "Lucky for them other motherfuckers, that they wasn't there."

"Or they would be dead too," Julie says and smiles.

Then Bre says, "After I killed Danny and we was rolling back to our block. I felt CJ move in my stomach, for the first time."

They're all quiet for a moment. Then Renee gets their attention again.

She says, "Speaking of moving. It's nine o'clock. Our group is to be at the chamber for ten. Let's hit it."

"Yea," Lynn says, "Like CJ did back then? Let's move."

They all laugh as they head out to their vehicles and load up.

The Chamber. 10am

When Renee and the girls arrive, they see that Ajay, Ebony and Lil Ajay are here. Tank, Nina, T-baby, Wes, Lil Rich, Rebbie and June are here too. Everyone who was here earlier with Chill and Chester, are still here. Including Lil Kenny, Chaundra, Charlotte and Brandon. Not to mention, Jessie Mae, Jeb Jr and Albert have returned. So has mama Rena, big Archie, Jacobson and Genia. It is evident that Old Jake, Tim, Draper and Justin will be dying very soon. Chill has already supplied each crew member with their weapon of choice. They can hear the front door opening.

A minute later, big Al and John appears. With them, they've brought along Ida Mae Graves. Old Jake is shocked to see her with them. Big Al just looks at him and smiles.

5 minutes after securing all doors, Arthur, Rob, Jb and Jr come straight back to the killing floor and grab their weapons. They brought

304

Charles and David back in with them and supply them with a weapon of their liking too. Black smiles at David and Charles. She knew they would be down for this type of action. And being that they're males, she knew they would be allowed to come. But Yolanda isn't. Not at this time. But Black is sure she'll be all the way in by the time Angel is hung from these rafters.

From the start, Ajay walks up under where Tim is hanging. He looks up and him.

He says, "I'm about to bring you down to the floor and we not having no kind of conversation either, you bitch. You're dying this round."

After KeJuan lowers Tim to the floor, at Ajay's request. Lil Ajay walks up to Tim and says, "You the bitch ass nigger that got my pops shot. Right?"

Tim is afraid. He doesn't say anything. Lil Ajay chokes up on the baseball bat, he's holding. He swings it with all of his might and hits Tim in the abdomen. Tim chokes, then coughs uncontrollably. Lil Ajay cracked a rib.

Lil Ajay says, "You had plans of hurting my mama. See her, right there?"

Lil Ajay asks as he points to Ebony. Then he says, "That queen is my mama. She belongs to my daddy. The king of my home. I need you to tell me one thing. Was it worth losing your life, to do dirty work for this old man?"

"No," Tim answers in an almost whisper.

Lil Ajay hits him in the abdomen again. Tim chokes and coughs again. At that moment, Chill signals to Pac Man, Joe and Dre to lower Old Jake, Justin and Draper too.

Chill says, "Let's get this over with. We got a big wedding in two days. Poppa Jones and papa Brown just sent me a text. They'll be in here shortly. It's time to erase this part of our history. For *good*."

Everybody else agrees. Some even clap. By that time, papa Brown and Poppa Jones are heading onto the killing floor. They each have long razors.

"We're going to do our part, sixties style," Poppa Jones says with a chuckle.

Papa Brown says nothing. He just walks up to Old Jake and slits his throat. Afterwards, Jessie Mae, Rena and Jeb Jr pound on him with their bats, for a half minute or so. Albert takes his knife and approaches Old Jake, who's already bleeding profusely.

Albert asks, "Do you remember those days when you tried to sale me to the highest bidder? Because you knew I was a gay young man?"

Old Jake can't answer him. But in his eyes, he's still showing no remorse at all. He tries to smile. That's when Albert takes his knife and stabs him in the spot where his heart would be, if he had one.

Next up is Chester Lee. He doesn't have but a few words to say.

"This is for Cheston Wayne "Stoney" Coleman," Chester says as he hits Old Jake on his left side and ride side. Two times, each side with a bat. Chaundra and Charlotte swing their clubs and hits him in the head, a few times each. From there, Chill and Lil Kenny takeover and do the rest. They beat him with Billy Clubs until he's no longer breathing. They continue hitting him, even after it's *obvious* he's already dead. Then Chill steps back and stands next to Renee. But Lil Kenny continues to beat Old Jake's dead body.

"That's for my grandpa!" Lil Kenny yells and hits him again and again and again. As he yells, "That's for both of my great grandmothers! And that's for my uncle Stoney! You son of a bitch!"
Chaundra joins Lil Kenny and reps Old Jake several more times with her club. Old Jake is dead. There are 3 more less than ass deadbeats to go.

Ajay and Lil Ajay are still in front of Tim. That's when Ajay looks over at Ebony. She comes to him. He doesn't even have to call her name.
Ajay says, "You remember our night together, after that movie night?"
Ebony just shakes her head yes and lifts her golf club up and puts the tip of it, under Tim's nose. She pushes up on it and makes Tim look into her eyes. She asks, "Was your job for Old Jake, to rape me?"
Tim says nothing and turns his glace away from her. Ebony chokes up on her golf club. With that, Tim says, "That's what he wanted me to do. But I wasn't gonna do that."
Ebony whops him across his head and breaks the skin, *convincingly*.
Lil Ajay yells, "My mama's got a swing on her! She busts this deadbeats head open!"
He's laughing. He's impressed.
Ajay says, "You know your mama ain't no pussy, son. She just carries mine for me."
They laugh and so does several others in their crew. T-baby is pregnant but she wants in. So does Nina and Rebbie. Tank, June, Jb and Rob are already doing Justin in. While Jr, Arthur, Brandon and the rest are working on Draper. Every crew member gets involved with the remaining 3 enemies.
Wes says, "I knew I was connected to the right side of my black skin. I thank my big sister, *everyday!*"
Renee giggles as they all continue to beat, cut and brutalize Justin, Draper and Tim. Black is going from 1 to the other, on every swing of her bat.
She yells, "I'm telling y'all now. I've got several muafuckahs I want y'all to bring all the way to Cleveland and hang their asses up here. I'll do them assholes by myself. Y'all don't even have to put in no work."

Everybody is laughing and still doing work. It isn't long before Draper, Tim and Justin are as dead as doornails.

"I'm tired as fuck!" Chester says and laughs. He adds, "But hey! I wouldn't have wanted to miss this shit here, for the world! We got their air! Hell yea! Now let's get these bitch asses to the dirt, so I can get to some of that good ass food the women are cooking. I know how crew rolls *daily*. And this is Sunday *too*!"

Everybody laughs again but agrees, as Chill says, "Let's clean house."

With that, each of them precede with they duties of cleaning, wrapping and doing away with any and all signs that either Old Jake, Draper, Justin or Tim had even been here.

By 1pm, all the cleaning is done. It's time to do away with the burned and slaughtered remains of these four *has beens*. That's not going to be a problem at all. Joe and Dre had some more of their team to bring 2 of their vans. The bagged remains are ready to roll. Now it's time to move.

As everybody's rolling out, Rena tells Chaundra and Charlotte, "Let's head on over to CrewLand. Chaundra you're going to kick back, eat and chill with the other brides to be. Bridal shower *times* four is tonight."

That's when Nina says, "The four way bachelor party is tomorrow night. And y'all brides-to-be got to get busy finding out where it is. So let's hit it!"

All the females laugh while the males look at each other and shake their heads.

Lil Rich says, "The only bride to find out where her groom's party was, was auntie Ebony. That can't change. Right fellows?"

"That's right!!!" All the men yell as they chuckle and head out.

Dre, Joe, KeJuan, Pac Man and their teams are doing the disposals. They load into the 2 vans and their other vehicles. Leaving Draper's SRX inside the Chamber. Wayne, Rob, big Archie and Jr had already taken it apart and wrapped all of the parts separately. The descriptive parts are in the vans with what's left of the bodies. Those will be disposed of, as well. The unidentifiable parts will remain secured in the chamber until the crew can find use for them. Or give them away as donations, much later on down the line.

Crew's House of Soul Food, 2/12/2006 @ 3pm

All generations and crew families are gathered at *Crew's House* for dinner. Today is *crew only* day. Which is fine because there are more than enough crew to fill the restaurant to full capacity. And then some.

Chester Lee gets to see his ex-girl Jackie Coleman-Carr. Her and Jason are here. Justine is here. They have just been joined by her fiancée KeJuan, who's back from his dumping mission. Jason tells Jackie, Justine and KeJuan, they're going to sit with Chester, Charlotte and Brandon and catch up on some long overdue conversation. They all do just that. Chester likes this but he has to add some humor.

"I can already see that he's got some *real* good sense," Chester says to Jackie. He adds, "He managed to get you to do what you're told."

"Oh shut up," Jackie says and they all laugh.

Then Jason says, "It took awhile. But she's doing pretty good now."

"My stepmother is on the one," Justine says, "I love her to pieces."

Jackie says, "Same goes for you, Justine. I've been getting some great wedding ideas from this wedding that's going down, in two days. We'll be more than ready for you and KeJuan."

KeJuan just looks at Justine, then to Jacob and Chester. They all laugh before KeJuan says, "Bring it on, mom-in-law. Let me hear the juice."

"She can't tell you the bride side," Justine butts in. She adds, "But we'll let you know all of it. If you tell us where the bachelor party is going to be at, tomorrow night."

"Oh hell no," KeJuan says and cracks up laughing.

"They already trying to trap you up, brother," Chester says. Then he asks, "So you two are next in line to jump the broom, ha?"

KeJuan says, "That's what the word is."

"We *are*," Justine says as she laughs and holds her left hand out to Chester, so he can see her engagement ring.

"That's a *nice* diamond," Chester says, "Good job, brother man. So when is the date?"

"Less than a year from now," KeJuan says.

"January twentieth. Two thousand and seven," Justine finishes.

Jacob says, "As you can see. My daughter is already finishing his sentences. Did you peep that, Chester? Where'd she learn that from?"

"Your wife," Chester says and they all crack up laughing.

They laugh more and enjoy some great conversation and great food too.

Jessie Mae, Ida Mae, Jeb Jr and Albert are here and filling their stomachs with some good crew foods. They've been doing that since the day they arrived. Big mama, Poppa Jones, Papa Brown, Papa Joshua, Papa Charles and grandma Annabelle are all seated with them.

"Is this the old people's table?" Albert asks as he snickers. "I need to find a younger table, right now!"

"Get on up and go over there and sit with Black, Tameka, Bobby and Corey," big mama says and smiles. "We are *all* family here. And every member has his or her *own* space to live their lives, as they are comfortable living it. So long as you're do things, the crew way. So go on over there. Jessie Mae and Jeb can't hold you back."

"And they don't even want too," Poppa Jones says. "Get on over there. They can hear us telling you to join them. They know they're gonna have to find you some companionship."

Papa Joshua adds, "Indeed. Because we know a lot. But that's one area where us old folks are of no help, whatsoever."

They're all laughing as Corey overhears the conversation. He gets up from his table and heads right over to Albert.

He says, "Come on and sit with us. We'll make sure you enjoy your new life here in America. You'll be glad you came back."

"Word," Albert says as he waves bye to all at the table and heads off with Corey.

They all laugh and have a great time at dinner. Crew's House is packed and filled with laughter, cheers and relief.

Ajay looks up and sees Jarvis and Lil Jarvis coming in the door.

Ajay yells, "All the food is gone!"

"Please tell me you're joking, bro," Jarvis says, "We're starving and looking forward to the cuisine."

"I'll bet you are," Nina says and cuts her eyes over at Rebbie. Then adds, "I'll just bet you are."

Ebony, T-baby, Rebbie and Yolanda crack up laughing. Ebony is trying to play it off. She knows Jarvis is going to be seated at their table. She just wants to see where he's going to sit. She notice there are 2 empty seats next to Rebbie.

Now I know who she was saving those seats for.

Ebony just shakes her head and smiles. Nina, T-baby and Yolanda are giving each other the eyes while they're smiling too.

"Just sit down and eat, so we can get done and go," Ajay says in a joking manner.

"Okay bro," Jarvis says, "I already know you've got your game plan on the schedule. Just stay here long enough for me and my junior to grub. Coach Ebony, does he have time for us to have supper?"

Everybody laughs before Tank says, "Don't ask that question, Jarvis. The answer is always no. They're not gonna make it convenient for nothing

else that's in the same sentence as *game plan*. You should know that by now. You can tell the truth. You're crew bound!"

"Ebony's got a bridal shower to go to," Pam adds, "And my big brother is not gonna make her miss it. Right, Ajay."

"I'll get you a car, Pam," Ajay says and everybody laughs.

Pam says, "Oh. Okay. Ebony it's cool with us if you can't make it."

They're all still laughing as Pam turns to Ajay and pretends to whisper, "An Oh six, Benz Coupe. With everything inside and out."

The entire Crew's House of Soul Food are in great spirits. As the 5pm hour nears, they're still having great laughs, family fun and wonderful foods. But it will soon be time for the females to go their own separate way.

The quadruple bridal shower starts at 7pm, 2 hours from now. But before they can leave, the elders table gets all of their attention. They have some things to leave them with. Papa Brown takes the floor first.

He says, "This is a family meal. A *crew* family meal. There's nothing but love in this restaurant and it feels damn good to me. I wish my lovely Pearline was living to see and share this day with us. But I know she's smiling down, from ear to ear. I am the oldest member of this crew. And for the first time in my life, I feel completely stress free. I have my crew, all of you, to thank for that. To the first generation, all the way down to the youngest members of this crew, the triplets: Ariel, Arianne and April. I love you all. And I will always do everything within my power to keep you safe. Now I'm gonna turn the microphone over to brother Charles Wilson."

Papa Charles takes the microphone and says, "I'm gonna be short and sweet. Thank you all and I love you all. To the crew!"

"TO THE CREW!!" they all repeat back.

Papa Charles passes the microphone to Joshua Logan, Jr.

Papa Joshua says, "I'm the youngest in my crew. I wanna sit at a younger table."

They crowd erupts with laughter before he continues. He adds, "Just like Jackson, here. My one and only love, Sally Mae is still watching over us and she's smiling too. Her and Pearline winning all the cooking contest in heaven. I'll just let all of you know. Other than wishing Sally Mae was still here and all of my crew brothers and sisters that we lost, along the way. Even young Stoney. When it comes to needs in my life. The crew is all I need. Thank you all and I love you all."

They all cheer as papa Joshua hands the microphone to poppa Jones, who starts in with a joke.

He says "There's something missing up in here. I done looked from one wall

to the other. Where's the *band*? I need some horns in some *hands*. Some *strings*. Tenor and bass with some drums. If I gotta mic in my hands. That *means* y'all needs to be *entertained*."

They all start to cheer, very loudly.

Ebony leans into Ajay and says, "I miss those days, baby."

"We got the records," he says with a sexy look in his eyes. He adds, "If you skip the bridal shower. I'll play anything you wanna hear."

They giggle and continue to listen to Poppa Percy Jones.

Poppa Jones says, "I just wanna say this before we head out. When it comes to the crew. *The Legacy Lives on!*" The crowd cheers again. He points to Jessie Mae, Jeb Jr and Albert and says, "There is No More Exile!"

The crew crowd erupts in cheers again. Poppa Jones continues,

"From this day forward, we will live on, on our paths. We will get involved in the campaign for Senator Barack Obama and send him to the white house!"

They erupt with cheers as Eric yells out, "Amen! Fired up! Ready to Go!"

The entire restaurant starts the chant and carries it for a few minutes before Poppa Jones says, "Breaking The Cycle is what this crew was put on this earth to do. Get things back to Black village status. And we are going to do it. Y'all have a great and safe night. Poppa lives for you all. And I love each and every one of you. Have a blessed night!"

They stand and applaud. Soon they're chanting,

"First generation crew! First generation crew! We hear and we know what to do! Reach one and keep it true!"

The all hug and start to file out to their cars. The females are headed to Pam and Sam's estate in Jackson Heights. Right across the cul-de-sac from Ajay and Ebony's estate.

Before they pull away, Lil Ajay gives Ebony a hug and a kiss. He's going to hang out with his pops and the all male crew, at Stoney's Bar & Grill. Just before Ebony hops into the drivers seat of her 2006 Escalade, Ajay pulls her to him.

He leans down and whispers in her ear. He says, "You're gonna be right across the street from home. I got the Spurs tomorrow night. So I need you to hook me up with some of that sweet pussy you holding." He kisses her ear and whispers, "Is that a deal baby?"

"Ummm. Yes it is," she whispers back. "Baby, you know exactly what it takes to get me to come to you and *for* you. You just hit me up when you're done at Stoney's."

Ajay says, "One hour," and they both laugh before they kiss passionately.

Chapter 73

JERICA'S CREW

The Quadruple Wedding Celebration, 2/14/2006 @ noon

Ajay, Jarvis and the Cavaliers beat the Spurs last night at their home game and the first thing Ajay said in his post game interview was "Thank you, Ebony." Jarvis, Lebron and his whole team got *that* message and so did the crew. The *Cavs* made plenty of jokes about it once Ajay made it into the locker room.

It didn't end there. It continued right on into today's celebration. The celebration today is in honor of the 4th generation [led by Bruce Dalvin Wilson] of the crew's, 4 marriages. It's time to present the happy couples.
1. Kenneth Ramon *Lil Chill* Payne Jr & Chaundra Denise Coleman-Payne.
2. Shannon Tyreek *Da Reaper* Wilson & Brittany Neon James-Wilson.
3. Jesse Lee *Lil Man* Brown & Ruthie Nakia *Roo* Williams-Brown.
4. Samuel *Mr. Cupid* Logan Jr & Pamela Darius *PD* Jackson-Logan.

The wedding ceremony is done. For the past 5 hours, the crew has been celebrating at the reception at *Allen Saul Williams Sports & Recreation center*. It's 5pm and it's still going strong. The 4 newlywed couples were just chauffeured to the airport. They're going to honeymoon in *Mount Pocono Pennsylvania's, Paradise Stream*. Ajay had shared that idea with all 4 of the grooms, some time ago. He remembered how much his baby sister Pam wanted to go there since she viewed him and Ebony's pictures. Only today's 4 sets of newlyweds will get to spend the *entire* week there. Unlike Ajay and Ebony, who were only there for 4 days and 3 nights.

Now that the newlyweds are gone. The Chill Spot and The Chill Spot II are the next stops for those who want to continue their party.

The Chill Spot II goes right into effect with the *younger side* of the 4th generation of crew. Since it's still early, all the crew who are 6 years old or older are here too. With the huge wedding that just took place and today being Valentine's Day. *Romance* is in the air for the teens and preteens too.

Chill, Renee and all of their crew head into The Spot II. They're going to stay around until it's time to open up the adult spot. Ajay and Ebony are here. They're because Ebony and Ajay want to enjoy their crew awhile longer before they have to head home. Ajay and Jarvis have a very early flight in the morning for their game against the Celtics. Ajay is here because, not only is Lil Ajay and Alan Anthony here. But Lannie and Kimmie are here also and Chill's crew already knows the younger side of

Bruce's crew are going to show up and show out. While getting their names out there and known. They're going to make sure everyone knows whom their mates are and get their couple shine on too.

The oldest of the younger crew is Bradley Lee Wilson Jr known as Brad III. Him and his crew believe in being in *full* effect.

Brad III says, "It's time to formally introduce our half of this fourth generation of crew, up in this piece. Let's let it be known that our crew is twice the size of Chill's crew. *And* we need to handle this while all of us are in the same city at the same time and in our *spot*."

"You should grab the mic and announce us all by name, brother," Kilo Jr says. "It's time. Because then everybody will know that the crew is non-stop and *not* to step to *none* of our girls or us, in the wrong way."

"Announce the crew guys *with* their girl, Brad," Destiny says. "And we can lay that on out too."

"Yea Brad," Kilo Jr says while chuckling. He adds, "You heard what your girl said."

All 18 of them laugh at that comment.

Then Jerica looks at Destiny and adds, "That's right, crew sis. Let's let these guys *and* girls know not to step to *any* of us, in *any* way."

All 9 of the younger 4th generation couples laugh as they all head down to the 1st floor and to the right side of the stage. That's when Brad III let's Tank know, he needs to grab the mic and do an introduction for his half of the crew. The *younger 4th generation* of Bruce's Crew. Tank obliges and tells him to give him a minute to introduce him to the crew and then, he can take it from there.

"Cool," Brad III says to Tank.

Then he heads back over to his crew and lets them all know they're about to have their time to shine.

The 9 couples gather at the foot of the stage while Tank goes up and makes the DJ aware. The DJ is none other than Robert Leon Jenkins Sr with Jan by his side as usual. But Rob is big Rob now. He's no longer, *Lil Rob*. Him and Jan's son is present as well. Robert Leon Jenkins Jr has been 6 years old since New Year's day. He is now known as *Lil Rob*. He's already learning how to master music, same as his dad. Tank gives him a pound. Then big Rob hands the mic to Tank and Tank heads to center stage.

"What's up, Chill Spot Two!!!" Tank yells into the mic.

The crowd yells back as loud as they can, "Chill Spot two is the business!!!"

"Cool," Tank says with a chuckle.

After he has everyone's undivided attention, he says, "Y'all know all about

the crew and I must make sure y'all know that the crew is *still* large and very much, in charge."

The crowd cheers loudly. Olivia, Jaylisa, Shalom and Rioshauna are standing front and center. And as usual, they're vying for the attention of Lil Ajay and his crew brothers.

After calling the club to order again, Tank says, "I'm gonna bring to the mic, the leader of the four *and a half* generation of this crew."

He chuckles and adds, "See. Our third generation is *more* than eighteen strong too. But the fourth generation is twice the size of the third. Brad the third is gonna introduce y'all to *his* entire young crew, in his own way because it's time for the crew to put y'all in the know. Welcome to the stage, Bradley Lee Wilson the third!"

The crowd cheers as Brad III walks up and takes the mic from Tank. Tank exits to the left and keeps the video camera's recording. The other 17 members of Brad III's half of the crew are offstage and to the right.

Brad III starts with, "Chill spot two! What's the business!"

"It's all crew business! Ya *heard*!!" the crowd yells back.

"Damn right," Brad III says, "Well the same goes for these strong brothers and these nine beautiful and well put together females that will be coming to the stage. Hear me and hear me good. Pay attention to the intro's and respect them from this day forward and it will remain all good for you, when you're in *my* presence."

The Spot II crowd cheers. They know Brad III's reputation. He'll turn 15 years old in September but his street credibility is already *full* grown.

Brad III says, "First off, I wanna introduce y'all to *my* girl. Her name is Destiny Jalene Shante' Payne. Come on up here, baby."

Destiny will turn 13 this year. On July 5th, she will be full fledge crew. A moment she's looked forward to for her *entire* life. She prances onto the stage and goes straight to the right side of Brad III. He hands her the mic.

She says, "The Chill Spot two and CrewLand mall is where my business *and* my personal is and this is where it stays. For those who don't know? Learn it. For all who know it? Respect it and we'll be alright."

"Word!" Brad III yells as he cosigns her, then gives her a kiss on the cheek. He leans into the mic while Destiny holds it and adds,

"My girl will introduce the next in line and that person will keep it moving. Alright Destiny, baby. Do yo thang."

"The next crew brother is KeJuan Thomas junior aka Lil Kilo," Destiny says, "Show him love!"

Lil Kilo comes up and she passes the mic to him. KeJuan is already full

fledged crew. He'll turn 15 this year, same as Brad III. Lil Kilo's birthday is in 11 days, on the 25th of February.

Lil Kilo says, "Chill Spot two! And especially all the dudes and chicks in the building. Be at attention because the *next* crew sister is *my* girl. And you know the rest. Give a Chill spot two welcome to my heart! Chastity Jaquel Coleman better known to the world as CJ!"

CJ just met her grandfather Chester Lee today, *in person*. She'd visited him while he was in prison, 14 times or once per year. She'll turn 15 on October 11th. Her mama Breanna known as Bre made sure CJ kept a relationship with her grandfather. Especially since her father Stoney was killed before it was even known that CJ was in her womb.

CJ walks up and takes the mic from Lil Kilo. He gives her a kiss on the lips. The crowd cheers loudly. Libby, Jaylisa, Shalom and Rio do clap. But the happy smile all 3 of them enhance is fake.

CJ says, "For those who don't know. I live in Atlanta but I was born in C-town. This is where my crew started and this will *always* be home for me. For any dramatic thoughts you may have pertaining to *my* crew? Dismiss them or I will dismiss you."

The crowd erupts while all of her crew family, cheers and hoots. She goes on to introduce the next crew male.

CJ says, "I wanna make y'all familiar with my crew brother from H-town. Give it up for Jonathan Banks!"

Jon will turn 13 in September of this year. He daps to center stage. Many more cheers fill the club before he gets to say 1 word. Many girls are trying *hard* to get Jon's attention. But Jon has only 1 girl on his mind as he takes the mic from CJ.

He says, "I'm Jon. Born in Houston which was the first south side branch of this crew. My home is Atlanta now, along with my sister CJ. Atlanta is the second south side city of crew and we represent crew to the fullest. But Cleveland is the original home of the crew and it will become my home, *this* summer."

The girls cheer loudest of all, to that revelation.

Then Jon continues, "Y'all wanna know why I'm moving to C-town, don't you? Because my girl is here. Put yo hands together and welcome to the stage. The love of *my* life and my future! Miss Jerica Eloise Brown!"

Jerica skips onto the stage in rhythm. Her crew sisters and brothers start to bounce in rhythm with her. They're use to this action from her. Just like her mama Nina, Jerica is known to get the whole crowd dancing instantly. And thanks to her aunt-by-marriage Rebbie Wilson-James, Jerica is now

ranked in the top 5 nationally, for her dancers age group. Jerica will turn 12 on October 20, 2006. But she's already a full fledge crew member from both sides of her family.

Jerica shuffles her feet until she comes to a stop, right next to Jon. She stands on her tiptoes and leans her head toward him and backwards. Her face, facing the ceiling. That's when Jon leans down and gives her a sweet kiss. The crowd roars. That brings a smile to her face while her father Tank has to shake his head and chuckle.

Then Tank yells out, "I'm calling Nina, right now! We've gotta talk!"

Ajay, Chill, Ron, June, Jb and Wes have joined Tank by now. They're all laughing which makes Jerica smile shyly. Jon hands her the mic.

Jerica says, "Do I even have to introduce myself? *Not*! My man just put y'all onto the *important* info but before I go on with the introductions. I've gotta introduce a crew leader of the future, who's gonna run thangs just like his big sister. My Lil brother is in the spot tonight *and* he's in the deejay booth. What you thank that means?! That's right. He was born with that groove in him. His daddy, *my daddy*, runs *this* spot. Act like you know! Now hang on."

Jerica walks over to the DJ booth and straight toward her little brother, Jeremy Marcus Brown Jr aka *Lil Tank*. Who's already sliding out of his chair to come to her. The crowd is applauding and cheering and loving this encounter. Jerica brings Lil Tank to center stage. She starts to dance. Lil Tank starts dancing, right along with her. The crowd loves it and so do their parents. Tank is chuckling hard, along with Jb, Ajay, June and the rest of the adult crew. While Jerica is swinging out. Lil Tank is popping and locking. It's *very* entertaining. The crowd's enjoying this as they start to yell, *"Jerica's crew! Jerica's crew!"* Big Rob plays a sample of a dance beat. With that, Jerica breaks it down and starts to jam. And even though he won't turn 4 years old until the middle of May? Lil Tank is keeping up with her, very well. Jerica's crew sisters and brothers start to jam too. She has to stop so she can introduce the next crew member.

She yells into the mic, "Hold up! Hold up! We got some *more* crew to bring up, so chill out!"

The crowd cheers loudly. Then Jerica puts the mic down to Lil Tank and says, "What you wanna say to the crowd, Lil Bro?"

Lil Tank yells, "Jerica crew!!!!"

Everybody applauds and cheers. Lil Tank laughs as he looks at Tank, who's calling him over, so the young crew can continue. Lil Tank heads to his daddy and Jerica gets back to the introductions.

She says, "The next crew brother is the son of the best film man in the business. *Money Shot Owens*! So welcome to the stage, my crew brother DeMarcus Tremaine Owens!"

DeMarcus just turned 11 years old on the last day of January. But as it goes for all the male crew. He didn't have to wait until he turned 13 to party and hang out.

He takes the mic and says, "I'm here now and it feels like I've been here forever. Money Shot is my pops and a *real* man. Just know that's the same road I'll be on. Heard me! But this is the best part of the news. Have you ever had a hard time concentration on school work or anything else because your mind is so focused on something that just consumes it?"

The crowd agrees loudly.

DeMarcus says, "It's best you don't loose focus for the same reason I do."

Everybody cracks up laughing.

DeMarcus says, "So long as y'all got that point. You got it? Good! Now put your damn hands together and welcome the prettiest girl in this world, Orian Chanel James!"

June smiles and so does Ajay, Tank the rest of the adult crew. Orian is only 8 years old and she won't turn 9 until the 23rd day of May. And she's shy, for the most part but she's comfortable with her crew and her boyfriend too. She comes up to DeMarcus and he kisses her on the cheek. She smiles and takes the mic.

"Spot two is rocking tonight!!" Orian yells as the crowd cheers.

She says, "I'm *so* down with it. It's a crew thang and a crew party."

She looks at her parents, June and Rebbie, who are all smiles.

Orian says, "My mama can dance. She hooked Jerica up and just know this. I can jam too!"

She starts to 2-step. Instantly, Jerica and the rest of her crew join in and just like that, they're all dancing again. They have to stop again to get back to the introductions.

Orian gets back to her mic duties, saying, "Oh we've got more crew. You ain't know?! Give up that love to my crew brother and my first cousin, Richard Trevon Williams the third!"

Rich III will be 11 on the 30th of September. He's very laid back, as he Michael Jackson moonwalks onto the stage to very loud applause. He makes it to Jerica, who hands him the mic.

Rich III takes the mic and says "I'm Rich! End of story!"

Everybody laughs and claps. T-baby is seated in VIP, watching through the glass window. She giggles as her and Wes make eye contact. They start

pumping their fist in the air, then they give each other the "thumbs up."
Rich III says, "I can't wait, so I'm gonna go ahead and get to it. My girl is older than me. So you don't even have to wonder if I'm man enough."
Tank, Ajay, Jb and big Rob crack up laughing. They like that, *big time*! Rich III is 2½ years from 13 but he's already more mature than his paternal father, the deceased Richie Rich was at his age.
Rich III gets on with it, saying, "Y'all know that R&B song that says, *Rock the boat?*"
He just smiles and the crowd starts yelling, "*Aaliyah! Aaliyah! Aaliyah!*"
Rich III says, "You got that right. My beautiful girl has the same name and even more beauty. She was born in NYC but to be closer to me, she moved south. Welcome my girl to this stage like the star she is to me. Aaliyah Janeese Hamilton!"
 Aaliyah is the youngest niece of Cedric Hamilton, Bre's husband. She'll turn 13 on the 30th of August. Her older and only sister Valene Hamilton will turn 17 in October and she hangs out with the oldest half of this 4th generation of crew. Their parents were killed in what was labeled as the worst terrorist act on American soil, *The 9/11 massacre*. Both sisters have lived in Atlanta with Bre and Cedric or Ced for short, since that tragic month. But today is about romance, love and crew. Aaliyah takes the mic from Rich III. They embrace in a long hug as the crowd cheers. Then Aaliyah gives Rich III a kiss on the lips. Valene and her boyfriend Ron Jr are the loudest in the yelling crowd. Definitely showing their approval.
Aaliyah says, "I have the same initials as the famous Aaliyah! Out of respect to her. I'm going to sing a couple of lines from her song to my prince, right here. But just so y'all know. I'm changing the words to fit me and mister Rich." They cheer as she starts.
She sings, "*When I feel, what I feel. It's never hard to tell you so. You're always in the mood to share. Anything your girl don't know. You're at your best and you are loved!*"
She brings the entire spot II to singing mode. They start to sing the real tune while her and Rich III share a slow dance for a full minute. The adult crew applauds too. Until Aaliyah and Rich III both hold the mic and say, "Okay. That's all y'all getting!!"
That brings laughter as Aaliyah starts to introduce the next crew member. Aaliyah says, "It's time to bring another ATL crew brother to the stage. Put your hands together for my ATL chief, John Brown the third!!!"
 John Brown III or Lil Jb will just be turning 9 in May, same as Orian will. But again, he's male crew. His father is Jb, the oldest child of

big John and mama Pearl. His mother is Lynn. Olympic track star and the oldest child of big Al. The only thing little about Jb is his nickname. He's very well known in Atlanta. By pro athletes, famous rappers, singers and politicians too. Because those are the types who spend countless hours in his parents home. But Lil Jb is ready to keep Cleveland as his home and everybody in the crowd will soon know why. Aaliyah hands him the mic.

Lil Jb asks, "Who am I?"

The crowd yells, "The big John Brown!"

Lil Jb asks, "What am I?"

The crowd yells, "Crew for life!!!"

"So long as y'all got that," Lil Jb says, "I can be brief."

Everybody is laughing and applauding. Jb and Lynn are whooping and hollering.

Jb yells, "Set em straight, son!!"

Lynn yells, "So yo mama don't have to set it off, up in here!!"

The adult crew are laughing at them, of course. But Lil Jb is focused on his mission. Right now he's letting everybody know some history about his girl.

He says, "My girl is a lady. What I mean is. She's older than me but only by her birth certificate. She's one of a kind. Feel me?"

They all laugh and Ajay yells, "You the oldest, nephew!!"

Lil Jb gives Ajay a thumb up and a side glance with a smile. Then he proceeds.

He says, "My girl is the niece of one of the strongest females in the world and yep. She's my crew. Misses Renee Payne, the mother of one of the grooms today. Y'all know Lil Chill. He's her first cousin. And big Chill is her uncle. Now hear me clear. When you meet my girl, in a second? Just say hey and cheer. After that, stay yo ass *way* away from her."

The loud applause comes again.

Lil Jb says, "My lady! Jada Renee Stewart! Brown, in the future!"

The crowd howls as Jada makes her way to center stage. Jada will turn 13, the 21st day of November. She has the middle name and the same birthday as her aunt Renee. Right now her daddy Wes and her step-mom T-baby are yelling in competition with Chill and Renee. And all 4 of them are winning.

Lil Jb passes the mic to Jada and stands next to her while she speaks.

Jada says, "It's crew or nothing. That's how it is for me and for everybody who loves me. I always knew my daddy was the best man in the world. John has already let me know that he's going to change my mind on that part."

The crowd screams and claps. Wes is smiling big, as are Renee and T-baby.

Jada says, "I've been an only child, all of my life. But since I became crew. I have a younger brother. You know that Rich guy y'all met, a few minutes ago? That's my brother and his mother is *my* mother. I love her with all my heart. Before I turn thirteen, I'm gonna be a big sister, all over again. This crew life is platinum. I'll never change anything that's happened since I moved to Cleveland. Y'all got that? Good. Let's keep it moving. The next crew brother goes by the name of Jarvis Rhodes Junior!! Show love!"

7-year old Jarvis receives huge applause as he makes his way to center stage. He's a smaller version of his father and *very* handsome. Jarvis Sr is yelling "Bravo." Rebbie is screaming *louder* than Jarvis Sr, while she stands *next* to June. June knows his wife is partial to kids. He doesn't see anything bizarre about her going extra for this little boy. Jarvis Jr will turn 8 on the 12th of July. One day after Ajay's birthday. His father is hoping he'll know Rebbie as his new mother, by then too. Jada gives Lil Jarvis the mic and he goes to center stage.

He asks, "How y'all doing tonight?"

The crowd yells, "We awwright!!!"

"It's cool y'all know how to answer that," Lil Jarvis says. "Now the next time I see y'all. I'm gonna ask y'all what's the name of my girl. So listen to what I'm fixing to say to you. Cool?!"

"Cool!!!!" the audience repeats.

"My girl of the future goes by the name of Ashanti Diavonni Brown. Don't that sound sweet?!! Give it up for this princess!!"

Ashanti makes her way on stage as her dad, Steven Davon Brown and her mom, Alicia Mallory Wilson-Brown jump up and down while cheering her on. Ashanti was born October 1, 1998. Four years before the member of Chill's crew whom she shared birthdays with, took his own life. Rich III's father, Richard Trevon Williams Jr took his own life on Ashanti's 4th birthday. Which was *his* 27th birthday. Ashanti is 7, just like her future boyfriend, Lil Jarvis and just under 3 months younger than him. Lil Jarvis takes her right hand and kisses her wrist. The crowd cheers!! Then he passes her the microphone.

Ashanti smiles shyly and says, "My name is Ashanti and I'm crew. Jarvis junior is going to be my boyfriend when we get big. My mama and my daddy already said it, so y'all can't say nothing else about it. Okay?"

"Okay!!" the entire crowd yells as they laugh and applaud her.

Then she says, "I got to bring up the next crew brother, so are y'all ready?"

"Yes!!!"

"The next crew brother is from Chicago. But now he lives here. His

name is Alan Anthony McNair!!!" Ashanti screams as she giggles proudly.

As Alan heads up the steps to the stage, Ebony smiles while Ajay shows no emotion. He's just ready to get through and past *this* part. He bends down to Ebony's ear and says, "I think we should get Lannie and Kimmie and head on to the house."

Ebony smiles and says, "Anthony. Be fair. I know you wanna be here when Ant goes up there. And Kimmie has to be here for that. So you'll have to watch Lannie's introduction first. Right?"

"Well I'm going to the bathroom," Ajay says and he finally smiles. Ebony latches her elbow into his and holds him down. She can tell Atlantis is nervous already. She's looking at her daddy. Ebony pulls Ajay's arm and he looks at her.

She says, "Baby. Please don't make her scared. This is a new crew ritual and she has to take part in it too. Right?"

"Uh huh," is all Ajay says as his eyes only leave Atlantis, long enough to look at Alan.

Ebony smiles. She's just happy knowing Ajay hasn't gone up on stage and stopped this whole program before it even got to this part where their twin and oldest daughter gets introduced as crew.

9-year old Alan who had his birthday 2 days ago, February 12, makes his way to center stage. Orian hands him the mic and he precedes.

"My first name is Alan," he says, "Sounds just like the name of the grandfather of the only *girl* I've ever liked. It's just spelled different. My middle is Anthony. The exact same name and spelling as the father of the girl I like. Everyday since I first met her. I've wanted her to like me and I still do. I'll do *anything* to be good enough for her. For anybody that ain't *crew*? Don't go near her. Not even to be her friend. If she wants you to be her friend? She'll tell you. Her twin brother is my best friend, so just know this. If you ever make my girl sad. I'm coming for you. That's the *only* warning I'm giving you."

Ebony smiles. She's heard similar words said by the man who's arm she's locked onto. She looks at Ajay. He's sort of smiling but it's not evident. She knows he's okay though.

That's when Alan locks eyes with Ajay as he continues, "There's a song by this old school group called *The Isley Brothers*. The name of that song is the name of the *only* girl that I've *ever* looked at in this way. I'm so happy my big brother Eric signed with the Cleveland Browns."

The crowd cheers. Alan adds, "That song title is her first name. Cleveland's pro football team is her other grandparents, *last* name. I want the loudest

cheer I've heard in here all night, when I say her name. I need to know, are y'all ready?"

"Yea!!!!!!!!!!!!!!!!!" the crowd yells.

Alan says, "Show some crew love to the prettiest girl I've ever laid my eyes on. One day, the name of my voyage will be, Atlantis Shalon Jackson!!"

Lannie heads to the center of the stage. She's going to turn 7 years old on the 25th day of July. Public appearances are not a favorite of hers. But just like her mom and dad, she's good at everything she puts her time into *and* she's a perfectionist. So she's going to pull this off to the best of her ability. She's going to do this in a way that will help Alan relax, make her mother proud of her and make sure that her daddy knows she's not in *any* hurry. When she reaches Alan, he lifts each of her wrist, 1 at a time and kisses them both. Then he passes the mic to her.

"Atlantis is my name," she says in her regular voice.

She never felt like she had to yell. Tonight is no different. After all, she has a microphone in her hand.

She says, "But my parents, my crew and everybody else calls me Lannie. That's what you all can call me too."

The crowd yells, "Lannie!!!"

Ebony and Ajay are apart of that yelling crowd and so is Lil Ajay and Lea.

Lannie says, "But there *is* one person. Only one male in this world, who will call me Atlantis. Did y'all just hear who called me Atlantis?"

The crowd roars, "Alan Anthony!! Yeah!!!!"

Ebony smiles. Ajay can't help but smile too. He's seeing visuals of his sister Lynn, when she was younger. While at the same time. He can see Ebony's soft tough when speaking but getting straight to the truth and her wishes.

Lannie says, "My papa's name is Allen with two ell's and an E. My daddy's name is Anthony but only my mother can call him that. The world knows him as Ajay. The crew brother who introduced me, has both of those names and he's best friends with my brother who came into this world *six* minutes before me. The guy who introduced me, admires my daddy and both of my grand daddies and great grandfathers too. *How* can he loose?"

Ebony screams, "Tell em Lannie!!"

To Ebony, Ajay says, "That's pretty good. Pretty good."

Then he yells to Lannie, "Go ahead and wrap it up!" as the crowd laughs and cheers too. Tank has to pop Ajay on the other elbow for that comment. They both laugh as Lannie starts to wrap it up.

She says, "Now the next crew brother is my twin brother and my best friend in this *whole* world. Y'all don't know this part of it but I know what

he's thinking before he says it. And yes. He knows my thoughts, the same way."

Everybody laughs.

Lannie says, "He has the same name as my daddy. Except he's a junior. But there's nothing junior about my twin. He's a man trapped in a boy's age group. For *real*. I'll ask y'all this. Who knows Ant?!!"

The crowd erupts yelling, *"I do!" "Me!" "We do!"* and *"I know him!"*

Or *"I wanna know him better!!"* many of the girls yell.

Libby, Shalom, Rio and Jaylisa want to be sure and be heard. They're yelling and jumping up and down at the same time.

Lannie says, "Keep cheering like that and be louder than you've been, *all* night, if you want him up here. Be heard like you're crew. Are y'all ready?"

"Yeah!!!"

She says, "I'm not gonna scream. Tell *me* who's coming up next. Now."

"Anthony Devante Jackson Junior!!!!!" the crowd all yells.

Ebony and Ajay are the loudest yellers. Lil Ajay is stalling. He wants the crowd to yell louder, so he stays exactly where he is. This is when Ajay heads to the front of the stage and reaches for the mic. Atlantis passes it to him, of course.

Speaking into the mic, Ajay says, "Look. I've got a flight *early* in the morning. So if y'all want my son to come on this stage. You'd better make the walls rattle in this bitch!"

The crowd goes wild. Everybody starts jumping up and down. Including the crew who are already introduced and waiting on stage. From the oldest crew member, big Chill. To the youngest who's present, Lil Tank and Lea. There's not a still or quiet person in the entire building. Kimmie is cheering and smiling big too. Lil Ajay is standing next to her. It would be fine with her, if he didn't move 1 muscle. But now she knows that when he does move. He's going to go on stage and she'll be the only person left standing at the foot of the steps. She'll be left alone. That's when she gets it.

He's going to say my name and tell me to come up there and stand by him. He likes me! He's gonna tell everybody that I have to be his girlfriend. I'm gonna go up there, I know that much. But I'm probably too little for him. I hope not. I don't know what to say next.

Lil Ajay makes it to Lannie, gives her a hug and takes the microphone.

Calmly, he says, "What's up, CrewLand?"

The crowd cheers, claps and yells as loud as they can.

Libby screams out, "You're what's up, sexy baby! You are!!!"

Lil Ajay says, "If this question has nothing to do with you. Then be very quiet. Is there anybody in here who *don't* know me?"

The Chill Spot II is absolutely quiet. Ajay smiles big.

"Cool," Lil Ajay says. "Now I need y'all to just stay quiet and listen. I'll let y'all know when to get loud again because I need to put y'all up on a few things. Y'all need to pay attention because I will not tell you *any* of this again. Unless you do something fucked up and I have to meet up with you."

Ebony looks at Ajay and shakes her head.

Ajay says, "Just be patient, baby. He's gonna bring it in a way which will make you proud."

"Well he'd best hurry up and get there." Ebony says.

Lil Ajay says, "In my history, things are done in order to change and then *protect* our past history. Every generation has to add something new. While adding more to the work that we was born into to keep it strong and lasting. I'm with that, all the way. Check this out. Every man in the crew family before me, had an order to abide by. I have the same. Through my father, I learned how the female who's gonna be my one and only, is suppose to be treated. Ebony Brown-Jackson is my mama and she's a queen."

Ebony smiles as her eyes become misty. Ajay just smiles and keeps listening.

Lil Ajay says, "My mama is crew, no doubt. But she's more than that. My mama, along with my aunt Nina and my second cousins, T-baby and Rebbie are called the awesome foursome of big Chill's crew. I'm in Bruce's crew. But there's thirty six of us, so we broke it down to two crews. Brad the third is the male head and Destiny is his girl. That's *true* crew history because their parents Chill, Renee, Junior and Tonya have been friends since birth. But there's more. Earlier, everybody was screaming *Jerica's* crew. Brad the third and Destiny told me to make sure y'all know, we're gonna roll with that. Her parents, Nina and Tank are my aunt and uncle on both sides of my family. That counts for everything."

Then he turns to Jerica and says, "We are your crew, from now on."

Everybody applauds and Lil Ajay continues,

"My crew was raised to protect our females and that's exactly what I'm gonna do. My pops treats my mama like a queen. I'm gonna treat my lady the same way. I know whom that lady is *already*. And by the look on her face, right now. I think she just now got the hint. Her first name is Kimora but only *I* will call her that. She's Kimmie to everybody else. She just turned six, last month. I'll be seven in July. Kimora's middle name is Eloise. That's my mama's middle name and my big mama's first name. What that says to me, is she's a perfect fit. Plus I just like to see her smile. That's the

same thing my pops told me, he wanted and still wants from my mama. Just to see her with a smile on her beautiful face. So there you have it. The girl that I wanna make smile and that I want to be my lady? Goes my the name of Kimora Eloise McNair but y'all will call her Kimmie. Now show her some love."

The crowd starts to cheer. Even Libby, Rio, Jaylisa and Shalom are cheering but they all still have plans on that being them, in the spot Kimmie is in right now. Lil Ajay walks to the steps and then down to where Kimmie stands. He takes her hand and brings her on stage with him. They're hand in hand as Lil Ajay brings her to the center of the stage. Libby, Rio, Jaylisa and Shalom are watching them closely. They don't like that it isn't either of them that Lil Ajay has just escorted. And they're whispering amongst each other, about what they're planning to do to change it.

By now, Lil Ajay and Kimmie are at center stage. He looks down at her and asks, "Before I hand this microphone to you. Tell me, what do you want me to do after you have it?"

Kimmie says, "Hold my hand and stay here with me. I don't wanna stand here by myself."

"This is exactly where I wanna be," Lil Ajay says and smiles.

He hands her the mic and stays right next to her while holding her hand.

Kimmie looks up at Lil Ajay and says, "I like how you say my whole first name. Will you say it again?"

"Kimora," Lil Ajay says as he leans into the mic.

Everyone starts to cheer but Lil Ajay signals for them to stay quiet while his girl speaks.

"I'm just glad that I live here with my big brother Eric and my auntie Erica," Kimmie says, "All I wanna do is play with my best friends everyday. Lannie, Ashanti and Orian are my best friends."

She looks up at Lil Ajay and asks, "That's so neat, ha?"

Lil Ajay smiles and says, "It is."

"But you're my only friend that's a boy," Kimmie says, "Other than my brother Alan."

"And I want you to keep it that way," Lil Ajay says sternly. "All the crew will be okay with that because they know that's how I want it to be. What anybody, who's not crew want? Don't matter. Okay?"

"Okay," Kimmie says and smiles.

She's relieved. Then she asks Lil Ajay, "Can I just talk to you and you by yourself? I don't wanna keep talking to everybody. Its too many people in here and they all keep looking at me."

"Because you're beautiful," Lil Ajay says, "Let's give the mic to big Chill and fall back with our crew."

"Okay," Kimmie says and giggles before handing the mic back to Lil Ajay.

Chill's crew cracks up laughing and starts to cheer and applaud. The entire crowd follows suit and before long, everybody's cheering.

Ebony feels the conversation between Lannie and Alan was very respectful, on his part. Very relieving on Lannie's part. As for Lil Ajay and Kimmie. The conversation was innocent and very sweet on Kimmie's part. And very protective on Lil Ajay's part. Alan wants Lannie to be whomever she wants to be, in her own time and he's going to make sure that no one interferes. The same goes for Kimmie and Lil Ajay.

Ajay stands there watching as big Rob and Jan starts the music back. Brad III and his entire crew starts to dance on stage. Lil Ajay is dancing with Kimmie. Something he has never done in public until this early evening. Kimmie only wants to talk to Lil Ajay. Ajay knows that's what his son wanted her to say. Because that's the same thing Ajay has always wanted from Ebony. And the same way Ebony was with him.

Now that all of the introductions are done, Ajay is ready to head home.

"Now can we get on to the house?" he asks Ebony with a seductive grin. He adds, "I need to get on with my game plan."
Ebony giggles and whispers in his ear.
She says, "Yes we can, baby. All this future romance *really* put me in the mood."
Ajay picks Lea up instantly.
Then he whispers in Ebony's ear, "Let's get Lannie and Kimmie and get on the road. Your fourteen inch property is showing through my tuxedo pants. I can't hold it back no more."

"I don't even want you to," Ebony whispers back. "Let's hit it."

"I'm gonna hit it, for damn sho," he says. "The world knows that."
With that, Ebony gets Lannie and Kimmie into their coats, hats and gloves. Her and Ajay say their goodnights to all of their crew. Ajay lets Ebony know he's already started her 2006 Cadillac Escalade.
"You know it's remote. I told you it was gonna be ready to go, at a moments notice," Ajay says of Ebony's SUV, as he smiles very seductively.
Ebony giggles. Then she asks, "Are we bringing Ant and Alan too?"
Ajay laughs hard before he says, "We're only bringing these three girls to *our* place. Cause they'll go to bed early."

CHAPTER 74

THE REVELATION

Ajay, Jarvis and the Cavaliers beat the Celtics in double overtime, 2 nights ago. Their next game is at home too. It'll be on the 21st against the Orlando Magic. Ajay is extra excited about being *in-town* for several days in a row. Because now that longtime nemesis Old Jake Johnson is dead and gone. Ajay is feeling warmed up but he wants to be totally hot. He and Lil Ajay are both ready to add some more movement to the cleansing of their crew's *beef plate*. They're putting more fuel in their mission tank, by keeping Angel Taylor thinking that forgiveness and acceptance of her, is even possible. All Ajay and Lil Ajay want for Angel now, is an *earlier* release date than 2007.

Today is Friday, February 17, 2006. All the out-of-town crew began their return home. Ron and Carolyn will be here awhile longer. They'll return to Houston after the Cavaliers game on Tuesday.

Jessie Mae, Jeb Jr and Albert aren't planning to move back to England. Now that Old Jake is deceased, they feel they can reside back at home without daily interference. Chill and Renee have already offered them big Paul's home across the street from big John and big Al. Justine and Kilo are residing in it, right now. But they, along with Arthur and Michelle, will be moving into new homes in Jackson Heights, come first spring. Until then, Jessie Mae, Jeb Jr and Albert will reside in the condo's.

Black, Yolanda, David and Charles will fly home today. Chill's crew gets together with them at *Crew's House* before they have to carry them to the airport. That's when Charles lets Ajay know he'd heard about Ebony getting her wedding bouquet back, which April had caught at their wedding. He tells Ajay, he's going to mail him the garter belt back too. Which he'd caught. Charles let the crew know he has no hope of meeting any woman who will take April's place. Then Black assures them that she will keep them informed on the hurricane Katrina recovery and the Jessie Lee Williams Jr death case story too. Yolanda and David didn't have any pertinent news. They just giggled a lot, while telling the crew they're going to be together forever. Chill's crew promises to keep their pact with Black, about visiting her in Gulfport. After their fun and hearty breakfast, the crew gets them to the airport and they depart on time.

Today is Saturday the 18th, 4 days since the wedding which was a huge celebration for the entire crew. And 5 days since to removal of Old Jake Johnson, Draper Watts, Timothy "Tim" Murphy and Justin Warner.

The majority of the crew are still feeling blessed plus closer than ever. But not Rebbie. She's ready to let June know she wants a divorce.

On this early Saturday morning, she's at her dance studio with plans of meeting Jarvis for lunch. But she wants to have some good news to share with him, when they meet up. She only left home and came into her studio to get her final thoughts in order. Before she has to sit down with June and give him this news. She'd told June to meet her for breakfast at Crew's House because she didn't feel she could ask him for a divorce, at home alone. Not without a huge emotional blowup by him. She also knows Jarvis is concerned about her safety. So she figured the best way to let June know, was to do it with some elders of the crew, at hand.

As she leaves her dance studio, heading to Crew's House, her cell phone starts to ring. She looks at her phone and smiles. It's a call from big Jarvis.

"Hello," Rebbie answers.

"Good morning," Jarvis says and she can tell he's smiling.

"Good morning to you," she say as she giggles. She adds, "I truly hope it's still a good one *after* this breakfast meeting I'm about the have."

Jarvis smiles and says, "Just stay relaxed and don't expect him to be nice. You remember how mine went with Gwen, that night. So I don't expect him to just say okay and bye, either. I just wanted to check on you and make sure I let you know that I'm here for you, if you need me. And if you want me to, I'll come to the restaurant......"

"No," Rebbie says, cutting him off. She adds, "I don't want you to come because Brian doesn't know anything about us. And if he gets loud on me. I know you're gonna react, in kind. I don't want that to happen, baby. So please. After this breakfast meeting, I'm gonna need some peace of mind. I know you're that, for me. So just relax until I call you back. Okay?"

Jarvis sighs and says, "I'll say yes but I don't even know if I *can* relax. I don't know how he's gonna react."

Rebbie says, "Most likely, he's gonna get loud. That's why I wanted us to meet at Crew's House. The elders are there and they'll make sure it doesn't get out of hand. Plus I invited my brother Greg junior and his girl Patricia, to meet us there too."

"I'm glad your brother will be at that table," Jarvis says, "That's a good insurance plan. That helps me to relax, some. I just wanna know that you're okay. That's all I'm concerned with."

While on the phone, Rebbie drives into the parking lot of CrewLand and parks her 2006 Navigator. She can see that June is already here, parked

and inside of Crew's House. She also notices Greg Jr and Patricia when they turn into the mall parking lot.

She tells Jarvis, "Brian is already inside. And I see my brother and his girl pulling up. I'll call you as soon as it's over."

"I'll be waiting to hear that you're okay," Jarvis says again. "I really wanna talk to Ajay right now. He always knows how to handle every type of situation. I really want him to be at that table. Can I let him know what's going down, up there?"

Rebbie says, "I told my awesome foursome sisters. So I'm sure Ebony has already shared it with Ajay." Then she starts to giggle and adds, "Ajay's two seat Benz coupe is turning in, right now."

"Cool," Jarvis says. "I can relax now."

"I'll call you when I'm done," Rebbie says and they end their call.

The Chill Spot. Renee's Office, @8:30am

T-baby and Wes have arrived at Renee's office for their meeting with Keno Madison, from Mentor-By-The-Lake. Keno and her assistant, Toni Landry arrives and heads to the side door. Renee meets them at the side entrance. When she opens the door, she's pleased to see Ebony and Ajay standing there with them. She greets them all. Then they head to the elevator and up to her office, where T-baby and Wes are seated and waiting. Once everybody's inside and seated. Renee gets right to the point of the meeting.

"So Keno," Renee says, "I expected to see your husband here. Was he not available?"

Her assistant is speaking for Keno to avoid the broken English responses.

"I'll be translating for misses Keno Madison," Toni Landry says. "Her English language speaking isn't quite up to par, for a meeting of this magnitude. So I'm just here to help her come to an agreement with you all."

"But I expected *mister* Madison to be here," Renee says, "At least, that's the impression we got from the memo which was faxed to me. I've never heard anything verbal from him. Yet his name is on the agreement document which Rich wrote and left with you. Is there a reason mister Madison isn't attending this important meeting?"

Keno shakes her head negatively. Then she looks at Toni Landry.

Toni says, "Mister Madison isn't going to attend *any* meetings about this matter. He only signed the documents because he was in debt to Richard Williams. And this was the form of repayment Richard wanted. At this

329

point, Keno just wants to get to a conclusion. So we can all move forward."

"Meaning what?" T-baby asks with impatience on her face.

Toni says, "Misses Madison is hoping that Mister Williams' family, you guys, will honor his wishes and publish his last will, as he requested."

"If he wanted us to publish this," Ajay says to Keno, "Then why did he give it to you and your husband?"

"As a last resort," Toni answers, "It's obviously some last words and things which he wanted to get off his chest. But of course, his life ended before he could do so. And he had brought it to my boss and his wife here. He asked them to make sure it gets published."

Before anyone from the crew can respond to Toni's last comment, they are interrupted by a hard knock on Renee's office door. Then the door swings open. It's Chill.

Chill says, "Let's head over to the restaurant, crew."

He leaves swiftly. Ajay, Ebony, T-baby and Wes hop up and head out the door behind Chill. Renee let's Keno and Toni know, they'll have to end the meeting here.

She says, "We can resume it later. Or if you two would like to wait here, in one of our conference rooms. You can do that."

"We'll wait," Toni says, "If that's okay."

Renee escorts them out into the hallway. She'd already beeped Courtney which let's Courtney know there's a babysitting job for her.

Then with salutation, Renee says, "Remain here. I have Courtney Freeman coming up now. She'll keep you comfortable until we return. We'll return as soon as possible."

With that, Renee heads out. She alerts Courtney and Wayne to keep close watch on these guest. Then she takes the stairs so she can catch up with Chill and the rest.

As soon as Renee gets outside, she can hear loud voices coming from the area where Crew's House of Soul Food is located. She runs to see where Chill and the rest are.

When she makes it out front, she can see Chill, Ajay, Ebony, T-baby and Wes. Chill, Ajay and Wes are trying to keep big June and Greg Jr away from each other. Ebony and T-baby are on the sidewalk in front of Crew's House with Rebbie, Patricia, big mama and grandma Annabelle. First, Renee hurries over to the men.

"What's going on?" Renee asks Chill.

"June and Greg junior just came to blows in Crew's House," he says as he shakes his head negatively.

"What?!" Renee asks, "Why? What the heck is going on?"
Renee looks for a vision through Rebbie. She wants to see what her present mood looks like.

Rebbie is looking traumatized. Renee heads over to Rebbie and the crew females. She has to get to the bottom of this, immediately.

When she makes it over to where the females are, she notice that Rebbie is really upset.
Renee asks, "Rebbie, what's going on?"

"Brian was about to hit me while we was at our table," Rebbie says, "And when Greg junior saw that. He jumped in between us and just punched him. That turned into a big fight. They was turning over tables and all. But papa Brown and poppa Jones got involved and made them stop. Then they brought them outside to calm down."

"Why were they fighting?" Renee asks.

"I told Brian I want a divorce," Rebbie says.
She unwraps a note which she's holding in hand and hands to Renee.
She says, "I gave this note to him. Instead of saying it, in front of people. I decided to write it down, just so I can get my words in. Because you know he *never* listens to me. But when Brian read it. He flipped out. He pushed the table away from him and into us and he was heading *straight* toward me. That's when Greg junior jumped up and got between us. But Brian pushed him very hard and told him to mind his fuckin business. That's when Greg junior punched him and they started fighting."
Renee reads the note. Then she says,
"Well now I can *see* why all of that would happen."
She just shakes her head and looks at the other females.
Patricia looks dumbfounded. It's obvious she doesn't have a clue as to why their breakfast meeting turned into a fight. Ebony and T-baby are standing there and neither 1 of them are commenting. And to Renee, both Ebony and T-baby look like they already know what the confrontation was about.

Ebony and T-baby knew Rebbie was planning to ask for a divorce. And they also know why she was asking. At this moment, they just want to get Rebbie somewhere away from where June is located, so they can find out how much was exposed. Ebony wants to avoid this public display also.
She turns to Renee and asks, "Renee, can we take Rebbie down by the spot or inside one of these other businesses? So we can calm this down."

"For real," T-baby says, "There are *way* too many people out here for us to have our business owners behaving like this."

"Sure we can," Renee says, "Let's head to the spot."

The 4 of them and Patricia start to walk away. That's when June notice Rebbie leaving. That's when he tears away from Ajay and Wes and runs full speed toward the 5 ladies. Ajay and Wes are running behind him but June catches up to the 5 ladies before Ajay and Wes can get to him.

"Where you going, Rebbie?!!" June yells, "Who the fuck are you seeing? Who the fuck are you trying to leave me for?!!"
It's at that time when Greg Jr gets away from Chill and security. He sprints over and catches up to them too. Ajay and Wes makes it to June, just before Greg Jr gets there.
Greg Jr yells, "Don't go at my sister, no more! I ain't bullshitting, June! Man, you dead wrong to be accusing Rebbie of fucking up! You the one that fucked up! Over and over!"
"I ain't fucking wit nobody!" June yells back.
Chill has made it over to all of them now and he's heard enough. He wants to bring this mêlée to order, right now.

"Let's head to my office, crew!" Chill yells, "Right now! Let's go!"
Ajay grabs June by the elbow and says, "Let's go, man. Come on."
Wes does the same with Greg Jr. Renee, Rebbie, Patricia, Ebony and T-baby walks behind the males. Chill is in front. Ajay is guiding June while making sure he stays a good distance from both Rebbie and Greg Jr. Wes is between Ajay and June. He's guiding Greg Jr. All 10 of them head into the side door of The Chill Spot. It's time to get this matter out into the open, up front and over with. So they can get on with that meeting about Rich's last wishes.

All 10 of them go into Chill's office. Courtney had already taken Keno and Toni down to the conference room, so they could be comfortable until their meeting resumes. Now that Chill and Renee have them inside and some seated, they can get to the bottom of the drama.
"What is this about?" Chill asks.
Big June yells, "Rebbie handed me a damn note asking me for a divorce! What kind of shit is that to do?!"
Chill says, "You need to lower your voice, brother. And calm down. We will get to the bottom of this. Just breathe in and calm down."
Once things start to get milder, Chill looks from June to Greg Jr. Then he asks, "Why the fuck was the two of y'all fighting?"

"He was about to hit my sister, Chill," Greg Jr says. "What else was I suppose to do? It really bugs me that my sister even feels like she has to end her marriage. Rebbie has always been committed to whatever she stepped out to do. June done fucked up on her, several times."

June tries to interrupt but Chill holds his hand up in June's direction and June stays quiet.

Greg continues, "I remember the first and last encounter that me and June had. That was about me and my messing around. When I was still with Erica. But what I tried to explain to him then. Is I *wasn't* married and I grew up *crew too*. Watching and learning from the males before me. I learned and I know, that the only time it will be okay with our elders for us to see another female. Is before we're married. But it still hurts your girlfriend. I learned from that bullshit, back then. I lost Erica. Then I met Kelly and she was killed. For awhile, I was thinking that it had to be a message from God or something. Saying that I would always be single. But then, I met Patricia. I'm blessed to have a lady that I truly love, in my life again. A woman that I wanna spend *all* of my free time with. My big sister use to be the same way about you, June. The only person in this *world* who could've changed those feelings for her, was you. Nobody else but you. It would take a lot for Rebbie to *even* want a divorce from you. So why don't you tell us what happened?"

Chill looks at June and asks, "I'm gonna asked you this. Even though, I already know the answer. Are you cheating?"

"No," June says, "Not since Diana Keyes. Rebbie knows about that. And she know I ended it on the same day that she told me to end it."

"She shouldn't have had to tell you, June," T-baby says, "Back then, I was apart of that loop too. Richard and you. Y'all kept me and Rebbie on the phone with each other. We stayed pissed off. Crying. Fussing. But Ebony here and Nina. They never had to deal with the type of BS that me and Rebbie had to deal with."

"*Well Ebony didn't,*" Nina says as she enters Chill's office. Her and Tank got word about the altercation and headed in, from home. They grab a seat and Nina continues, "I had less than T-baby and Rebbie. Yes. But now T-baby is as happy as all us other wives are. Why can't Rebbie have the same happiness?"

"She can and she does," June tries. "I've been faithful to her since that incident with Diana Keyes."

"Not with you, I can't be happy and I don't even wanna try to," Rebbie says suddenly, "Not anymore. I'm done, Brian. I cannot live a lie, *anymore*. I never got over that Diana Keyes situation. I wanna be able to converse. I wanna be happy. Don't I deserve to be happy?"

Sadly, June says, "You're not happy with me, Rebbie?"

"I'm not happy, Brian," she admits, "I haven't been, for a long

time. When I saw your *Acura* parked at her apartment. That wasn't the first time I've known you to be with her. And I don't even think you cared enough to asked me, *how* I knew it was *her* apartment. Because I learned her car, *ten* years ago and you've never asked me, once. How did I know who's place you were at. Let me just put you up on *how* I knew who you was with. I learned what car she drove when you was still in college. She was going all the way down to Cincinnati to be with you. And you was fucking her, *then*. I've *seen* you and her together. I just never bothered to tell you that I did. But I did and that was before we even got married. But the day my feelings ended, was the day I saw you at the U. I called your phone and you answered it. You lied to me about where you were. That was the beginning of the end of me, *ever* being able to trust you and love you, one hundred percent. We were married and Orian was already in this world. So me knowing that you were still doing the same whore that you was doing *before* we got married. That did it for me. Brian, our twin boys are the only reason we've lasted *this* long. Seeing that you was still cheating with the same woman, *after* we were married. That I'd seen you going into a hotel with, *before* we were marriage. That took every little bit of my faith and my security away of our relationship. I am not going to live a lie."

"Who told you she was visiting me in *Natti*?" June asks.

He's only trying to find out if someone told her, he was cheating. Instead of trying to admit to and get passed the fact that he *was* cheating.

Ajay doesn't want this to come down to Rebbie mentioning Jarvis Sr. He wants to change this line of questioning and move away from discussing anything that could lead to Jarvis' name being brought up.

He says, "Nobody in this crew would tell on you, June. And if you're not careful. You're going to be telling on yourself. I think y'all should give this some time."

Tank looks at June and says, "Give her some space, June. Let her have time to process it all. Just give her room. Because if you stay confrontational. She will certainly not change her mind."

"I'm not going to change my mind," Rebbie says emphatically. "I did that, back then. I gave you my heart and my undivided attention. I trusted you, Brian. Because I wanted to and I loved you. I'm not in love anymore. Please accept that and let's just move on. *Please*."

June looks at Rebbie. He has tears in his eyes but he's not saying anything. He's just staring at her. He's finally quiet for the first time *ever*, when Rebbie is involved in a disagreement with him.

Chill says, "I'm very disappointed in June and Greg junior, coming to

blows. What's worse is y'all did it inside of Crew's House. *Our* business property. The last time when y'all almost came to blows. Y'all was in this club. Do y'all remember that?"

June shakes his head, "Yes."

Greg Jr says, "I definitely remember it. That's what I was about to comment on when I was speaking before. That night June was going off on me because I was talking to Mya Dean while Erica was in here too. And he called me the N word. That not only pissed me off. Because niggers are not allowed in nor around this crew. Not even the nigger mentality. So I was pissed when he called me that. But I was hurt too. Chill, your whole crew was our big brothers and sisters. To be called a nigger by a crew member. Made me feel like I wasn't crew-like or accepted. It took me a long time to live that down."

"I'm sorry I said that, Greg junior," June says suddenly, "That was dead wrong and I apologize. I should've apologized a long time ago. I'm sorry."

"I accept your apology," Greg Jr says, "And I don't want us to *ever* get into it again. That's not crew ways, by a long shot. And I agree with Ajay and Tank. I need you to give my big sister some space. Just like Ajay and Tank just said. Because Rebbie hasn't been herself for a long time. And today, I finally know why. Just give her some space."

Then Greg Jr turns to Rebbie. He says. "Are you okay? Are you gonna be able to stay at home until y'all get this situation solved or ended?"

"I'm good, Greg," Rebbie says, "I'm not gonna stay at our house, if Brian wants to stay there."

June says, "You don't have to leave our home, Rebbie. It's big enough for us and our three children to be in there and not be in each others space."

"I don't wanna be away from my kids," Rebbie says, "That's a fact. But I can bring them with me, if necessary. I just need some private time and space."

"I can go stay out at the condo that we own," June says, "I'm definitely not gonna make my wife or my kids leave the only home they have. And where our kids are concerned. It's the only home they know."

Rebbie looks at June. She knows he's being kind and considerate, for a change. But she's not going to be okay with him moving *to CrewLand Luxury Suites and Condominiums.* No way!! That's her and Jarvis' meeting place. And she knows she can't bring Jarvis to the house. Not with her kids there and certainly not before she's divorced. She has to throw in a quick idea. She's going to go with what June said initially.

"We can both stay at the house, Brian," she says.

That gives June a feeling of relief. Maybe if they're both still staying together. He might be able to change her mind and fix their marriage.

"Thank you, Rebbie," June says.

"You're welcome," she says, "I didn't say that for you or for myself. I just know that would be the best thing for our kids. I don't want them to be without either one of us. We're not leaving them. I think we should build another home in Jackson Heights. By the time it's complete. We will have figured out who will have it. It doesn't matter to me. So long as our kids can see both of us, regularly. We're gonna have to add all of our property in our future divorce decree, anyway. So we can decide who gets which house and so on, *then*. Does that sound reasonable?"

"It does," June says calmly. He adds, "And you and all of y'all are right. I should've listened to you more. I didn't, baby and I know that's the reason you wanna split up. I just want you to know that I do love you and I will do everything in my power to fix what I've broken. I'll respect your wishes. I give you my word."

"Thank you, Brian," Rebbie says, "I haven't heard anything like that, since back then. When you knew I had caught you cheating. So thank you because this time, I know you mean it. But look what it took. I know you haven't been cheating, *this* time. I just wanna make that clear to everybody in this room. I believe Brian has been faithful since that last time when I saw him at Diana Keyes apartment. But look where *all* of these years of you *not* even respecting my voice or even giving me a voice when it came to decisions from us and our part of this crew, has taken us. We've rarely had a conversation about what was on *my* mind. It was always about what was bothering you. Or what you accomplished. Or what your dreams were. I would have to call my girls or my mama. Or even Ally. Just so I could relieve my mind of whatever I was thinking about pursuing in my life. Or when I was depressed or pissed off. The most I've *ever* known you to be there for me, in the same way I've been there for you. Was when I was in New York on Nine Eleven. You was really worried."

"I was," June says.

"And that's the very reason I found the news media and asked if I could go on camera," Rebbie says, "Because I wanted to make sure you, my husband, wasn't stressed out and worried. So I know you care. I'll never say you didn't. But I cared everyday and all day. And in *everyway*. I just wanted you to love and appreciate me, for me. Not just because of crew rules. Because if the crew wasn't around today. *Right now*. Then this

conversation would not have been this calm. It would've continued the same way it started out in Crew's House. That's how it's been when we disagreed at home. Without the hitting, of course. But we've had moments when you were ready to bite my head off when I disagreed with you about a topic discussion we'd had. I would just stop talking. Or shut up, like you would tell me to do. That's what I'm divorcing, Brian. And I am moving on with my life. I want the same for you."

Everybody in Chill's office is quiet. They're looking from Rebbie to June. Rebbie and June are looking at each other. Eye to eye.

Ebony feels more relief then sadness. She's very proud of Rebbie and she understands equal love, even more now than *ever* before. Every member of her crew hasn't had the same true love which she has with Ajay. She's even more relieved that the true reason for Rebbie wanting a divorce. Didn't come out today. Because even though June has been unfaithful. And his unfaithfulness is what brought Jarvis into Rebbie's life. He still doesn't know about Rebbie and Jarvis. It *will* come out. Ebony just hope it's later and not sooner. Like after Rebbie and June's marriage is over. Because though June asked her who was she leaving him for. Rebbie never responded. But Ebony, Nina and T-baby know Jarvis is *The Revelation* to the marriage of June and Rebbie. But for now, Ebony is just glad this revealing meeting is adjourned.

The Chill Spot, Conference room 1 @10am

All who were in Chill's office have now moved down to the conference room to finish the meeting with Keno and Toni Landry. The crew are already wide open from June and Rebbie's meeting. So they get right to the point.

"I'll publish this for Rich," Renee says immediately, "But my crew will decide *when* it's published."

She points to T-baby and says, "This was his wife until the day he past away. He has a son and a daughter too. I'm gonna make sure that nothing harms them. All *three* of them. So I have an idea."

"Let's us hear what you have," Toni says.

Renee says, "We're his family. I think we should do a documentary type of book, on his *entire* life. Not just this stuff or the bad stuff. His *whole* life. Can we agree on that?"

Keno nods yes and Toni says, "She thinks that will be fine."

That's when Chill takes over and says, "Okay. We'll set up for another

meeting with you ladies, so we can get your side of Rich's life. We'll want to include all of it. Will that work for you two?"

"Yes," Toni says as her and Keno smile big.

Chill asks, "T-baby, is this okay with you?"

"Yes," T-baby says, "It will be fine with me. I know it all, already. Or at least, I think I do."

Then she turns to Keno. She asks,

"Where you in a relationship with Richard?"

It takes Keno a moment to answer. She's acting as though she didn't fully comprehend what T-baby asked her.

That's when T-baby asks, "Do you want to include your *sexual* relationship with Richard, as well?"

"I do. Yes. I do," Keno responds in *very* plain English.

T-baby looks at Chill and Renee. Then she looks at all the others in the room. Then she stares at Rebbie. Then June.

She says, "See, June. The revelations will always come out. You don't even have to be alive. So it turned out much better for you, today. You agree?"

"I do," June says, "I agree fully. Because I didn't even know about *this* one."

Ebony and Ajay just shake their heads. Ajay is ready to go home. So is Ebony. She wants her and Ajay to get back to *their* time at home. With just their children and their 2 dogs. Ajay senses it, right away.

He says, "So is this meeting over? I'm ready to go. I'll be back when we can get on to the next revelation. Like that book of revelations from the bible. When we all get to see the faces of devils that's been portrayed as angels. Let's hurry up and get that damn cleansing done."

All of his crew knows whom he's talking about and what meeting he wants to be the next one. That's when Ajay laughs. Which makes everybody else laugh too. His crew know he's ready to get to Angel Taylor. They are, as well. But for now. It's time to get back to crew business. This meeting is adjourned.

Parma @noon

Alana, Farah and Darlene are at home and enjoying this chilly Saturday, early afternoon. Olivia, Rio and Jaylisa had spent the night with Shalom. So it's just these 3 grown *thangs*, kicked back and relaxing when the phone rings. Alana looks at the caller ID. Then she looks at Darlene.

"Is it for me?" Darlene asks.

"No, auntie," Alana says, "Not unless you wanna speak to Angel."

"Oh I *will* today," Darlene says, "I need to make sure she knows, she can stay her ass in the prison. Because I'm on Ajay's list again. And when he's not with his wife. I'm the *only* other woman who's gonna get his time."

"Oh my," Farah says and giggles, "I just wanna make sure you remember to get me in on some crew dick too. And you *know* who's dick I want."

"Chill's!!!" Darlene yells.

"Y'all be quiet so I can answer this call," Alana says as they all giggle.

She takes the call from Angel. From the moment Angel starts talking, Alana can tell she's in a great mood.

"*Damn*, Angel," Alana says, "You're in a good mood today. What's going on with you?"

Angel says, "I just found out that I have a parole meeting. And it's about getting time off for my good behavior!"

"What?!!!" Alana asks loudly.

Angel says, "Yes, friend. I think I can get out before next year. That made my damn day! And guess what lawyer is representing me at that parole hearing?"

"Hell, I don't know," Alana says, "Just tell me."

They both giggle and Angel says, "Attorney George Wheeler. I know you know whom he represented at our first case."

"He's the lawyer for the crew," Alana says in shock.

"*Yes*, he is," Angel says and giggles. She adds, "He met with me. He told me that the first generation of the crew was okay with him representing me. And he said the crew feels like I've done my time and that I'm in remorse for what I did to Ajay and his wife."

"Her name is Ebony," Alana says, "You still won't even say her damn name."

"Yea, Ebony," Angel says in a dry tone. She goes on to say, "But anyway. She must've forgiven me. Because their lawyer is now *my* lawyer. And her son and me, we talk on the phone every time Ajay is in town. Ajay be in the background. I really think they done got over my mistake. They know I wasn't trying to kill nobody. I was in love with Ajay. I still am. And lord knows if he's desperate enough to be fucking Darlene's *old* ass. Then he's out there again and you know I'm ready to get back out there too."

Curios now, Alana asks, "When are you suppose to get out?"

That question makes Darlene and Farah sit up in their seats. They're trying

to get Alana to put the call on speakerphone but she's not going to do that. She wants this news first.

Angel says, "I don't have a date yet. But I just hope it's soon. I'm so ready to get out of prison and get on with my life. I'll turn thirty one, this year. I've been locked up since I was twenty years old. I'm the same age as Ajay's wife. Ebony. And you know I told you, me and their son talk on the phone every week. Sometimes four or five times. I think Ajay has forgiven me."

"Ebony must have too," Alana says, "If they allow him to talk to you. The crew *has* grown a lot since you've been locked up. I mean, maybe they *have* forgiven you. You have done time for it. And as for me. They made me leave the city for three years. And now, I *work* for them."

"So thinking of it like that," Angel says, "Then I know you can feel where I'm coming from. Because you was my best friend and they hired you in their place of business."

"True," Alana says, "I'm floored girl. I'm happy for you, though. I can't wait to find out when you're getting out. I told you, Michelle and Tameka are my friends again. And I know they come and visit you. Right?"

"They've been here twice," Angel says, "And Julie Von Reese came to visit me, less than two weeks ago. When she was here for that big crew wedding."

"Things are looking up, *finally*," Alana says and laughs.

"They sure are," Angel says and giggles too.

They have a minute left on their call.

Angel says, "I'll keep you informed on how things are going for me. You keep doing the same for me. It won't be long before we can hang together again."

"I can't wait," Alana says and giggles.

"I love you, friend," Angel says.

"I love you too, friend," Alana says and the call ends.

Alana hangs up with Angel and commences her conversation with Farah and Darlene.

Darlene has to know what that total conversation was about.

She asks Alana, "Did I hear you answering to something about her saying she's getting out of jail?"

"Seemed like that to me too," Farah adds.

Alana says, "That's what she just said. She don't know when it will be. But the kicker part of it all. Is the crew's attorney is now representing her."

"What?!!" Farah yells and nearly knocks over her ice tea.

She adds, "There's *got* to be something more. Or something very wrong

with that picture. I haven't been here as long as the two of you have. But even I know there was very bad blood between Angel and Ajay's crew."

"Hell! And Ajay too," Darlene says.

Then she remembers Ajay had instructed her not to give any info about their actual discussions. But he said she can fabricate the sex talk, all she wants too. And Ajay told her if she's able convince Angel and Katrina to stay far away from the crew. Then she might be able to get back to the sexual side with him. Ajay knows it will never happen. But Darlene can believe it will, if that will get her on her mission of having a public dual with Angel, once she's out of prison. Ajay was just saying anything it would take to get Darlene's mind on making sure that Angel would never have access to him and his family again. Because that's what Ajay wants Darlene and law enforcement to think.

Ajay and Ebony's Estate. 2pm

Lil Ajay has already left home. Him and Alan Anthony are kicking it with their crew, out at Greg Jr's condo. And just like always. Libby, Rio, Shalom and Jaylisa have found their *own* way to them. Which is something *non-crew type* girls *have* to do, if they're even allowed to be in the presence of crew males. While the little *crew girls* which have Lil Ajay and Alan Anthony's *immediate* attention, are at Ajay and Ebony's home. Lannie and Kimmie are upstairs in the playroom enjoying playtime with Lea. The 2 Nana's, Pearl and Jo have the triplets today. While Eric and Erica have Ike and Tina, the twin Pekinese of *The Jackson Estate*. Ajay had practice after their meetings at The Chill spot. Immediately after practice, he brought Jarvis up on the meeting with Rebbie and June. He felt he had to tell him something. Jarvis was all over him, wanting details. Because he hadn't heard from Rebbie, by practice time and he felt desperate. Ajay tried to assure Jarvis that Rebbie was going to tell him about it during their next get together. Ajay figures she's most likely with him, right now.

Ajay arrived home from practice and took a shower. He has just joined Ebony in their master bedroom. Their getting ready to talk and enjoy their alone time. They have a lot to discuss, so they get right to it.

"I like how Rebbie handled June in that meeting today," Ajay says with a chuckle.

"So do I," Ebony says and smiles. She adds, "Baby, I wanted all of our crew marriages to last *forever*. Especially my awesome foursome sisters. But first and foremost. I want everybody to be as happy as we are."

"Then they should watch us and learn," Ajay says and they both giggle. He adds, "I feel sorry for June, in a way. But in my opinion. He took their *entire* relationship for granted. He acted like Rebbie was slow. Or she was not gonna figure him out. That's how I see it. But she has always been brain smart. And she was *always* faithful too."

"And June was *always* cheating," Ebony says and they laugh again. She adds, "I'm *so* glad that we're blessed. Any problems we had *before* we got married. We fixed them."

"Yes we did," he says, "We discussed *everything*, baby. That's the way it's suppose to be done. If either member of a relationship has things in their life which bothers them. They have to bring their future mate up on it. We did that. We got it out in the open. And got it out the damn way."
They smile and kiss.

Next, they chat about their odd meeting with Keno Madison and her assistant. Keno's demeanor seemed desperate to both of them.

"I knew she was fucking Rich," Ajay says.

"We all know it now," Ebony says, "That explains why he spent so much time out there."

"Other than to smoke crack?" Ajay asks and he's not smiling.
Ebony says, "Baby, he had a problem but he was still crew. Crew from birth."

"I know that part," Ajay says, "And about this book we're suppose to do about Rich's life story. I want them to include all of his bad shit too. Then it can be made clear why I'm not able to grieve for him, like a normal cousin would. It wasn't shit normal about him trying to fuck with my girl. And he did that shit, for your entire life. Let's be sure and put that out there."

"I know he did, baby," Ebony says, "I was never close to him, for that very reason. I knew he didn't want Jb, Tank or you to know how he was acting when y'all wasn't around. And you know what? I don't care if they put all of that in the book either. I'm over it. *Totally*. I'm just relieved that I wasn't experienced enough to know he liked me, back then. You made me aware of it, that first time you beat him up. When he hurt Sparky. But baby, you know you had my full attention, *even* back then. That was something he could never have gotten. He wasn't mature enough *and* he wasn't you."
They smile at each other again. Then Ajay says,
"I had your attention, fasho! For me, that was something I couldn't allow *no* other motherfucker to have. Truth be told. I needed your attention, so I

342

could stay focused on what I needed to get accomplished in my life. I wasn't gonna be able to rest if another male had your complete attention. Other than big John, pops and your papa's. Tank *and* Jb will tell you that part. No male was gonna be in your life trying to date you. Not and live. I was not gonna be okay with *anybody* else having your undivided attention, baby. Not more than me."

He chuckles and adds, "Well, not until I made you a mother."

"That's so true," she says and smiles. She adds, "I love my life, Anthony. I know we're gonna be together forever."

"Yes indeed, baby," he says and gives her a quick kiss on the lips. He adds, "We'll definitely be together forever. Even *after* breath. We said that in our vows."

They giggle and Ebony agrees, saying, "We sure did. And about the book. I think the title of Rich's book should be, *The Revelation*."

"There will surely be a lot of that," Ajay agrees and chuckles.

She asks, "Now I really wanna discuss this next phase of our crew problem. How do you think Angel is handling the news that attorney Wheeler just recently brought to her?"

"Like she's forgiven and out of the woods," Ajay says with a very stern face. He adds, "That's how I want her to think. I want her to think that we've forgiven her because that way. She'll start with that stalking shit again. And I'll make sure she goes to hell, the next time she leaves the streets."

"*Baby*, Ant is *so* motivated about taking her life that it frightens me," Ebony says. "But he *is* our son. So I knew he would be capable of taking a life to protect those he love. I know he's carrying anger for her. But he's so smooth with the way he's got her thinking that they're friends."

"He's got his daddy's charm and his momma's wisdom," Ajay says.

"Umm," she moans, "You're making me hot."

Ajay says, "And I'm ready to get you back to lukewarm too."

They giggle before Ajay says, "But devil should be out of jail by August. She don't know that yet. The crew will know every move she gets before she'll know. The way it's been since she's been in there. August is the month I'm setting *all* of my plans around. Because I know Wheeler is gonna bring her bitch ass right on out here to me. In the way that I want her. And that's when the beef between her and Darlene can go *fulltime*. Me and Ant already got the brothers in gear, for the rest of it."

Ebony raises her eyebrows and says, "And Darlene is thinking she's gonna get some of my fifteen. Her *and* Angel *and* Katrina Dobbs too."

"And not one of them ho's realize that this dick belongs to a lady who can take all of their *nothing* asses out of the game of life," Ajay says while looking at her in a seductive way.

"And they won't know until it's too late," she says and blushes.

Ajay's eyes get lower on that comment. He has that *'I need to get close to my pussy'* look in his eyes. Ebony dares to be boastful and speak again.

She whispers, "I know those eyes, baby. This clitoris that I carry for you. Throbs when your eyes hold that stare."

Ajay pulls her to him and starts to kiss her, very aggressively. The way she likes it.

He whispers in her ear, saying, "Tre' is with their grandmothers. Ant is out wit crew. The big girls are here. So I'm gonna try not make you scream *too* loud."

Ebony smiles while shivering behind that comment. Ajay's words always go right through her and she loves it. He's kissing her ear now.

He whispers, "Your body's shivering but you're not cold. That means it's time for me to kiss and lick my sweet pussy."

"Umm baby," she moans as Ajay heads south.

She whispers, "You know me, *so* well."

She continues her whisper, asking, "Can we have some sixty nine action, baby? I wanna taste you too."

"It's your property," he whispers while kissing her pussy.

He adds, "I'll let you make that decision today. Because you know my rule."

She smiles as she starts rotating her body in the opposite direction. He's just staring at her. Waiting on her to respond to him. She's still rotating. He's still watching. Once she gets her face to within 2 feet of his penis, she looks back at him.

She whispers, "I've got enough milk pumped to last until the night of the Orlando game. *Four* nights."

She starts to massage his dick. He's still watching her but he's no longer waiting for an answer. She gave him the answer he wanted to hear. She now has his permission, to get up close and personal with the dick *he* carries for her, when she said she has breast milk already pumped and waiting for Tre'. She answered his stare correctly too. Now she wants to suck some of the brawl out this 14 ½ inch beast which she's staring down.

They're both on their sides now. With their heads at opposite ends of their bed. She's still massaging *her* dick. She's still staring at him. He's kissing her pussy and inner thighs while rubbing and massaging her legs. She kissing the head of his dick, ever so gently. Then she licks the tip.

He moans. She loves that sound from her man. It assures her that she's doing the right thing.

Then while staring at *her* dick, she whispers to it, saying,

"I'm not ever gonna allow another to touch you. *No one*. Besides me and my man, whom you're connected too. And he won't even let me touch you as much as I want too. So I'm gonna be real good to you today. That way. He'll allow us to be closer friends."

She smiles and gives it a kiss. Ajay is watching her again. But his stare is very different than it was. He's turned on to the max. She looks at him. He just smiles. She holds his dick and licks the head of it while she's still looking at him. His stare intensifies. He's no longer smiling. He's *very* ready to get to the good part.

He separates her legs and dives in. She takes his dick into her mouth and starts to suck it, at a fast pace. He moans harder which goes right through her with force.

"Oh!!!" she yells.

He's got her clitoris held hostage to his tongue. She counters by sucking him as hard and as fast as she can. Only breaking her sucking action to lick the tip of it and down each side. The moaning is going both ways now. Ebony can feel that familiar feeling already. That tightening of her thigh muscles. Which are no match for her man's tongue and lips. Ajay has mastered this skill. He knows Ebony's body. He knows what it's likes and dislikes as well, if not better than she does.

He whispers, "I love the way it feels, baby. And I love how this clit starts to swell when I put my tongue to it."

He starts licking her very fast. Holding her clitoris in between his lips. He's massaging it.

"Ooooo," she oozes.

She tries to reciprocate the feeling she's having, back to him. She wants to hear him moan like she's doing now and always does. She squeals. Screams, even. She has to get him to that point before he makes her cum. She wants them to be *sexually* even. And she wants him to demand that she give him head, every time he eats her pussy. Because if it's as intense as his pussy eating. He'll want it every time they have sex. The same way he gives it to her. She has to get his attention right now because if she doesn't. He's going to make her cum. She can already feel it easing up on her and after she cums. He's going to put this dick that she's sucking, into the 1 spot that it truly loves and enjoys. Her sweet pussy. So right now she's thinking of a master plan. She knows 1 of the things that turns her on from him, is when

he talks sexy to her *while* he's doing her. The way he's doing, right now.

"My sweet pussy is throbbing, baby," he whispers, "It wants to give my mouth and tongue a shower…with that sweet juice you're packing, baby girl. Bring it to me, sugar."

She moans and then counters with, "My strong dick wants to drench my mouth with that white honey that shoots out *strong* enough to scratch my throat."

Ajay likes that!

He moans. Then he starts to suck her clitoris at double the rate of speed. While at the same time, he reaches his hand up to her chest and starts to massage her breast. She moans hard. Then she moves 1 of her hands up to his stomach and finds his naval. She starts to massage it. Ajay is licking her so swiftly that she can hear his tongue moving. She moans and takes his dick to the back of her throat. He moans hard. She's proud of herself. She knows he liked *that* move. This time she has to say it out loud.

She whispers, "Did you like that, baby? Huh?"

"Yesss, baby," he manages as he moans again. "Suck that shit. Ooooo, baby. That feels good. *Good*!"

"You feel so good to me, daddy," she drools, "I can feel my stomach tightening up. Mmmm. I wanna get a nut out of this power tool. It's mine. I want it. All of it."

Ajay is really feeling her boldness but this is the 1 war game that he always has to win. He rolls her over on top of him and takes her captive from her hips to her knees. She can't move away from him anymore.

He whispers, "You gotta play fair, baby. You can't move my sweet pussy away from me while you play catch up. This is my shit. Do you hear me?"

He goes for broke. She's still sucking him hard but she can feel her climax. It's inching into the forefront. She's grabs his dick with both hands. She goes up and down on it at a maximum pace. As fast as she can without it choking her. But she's about to get her orgasm. If she does. That's going to make her open her mouth for the screaming and moaning that she's surely going to be doing.

What can I do to keep up with his pace? Oh! I got it.

She keeps sucking at a fast pace. But she takes 1 of her hands and brushes it across his nuts. His *sensitive* balls. She remembers Renee and Tonya telling her and her crew sisters that *this move* is a winning one.

"Ahhh," Ajay moans but he's still licking her like the pro that he is.

346

Please let him cum before me. Mine is right there. I want us to come together, orally. That would be new.

Ajay has another move. One that he knows will bring that sweet nectar to his lips, right away. He takes his middle finger and slides it into her pussy which is already vibrating next to his nose.
That did it. He won. Damn!

"Ahhhhhhhhhh, Anthony!!!!!"
Ebony is in that erotic cloud. The 1 where her body starts to shake, tremble, stretch and tighten. She's in ecstasy. Ajay lifts up and turns around quickly. He pounces on top of her and shoves his dick into her moist and ecstasy alerted tunnel.
"Oh Anthony! Oh baby! I'm Cuming, baby! Oh my god!! It's so good," she yells.
Ajay whispers, "Our girls are hearing you, sugar. Get that shit, Ebony. I love to see your face when you cum, baby. You're so fuckin sexy. *Sexy!*"
He's pounding her pussy with full force. She's cuming and screaming, at the same time.
"I gotta get it all, Ebony. This tight ass pussy is hugging it's dick," Ajay whispers which makes her orgasm *even* stronger.
He's making her cum harder. It's not easing off at all. Nowhere near it. She's at a constant moan right now. Ajay starts to kiss her hard. He sucks on her neck. Her nipples. He licks her from her neck to her chin.
"Anthony!!!!"
"Damn right it's me, baby," he whispers as he looks down at her face.
Then he looks down to watch his work. His dick is wet with her juices. He's exactly where he wants to be and she's exactly where he wants her to be. In *fucking* heaven! He can feel his nut coming and he wants it. He wants to join his woman in the heaven she's in, right now. He can feel his back arching. He can't hold this nut back *any* longer.
"Ah shit!!!" he says with force.
Ebony is just holding onto him while he beats her pussy like it made him angry. He's pounding her with maximum force. While he's watching her facial expressions.
"Ouwha!" she screams from the pain of each of his strokes.
"Take it baby!" he demands, "Take yo dick! It's all yours, sugar. I've gotta give you all of it. Right?"

347

"Yes!! Ouwha!! Ooooo Anthony!!"

"You fuck me sooooo good baby!" he yells.

That's when he throws his head back but he's still pounding his dick into her with every ounce of energy he has. He's pulling her hips to him. He knows his nut is right there on the edge and he's going to get it, very soon. But he wants to pound every ounce of energy out of his wife before he gets his nut. He wants her to be ready to take a nap when this session is done. Because he knows he's going to need some rest before he can get his dick ready to go back inside of this pleasure pussy again. But he's still talking loud.

With force, he says, "I wanna drench this sweet ass pussy, baby. It's got me feeling like I own it."

"Oh baby! You're way deep in me! Ooooo Anthony! Cum! *Please*!"

He can't hold it off any longer. He's biting his own lip now, as his head goes toward the ceiling and his body starts to tremble.

"Aaaaaaaaaah!! Oooooo!" Ajay yells.

He's still trying to fight it but he can't hold this nut back any longer.

"There it is, baby! Take this nut, Ebony! You pulled it right on outta me! Sssssssssss Oooooo! Aaaaaaaaaaah!"

He's letting it go now. Because if he tried to hold it any longer. He would've had a massive stroke, headache and then some. His dick is still stirring in her pussy while it unloads. Ebony is just seething and trying to hold onto him. But she's digging her nails into his back. He can't move her hands because he's still holding her hips. He's still emptying his nut sack. He's still in blissful heaven. Enjoying it with the woman he loves more than his own life. He just lays his head down on her shoulder and lets it all go.

Moments later, he lifts his head and looks at Ebony. She has those usual tears. He wipes them away as he usually does. Their both out of breath but he has to let her know something about the way he's feeling, right now.

He whispers, "Now do you understand why I'm so hooked on you?"

"Yes baby," she mutters.

Her strength is gone. She's just holding onto him and trying to kiss on whichever part of his face is closest to her.

He whispers, "I love what you just did. And you almost got me before I got that double nut out of you. Sending you to ecstasy? That's my mission in life, baby. That's what *you* inspire. I'm *your* man and that's my job. Every ounce of my energy *is* and has always been about making sure *you* win.

And when I make you cum before I do. That's your win. You please me, just by looking at me and smiling when you see me. This dick I'm carrying for you, goes into full attention mode just at the sight of you. This is as real as it can ever be. I have to make sure you enjoy sex before I do. Do you understand that?"

"I do, Anthony," she whispers, "I've known that since the first time you touched me. The first time you held me. I could feel it, baby. I just want you to understand that I will *always* want to give you the same thing."

"Oh you do, baby," he whispers, "You do that *every* time. That's why my first mission is to make sure you get yours before me. Because I know you're gonna give me mine. You always have. I can get a nut just by thinking about you, baby. Do you hear me?"

"Yes baby," she whispers and smiles.

He smiles and whispers, "This is heaven right here. This is the most peaceful and the most enjoyable thing I've *ever* done in my *whole* life. Pleasing you. And it ain't no way in *hell* I'm ever gonna allow that shit to change. I've tried to cum before you but my body wouldn't let it happen. I know it's because I'd feel like I didn't give *you*, all of me. And baby, all of me is for you. All of me."

"I know that's the truth, Anthony," she whispers, "You are the man. A *whole* man, Anthony. My man. A real man. That's why I would never allow any other person to come between us or ruin this real love that we have. There was never gonna be another man for me. As I said on our wedding day. You complete me."

"And you do the same for me," he whispers, "Everything I needed in my life. You brought it."

"We were born to be together," she whispers, "The way my daddy reacted to us when he first found out that I liked you? Was what let me know that he wanted us to be together."

"He made sure I knew what it was gonna take," Ajay whispers and smiles. "Him and pops use to make sure I had my ducks in a row, when it came to you, your time and your attention."

"You had my attention from day one," she whispers, "Baby, you have always had a way about you that was just interesting. No matter what it was that you were doing. You demanded attention. And when you saw me. You would always stop whatever you was doing and either watch me. Or come to me and start a conversation. I felt so special to you and so protected by you. All at the same time."

"And that was and still is my mission, baby girl," he whispers.

He puts his index and middle fingers under her chin and lifts it up. Then he starts to kiss her with passion. She puts her arms around him and kisses him back, as hard as she can. This moment is very pleasant and the most natural thing to both of them. Ajay is moaning again and she knows what that means. He's ready for round 2 and she's going to let him have as many rounds as it takes, to rest his mind and body. That's her job and she loves her job, just as much as she loves this man who puts all of her needs before his own.

"Mmmm," she moans.

"Mmmm," he moans right back.

They continue kissing. He starts rubbing her body again. She relaxes herself as much as she can. She's very familiar with where he's headed. To his fantasy world. His heaven. It's her heaven too. That's a revelation that they both found, 2 whole decades ago.

He pauses the kiss and lifts his head up so he can look into her teary eyes.

He says, "I love you, Ebony."

"I love you too, Anthony," she says.

He's about to head south but his text alert goes off. It's Lil Ajay's text tone. He looks into Ebony's eyes, to find her looking back at him.

She asks in a whisper, "Is he about to *ask* for advice. Or give *you* advice?"

"A little bit of both," he whispers back and smiles.

He grabs his phone and reads the text message from his son. He raises up off of Ebony and sits up on the bed. He sends a text back to Lil Ajay. Ebony can tell this is something serious.

She asks, "What is it?"

"He said Rioshauna has a nine millimeter," he says as he sends another text.

"What?!" Ebony asks in a startled tone. "She has a gun?! Why?"

Ajay says, "She told him that her mama gave it to her for her protection. Since her daddy Draper has been missing for six days. Nobody knows where him or Old Jake is. Rio told Ant that her mama told her not to trust nobody."

"Mallory Fields gave her daughter a gun?" Ebony asks.

Ajay says, "Yep. Ant just took it from her. He told her, he was gonna make sure she's protected and she won't need a gun."

"And what did she say to that?" Ebony asks.

"She asked him why does her mama think that she needs to protect herself around him," Ajay says and chuckles.

Ebony asks, "Is she trying to do harm to him? Please tell me that part."

"No she's not," Ajay says, "He's got the gun now. He gave it to Brandon and told him to put it up. He told Rio that he was going to protect her. If anybody tries to harm her. He's gonna take care of them."

"Did she go for that?" Ebony asks.

Ajay says, "He said she asked him, *would he ever want to hurt her*. He says he told her, no."

"Does she believe him?" Ebony asks.

Ajay says, "Hang on. He's texting me back right now."

Ebony sits up so she can read his phone. She's waiting for the response from their son to come through. Ajay is waiting for it as well. Ebony can sense that Ajay isn't as calm as usual.

"Are you nervous, Anthony?" she asks.

He looks at her. Then he smiles and says, "About what his next action might be. Yes. About him being harmed. No."

"I don't want him to do anything to her," Ebony says, "Not now. Not right after her father and Old Jake went missing. The two of them plus Tim and Justin's story, *stays* on the news. Please tell me that Ant is going to be able to get through this without letting anything go. Or taking her life. Tell me what you're thinking, Anthony."

"Ant won't do anything to her," he says, "Unless he has too. And he already got the gun from her. Wait. His text is coming through."

He reads the text from his son. Then he looks at Ebony. He smiles.

"What does it say?" she asks as she leans in to see the text message.

Ajay says, "His text says, '*Rio said her mama told her that you and my family did something to her daddy and to her papa Jake. I told her that her mama must be crazy because my pops and my family don't have no reason to do nothing to neither 1 of them. They always wanted to hurt my family but they couldn't get past our security.*' He handled that answer really well."

"Do you think she believes him?" Ebony asks.

Another text is coming in. Ajay and Ebony reads it and they both start to giggle. Ebony reads the text aloud this time.

She reads, "*She just told me that her mama would have to be crazy to think that she's gonna do something to hurt me. Because she just said she's in love with me. She even said, if her mama try to insist that she can't be with me. She's gonna do her mama in.*"

Ebony says, "Oh she's got it bad. Ant already said Kimmie is his future. And Rio is ready to kill her own mama to be with him."

"Ant is *definitely* my son," Ajay says and chuckles.

"Yes he is," Ebony says, "So how do your think this afternoon is going to go, from this point?"

"He's gonna fuel her anger against her mama," Ajay says. "He's gonna make sure that she stays on his team and on his side. So he's gonna make her feel like she's his."

"Like she's his," Ebony says, "And she'll end up turning against her own mama to spend time with our son."

Ebony shakes her head. Then she smiles.

She says, "I must give Ant the same type of credit that I've always given to you. Because he's wise beyond his years. Very wise. Just like you, Anthony. He's handling this situation like a *grown* man."

"Baby, he is," Ajay says, "He's a Jackson man. That's a natural thing for us. He's gonna spend a lot of time with her today. Probably all night. Or until he knows she's down with him, all the way. I'll bet you the rest of those girls out there are mad. Because Ant is in the room with Rio and he ain't spending *no* time with the rest of them. Right now, he has got to make sure Rio trusts him completely. But at the same time, she already knows that she's not his girlfriend."

"So what will he do now?" Ebony asks as she rolls her eyes up to the ceiling.

Ajay says, "He's gonna give her the time that it takes to pull her all the way in. While making sure she knows that he don't want no girlfriend. But if she's okay with spending his free time, with him. Then he's going to allow that. But she will have to know that he is not going to be loyal to her. Not when it comes to having his needs met because his needs are going to come first. If she's okay with that. Then he can see her and fuck her. But she will not be able to change his mind about what he wants or who he wants."

"He is *definitely* your son," Ebony says and laughs. "Because I know you use to say that to Darlene, Angel and all of them, *has beens*. And not one of them has gone away."

"That's why a Jackson man will never want them," he says and laughs, "Because we have to have a strong and intelligent woman. One who is determined to be, whom she is. We just have to figure out what it takes to get and then keep her attention. We don't want a girl who's ready to do any and everything just to be around us. And Rio done turned against her own mama. She didn't even like her daddy."

"And she's ready to do whatever Ant wants," Ebony says.

"And he's gonna put her ass to work too," Ajay says and laughs. "It is only a matter of time before he gets tired of her though."

"And then what?" Ebony asks.

Ajay chuckles and says, "She's gonna go into that Darlene and Angel category. Ant is going to stop allowing her to be in his space. He won't even go hang out where she's going to be. If that's what it takes."

"And she's gonna start coming to wherever she thinks he is," Ebony shakes her head and says, "Just so she can see him. And try to get with him."

"She's older than him," Ajay says, "She's near teen years. So she'll be more like Darlene has been in my life. When Ant is totally done with Rio. Rio is going to stay out of the way but she's not gonna go away. Not completely. She'll always be in the background. Looking for away to please him and to get his attention again."

"Just like Darlene is right now, ha?" Ebony says.

"Yes," Ajay says, "Darlene will be ready to do Angel's ass in. If she thinks that will get her some time with me. You know I've already started setting that shit up."

"I know," Ebony says and smiles, "She really thinks she's gonna be able to get to *my* property."

"Hell yea, she do," Ajay says, "When all the time, the only thing she's going to be. Is a prime suspect."

The End of Part 6
COPYRIGHTED 2015!

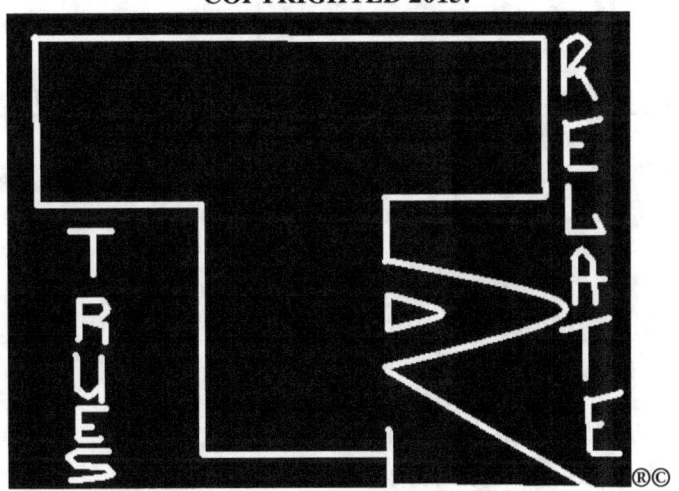

===

If you were charged more than $25(US dollars) and shipping & handling was not included, contact us immediately:
[Black Coffee's websites]
www.blackdollone.com or www.truesrelatepublishing.com

THE TIME WILL REVEAL SERIES READING ORDER:

Time To Learn-RELOADED-part 1>novel
More Than 4 Admirers-RELOADED-"The Threat to a Legacy" short 1
Mr. Wrong and the Rats-RELOADED-"Sweet Ray, Sonya, Shuntay & Tina" short 2
Time To Grow-RELOADED-part 2>novel
Time To Love-RELOADED-part 3>novel
Time To Know-RELOADED-part 4>novel
Time To Feel-RELOADED part 5>novel
The Making of AJAY-Every Man-RELOADED>novel
Time To Show-RELOADED part 6>novel
Crew Males + 1st Priority= Crew Females- "Goodbye Deviled Angel {summer 2015}
Ajay & Ebony-Time To Give-RELOADED part 7 [2016]
Ajay & Ebony -Time To Live-Time Will Reveal 8 [TBA]

THE ORGANIZATION SERIES READING ORDER:
All By My Lonely-The Organization-part one
Still.., All By My Lonely-The Organization-part two
The Real Family-The Organization-part three

[Black Coffee's websites]
www.blackdollone.com or www.truesrelatepublishing.com
Twitter: http://twitter.com/AuthorBlkCoffee
INSTAGRAM: AuthorBlkCoffee
Linked-In: Author Black Coffee
Facebook: Lovely T. Brown

Facebook Groups:
The Time Will Reveal-RELOADED series Crew Nation #Crew4Life
The Organization
Facebook page:
Author Black Coffee & True's Relate Publishing, LLC
All books are available in print and eBooks
On ALL online sellers

Look for these future releases by Black Coffee [TBA]
The Foe, The Friend-Poetry [print & audio]
To Hell and Back [3 recovering addicts]
Set up to Fail
Katrina-The Catastrophe heard around the world
To Strong to fall Off
How the Internet challenged Privacy
Bigotry bleeds and breeds
The Jessie Lee Williams Jr story
9/11-The homegrown terror

Contact me online and let me know what you think!
-Black Coffee
"Stay Blessed and Vigilant"
#NoJusticeNoPeace
#ByAnyMeansNecessary